Love *and* DEATH

in Dallas

Bruce J. Gevirtzman

Black Rose Writing

www.blackrosewriting.com

The final approval for this literary material is granted by the author.

First printing

This book is based on events that occurred on November 22, 1963. References to, and reproductions of, any actual conversations that may have taken place are speculative. Most of the characters depicted in this story are fictitious. Any resemblance to real persons, living or dead, is purely coincidental.

ISBN: 978-0-9825823-3-6

PUBLISHED BY BLACK ROSE WRITING

www.blackrosewriting.com

Printed in the United States of America

Love and Death in Dallas is printed in 12-point Times New Roman

NOTES FROM THE AUTHOR

In any work of fiction told against a historical landscape, it is often difficult for a reader to separate facts from make-believe.

Certain *facts* presented in this book are indisputable: John Fitzgerald Kennedy, the 35th president of the United States, was assassinated in Dallas, Texas, around 12:30 in the afternoon, on November 22, 1963. Less than an hour later, twenty-three year-old book order filler, Lee Harvey Oswald, was arrested for murdering Dallas policeman J.D. Tippit on a suburban street corner. Two days later during Oswald's transfer from the city to the county jail, local nightclub owner Jack Ruby shot and killed the suspect, as a live national T.V. audience looked on in disbelief.

Several other actual events are described in this story. But what really happened in Dallas that Friday is a matter of conjecture, supposition, theory, and opinion. This book, a work of fiction, utilizes many historical truths along with some of those conjectures, suppositions, theories, and opinions—combining them in a yarn about fictional characters and an imaginary high school debate squad from Southern California.

My deepest gratitude goes out to my friends and family for supporting me throughout this risky endeavor. Their patience was amazing! Over the years they discussed the Kennedy assassination with me until some of them were ready to whack me over the head with a large mallet. But, fortunately, no one ever did.

To my publicist and the creator of Phantom Projects, a magnificent youth theater group that helped to put me on the literary radar, Steve Cisneros: thanks for all your support, hard work, and, when necessary, your helpful criticism.

Reagan Rothe, my editor at Black Rose Writing, took a chance on this, and I am indebted to him.

And finally, to my wife Janis and my two children, Aiko and Viktor: You are the motivation for my writing and the reason I am still alive, even though I am 150 years old. I love you.

Bruce J. Gevirtzman
December 31, 2009

—PROLOGUE—

Throughout his sixteen years of life, he had never experienced a similar surge of excitement. Tinged with a nervous energy that helped him to bounce briskly up the small slope, he felt his heart beating away, a thumping caused more by enthralled anticipation, than by sudden exertion.

In less than a minute, Randall Walter Whitman's life would be changed forever.

And on a much broader scale, the United States of America, too, would be permanently transformed.

For most Americans Friday, November 22, 1963, began as an ordinary morning. A little more than a year earlier, the Russians backed down from their run at international intimidation, dismantling the menacing nuclear missiles they had strategically planted in Cuba. A heavy anxiety over the ominous threat of nuclear war had been relieved.

Americans breathed easier over the prospects for their future. Tending to school, traveling to work, and taking care of children were once again normal routines, with Friday night's high school football games looming very big in the weekend plans of most Texans.

But when Randall Whitman reached the low concrete barrier at the top of the grassy hill, time suddenly stood still. He had the sensation of his heart tumbling to the bottom of his feet. His body froze; his mouth fell open.

Although he didn't know it at the time, events perpetuating a living nightmare in his life were already set in motion.

—CHAPTER 1—

At the age of ten, Randall Whitman bravely stood up to the fourth grade bully.

With very little success in the actual fight (his black eye and a bloody nose to show for it), at least Randall had made a name for himself at school. After that momentous afternoon, some of Randall's classmates came up to him and made comments like, "You're the guy who took on Sledge. Cool!"

Although Randall lay flat on his back nurturing a bloody nose throughout most of the ordeal, Randall *had* taken on the fourth grade bully. From then on his reputation exceeded itself. Everyone at school now recognized Randall Whitman, even though Randall planned to excel in areas that had nothing to do with physical violence or cruelty.

"I didn't like what Sledge said about Cheryl," Randall told his school's principal. "He called her a bad name."

"What did he call her?" Mr. Trask asked him.

"I'm not going to repeat it."

"It must have been really bad for you to jump on Sledge, uh, Reggie Johnson like that, Randy. He darn near broke your nose."

"Well," Randall shrugged sheepishly, his head hanging forward. "I don't like it when boys pick on girls. I just don't. It's not right. Besides, Cheryl Tigretti is a very nice girl."

"Do you like fighting?"

"No!" Randy recoiled. "I hate fighting! I hate it! But he was mean, and he started it!"

Randall Walter Whitman, known by his friends as *Randy* and, unfortunately, middle-named *Walter* by his parents, often struggled with threats of physical intimidation—that is, until he became bigger and stronger. His increase in height from ages ten to thirteen began a spurt no one expected (all of his blood relations had barely grown), and he packed some beef on his bones through an intensive karate program, accompanied by his *sensei's* orders for mandatory trips to the weight room.

By the time he turned sixteen, Randy stood almost six feet tall and weighed a sinewy 180 pounds, not bad for a boy everyone thought would be taunted all his life for looking unbearably scrawny, and whose "fight" with the fourth grade bully lasted barely five seconds—if that.

Despite Randy's newfound self-respect due to his growth spurt and intense immersion in karate classes, he instructed himself to stay away from activities involving competitive violence.

A braggart about his own pacifist philosophies, one of Randy's good friends, Ira Cushman, often challenged Randy for his apparent tendencies to like violence. Ira looked at Randy and identified what he believed to be some lurking hypocrisies. "Non-violent?" Ira chimed with a sardonic grin. " What else do you guys do in karate, other than punch and kick each other around?"

Randy remained stoic. "We're taught *not* to punch and kick people around."

"Could have fooled *me*."

"Have you ever seen me punch or kick anyone?" Randy asked. He was a tad irked by Ira's ignorance. "The most important thing in karate is being able to defend yourself."

"And what a loada' crap *that* is, man! I saw *Dr. No*—and how those guys trained their hands and feet to be lethal weapons. I saw that!"

Randy nodded. "They had to defend themselves against the bad guys. I haven't been challenged to a fight since I took up karate."

"And since you sprang up six inches," squawked the much shorter and slighter Ira Cushman.

"I don't like playing sports where the object is to hurt your opponent. That's why I don't like boxing either," Randy clarified, increasingly frustrated by this conversation with Ira.

To quench his thirst for non-violent combat, Randy joined Ira on their high school's debate team. His Long Beach, California, school bragged of one of the best debate programs in the nation.

Almost a dozen former competitors from Long Beach High School had earned lucrative scholarships to colleges and universities wishing to recruit them to embellish their own intercollegiate competitive debate teams.

Randy's girlfriend, however, served as a distraction. She treated him poorly, and he stumbled and bumbled in her presence. But Randy called Carmen Pedro his girlfriend, and he and Carmen did things boyfriends and girlfriends usually did together.

Save one.

On the doorstep of her house after their third date, the formal Christmas Dance, Carmen shoved him away. It was a resounding gesture of rejection just before the requisite goodnight kiss. In no uncertain terms she had said to Randy: "We're going too fast. Let's cool it a little bit."

Not that Randy knew this for a fact, but he was almost sure they weren't "going too fast." Some of his friends and several other annoying boys in his sophomore gym class boasted all the time about their exploits with girls. *They* were going too fast! Carmen Pedro, dark features, exotic, had the pick of any boy at school, but she had chosen to pursue a romantic connection with Randall Whitman. And for the first couple of dates, it had gone rather well: nothing more than a few last minute, quick, clumsy kisses on her front porch. He certainly enjoyed those experiences and figured she had, too!

But too *fast*?

Randy didn't dispute her claim at first, but he later brought it up in a conversation. When they were alone and enjoying each other's company in a frivolous, casual way at McDonald's, he asked her, "I've been thinking—wondering about it for a couple of days—and I just wanted to ask you what you meant last week when you said that we were going too fast. I mean, I respect that; I do. But you kissed me on our very first date—and *you* were the one who initiated the kiss. So I was just wondering…"

Randy's voice trailed off, because he didn't know what else to say. He had said all that he wanted and maybe had said too much.

To his amazement, Carmen succumbed to his openness. She

didn't expect Randy to bring up her rebuke, and her utter surprise had restrained her from erupting. She said sweetly, "I just didn't want you to think I was the type of girl who would let you feel me up by the third date."

"I never thought that you were."

"Well," she grinned, "you might have. If I were to let you do whatever you wanted with me whenever you wanted it, you would now have the wrong idea. Boys get the wrong idea about me all the time."

"Really?" Randy asked, raising his eyebrows very high.

"And I am only a tenth grader!" she smiled mischievously.

"You want to let me in on that—just a little?" Randy played along.

"No names."

"Ah," he relaxed.

With Carmen, it wasn't all fun and games. As the days ticked off, their relationship became more complicated. Randy's parents had grown up in a time of racial segregation and homogeneous courting. Men and women did not date—let alone marry—someone of a dissimilar race, different nationality, or another religion.

Carmen Pedro's roots went back to Puerto Rico. Her parents came to America during World War II, and her father immediately joined the United States Army. He spent over two years on the Pacific Front and would have been deployed for an invasion of Japan, had President Truman not ordered atomic bombs dropped on Hiroshima and Nagasaki.

As for Mr. Pedro, a Puerto Rican national and eventually a certified citizen of the United States, no one had the right to question his patriotism to America. He did, however, adhere to old-fashioned views on culture and race, believing that no boy in this entire solar system was good enough to date his daughter. The only chance a boy had with Carmen—his lone exception—came from the boy being Puerto Rican.

Which, of course, Randy Whitman was not.

Unfortunately, with people like Randy's mother and father, older, more archaic values dominated their way of thinking. The prospect of allowing someone with brown skin into their family (as the wife of their only son) crossed the line of absolute blasphemy.

Melissa, Randy's older sister, usually brought some reason to the situation. Once, with the Whitmans congregated at the dinner table for a meal, Mrs. Whitman asked her son, "Randy, are you going out tonight with that what's-her-name girl again?"

Randy worked to force a smile—and failed. "She has a name, Mom."

Mrs. Whitman shrugged. "All those people have about the same name, don't they? It's hard to tell one from another, isn't it?"

Randy had become familiar with his parent's latent bigotry, but each time they actually displayed it, the ugliness of it all, its indecency, angered him. Randy had never thought of his parents as ignorant—or worse. But when their lack of acceptance for minorities reared its ugly head—as it did from time to time—he found himself recalculating his assessment of his parents' humanity. When their bigotry affected him personally, as it had in the case of Carmen, Randy became infused with anger, a righteous resentment he would have to control.

As a response to his mother's last dig, Randy's shoulders sagged at the dinner table. His feelings of disgust lingering, he said nothing.

But Melissa came to his rescue. "What do you mean by *those people*, Mother? Who are *those people*? They have names; they have identities."

"You know what I'm talking about," their mother grinned passively. "Those Mexicans: they all have similar names. Honey, I'm not criticizing them. I'm just pointing out a fact."

Randy couldn't believe how boorish his mother sounded. For a woman who held a college degree (in theater), she reeked of ignorance. At one time Randy had figured people in the arts were more liberal, more open-minded, and even more intelligent than others.

Perhaps his mother once had been more liberal and more open-minded and more intelligent than she now sounded. Perhaps his father, who studied Business Administration in college but never earned a degree in anything, had contaminated his wife with his oppressive, narrow-minded views of people who appeared different from those in their own extended family.

He looked directly into his mother's eyes and said, "Carmen is not Mexican, Mom. She's Puerto Rican. But actually, if you want the real lowdown on her, she's *American*. She was born right here in California. Just like you, Mother. She's just as American as you are."

Mrs. Whitman let her son's words of wisdom roll off her. "Yes, well, that's your opinion."

"In *fact*," Melissa added, the excitement level of her voice increasing, "she's more Californian than any of us. You and Dad met in Birmingham, and then you guys *moved* here. From what I understand, Carmen was *born* in California. She's as Californian as you can get!"

"So," Randy continued, picking up the tempo, playing off his sister's comments as though she had set him up for a strategic spike during a game of volleyball. "What it comes down to—what it's all about for us—is that the only thing that makes us so different is our *skin color*. That's it. Her skin is darker than mine—than yours—and she stands out to you because of *that*?"

Rather than respond directly with another one of his offhand, bigoted analogies, Mr. Whitman brought his lips together and reached for a bowl of buttered corn. He said, "You know, Randy, pulling your old debater tricks on me or your mother is not a good way to make your point. This is the real world, Son, not your world of verbal diarrhea."

Part of Randy wanted to laugh. Another part of him wanted to cry. His generation was determined to be less bigoted than his parents' generation, and that was a good thing. With President Kennedy in office and his push for substantial, sweeping civil rights legislation, things were bound to change for the better. Perhaps the racist tenor of society for the current crusty cluster of narrow-minded adults could not be swayed, but at least their children would be subjected to more enlightened attitudes.

In California, the immigrants from South of the Border, particularly Mexicans, faced the toughest challenges. But overall, no group of Americans had suffered more at the hands of racism than Colored People. Negroes in the South were lower than second-class citizens. Negroes were forced to drink water from separate fountains, attend all Colored schools, and ride only in the back of the bus. These had been trademarks of Southern bigotry for decades. American Negroes lived better in California. But pocketed in the ghettoes of Los Angeles, San Francisco, and Sacramento, they were entrenched in appalling poverty.

The Whitman family was one of privilege, largely due to Randy's parents' commitment to getting an education, but also due to dumb luck. The Whitmans were white. The ancestry of the family could be traced to hard work and heredity of money lines through lucrative small business ventures that had been passed down to each successive generation of Whitmans.

Randy knew his parents well. He recognized their bigotry and where it came from. He simply did not like it. And now that a beautiful girl like Carmen had personalized these issues in his life, he grew less and less tolerant of people who dismissed others because of the shade of their skin.

However, Carmen had become another issue altogether. It had nothing to do with her Puerto Rican values, her parents, or her inability to cope with Randy's parents' rejection of her. Carmen radiated a social dominance that most young females did not dare approach. Her assertiveness never went unnoticed. She did not think boys and girls were equal; she believed that girls were *better*: Girls should establish all the rules of dating etiquette. Girls should call the shots. Girls should determine the future of a relationship and where it would (or would not) be headed.

Randy believed that Carmen's arrogance reflected a backlash to the way her father treated her mother. In her culture there was no question about who wore the pants in a marriage or even in a dating relationship. Males were far superior to females. God had intended it to be that way. The *men* in families controlled money, education, and social customs. Life-altering decisions affecting great familial changes both began and ended with words of great wisdom from the man.

So Randy believed that Carmen, encumbered by the cultural confinements of her family, was making up for lost time. And he found this increasingly difficult to deal with.

"When we get married," Carmen had told him, "I want to live in Puerto Rico—at least, for the first few years, until we have our children. Our children who are born in Puerto Rico will still be Americans by birth."

Randy squirmed in his seat behind the steering wheel of his father's 1961 Plymouth Fury, an inordinately large, white automobile with obnoxious looking fins that jutted from both sides of its rear. "This is the first time you mentioned that to me."

"There has to be a first time for everything, Randy."

"Well, I don't know if I'd be okay with that, Carmen. My family is in America. And you don't have roots in Puerto Rico. Your roots are *here*."

"Most of my family is still in Puerto Rico," she corrected him.

"But there are also other things to think about: my career. I want to be a lawyer. How am I going to practice law in Puerto Rico?"

"You can practice law in Puerto Rico," she replied, smiling. "Puerto Rico needs lawyers. We have bad people there who need defending, too."

"And another ambition that I have—I've told you about this before, Carmen," Randy stumbled.

Randy paused to let her recall that second ambition of his, one he had mentioned on numerous occasions. But Carmen could not remember it. She rarely paid close attention to Randy while he talked about himself or his family.

"Remember?" he coaxed. "I want to shake hands with President Kennedy before he leaves office in 1969. How can I do that in Puerto Rico?"

"Silly," Carmen chided him, as she slapped him lightly on his shoulder. "All you have to do is shake hands with President Kennedy before we get married. We are both going to college first, anyway. See, Randy? Just shake hands with President Kennedy before, uh, 1968."

Carmen, with her patented rapid-fire delivery, had an answer to everything. Sometimes she was right, but often her ideas made little practical sense. According to Carmen, if Randy wanted to shake hands with President Kennedy, he still had five or six years —before he married her—to make that happen.

Randy and Carmen had this discussion about Puerto Rico and marriage and college and President Kennedy in the summer of 1963. In less than four months, President Kennedy would be dead, a victim of assassins' bullets. Shortly thereafter, in a manner far beyond even her ability to take control, Carmen would be sliding away from Randy's life.

And Randall Walter Whitman, at the tender age of sixteen, would be descending swiftly into hell.

—CHAPTER 2—

The Boss never had been one to mince words.

His tongue lashing of the dark-skinned Cuban should have been recorded for posterity.

Anyone with even a minimal sense of self-preservation, not to mention self-respect and dignity, who listened to that recording would have trembled. It was a humbling experience, bordering between awesome admiration and blatant fear.

But too many men knew about their mission, and some of these men could not be trusted. It wasn't that any of their cohorts gave The Boss solid reasons to distrust them, but The Boss preferred much greater scrutiny of, and ultimate control over, the decision-making process. Selecting the right people for the job should not have been a frivolous endeavor.

The Boss's New Orleans office in a benign-looking, high-rise office building, one smelling of Lysol and inexpensive soap scrubbing agents, did not intimidate Ricardo.

Only The Boss intimidated Ricardo.

No one else in the world had the power to do that. Ricardo, a tall, lithe, handsome man in his early forties, personified the essence of Latin terror in the Caribbean during the last several years. A period of revolution, violence, and political haymakers left standing only the strongest and most enduring. And Ricardo had been one of those who had not only survived but also wound up near the very top of the revolutionary hierarchy.

The Boss ended his tirade against the normally irascible Latin by telling him, "I'll be honest with you, Ricardo. I came this close…" He held up his right hand, pinching his thumb to his forefinger. "…To having *you* disposed of! But I don't know who you've already involved, so offing you would have done no good, not in a practical sense. Do you know what I mean?"

Ricardo, who often sported a grin, would not bow his head in deference to anyone. He did, however, lower his voice. Nobody else ever spoke to him this way. He mumbled, "Yes, I understand your concern. My part of the mission was to recruit and control our soldiers. That is what you told me."

"Yes, and you were given a deadline. But that deadline is several weeks from now, at least a couple of months before our serious meetings will begin. It's still early."

Ricardo nodded. Oh, how he wanted a cigar right now! Watching The Boss devour several cigarettes made his cravings only worse. "I saw a need to get things in place in case we have to make a few personnel changes."

"It's only summer," The Boss sneered. "We have until the fall—maybe the winter. Your haste could have created serious problems." He narrowed his eyes into their infamous scolding alignment. "I'm simply reminding you of your obligation to second guess nothing yourself, and to preempt any need for remorse by placing all responsibility on *my* shoulders."

"Yes, I will be more patient. I take back any urgency."

"It *is* urgent, Ricardo," the Boss reminded him. "But urgency doesn't have to be defined by impatient acts of stupidity."

"I get it."

"Or carelessness."

"I understand."

This time Ricardo truly understood. The Boss reigned over tens of thousands who depended on his leadership capabilities: his iron fist guarded their standard of living, their ability to buy a car, and the amount of food their children could put in their bellies. Before his recent acquaintance with The Boss, Ricardo usually had deflected ideas offering theories and opinions contrary to his own. Implanted in a position of audacious authority, Ricardo saw little need to revere anyone else's way of conducting business.

But dealing with The Boss in New Orleans had abruptly changed Ricardo's philosophy about power and authority and deference, exposing to himself his personal vulnerability at levels he wished he never had become familiar.

—CHAPTER 3—

Across the Atlantic Ocean, a young quartet had just broken into the rock music world. Four shaggy-haired, young men calling themselves The Beatles created an exceptional stir in Liverpool but had not been accepted by audiences in the United States.

In America in 1963, surf music became a phenomenon, with groups like Dick Dale and the Deltones leaving their exclamation mark on the genre. Phil Spector produced a couple of talented female groups, The Ronnettes and The Crystals, while bands like the Ran-Dells offered up innovative faire in the form of songs like "The Martian Hop."

Novelty television programming was also in order in 1963: *Mr. Ed* (a talking horse), and *The Beverly Hillbillies* (the nuttiness of the title speaks for itself) led the way in the ratings. This period also marked the debut of *The Fugitive* and popular T.V. doctor shows, *Ben Casey*, and *Dr. Kildare*.

In 1963, American pop culture was teeming with the freedom of creativity, yet bound by the security of tradition.

One of the most popular recordings of this era was an album recorded by comedian Vaughn Meader. Meader eagerly took advantage of the uniqueness of the Kennedy Administration's youth, handsomeness, and vigor, by creating a parody of those who dominated the news in the early 1960s. Meader's album, *The First Family*, a vinyl disc played by a needle at thirty-three revolutions per minute, extracted knowing chuckles and easy laughs from those in all walks of American life. Love them or hate them, this spoof of the Kennedys—and the way they talked and the way they thought and the way they ran the country—raked in millions of dollars and stood above all other records of that genre as the biggest money-maker to date.

Randy loved this recording almost as much as he loved the

real President Kennedy. He couldn't listen to it enough. According to Randy, Meader's impersonation of President Kennedy helped to infuse the country with a certain youthful vitality and sense of humor it had been missing for a long time—from Presidents Hoover, Roosevelt, Truman, and Eisenhower, until the present day. Apart from debating the effectiveness of these leaders, one could not dispute that they had all been *old* while they sat in the White House.

John Fitzgerald Kennedy: his wit at press conferences; his home movies of a beautiful, fashionably dressed wife and adorable, doting children; his youthful athleticism, with an appetite for competitive touch football on the White House lawn, bucked the trend of aged leaders in the executive branch of government and welcomed the anomaly of young people serving in positions of American leadership.

****

"Randy," Mr. Lott called, jolting Randall Whitman awake from a disturbing daydream about Carmen, "Are you planning for your best year—your best year *ever*?"

Randy always recognized trick questions. An obvious answer, of course, should have been *yes*. But Mr. Lott, the team's teacher and debate coach, had an ulterior motive: *Are you one of those losers who thinks his best year should only come during the senior year*?

Late summer debate meetings were not only for organizational purposes. Mr. Lott used them to generate enthusiasm in his team and to indicate what lay ahead: their goals, their expectations, and the championship caliber tournaments they might attend. These meetings, held in Mr. Lott's modest home in an upscale Los Angeles County suburb, filled the teenagers with excitement and anticipation. But their discussions also caused the debaters some angst, for they all knew that they would have to work hard, compromise their temptations, and sacrifice their leisure time to achieve those goals.

"Well, Mr. Lott," Randy said, jarred from his thoughts by

Mr. Lott's trick question, "I want to have the best year I've had *so far.*"

Not the right answer, at least, according to Mr. Lott.

Mr. Richard Lott, a steely-eyed, dark-haired man in his early forties, glared in the direction of another debater in the room: a skinny, anemic-looking kid by the name of Ruther Gardner. Ruther, who always looked on the verge of death, had the misfortune of having a face covered by acne, *and* being stuck with the name *Ruther.* But in this dog-eat-dog world of academic debate, where the quest for college scholarships and for national prestige came together in one room, no one would be feeling sorry for Ruther Gardner.

"What do you say, Ruth?" Mr. Lott asked Ruther Gardner, committing the cardinal sin of referring to him as *Ruth.*

"I think," Ruther answered tentatively, "that *this* will be the best year—for me, the best. Yes."

Maybe this was the right response, the answer Mr. Lott coveted. An English teacher and the squad's debate coach, he paced in front of a dozen students who had congregated in his living room and littered the space with Cheetos, pretzel snacks, Cokes, and their own bodies. Clad in their cool summer attire, the kids had prepared for their next stop after the debate meeting: the backyard swimming pool belonging to the parents of one of their team members, Margie Pendergrass.

Mr. Lott looked older than his years, but he breathed youthful enthusiasm into a once dying high school debate program. During the three years he directed the squad's activities, the team had risen to one of the leading chapters in the National Forensic League, the master organization for high schools involved in competitive speech and debate. Here the letters N.F.L. did not stand for the National Football League. Mistaking this acronym had become a standard irritation among those who knew better.

Mr. Lott gave Ruther a patronizing pat on the top of his head and spoke to everyone in the room, using his booming speaking voice even in these small confines. "You're going to have your best year? *Duh!* From you juniors, that sounds especially stupid. You're dismissing the possibility that *next* year can be an even better one. Do you see what I'm saying?"

Most of the debaters nodded.

"So," Mr. Lott continued, "let's just count on *this* being your best year ever. At this time next year in this same room, when I ask this same question, you will adjust your answers accordingly. Besides, what if this year is our last year?"

Perplexed by Mr. Lott's question, the debaters ignored it. These students were too smart not to recognize their coach's hokey approach to generating confidence and enthusiasm. But they played along. Summer had almost gone by, and these young people were ready to start thinking about another year of competitive debate. Looming tournaments were often the catalyst for these kids to do well in school. The thrill of debate competition, like sports, often got them to school in the first place.

And when Mr. Lott then made a surprising announcement, Randy Whitman thought he would, indeed, have his best year ever, not only in debate, but also in school as a whole.

Mr. Lott grinned sheepishly and said, "How would you guys like to go to Southern Methodist University to compete in the Tournament of Champions? Huh? How does that sound to you?"

At first, none of the debaters responded. None could. Their mouths hung agape, and even Randy remained silent. Then it seemed as though they all began to speak at once. They interrupted each other with all the etiquette of little children clawing for the ice cream and cake at a toddler's birthday party.

Ira Cushman's voice caught Mr. Lott's immediate attention. He asked excitedly, "You mean all of us? You're talking about *Texas*?"

Others attempted to break through with questions of their own, but Mr. Lott put up his hand and dealt with each query in a diplomatic manner, much like a political candidate taming the throngs of eager reporters at an exciting press conference.

He replied to Ira first. "Our school has been invited. Only thirty schools in the entire nation received initial invitations. Southern Methodist keeps sending priority invites in the mail until thirty schools confirm. We have until September 15 to RSVP. As for how many of us will attend, here's the scoop: Only three debate teams per school are allowed to enter. That means, of course [with two person teams], six of you will be going to the Tournament of Champions at Southern Methodist in November."

Next, Maria Barquin, a dark-haired, brown-eyed sophomore asked, "Is this one of those tournaments that awards big college scholarships?"

"Not directly," Mr. Lott replied. "But the overall prestige of this event attracts all kinds of college recruiters—from Harvard, MIT, Stanford, and so on—which always leads to some really attractive scholarship offers about the time you graduate high school. In your case, Maria, you would be looking at those scholarships probably two years from now—although you may decide not to use any of them."

More questions:

"How will you determine which teams get to go?"

"We have eight established teams. Maybe we'll have some kind of round robin here at school."

"How much will it cost?"

"Too much."

"Where are we going to get the money from?"

"We have a supportive school board; they love our program. It brings accolades to the district."

"The school board will pay?"

"They always gave us money when I asked them before. This one is so cool, it'll knock their socks off! Trust me."

"Where is Southern Methodist University, anyway?"

"Dallas, Texas."

"When's the tournament? I sure hope it's not Thanksgiving weekend. My parents would never let me go during Thanksgiving. What's the date?"

"Don't worry about Thanksgiving, Margie. It's the weekend before. We'd fly out of Los Angeles on that Thursday morning and arrive at our hotel in the late afternoon. Your first round of competition would be on, uh—let's see—Friday evening, the twenty-second of November..."

Later as Randy stood in front of Mr. Lott's house waiting for his father to pick him up, another debater came up behind him and slapped him on the back—hard!

Tommy Wright looked more like a football player than a debater. Tall and sturdy, and adorned by a head of wavy blond hair, Tommy fashioned himself quite the ladies' man of the debate team. But none of the ladies on the debate team seemed to be interested in him. It wasn't his physical appearance that posed an obstacle for the girls; he was quite handsome. What troubled the females on the debate squad about Tommy: his crass, loud demeanor and a raucous personality that lent itself more to having friends who were in junior high school, instead of in high school.

Randy often found himself annoyed with Tommy Wright.

After receiving the smash on his back from Tommy, Randy forced a grin. It hurt, but he didn't want to look soft, especially around Tommy Wright, a boy who constantly searched for tactics that would annoy Randy.

"What's goin' on, Tommy?" he forced himself to ask.

"Nothing. Just wanted to pick your brain," Tommy replied, his face so close to Randy's that Randy could smell the barbecued potato chips on his breath.

"Pick my brain?"

"Yes," Tommy said. "You know something? You're such an asshole!"

Tommy's name-calling and use of profanity rarely surprised anyone, but Randy wondered why Tommy thought he was an asshole tonight, as opposed to, say, last night. "I'm an asshole?"

"Yeah. You know why." It was a statement, not a question.

"I do?"

"You should."

"What if I say that I don't?"

"Then you're a *lying* asshole!" Tommy chided him.

"That makes no sense, Tommy."

"Yeah? Well, Randy, you're going to Southern Methodist in November. You're a shoe-in; I'm not."

"What makes you think I'm a shoe-in?"

"Come on!" Tommy ranted. "You're the top debater on this team. Mr. Lott thinks you're Jesus Christ. You're going for sure!"

"So?" Randy shrugged. "Why are you mad at *me* for that?"

"I'm not mad at you, Randy," Tommy smiled. "You're just an asshole."

"What?"

"For being in such a great position. You can't lose. Now, on the other hand, Ira Cushman, your esteemed partner, is not nearly as good as you are. Maybe with a different partner Ira wouldn't be going to Dallas at all."

Shaking his head, Randy half-chuckled. "That's not true, Tommy. All you have to do is be in the top six. Ira's certainly in the top six."

"Yeah," Tommy sulked, "but I'm not. I'm probably around number eight."

"So," Randy mused, thinking Tommy had placed himself a little too low at number eight, "you want me to stop debating with Ira so he can become your partner—and then you'd be going to Dallas? Is that it?"

In the partial darkness of the street lamps, Randy detected Tommy's nod.

"Something like that," Tommy partially agreed.

"Only," he went on, "I don't want Ira Cushman for a debate partner. I want *you* for a debate partner."

Randy forced himself to remain stoic. "Me?"

"Yeah. That way I would be on the top team."

"Not necessarily."

"Yeah, I would," Tommy persisted. "I'd be on the number one team—and you know it. Anybody who has you for a debate colleague would be on the number one team. At the very least, I'd be going to the Tournament of Champions in Dallas—guaranteed."

"Mr. Lott makes those decisions, Tommy," was all that Randy said, all he could think of saying. Tommy's proposition had taken him by surprise, and it was utterly ridiculous. He could never debate with Tommy Wright as his partner. Tommy's personality rubbed him the wrong way, and his character came off to him as a bit creepy.

"Mr. Lott will pair you with whoever you want," Tommy said bitterly.

"No, he won't," Randy replied, although he thought maybe

Tommy was correct in his assessment about Mr. Lott granting him his wishes. Randy usually had his way with the coach.

Randy anticipated further nagging from Tommy, but Tommy decided to wait and think things over.

Then Tommy Wright folded his arms, sighed, and looked up into a clear, star-filled sky. "Okay. I can't force you to be my partner. But maybe I can get that swell looking babe—that freshman—to be my partner. Mr. Lott's thinks she's keen, too—wants to take her to Dallas no matter what."

Tommy Wright sounded crass, but Randy did have to agree on some level: Maria Barquin was a fantabulous looking babe—and smarter than anyone else on the debate team. Her lack of experience in the thick of championship debate competition presented her only liability.

Randy wanted to correct Tommy about Maria's class status (she, after all, was beginning her *sophomore* year), but he decided to let it go. Tommy Wright, for selfish purposes alone, had considered snaring Maria for a debate partner. He would ruin her in every way imaginable. And although Tommy demonstrated incredible immaturity and perpetual tactlessness, his good looks did have their potency. Some girls actually fell for boys like Tommy: handsome, aggressive, loud, troubled, and physically strong.

As he waited for his father to pick him up, Randy mulled over whether Maria Barquin possessed the potential for being attracted to boys like Tommy Wright. He shuddered at the possibility, the summer night suddenly becoming very cold.

****

It appeared—at least, for a while—that Randy's worries about Maria and Tommy would have no foundation.

Randy's mind was preoccupied with the beginning of school and the constant drama of Carmen Pedro. He really hadn't thought very much about Maria Barquin; that is, until the next debate squad meeting, this one on the night before Monday's fall opening of the school year. The get-together was mostly social, an annual function also attended by Mr. Lott; he would, unfortunately, don his turquoise bathing trunks at another swim party, again at the luxurious home of Margie Pendergrass.

When Mr. Lott later approached Randy, who was seated alone in a corner of the Pendergrass living room, Randy had just finished his bottle of Coca Cola and was thinking about a recent confrontation with Carmen. This time it was over Carmen's unwillingness to accompany him to the get-together at Margie's swimming pool. Even after Randy had assured Carmen that the others at this informal, non-academic, non-debaterish event would welcome her, she lashed out at him for what she argued was his condescending attitude and general lack of sensitivity towards her.

"Sure, you would take me to *this* meeting, Randy! I guess you don't think I'm smart enough to go to a *real* debate meeting!"

Despite Randy's frustration with trying to explain to Carmen that she would be utterly *bored* at a "real debate meeting"—only because she was not a debater—Carmen snarled at him anyway. "I suppose you would like for me to parade around your puny little brainy friends in my white bikini so you can show me off or something!"

Ironically, it had been Randy's celebrity in the debate realm that had first attracted Carmen to him. But now it created a wedge that occasionally drove them in separate directions. At first, sparked by Randy's verbal prowess and rising popularity on their campus, Carmen eagerly sought after him, absorbing him into her web of femininity and calculated flirtatiousness. But like a fly trapped in a spider's nest, his emotional flailing about served only to make matters worse. Carmen, and the problems she posed, had saturated Randy's thoughts.

Mr. Lott—thankfully, now fully dressed—sat down next to him on another leather loveseat chair, a quality of furniture no one else's parents on the debate squad could afford to bring into their homes.

"I have a proposition for you, Whitman."

Oh-oh. Whenever Mr. Lott addressed one of his debaters by only his last name, trouble brewed on the horizon.

"I'm listening," Randy lied. His mind was now frozen on an

image of his girlfriend parading around the Pendergrass's swimming pool in that white bikini she had alluded to in their most recent skirmish.

"Here it is," Mr. Lott told him, suddenly very business-like. "You're going to Southern Methodist in November. You're my top debater. I don't need some cockamamie round robin to tell me that. But…" Mr. Lott pinched his cheeks back simply by jutting his jaw and overlapping his lips. "You're not going to debate with Ira Cushman anymore. Ira is good, but he's not in your league; frankly, if anything, he's holding you down."

"But, Mr. Lott," Randy pleaded. "We won Berkeley last year. We took fourth at U.S.C., and we probably would have won the State Qualifier, if…"

Just as Randy's words trailed off, Mr. Lott finished his sentence. "If Ira hadn't dropped the plan attacks in the first affirmative rebuttal. Ira did that. Not you. Ira's good; you're much better. And how does a first affirmative rebuttal speech ignore the plan attacks, for God's sake!"

"Is Ira going at all? To Dallas, I mean."

"Only if he and his new partner pan out."

"Who's that?"

"Who's what?"

"Ira's new partner."

Mr. Lott laughed. "You're all hot and bothered about Ira? Wouldn't you like to know who *your* new partner is going to be for Southern Methodist? A guaranteed position at The Tournament of Champions!"

Oddly, Randy felt his lower lip twitching uncontrollably. He was not, after all, about to be indicted for murder by a grand jury. But the debate squad's logistical minutia—the various team pairings, tournament schedules, and housing arrangements—meant more to him than he ever openly admitted to anyone else.

"Maria," he heard Mr. Lott say.

"Huh?"

"Your new partner will be Maria."

"Maria Barquin?"

"The only Maria on the squad that I know about! Even

27

though she's only a sophomore, she's the second best debater on a very good squad. You were our second best debater at this time last year. Remember? *You* were only a sophomore."

Randy's emotions churned.

And he wondered why. Was it that he had never been teamed with anyone other than Ira Cushman, or that Maria did not measure up to the requisite standards for a championship caliber debater? Perhaps it was really something *else*.

Then he glanced out a window peering into the backyard and saw Maria Barquin in a green, one-piece bathing suit preparing for her dive into the swimming pool.

Randy now had a hunch about his teeming emotions—and raging hormones. He had never *consciously* viewed Maria in those terms before, but his epiphany allowed him some insight into what had been bothering him for almost a year: his inability to reconcile his intense, natural attraction to Maria with his required loyalty to Carmen.

Never before had he so carefully mulled over this conflict. But not until just now had he been assigned by his debate coach to work closely with the brilliant, dark-haired sophomore in the conservative, green bathing suit.

—CHAPTER 4—

Four very different men sat in the same room, surrounded by the dim lighting of incandescent light bulbs, flickering in the twilight of their life's expectancy. Late September heat in Southern Louisiana was still oppressive, and even the roaring fans, several of which were mounted to the ceiling, provided little relief in the wake of the waning Southern summer.

The man who wore a businessman's gray suit and oversize hat sat back and occasionally rubbed his free hand on his chin. He scowled while he huffed and puffed through a chain of cigarettes. "They know who I am. They like me. And I can make myself visible almost anywhere."

A second man, one who always seemed to be grinning, shrugged. "Only if and when the situation necessitates that kind of subterfuge, and only if the event transpires in your city. No location has been guaranteed. None."

The Hat Man removed the cigarette from his mouth. "Right now, Texas stands out as a pretty good possibility, doesn't it?" And he intentionally blew a string of smoke rings at the Grinning Man.

A third man radiated a seriousness the others camouflaged. He grimaced as he shook his head. "If his schedule changes—and it usually does—sure, there needs to be a backup; there need to be several backups. But the *means* must not change! We've studied this over and over. It gets to the point where we must be ready to go. Further study will waste time and immobilize us!"

The Hat Man nodded his head. "There may never be an opportunity as ripe as this one."

"So what?" a fourth man, one who stood six-and-a-half feet tall, said. "The schedule will probably be altered between now and October." He then scowled, his fiery eyes blazing at the Serious Man. The Tall Man's eyes would have destroyed the confidence of almost any other man. "Something tells me you're *too* willing to go—and that concerns me. The schedule could be changed, and we'd have to adjust."

As the other three bickered, the Grinning Man took notes. "It *will* be altered," he emphasized without looking up from his paper pad. "Plans for parades and motorcades and public appearances don't stay the same for very long. We should plan with great flexibility. As The Boss recently reminded me, October is not far off."

The Tall Man scolded, "That's right: backup plans, contingencies. There's no room for failure."

The Hat Man pulled out another cigarette from a package of many. "My position in the community gives us some of the flexibility you've been talking about."

The Grinning Man narrowed his eyes on the Hat Man. "This is why, if you screw up, or—if God forbid—you are deceiving us with a double-agent modality, you will be the first to die. The rest of us may be right behind you, but you will be the first. Is this clear?"

Because the other three did not have a full amount of trust in the Hat Man, they watched him carefully. After the Grinning Man's admonition, the Hat Man relaxed his bravado, stuffing his newly lit cigarette into an ashtray.

****

One of the perks of having a debate partner was that they would visit each other's homes. They ate good snacks together and enjoyed drinks prepared by their debate partner's mother.

If the partner was an attractive female, then what had been some nice perks suddenly became even a lot nicer.

Randall Walter Whitman now spent less and less time with Carmen, as he intensified his preparation for the Tournament of Champions in November. Naturally, this entailed working near and dear for many hours with Maria Barquin, at her house—and his.

One night in early October, Maria walked into Randy's home with a pile of books under her right arm and a briefcase in her left hand. Normally, Mr. and Mrs. Whitman ignored her presence, but tonight Mr. Whitman worked late. Mrs. Whitman approached her for the first time without the company of her husband.

"Randy's in his bedroom, Maria," she smiled cordially. "Mr. Whitman and I both agreed that it would be proper if you and Randy worked together down here in the living room—or even on the kitchen table, if you'd prefer. Or maybe you would just consent to keeping the bedroom door wide open."

Maria didn't blanche. "Oh, that's fine," she said as she put her books on a side table and rested her briefcase on the floor. "I think my parents would actually feel better about any of those arrangements, too. We do it like that at my house."

"Thank you for understanding."

"Of course," Maria smiled back.

"I know that you two are, well, just *colleagues*, but still…"

"Yes, we are just colleagues."

But as Maria described Randy's and her relationship as "just colleagues," Randy had reached the top of the stairwell and overheard her comment. For some reason these words drove what felt like a spear made from hot metal through his liver area.

Randy's defensive mechanisms came to life. "You're late," he scowled at Maria.

"Late?" she grimaced.

Randy found her crinkled, turned up nose irresistible. Something about petite, curvaceous, dark-haired, brown-eyed, young Hispanic women allured him in ways that he had not yet understood.

"Well," he stammered, "since you're usually early, being only on time *makes* you late."

Randy befuddled even himself with his own logic.

She half-grinned and said, "Yes, well, maybe the novelty of spending time with you has worn off, and I'm not so eager to get here early anymore."

Ouch!

That hurt!

Another blow to Randy's liver area!

Maria Estella Barquin's mother and father did not own their

American citizenship at the time of their daughter's birth. But these undocumented immigrants from Mexico introduced their precious baby Maria to the world while they lived in a small apartment in Pico Rivera, a suburb of Los Angeles, California. This provided the legal status they so purposefully had sought for her: a natural American citizen.

Staunchly Roman Catholic and determined to provide a better life for their (then) only child, Mr. Barquin taught himself tooling skills—buying, selling, and fixing. He eventually found his way to a favorable business climate that took him and his family from the comparably dreary confines of Pico Rivera to North Long Beach. More immediate opportunities for attracting clients and superior schools for his two children awaited them.

The year 1963 saw a plethora of stay-at-home mothers, and Mrs. Barquin endeared herself to her family as such a woman. She keenly observed her only daughter grow into a beautiful, though somewhat precocious, young lady who knew more about national politics at the age of twelve than her father had known during his entire lifetime.

High school debate competition sparkled as an obvious depository for Maria's analytical mind and blossoming oratory abilities. In her freshman year, she boasted of both academic and debate achievements, largely due to her disciplined study habits, her intense desire to succeed, and natural rhetoric skills. And when it came to winning over the judges in tight debates at tournaments, Maria's good looks were an attribute.

The 1963-64 high school debate season brought a new national topic, one that would be used at every tournament throughout the year: *Be it resolved, that the federal government should provide a guaranteed annual income for all American citizens*. Not exactly a subject for sexy discourse, the question of whether or not the government of the United States had the responsibility to make sure every citizen "earned" at least a minimum amount of money each year lent itself to some provocative areas for discussion: entitlements, bilking the system, racism, socialism, and the desperation of people mired in poverty.

The average, run-of-the-mill teenage mind did not spend too

much time giving serious consideration to these topics. But then again, high school debaters in 1963 did not own average, run-of-the-mill teenage minds—or vocabularies or work ethics.

Soon the minds of Randy Whitman and Maria Barquin began to concentrate less on profound topics related to government involvement in solving the poverty problem, and more on the politics of mutual attraction.

Maria playfully poked Randy in the arm when he made her laugh at his comment about girl debaters being better suited to deliver the first speech in a debate. He had said, "You girls can get your team off to a good start by flirting a little bit with the judge. You do give a good speech, Maria, but some flirting won't hurt."

"What if the judge is a woman?" Maria teased.

"Ah! Doesn't matter," Randy replied. "Women just respond better to that stuff no matter what. The women will just think you're friendly." And then he made the comment that precipitated her punch to his arm: "Even you can fake being nice, can't you?"

He didn't say it genuinely, and she didn't punch him hard. But Randy immediately reverted his thoughts to Carmen Pedro and quickly became solemn and introspective, putting an end to this short, flirtatious interlude with his debate partner.

The very next evening, his father, in Randy's estimation, crossed over the line.

Randy busily worked on his algebra homework from his usual perch at the kitchen table, when Mr. Whitman approached him. Most men who owned their own businesses established their own working conditions and set their own hours. Mr. Whitman usually returned home from his hardware store shortly after 6:00 P.M.—in time for dinner. Tonight, still adorned in his white shirt and thin black tie, Mr. Whitman arrived home almost an hour later than he usually did.

"You work hard, son," Mr. Whitman complimented Randy.

Randy glanced up and forced a grin. The cumulative hours of working on debate and keeping up with his daily homework had exhausted him. "Thanks. You're home late tonight."

"Yeah," Mr. Whitman sighed. "I had a long talk with Petie. Unfortunately, I had to let him go."

"You fired Petie?"

Petie had been an employee of Whitman's Hardware for almost a year. An immigrant from the bowels of Mexico—probably without legal papers—Petie was an affable, quiet man who struggled with a drinking problem.

Randy knew his father had contemplated firing Petie—and why—but he felt compelled to ask, "What happened?"

"Same ol,' same ol.'"

"At the store?" Randy was incredulous.

"He showed up drunk again this morning. He staggered through the day, and after lunch he fell asleep in the supply closet. No booze at the store, but those people don't do it like that. They tend to get drunk at night while they're watching television, until all the stations shut down for the night. And then they can't sleep it off by morning. That's just how they operate."

Randy didn't know what to say. He wasn't sure whether to smile, scream, or run. A rush of rage came up through his body, but he managed to block it in his throat. His father's brother, Leo, was a drunk—and a *white* guy. Ira's father—a *Jewish* white guy—drank to excess! "I don't know what you're talking about, Dad."

Mr. Whitman didn't intend to toy with his son, but evidently it appeared that way to Randy. Totally *serious*, Mr. Whitman wanted to change that perception: "Oh, come off it, Randy! You know how Mexicans are! They drink liquor like it's water. And most of the time they can't hold their booze, either. That's why it's so hard for them to keep a job after they sneak over here!"

Randy silently reminded himself to take very short breaths. He thought he loved his father, but the bigoted part of him—and of his mother—he didn't like or understand. "Dad, if this has been for my benefit, you can save your breath."

"It's not for your benefit. You asked me why I fired Petie."

"You've never even met Maria's father," Randy argued, exasperated. "This man—this man came over here with nothing. When he was a teenager he lived in old railroad cars while he worked in the fields. He finally taught himself a skill, something he's gotten very good at over the years. And he makes good money, enough to feed a family of four, while his wife stays home and takes care of the kids. His son is brilliant in school. He's only eleven, and already he wants to be a doctor. And Maria, well, Maria is one of the smartest people I've ever met. She's so incredibly nice—and *she* doesn't have a racist bone in her body."

Randy finally let out his breath.

"Are you done?" Mr. Whitman asked.

"Yes."

"Because if you're not—"

"I said I was done."

Shaking his head, Mr. Whitman sat down next to his distraught son. Randy hoped he would have something profound to say—perhaps, an apology; after all, his father now had shown such unfair judgment towards two extremely important people in his life.

But an apology was not in the offering.

"She's the Mexican one or the Puerto Rican?"

"What?" Randy's heart did a dive.

His father went on. "Maria? I think you said she came from Mexico."

"She was born *here*, Dad! She was born in California! You and Mom weren't born in California! If Maria is some kind of outsider, what does that make *you*?"

Despite their sizzling confrontation, Mr. Whitman displayed calm. "I'm not calling her anything, Randy; in fact, you're the one who brought Maria into the conversation. I was talking about Petie and how he has a problem that many Mexicans seem to have. And that's the truth. Maybe your Mexican girlfriend doesn't have that problem. Maybe her father is as dry as the desert. Just why are you being so defensive?"

For the life of him, Randy couldn't comprehend why his father didn't get it. "Never mind," he sighed. "Dad, I don't go out of my way to pick Hispanic girlfriends—even though Maria is not my girlfriend. Uh, you know—what's her—*Carmen* is my girlfriend. The thing is, these girls come from really nice families."

"Maybe," Mr. Whitman acknowledged. "But do you want to marry into a Puerto Rican family? Do you want to live in Puerto Rico—or Mexico—around all their relatives?"

"No."

"Well, that's where you'd be headed."

"Dad, I'm only sixteen years old!"

"I was sixteen when I met your mother."

"You don't marry every girl you meet."

"No," his father said, "you don't. But do you want to open yourself up to marrying one of them?"

At this point, Randy knew their discussion had to end. He had nothing left to say. Emotionally exhausted, he looked down and weakly inquired, "Dad, did you want to ask me something? Because I've got a lot of algebra left."

Mr. Whitman, his upper neck above the white shirt collar showing a beet red, rose from the wooden chair and shrugged. "Not really. I thought you'd been working too hard—that with all the debate work and homework you might like to take a break and go to the World Series with me tomorrow afternoon. I got tickets from a guy who comes into the store. Koufax is pitching against Jim Bouton."

In any other context on any other day, Randy would have gleefully leaped at the opportunity to go to a ballgame with his dad, especially a World Series game against the hated Yankees and with his beloved Sandy Koufax on the mound. But he suddenly wanted to steer clear from his father and rejected his invitation. After an unusually long pause, he lied in a weak voice, "No… sorry, but I have to go over to Maria's tomorrow and work on debate. Mr. Lott's going to hear us practice on Monday."

How Randy wished this were the truth! In actuality, Maria had been invited by a friend of her cousin to go to the movies with him.

A *boy*.

Alone.

At night.

Maria had even tried to coax Randy into asking Carmen to double date with them, but he didn't think he could handle watching another boy hold Maria's hand. Logically, this shouldn't have mattered to him, for he was still Carmen's beau. But logic, he discovered, had played no part in his feelings for Maria Barquin.

He still had to cope with his father's encore. Oblivious to Randy's lie about tomorrow's debate meeting with Maria, Mr. Whitman affectionately touched his son's shoulder. "I understand. I know how busy you are. I just thought you needed a break and, you know, the World Series and all…I'll ask your sister to go with me."

Just like that, totally impassive to this unpleasant encounter with his son, Mr. Whitman turned away. He ascended the stairs and made his way to his daughter's bedroom.

—CHAPTER 5—

The Grinning Man chewed on the remains of his Cuban cigar. In many ways the satisfaction that came from smoking cigars increased immeasurably each time a cigar's light disappeared, with only the burnt, smoldering stub nestled between the Grinning Man's lips.

In Southern Louisiana on a beautiful evening from which tourist brochures were created, the Grinning Man sat with the Tall Man in the small office of the Tall Man's kitchen supply store.

And the Tall Man was not happy.

The Grinning Man noticed the Tall Man's mouth, and only one thought entered his mind: Perhaps after this job had filed into the history books, the Tall Man would get his teeth done. He certainly would have enough money! The Tall Man's size provided a distraction from other flaws on his body. But up close, crooked and yellow, bad teeth always stood out.

The Tall Man sat back in a mahogany chair and folded his long arms over his barrel chest. "Our man in Dallas was right— looks like Texas is our target. He's an insider there and would lend support. And he knew it all along."

The Grinning Man paused to flick some sleep from the corner of his eye. As he wiped it away, he shrugged his sturdy shoulders. "But he was wrong about dates. Dates are crucial."

The Tall Man nodded. "But he did get the city right. And he has contacts there."

"Contacts—yes. But none of them have been brought into our plans."

"Not those kinds of contacts. Let's just say that these people would be horrified if they knew. But they'd still go along with us and not have a clue what they were doing."

The Grinning Man squinted. Looking at his notebook, which

was now full of dates and scribbles and cross outs, he sighed heavily. "So, the tour is now set for November. But we do not have exact dates—and certainly no times or routes or specific locations. We are sure he will begin his bid in Texas—probably in the Dallas area. We can only conjecture about everything else. His goal will be to get as friendly with the people as possible. He needs their votes. He needs Texas. This means a very personal appearance. And a very personal appearance means a lot of exposure, usually accompanied by an astonishing lack of security around him."

The Tall Man nodded. "I've always said that patience is the thing."

The Grinning Man suddenly stopped grinning. "And so is secrecy during the time we are being patient. I can count on one hand the number of people who know about this. The Boss has already told me that if anything goes wrong during these early stages, he is holding me personally responsible. Me. I must weed out the bad plants now."

The Tall Man, using his fanged teeth, bit at a fingernail. Immersed in deep thought, he then scratched under his chin. He said, "I'm worried about one of us."

"I know who you mean."

" I'm not referring to our man in Dallas."

"I know that," the Grinning Man confirmed. "I, too, felt the strangeness of his urgency, wanting to make immediate plans for an event that had not yet been scheduled. He was too eager, too willing. I know that he came highly recommended—as did you and the others—but I do not feel secure with this man."

"Then what do we do?"

"The Boss has money, plenty of money. I have means. My contacts only want to know how much they will be paid to take care of this—and when. They do not need to know *why*."

The Tall Man opened his eyes wide. "Then that's your decision?"

"I already have given this much thought."

"Can we get a trustworthy replacement soon?"

The Grinning Man began rolling another cigar. "The Boss said this would not be a problem, if we made a decision on such matters soon."

This time the Tall Man said nothing.

So the Grinning Man, his handsome Latin features suddenly radiant in this clandestine office setting of a Louisiana port city, waved his hand. "So it will be done. He will be taken care of."

"But we don't know for sure that we can't trust him," the Tall Man advised. "We could be wrong."

"Yes," the Grinning Man acknowledged. "We could be wrong. We do not know for sure. But we *must* be sure. Taking unnecessary chances is not an option. Having ambiguous trust in someone—now that can be fatal."

—CHAPTER 6—

Randy loved listening to contemporary rock-n-roll music. His favorite group was the Five Satins, and his favorite song their number one single, "In the Still of the Night." He also relished the sounds of Dion and the Belmonts, The Penguins, and a new group from Southern California, The Beach Boys. Their new hit single, "Surfin' Safari," had an enjoyable tune and a terrific beat that almost everyone enjoyed. But Randy, who fashioned himself a music aficionado, nervously predicted an unwelcome change in the style of American rock-in-roll music.

As he listened to the melodic lyrics of the Danleers and a dreamy romantic ballad, "One Summer Night," he glanced at Maria, who sat on the edge of his bed with a yellow legal pad in her hand. She took notes from a book about state/federal welfare programs. The material would later be transferred to 4 by 6 index cards and used as evidence to support their arguments during debate rounds.

For a few precious moments, the climate around Randy Whitman defined a highpoint in his life: in his own bedroom; working on an activity he loved so intensely; surrounded by the magnificence of a gorgeous girl with more brains and giftedness for debate than anyone else on the team (besides him, of course); accompanied by the blissful notes of one of the most talented doo-wop groups in American music.

And she was *his* debate partner!

And she was *his* to talk to, and confide in…

But nothing more than a colleague in their pursuit of a competitive goal, Maria Barquin presented to Randy frustration he could not describe to anyone else, even to his best friend Ira Cushman.

His stare bounced off Maria just as she looked at him and

asked, "Do you want me to type your evidence cards?"

"I can do that," Randy replied, thinking to himself, *what a sweetheart for asking! Ira never volunteered to type anything for me!*

"I just like writing mine out. I can print them faster that way. But if you prefer, I will type yours. You might have trouble reading my printing."

"I doubt it," Randy smiled. "You print great. Anybody could read your printing."

His last few words drifted off into oblivion, as the sounds of the Danleers faded contemporaneous to his loss of focus on debate work. Around Maria, Randy often lost his desire to speak—or, perhaps, it was his *capability* to speak that he had lost. Randy had read books and seen movies about men who felt like putty in a woman's presence. While he spent time with Maria, Randy saw this happening to him.

But there were those moments Randy had invented exciting, new ideas that would probably help them in their debates. When he did so, his testosterone level soared to new heights. His considerable size for his age, even his impressive musculature, did not compare to his strengths in debate. In the debate world, he led the fold: impressive speaking skills, an acute sense of what truly mattered, an ability to quickly and logically process—then respond to—opponents' arguments, and an intense desire to succeed in the competition.

Randy wondered what Maria thought of him. Sure, he knew she admired his skills as a debater and his tough work ethic. But he doubted *she* had stared at *him* while he worked and thought about how beautiful *he* was—or how handsome. Much of Randy's time had been preoccupied with images of Maria and him as a couple. And he both admired himself and hated himself for those fantasies.

As another ballad started to spin, the Classics' "Till Then," Randy's head began to swirl. He smelled the fragrance of Maria's cologne and the unique, delicate scent of her hair. Debate work suddenly faded into the far reaches of his mind, and for an instant he even forgot the National Debate Topic. Someone might have asked him his name, and he would have had to pause and think about it.

Then the ringing of the downstairs telephone jarred Randy from his obsession, blemishing the perfection of his daydreams.

"Randy," the familiar voice of his mother reverberated from the foot of the stairs. "It's Carmen."

Randy immediately glanced at Maria for a reaction and saw her grimace, although she didn't look up from her work. The magazines and books she'd been pouring through were piled in front of her.

"Gotta' take it," he told her with a hint of resignation in his voice. He scooted from the bed and made his way downstairs to the phone his mother was holding. She handed the receiver to her son.

"Hi, tough guy!" he heard Carmen say on the other end.

"Hi," Randy said, slightly out of breath. For a brief instant he regretted not having feigned enthusiasm.

"Whatcha' doin?" she spoke in a vernacular completely inconsistent with her speech patterns.

Oddly, a truthful answer from Randy—threatened Randy: "Working," he replied sheepishly.

"Debate?"

Of course, Carmen knew he had been working nonstop on debate—with a little classroom homework thrown in—for over a month now.

"Yeah, debate," Randy affirmed. "We've been researching for evidence cards [Carmen didn't know what that meant.], and we'll be done pretty soon."

Carmen's voice rang of desperate sweetness. "What time?"

"Huh?"

"What time will you be done—working? I need to see you."

Randy hurriedly calculated in his head, "Uh, around 8:30 or 9:00 or so."

"Okay, I will be over," Carmen said abruptly. And she hung up before Randy could respond.

Did that mean she was coming over at 8:30 or closer to 9:00? And did it really matter if Carmen and Maria came together for the first time in *this* setting? Why did Randy care if Carmen arrived at his home while Maria performed the mundane task of copying quotations and statistics from magazines?

Here lay the real difficulty: Randy had to convince himself there was absolutely nothing wrong with going back to his room and telling Maria that *his girlfriend was coming over*…to talk to him about a personal problem, of course.

Carmen had sounded impatient on the telephone. Perhaps she had finally become confrontational about a smart, talented, pretty, *Mexican* girl spending inordinate amounts of time with her boyfriend—much of it in their respective bedrooms—supposedly working on debate cases and arguments.

Which had been the truth. They *were* working on debate cases and arguments.

Weren't they?

It was totally innocent and professional.

Wasn't it?

Randy recalled his negative thoughts and feelings at the very moment Carmen had summoned him on the telephone, and he shuddered with guilt.

"Uh, Maria," Randy forced a smile. "We gotta' wrap this up. It's getting late."

Maria, always compliant with Randy's parents' demands for taking back their house at a reasonable hour, assumed that this dictate to end their work session had come from either Mr. or Mrs. Whitman, not Randy's girlfriend.

As Randy saw Maria sliding papers and writing implements into briefcases and folders, he thought about telling her the truthful reason for an abrupt end to their meeting.

He wondered if he detected a perceptible sadness in Maria. Perhaps she looked a bit dejected because she had grown tired. Maybe, Randy thought to himself with an unreasonableness associated with youthful, blind passion, Maria had suddenly darned melancholy because she was forced to go home now and would not see Randy again until tomorrow morning!

Or maybe she knew *exactly* why Randy was getting rid of her.

"Carmen's coming over." Randy told her point-blank.

"Carmen?"

Had she forgotten?

"My—friend: she has a problem. She needs to talk. I guess it's kind of an emergency or something—a problem at home or something. Carmen's family is kind of messed up. Her father drinks a lot."

Oh, how he rambled!

Then Maria flashed what Randy hoped to be an insincere smile. "Randy, it is all right. You don't have to feel bad about this. I know Carmen is your girlfriend. And from what I have seen at school, she is very beautiful. You should help her with whatever problems she has."

Maria's reaction could not have been any more awful. Had she yelled and screamed and stamped her feet in a wild jealous rage, these emotional responses to Carmen's presence would have been preferable; instead, she was being too understanding and cooperative.

So Randy proceeded to say something incredibly dopey: "You know, Maria, Carmen is not my girlfriend."

Which not only came off as unbelievably stupid, but also as a blatant lie. Maybe Randy wished he *hadn't* asked Carmen to go steady with him. But universally, and across the Long Beach High School campus for almost six months, Randall Whitman and Carmen Pedro were linked as boyfriend and girlfriend. And Randy had supported his boyfriend status with Carmen Pedro, building a barricade of verbal defenses against his parents' racial hostilities. He had, indeed, established a record of protecting his woman.

In front of Maria in a couple of instances, he had referred to Carmen as his *girlfriend*. To now brand her otherwise colored him as a deceptive, whiney, immature adolescent. And all of these—to a girl of Maria's caliber—were not attractive qualities in a boy.

"It doesn't matter, Randy," Maria patiently responded to his "not my girlfriend" insanity. "She needs to talk with you. This is what friends are for. We can work on this debate material anytime. We still have almost a month until the tournament."

Randy didn't know for sure; perhaps, Carmen's father had started drinking again and she *did* need Randy to console her. If

45

Carmen needed help, Randy would be there to listen and advise. Postponing some useless—in the scheme of things—debate research to meet the personal needs of his girlfriend necessitated a very minor sacrifice on his part.

But watching Maria pack up the hordes of materials they had strewn about the room tore at his heart. He started to irrationally believe that Maria was forever walking out of his life.

He said, "Maria, I don't want you to go now. We're not done."

"What is it that we were we supposed to finish?"

"You know."

"No, I didn't realize we had a specific goal for tonight."

Randy desperately grasped at straws. "Just let me *read* the cards you wrote up for me. We don't need to do anymore original research."

"You can do that later," Maria retorted, finding herself opening a couple of compartments in one of the briefcases she had previously closed.

"No, please—now," Randy insisted, sounding as though his life depended on their being together another twenty minutes. Whether Carmen walked in on them or not, it only mattered to Randy that they had committed themselves to a specific objective and then met that objective, all unaffected by Randy's *friend's* impending visit.

"I just want to read and file the cards," Randy told her. "I'd feel a lot better—like we accomplished something tonight—like *I* accomplished something tonight, if I read those cards."

"There are a lot of them."

Randy was slightly surprised. "How many?"

"Maybe twenty pieces."

Randy sighed. This was good. He really *would* come away from the evening with constructive output.

Maria shrugged and handed Randy a clump of white index cards on which she had scrawled notes, data, and expert testimony from authority figures on the poverty topic. She then opened a few books and added information to another cluster of notes she had decided to utilize herself. Later she would put those notes on cards, using her mother's new Royal Typewriter.

Randy began to nervously scan the cards, ignoring what Maria had written on them—only thinking about the moment Carmen would arrive at his home and find Maria still there. He occasionally peeked at Maria, who appeared to be working calmly, not at all in tune with what he was going through. His two worlds were about to collide, and neither girl had the slightest notion as to what impact this collision would have on Randall Whitman's life.

Just as the song, "Surfin' Safari," blared from the radio, Carmen rang the doorbell, bid a few stiff greetings after being let in the house by Randy's parents, and made her way up the stairs to his bedroom.

Maria, at the sound of Carmen's voice from downstairs, did not comment to Randy. But she hurriedly stuffed her notes and cards into their appropriate compartments in her file system, apparently surprised Carmen arrived less than thirty minutes after she had called Randy.

Carmen didn't look at Maria—not even a glance in her direction—but, of course, knew of her presence; instead, she threw her face into Randy's face and gave him a hard kiss on his lips. It was not a long kiss, but one that made a distinct impression she had marked her territory.

Randy stepped aside and gestured to Maria, who had stood up and prepared to exit. "Carmen, this is my debate partner."

The two high school girls cordially whisked hands. Maria said, "I've heard a lot about you. Randy has told me how wonderful you are."

Randy didn't think he had done that but, nonetheless, was glad Maria said as much to Carmen; in fact, Randy was positive he had not—in any sense—praised Carmen to Maria. He didn't wish to give her the impression he was involved in a signed, sealed, and cemented romantic relationship with Carmen Pedro—or with anyone else.

Then Carmen, pleased by Maria's generous comments, outright lied: "Thank you. Randy has told me a lot about you, too —that you are the best debater he has ever heard."

Randy had never told anyone such a thing, especially not

Carmen, who would not have had a stake in the matter and certainly would not have cared about the best debater Randy ever heard. Even with the competitive potential she had displayed to Randy, Mr. Lott, and other debaters on the team, Maria was only a sophomore and had not collected nearly enough experience to be "the best debater" Randy ever heard.

Aware of the dubious veracity of Carmen's comments, Maria responded, "Well, if that is true, he hasn't heard very many debaters."

After several seconds of awkward silence, Maria graciously excused herself.

Randy, crushed by his despondency over watching Maria leave his room, and anxious about an impending private talk with his girlfriend, sat back and folded his arms. He nervously waited for Carmen to disclose why she had come.

The best-case scenario, Randy thought just before Carmen began to verbally unload, would be that Carmen had come here to break up with him, to gently end their relationship. For without a girl named Carmen Pedro knocking on the door to his future, he could breathe—and reclaim some of his long lost dignity.

Randy suddenly realized that having a girlfriend like Carmen Pedro was infinitely worse than having no girlfriend at all.

—CHAPTER 7—

Almost two thousand miles from California, in New Orleans, Louisiana, events began to spiral at a breath-taking pace. Even the unexpected occurred, bringing more conflict within a group of men already fraught with disagreement.

The Serious Man emerged from his office on Market Street. Although the streets were dimly light, the Serious Man's familiarity with the area allowed him to find his automobile in the gravel parking lot about a hundred yards from the door to his office. One dollar a day parking lots dotted the long, nearly barren streets. But most buildings had closed down hours before, so those parking spaces had been virtually empty for a long time.

The Serious Man had been forced to work late that evening. Tired and hungry, he thought about stopping for a hot roast beef sandwich at his favorite diner. Taking in a gulp of fresh air, he felt the heat of summer still lingering in the early fall. Sometimes it was like that in the South. After a few consecutive years of four seasons, there would be a number of years with only two seasons: summer and a variation of summer. Perhaps this was going to be one of those years.

The Serious Man welcomed pleasant distractions. Potential maladies weighed heavily on his mind. He wanted nothing more than to stop for dinner, go home, and fix a soothing bath. Already today, he had entertained numerous risky phone calls; and already today, he had discussed grave business dealings with men he did not really know or trust or believe in.

Just as the Serious Man spied his automobile in the gravel lot, he sensed someone trailing behind him. What sounded like a trot may have been a brisk walk, but the Serious Man definitely noted sounds that made him uneasy. He picked up his pace until he came upon his own car.

The Guy In The Black T-Shirt called the Serious Man by name, and the Serious Man automatically turned to face him.

"Yeah?" he responded, suddenly filled with panic.

The Guy In The Black T-Shirt did not utter another sound. Having identified his prey, he decided any further confirmation was unnecessary.

With escalating horror, the Serious Man, who had back peddled into the side of his own car, watched the Guy In The Black T-Shirt raise a small caliber revolver and point it directly at him. Stunned, and without opportunity for escape, the Serious Man bowed to his fate.

After unloading three bullets into the chest of the Serious Man, the Guy In The Black T-shirt turned and calmly began his walk to the curb. The Tall Man, sitting behind the steering wheel of a red Cadillac, waited there for him to return.

****

"She is cute," Carmen told Randy, after Maria had left.

He shrugged his shoulders. He thought better of saying or doing anything else.

"Adorable, actually," Carmen added with both brows raised.

You don't know the half of it, Randy wanted to say. But as before, he clammed up, offering a begrudging nod.

Inexplicably and awkwardly, "My Boyfriend's Back," by The Angels, blasted on the radio. The moment struck Randy as being quite humorous. He wondered if Carmen felt the same, and he briefly thought about asking her.

Up until now Randy had pondered long and hard what he would tell Carmen if she confronted him about Maria. But he wasn't sure about Maria; he didn't know of any relationship they may have been tending beyond their pairing as debate colleagues. Still, he decided he would reveal all this to Carmen: his feelings for Maria, his intentions, and the fact that he no longer wished to go steady with her.

But as he sat there in front of Carmen, sincerely ready, if not eager, to bare his soul, the absurdity of it all barreled into him like a runaway truck tumbling from a freeway off ramp. Carmen was a nice girl, albeit occasionally impudent and insensitive. But who wasn't occasionally impudent and insensitive? Why throw away his friendship with Carmen to fly into the arms of another girl, his *debate* partner—who may wish to remain nothing more than, well, his debate partner?

So he treaded water a tad more lightly than he had originally intended.

"Yeah, she's cute, Carmen. So what? Is that what you had to tell me?"

"No," Carmen answered quietly. Suddenly her nostrils flared, and Randy saw that it detracted from her otherwise attractive features. "You are just spending an awful lot of time with her, you know?"

"She's my debate partner. I spent a lot of time with Ira Cushman, too, when he was my debate partner."

"Yes," Carmen smiled, "but Ira doesn't look like this girl!"

Fighting an urge to share her smile, Randy asked, "What do you want me to do, Carmen? You want me to get an *ugly* partner?"

"No. No, that's not what I want."

Randy was glad she answered that question in the negative. "Then what?"

"I—I just want you to make a little more time for me. Make *some* time for me. Even the weekends you're too busy."

Randy didn't think he was too busy—just too tired for Carmen or anyone else. "I'm so tired by the time Friday night rolls around, Carmen. I mean, if you'd be okay with just coming over and watching T.V. or something, that'd be cool. But I'm not in any shape to go out to a movie or anything like that. By the end of the week, I'm zonked!"

Carmen perked up a bit. "Lately, you don't even want to do things like television. Sometimes I even get suspicious that you are out with...her. I mean, I know you're not, because you tell me you're not. But I don't get how you never want to go out anymore with *me*."

"Come over here Friday night, and we'll watch some T.V. together. Just don't bring that creepy cousin of yours, that guy who's living with you," Randy finished with a subtle smile.

He saw the transformation come over Carmen's face. Her look of consternation had turned to despondency but didn't sadden him; it irritated him. "That's the truth, Carmen. If you want to come over and study, too, that's fine. But you never like to study or do homework, and I have a Great Books exam next week. I need to get ready, and there's no time during the week. Mr. Lott's got us hopping."

"Just some time together like the old days. That's all I want, Randy." Carmen narrowed her eyes, slowed her rate, and lowered her volume. "Wouldn't you want that, too, Randy? How would you like it if I was out every night with a really handsome boy, even if we were working together on a project for school? Wouldn't it bother you?"

Randy suddenly realized that this *wouldn't* bother him. Not anymore. In fact, Randy now *hoped* for something like that to happen. Carmen would find a handsome boy she liked a whole lot and wanted to spend enormous amounts of time with him. Two months ago Randy would not have liked this—maybe not even two weeks ago.

But it occurred to him that he liked this idea *now*.

However, he replied to Carmen's assessment of the situation with another lie. "No, I wouldn't like that," he answered her softly with a hint of understanding in his voice. "You're right. I haven't been very nice or very considerate lately. Let's go to a drive-in movie Friday night. We haven't done that in a long time. Maybe we can see *Mad Mad World* or something."

Carmen nodded; she paused, suddenly purring like a kitten. And then, referring to the messy debate materials strewn on the floor, she commanded in a loud, unfeminine voice, "Now you need to clean up this room! All this boring debater junk all over the floor —pick it up!"

—CHAPTER 8—

John Fitzgerald Kennedy had won the 1960 Presidential election, but barely.

Only after all the votes in the state of Illinois had been counted and recounted, and only after all precincts from California were tallied, had the young, handsome United States Senator from Massachusetts secured enough electoral votes to be declared the 35th President of the United States.

Richard Nixon, Vice-President for eight years during the administration of President Dwight Eisenhower, was a formidable opponent; however, in the end—especially after the televised debates in which an unhealthy-looking Nixon pallor compared miserably with a tanned Kennedy radiance—the Senator won a narrow victory over the Vice-President.

John Kennedy captured the trust and admiration of young people. In a national poll conducted in early 1963, ninth grade students were asked to name an adult they most admired of anyone in the entire country. A majority of the youthful respondents chose President Kennedy (even after considering their own parents).

Kennedy's family, his wife Jacqueline, daughter Caroline, and toddler son John-John quickly became a Hallmark card for family togetherness and loyalty. Perhaps even more important for the nation, they symbolized youth and vigor, moving forward into what the President himself described in his inauguration speech as, "The New Frontier." The tension over the Cuban Missile Crisis had dissipated, but the new President still had to face other issues of grave concern: pervasive racial segregation, international cries for nuclear disarmament, poverty, unsettling relations with Cuba, and growing political and military unrest in Southeast Asia. There seemed, however, to be a budding optimism in America. Adults looked to the Kennedys as their saviors, and young people saw them as awesome inspiration for greeting a brighter future. The White House, and the entire aura surrounding it, became known as *Camelot*. The flash and tinsel of a fine-looking family came to represent all that *Camelot* embodied, as the new King sat on the throne of a benevolent democratic government.

In his crusade against international Communism, the young President battled conflicting ideologies in Cuba, China, Russia, South America—and later—Vietnam. When Soviet Premier Nikita Khrushchev angrily rapped his shoe on the table of the United Nations or claimed in an international economic summit, "We will bury you!" Americans took him seriously. Severe challenges awaited the new Administration. Hard, steadfast decisions would be made soon, even as the young leader contemplated organizational plans for a reelection campaign just over two years into his Presidency.

The gallant warrior from Brookshire, riding his way through the politically charged forest on the white horse of Sir Lancelot, had not only impacted politics and culture, he also fortressed the United States from evils abroad—without creating that fortress. On the contrary, American participation around the globe expanded, as the great superpower thwarted Communism at every opportunity and spread economic assistance with every request.

Certain failures of the President resounded across the globe: the Bay of Pigs invasion, an inability to march major legislation through Congress, and getting sucked into the morass of French Indochina. Kennedy's image may have glittered with style over substance, sophistry over accomplishment—but the people liked it; they breathed in it. America, with its eyes peeled on the future, seemed more than satisfied to bask in the sunlight of Camelot's promises.

The Kennedy Presidency was the closest America had come to a royal dynasty. But as political enemies of the Kennedys and ideologues of the Republican Party had planned to defeat him in his reelection bid in 1964, other adversarial forces deliberated a far more sinister method of eliminating Camelot from the world's landscape.

—CHAPTER 9—

In 1963 several spacious hotels stood in the shadows of Southern Methodist University, but the Long Beach High School debate team, considering their modest personal means and limited school budget, could not afford to stay in any of those hotels.

Motel 6 charged $9.95 per night for a room. Both girls on the team, Maria Barquin and Margie Pendergrass, roomed together. Ruther Gardner stayed with Tommy Wright (his partner for the tournament). Ira Cushman and Randy shared a room, and Mr. Lott took one for himself.

Aside from the Tournament of Champions debate tournament, one other occasion, a complete surprise, filled Randall Whitman with excitement. For Randy this event was more electrifying than even the tournament itself.

The people of Dallas expected President Kennedy to visit their city on Friday morning.

As part of a tour kicking off his 1964 reelection campaign, the President had promised to fly into Dallas and cruise through downtown in a motorcade. Kennedy was headed to a speaking engagement at the Dallas Trade Mart.

As soon as the debate team arrived at the hotel on Thursday afternoon, Randy read on the front page of the *Dallas Morning News* about the President's planned appearance. He immediately made phone calls to the Dallas Chamber of Commerce and received information on the parade route. A map had already been published a few days before in the local newspaper. He discovered some amazing details: President Kennedy would be riding in an open-top limousine (if it didn't rain), with people allowed to crowd along the sides of the roads, in some spots within ten feet from his car!

Randy couldn't believe his good luck!

Without much trouble he convinced Mr. Lott to take the six teenagers to the parade route. They would leave for a place called Dealey Plaza at about ten o'clock in the morning and camp out at the intersection of Elm and Houston, a location near the end of the motorcade's itinerary. The Chamber expected the President to pass through this area around noon.

On Thursday night, November 21, the night before the first day of competition, all seven representatives of the Long Beach High School Pilots debate squad met together in Mr. Lott's room to go over last minute debate strategies. They spent three hours blocking arguments, exchanging evidence cards, and talking about various styles they would assume against different opponents.

At 10:30 P.M, the general meeting concluded.

But Mr. Lott then asked to speak privately with the team of Whitman and Barquin.

When Randy and Maria found themselves alone with their coach, they both detected a strange, acrid smell on his breath. Randy saw that an abnormal, gray tinge had infested Mr. Lott's eyes, tainting the white areas, a peculiarity they couldn't detect from across the room.

Mr. Lott began in almost solemn tones, as though he were going to announce the location of someone's funeral. "I wanted to talk to my number one debate team. You're my number one team, aren't you?"

Neither Maria nor Randy knew what to say. How do you agree that you're number one in someone else's eyes? But that's the way Mr. Lott began the conversation, so eventually Randy nodded.

Mr. Lott looked at him. "It's no secret, Randy. I put you two together a couple of months ago to create a number one team—to prepare you to win the Tournament of Champions. Do you think you can do that for me?"

A rather odd way to phrase the question, Randy thought. Do it for *him*?

But both Randy and Maria nodded tentatively.

Mr. Lott then rose from a chair and went to a small refrigerator near the door of the motel room. It took him less than three seconds to reach in and remove a can of beer. As the surprised teenagers watched, he popped it open and drank from the can. Although expecting an invitation (that never came) to join him with a Coca Cola or something, Maria and Randy remained speechless.

Mr. Lott downed all the beer in the can. He then tossed the empty into a small trash receptacle under a cheap business desk and went through the process of procuring, and then drinking, another beer. During the entire evening of debate work, there had been plenty of soda and chips. But this was the first sight of any alcohol; in fact, never before had Maria or Randy seen Mr. Lott consume anything with alcohol.

"I have leukemia," Mr. Lott said, breaking the silence.

And then, of course, everything had been explained: Mr. Lott's odd behavior, his physical deterioration, and his recent lackluster performances in critiquing practice debates. But wasn't leukemia supposed to be a young person's cancer? Since when did forty-something year-old men contract leukemia?

Tears appeared in Maria's eyes. She didn't know what to say.

But Randy tried. "You have leukemia? For how long?"

Mr. Lott looked at both of them. "The test results came back last Monday. But I've known since the end of summer that something wasn't right. I've been so tired. The only thing that seems to spur me on is you guys—debate. Getting you ready for the Tournament of Champions has been my inspiration."

"What did they tell you, Mr. Lott?" Randy asked, also fighting back his emotions. "What have the doctors told you to do? What's their strategy?"

Mr. Lott, looking sadder than Randy had ever seen him, shrugged. "Right after we get back to California I'm having a blood transfusion; then they're going to look at other possibilities. Radiation is a relatively new therapy used for other cancers, but blood cancer is usually treated with all kinds of transfusions and new medicines."

Finally, Maria spoke up. "Mr. Lott, shouldn't you be having that transfusion right now? I mean, shouldn't you have had it *yesterday*? It seems to me—I mean, I really do not know anything about this, but is not time of the essence?"

Mr. Lott saw the apprehension in her eyes, and he smiled. "See, Maria. Right *there*: the fact that you love me so much. I didn't want any medical treatments that required hospitalization this week. I needed to be *here*. For you. For the Tournament of Champions."

Mr. Lott smiled easily again, and for a split second Randy felt guilty. For an instant he thought Mr. Lott had concocted this whole story in order to bully his debate team into winning the big tournament this weekend.

Randy quickly dismissed that thought.

Mr. Lott crossed his arms. "Don't tell the others. This is just between us."

Randy shook his head. "Shouldn't they all know about this, Mr. Lott?"

"Eventually, but not now. That could be counter-productive. You're the team that has a chance. The others will win some debates. You two have a chance to win the whole thing."

Randy was conflicted. On the one hand, he already sensed an urgency to win every debate in this tournament; on the other hand, he felt some resentment toward Mr. Lott for putting Maria and him on the spot. And on the third hand (if there were such a thing), Randy suddenly entertained such apathy for the meaning of *any* debate tournament, he no longer felt like competing in Dallas.

Randy sighed and then tried to say with the greatest amount of delicacy, "Mr. Lott, of course we're going to do our best. Maria and I have talked about this over and over: We want to win. If you could tell us what else to do—anything more—we'll do it. But I think we're ready. We're as prepared for this as we're ever going to get."

Mr. Lott's bloodshot eyes turned sympathetic. "I know you two are ready. And I wasn't going to say anything to you. But I've never been married, and almost everyone else in my family is either crazy or dead. This is more for me than it is for you. I know how hard you've been working, so maybe there's nothing more that can be done. I appreciate that, too. But here's the scoop: Be fair. Have dignity. And make it *real*—no games. If what you say doesn't matter to you at the time you're saying it, it probably doesn't matter at all. Not really. Not in the real world, the one you live in each and every day of your lives. So…tomorrow night, this weekend, don't leave any stone unturned."

The teenagers both nodded, tentatively, because they were still unclear as to what Mr. Lott really wanted them to do.

Leaving their fixation on disease and morbidity and the ultimate meaning of a debate tournament, the threesome's attention finally turned to more pleasant considerations, such as the squad's pending visit to Dealey Plaza and the route of President Kennedy's motorcade.

—CHAPTER 10—

Alex Hidell walked into his bedroom and found his young, Russian born wife reclining on their bed. With pillows propped behind her, she started attentively at their small black and white portable television set, sitting atop a dresser at the other end of the room.

"Lee," she said to Hidell without taking her eyes off the T.V., "President Kennedy is coming to town tomorrow!"

Hidell already knew that. He went to a closet and began to retrieve clothes for the following day of work. Fridays were always tougher, more rigorous, than the other days of the week.

"I know," he grunted without looking at her.

Hidell did not live with his wife and children anymore. He rented a bedroom in a boardinghouse several miles away from his family. He returned to his former home and his wife only on the weekends, so he could wash clothes and play with his kids.

"It is exciting. Do you know he is going to be in a parade right near the place where you work?"

Hidell's wife's Russian accent was still thick and her English broken. She had taken the responsibility to learn English herself, but it was a harder chore than she had anticipated. Just after her twentieth birthday, she heard from her friends and neighbors how much easier it is to learn a new language when you're a child: a truth, but not helpful information at this point in her now adult life.

"Check the news," she said to her husband. "Find out what time he will pass your building."

"I don't care about President Kennedy," Hidell said. "I want to work in peace."

"But it is a one in a million chance!" she exclaimed.

"I don't care!" Hidell's voice rose with authority. Even though he was only twenty-three years old, he acted the part of a much older man—one in control: of his wife, of his friends, of the children he had created with his young bride, a woman he married in the Soviet Union and then brought to America.

"I told you before," he repeated with an exaggerated but seemingly unprovoked annoyance, "I am not interested in politics or celebrities. They bore me. I have so much work to do. My job is hard. I go to work and earn only a dollar an hour. What do you think I have time for? If I don't work on crating the books, they won't pay me. They might even fire me. Would you like that, Marina? Huh? Would you like for the only breadwinner in your family to lose his job so there is no food or milk on your table?"

Alex Hidell and his wife didn't speak with each other for the rest of the evening. Around eleven, Hidell crawled into bed next to his sleeping wife and kissed her on the cheek, a rarity, considering their fractured relationship and separate living arrangements. Earlier, he quietly had removed his wedding ring—something he had never done before, despite Marina's insistence that he find residence somewhere else—and put it on top of the bedroom dresser. Underneath the ring, Hidell slid $124.17 in cash, all the money he had to his name.

******

During breakfast the next morning, a few silly events that would later prove to be inconsequential crept into the debaters' world. Old pranksters never die, especially if they are teenagers.

At about the time Mr. Lott was ready to go to bed the night before, he couldn't find his pillow. Mr. Lott always brought his personal pillow on trips. He loved his pillow. One of Mr. Lott's well-known displays of neurosis was his going ballistic over anyone or anything touching his bed pillow. If, for example, the pillow fell off his bed and hit the floor, he immediately washed the pillowcase. Some of the debaters kidded him about his pillow taking the place of a wife, contending that Mr. Lott would never be able to stay married, because any woman he lived with would become insanely jealous of his pillow.

After ten minutes of searching throughout his room, Mr. Lott finally found his pillow on the dirty carpet in the corridor. Furious, he returned to his room. How had one of the debaters stolen the pillow from his room without his knowing? Much more serious and profound mysteries soon would follow, but for now, Mr. Lott's most pressing quest: to somehow get his pillowcase washed and dried that day, and to make sure the wicked pillow pranksters had run their course.

At breakfast, Mr. Lott steamed over the pillow incident. And then he fell victim to a practical joke of potentially more serious consequences.

After the debate team had ordered their meals from the moderately priced diner adjacent to the Motel 6, Ruther Gardner excused himself to go to the bathroom.

When he finished using the restroom facilities, Ruther went back to the breakfast table and announced, "Mr. Lott, the manager of our motel is standing at the cash register. He said that he wants to see you about something. He looks pretty serious."

Ruther escorted Mr. Lott to the front of the restaurant, where, of course, no one waited to speak with him.

"Hmm…" Ruther feigned, forcing himself to look around. "I guess he left. He'll probably see you back at the motel."

Later, Ruther would not be able to point to any man who had identified himself in the restaurant as the motel manager.

"Did he say what this was about?"

"No."

Meanwhile at the breakfast table, Tommy had surreptitiously dropped half a dozen Ex-Lax chocolate laxatives into Mr. Lott's hot coca cup, stirred, and blended them into the Nestlé's Quick. Since Mr. Lott and the debaters planned to be away from the motel attending the President's motorcade in Dealey Plaza, those who were let in on the Ex-Lax prank contemplated the hysterics that would ensue later and began laughing aloud just at the thought of it. As the speech team filed from the restaurant and boarded their rented ten-person station wagon, Tommy nudged Ruther with his elbow. Both boys giggled in knowing amusement.

Randy saw their mischievous display and wondered what it was all about.

Navigating to Dealey Plaza proved to be a difficult task,

since many of the city streets were closed. By almost ten o'clock, thousands of men, women, and children had already lined the parade route, so they could get a close look at the second youngest man ever to be elected President of the United States. Kennedy would be so near they could practically reach out and touch him. Who knows when they would ever get another opportunity to see this President—or any other President—so up close and personal!

Throughout the pomp and circumstance of merely waiting for the motorcade, Randy seemed most at ease. After all, he was one happy boy: two thousand miles from home with Maria at his side, prepared to compete in a tournament most high school debaters only dreamed about entering, and about to get a good look at his idol, President John F. Kennedy!

True, Randy would not be able to shake his hand this time. But later he would; he was sure of it. And maybe that time he would look Mr. Kennedy in the eye and smile and say, "Mr. President, you may not remember me, but I was one of the young men standing on the street who waved to you while you were riding in a motorcade back in 1963 in Dallas, Texas!"

And, of course, President Kennedy would nod and say, "You know, I actually *do* remember you! I seem to have an imprint of your beaming face and hearty wave in my mind—and I have kept it there for the last few years." And then he would clasp Randy's hand with a firm hold and display his pearly, white teeth and say, "Hi, I'm Jack Kennedy. And you are?"

"I'm Randall Walter Whitman. My debate partner then—and now my fiancé—won First Place at the Tournament of Champions at Southern Methodist University, just after we saw your parade in Dallas."

"Well, I'm pleased—very pleased—to meet you, Randall! I'd be honored if you'd accept my invitation for you and your lucky wife to join Jackie and me at the White House for a Sunday barbecue and touch football game."

"Yes, Mr. President!"

And then President Kennedy would quietly say in that legendary Boston accent Randy had heard the comedian Vaughn Meader impersonate so many times on his *First Family* parody record, "*Jack*. Call me *Jack*. Meeting a fine young man like you has been a real pleasure for me, I'm sure!"

Kennedy would clasp his hand again and shake it again, this time more warmly than the last, with an intensity that told Randy President Kennedy knew he was shaking the hand of a future President of the United States.

—CHAPTER 11—

"Why do we have to be way over here?" Tommy Wright grumbled. "Nobody's here! Are you sure the motorcade is coming by this spot? There's nothing here but a hill and a freeway onramp and that— that—ugly building across the street!"

The spot to which Tommy Wright referred was near a street corner, more isolated from the central city than the rest of the route. Only a few dozen people congregated around the winding curb; some areas were left unoccupied, wide-open. To the debaters' right stood a large, tall structure called the Dallas Records Building. Its namesake for the city was self-explanatory, although it functioned mainly to store police records and court documents. Across the street sat a large building, its name indicated by a sign over the double doors on the first floor: *Texas School Book Depository.* On the same side of the street, to the right of the book building and slightly behind it, sloped a small grassy hill. It was less than steep but led up to a white concrete barrier and a few monuments near the top.

On the far reaches of the hill, a wooden brown fence divided Dealey Plaza from a large parking lot and a cluster of railroad tracks. To the debaters' immediate left and across the street from them was a sign that read *Stemmons Freeway,* and, of course, an entrance ramp accommodating traffic onto the freeway.

Ira Cushman responded to Tommy's gripe about the senselessness of their location. "This is a great spot. We got to park pretty close. There's nobody blocking our view, and the President and Vice-President are going to be right *there*." He pointed to the street only a few feet from where he stood.

"How do we know that, Ira? We don't know that." Tommy persisted.

Ira pointed to the Stemmons freeway sign. "The motorcade

is going up that ramp. Just ask Randy."

Randy stood next to Ira, but he leaned over so Tommy could hear him. "President Kennedy has a speaking engagement this afternoon at the Dallas Trade Mart, so he has to get on the freeway right *here*."

"How do you know all this?" Tommy asked in a challenging tenor.

Randy pointed to his heart. "I'm a Kennedy fan, man! I've been studying him for months. I called the Dallas Chamber of Commerce. I know everything." Percolating with excitement, he looked at his wristwatch. "Such as, the motorcade will be here in thirty-five minutes!"

Tommy Wright did a gagging sound, a sudden wretch filled with antipathy. He chided, "If you ask me, Randy, you're not a Kennedy fan. You're a Kennedy queer!"

Randy ignored Tommy Wright's slur.

But Maria Barquin heard Tommy's loud, derogatory remark and did not ignore it. She came to Randy's rescue. "Tommy's gonna' get jealous!" Maria kidded, as she moved in from a spot behind them.

"Ah, man, give me a break!" Tommy waved her off.

"Randy's greatest ambition in life," she smiled, "is to shake hands with President Kennedy."

"His greatest ambition?" Tommy questioned sardonically. And then he made an obscene motion with one hand, adding, "His greatest ambition is to shake *something* of President Kennedy's— and it ain't his hand!"

Randy sighed, shaking his head.

Maria acted as though she didn't understand the double entendre, faking bewilderment.

Ira intervened, "I don't think you ought to be saying stuff like that in front of the girls on the team, Tommy."

"Yeah, right, Ira."

"Really."

"You're right, friend."

"It's not cool."

"And you're *so* cool, Ira. Mr. Cool!"

"If cool means having no respect for anybody else and acting like an ass, yeah, Tommy, I'm not cool!"

"Oh, bite me, Ira!"

"Bite you? Gag me!"

"Yeah? You wanna' make something out of it? You wanna' *go*? Right *here*, Ira, you little twerp!"

Maria raised her voice so that Mr. Lott and the others could hear her. She yelled, "Tommy, just leave Ira alone! Why are you being so mean?"

Mr. Lott came up behind them and grabbed Tommy by his shoulders. "Tommy, stop being—*yourself*. Come on!"

Annoyed, Tommy pulled back. "Hey, Mr. Lott! What's up, man?"

"You're tired, Tommy. You're under stress, and you're bound to say things you'll regret later. Why don't you just keep quiet and let these folks have a good time."

Randy shrugged. "This is no big deal, Mr. Lott. Really, it's not."

"He's calling Randy a queer because he admires President Kennedy so much," Maria asserted.

"I am not!" Tommy barked with indignation. "You gotta' be kidding me!"

"It's okay, Mr. Lott. I think he was just messing around," Randy said quietly, trying to appease everyone. "Really. Forget it."

Mr. Lott's body sagged, and with disappointment he eyed Maria.

Maria, however, struck a bulging pair of eyeballs in Randy's direction. "You heard what he said, Randy. Tell Mr. Lott. It was disgusting! Why are you defending Tommy?"

Mortified, Randy forced a grin. "It was nothing, Mr. Lott. Really."

Maria's brown eyes blistered. "Randy, Mr. Lott thinks I am over-reacting. Tell him the truth."

Mr. Lott looked at Randy. Randy paused and glanced at Tommy, who stared down at the ground.

"We can work this out, Mr. Lott. Like I said, it was no big deal," Randy insisted, despite the surge of panic he felt when he noticed that Maria was clearly fuming. In a weak, stubborn defense of an offensive, irrational Tommy, why had he let Maria down? Tommy meant nothing to him. Maria now meant everything to him. What was he doing?

Nobody spoke with Randy for the next several minutes; in fact, all the debaters had clammed up. Mr. Lott actually welcomed this opportunity as his lone chance to focus, undistracted, on his surroundings. He happily soaked up the idea of being so close to the President and Vice-President of the United States, although he didn't vote for them in the previous election.

More people now were pouring into Dealey Plaza. But even with larger gatherings along the streets, the Long Beach group maintained an unfettered view of the Presidential motorcade.

Around 12:15, a buzz went through the crowd. The approach of the President had already sent electricity down the parade route. Randy's tension over the confrontation involving Maria and Tommy had been temporarily diffused by the growing excitement over President Kennedy's imminent presence. For a few moments he even forgot where Maria ultimately had wound up to watch the motorcade.

Ira interrupted his thoughts. "Randy, if you take pictures from across the street, I can take them from here. That way we'd have pictures of the President from both sides of the parade. And Vice-President Johnson, too. We'll share them later."

There was nothing Randy would have liked more than to have all those pictures of President Kennedy. And photos from both sides would be even better! Only a sparse gathering of people waited in the grassy area directly across the street, although the throngs located right in front of the old brick schoolbook building were now thickening.

But Randy frowned. "I want to be *here*, Ira. That way I can get a better look at Kennedy."

Ira disagreed, pointing at the top of the grassy hill. "If you go up there near those monuments, you can get full view pictures of Kennedy, Johnson, and the Secret Service cars. And you're still gonna' be close. You'll be behind your camera taking pictures anyway, so what difference does it make?"

68

"I also want pictures from *this* side."

"I'll take pictures from this side; you from that side. My camera is going to get only one or two cars at a time. Yours will get practically the whole motorcade."

Randy, rattled by Ira's suggestion—mainly because he actually saw his point—said, "Why don't *you* go across the street? I'll stay here."

Ira winced. "Because I'm a coward. For some weird reason I don't want the cops to shoot me. I guess I'm funny that way."

Randy laughed. He appreciated Ira's honesty but felt uncomfortable with his idea. He nodded in concurrence, but rather than risk getting into trouble—even though others were crossing at the corner—he silently decided to forgo having even better, and additional, pictures of the motorcade. After all, the purpose of their visit to Dealey Plaza was to *see* the President, not necessarily to *photograph* him from sixty sides and two thousand angles. But he said nothing further, hoping Ira would not badger him anymore about the photographic perks of crossing Elm Street.

Randy noticed that a few more motorcycle policeman had arrived to patrol the area and hoped there would not be too many more cops on the street by the time President Kennedy arrived. If he decided to cross the street, Randy didn't want the police to swarm him, throw him to the ground, pull out their nightsticks, and bash his head in. This did not loom as an attractive option.

"Better go now, Randy," Ira advised. "Maybe they won't let you cross later."

"Yeah, maybe," Randy sighed. But he hated to part with the group and already had decided to stay put. Besides, photographing the motorcade from afar, Randy's sole purpose for hopping over to the other side of the street, did not figure to be enough motivation for such an audacious venture.

And then a seemingly innocuous argument occurred, starting a chain of horrific events that would require patience, strength, and enormous courage in the young life of Randall Walter Whitman.

—CHAPTER 12—

At noon the temperature in Dealey Plaza was 64 degrees. After a substantial, though brief, morning rain, the sun came out, and the clouds began to dissipate. Scattered, fluffy clouds lay on the northern horizon. Relief from the fear of more rain—and thus a dampening of the President's motorcade—had cheered up the masses of men, women, and children who lined the streets of Downtown Dallas.

Alex Hidell sat on the wooden floor in a small crease sealed by surrounding empty book cartons. Near him, an open window brought in the bass sounds of adult mumblings and the tenor cries of children's voices from the streets six stories below. Beads of perspiration lined his forehead. Droppings of sweat fell from his armpits and then absorbed into his dark T-shirt. The boxes had created a fortress around him, blocking Hidell from the view of others, unless a curious worker peered over the cartons.

Positioning both his knees on the floor, huddling down in his makeshift-hiding place, Hidell assembled the Italian Mannlicher-Carcano rifle, sliding the sight scope into its proper place. He sighed—half from impatience, and the other half from a strange conglomeration of trepidation, suspense, and excitement.

****

Since early in the morning, a workman had occupied Judd's office in the Dallas Records Building. The Celestial Electrical Company claimed they needed the room to repair dangerous wiring embedded in its ceiling. Hundreds of folders, all containing materials relevant to court documents and police arrests in Dallas County, had been haphazardly tucked into drawers and throw baskets, so the repairman would have an uncluttered work area.

70

"Fire hazard," a very tall man in blue corduroy pants had cautioned Judd three days ago during a routine inspection of the room's electrical wiring.

"It'll probably hold for a while," he had advised. "But it's not a good idea to mess with it for very long."

He then told Judd that the city would not approve of going more than ten days without repairing the faulty connections. "Ten days..." he babbled, looking at the heavily marked paper on his clipboard. "Hmmm...Hard to fit you guys in during the next ten days...so busy and all. I guess I'm going to have to recommend closure."

He sighed.

Then: "*But*! We *could* get over in—I have a cancellation for —that would be this Friday."

He said that somewhere around ten o'clock in the morning on November 22, he would come by—at least, *somebody* from the company would come by—to fix the wiring and prevent having to close the entire floor of the building. It would take a few hours, but if he didn't fix it then, he wouldn't have time to fix it for a while.

Judd transferred many of the work-related documents to an empty office down the hall. There he set up shop. He was slightly surprised the very tall man with the toolboxes preferred to have the door locked during the time he worked, "For fear of someone entering and touching electrical wiring. It could light him up like the White House Christmas tree!" he sternly warned.

At noon on Friday, Judd returned to his office in order to retrieve his mail. After Judd knocked, The Tall Man answered the door. Judd peered into his own office behind the Tall Man and noticed electrical wiring and lights scattered about the floor; a short ladder was in place near the window. Judd assumed the Tall Man worked near an opening, a hole he had made in the ceiling. He acknowledged the Tall Man's rigorous efforts, grabbed his mail, and slid out the door as quickly as possible. He didn't relish the thought of lighting up like the White House Christmas tree.

The Tall Man found a small briefcase and opened it. The various components of the rifle had been explained repeatedly to him, and he had practiced their assembly over and over, attempting to thwart previous record times on each successive attempt. Now that the reality of cold steel stared him in the face, he recoiled in a momentary panic, feeling alone and slighted by the people who had led him to this scary climax.

But there could be no turning back now.

****

Howard and his cohorts, Joey and Craig, had not shaved for a couple of weeks. Somewhat doubtful that the stubble on their faces and their ramshackle clothing disguised their actual socio-economic status—they were attired in old slacks and shaggy shirts; one of them wore a white, holey, unlaundered dress shirt—they inched forward down the grassy hill from the railroad tracks that ran behind the book building. Carrying the bags of the homeless, they lingered about the grassy hill for almost ten minutes. As a few other people in the area took their places to watch the motorcade, the hobo-looking guys appeared to scatter.

And eventually they disappeared.

—CHAPTER 13—

They could hear a smattering of applause—a few screams, and excited, hoarse cheers in the distance.

The Long Beach High School debaters and their coach knew the motorcade was approaching.

Mr. Lott, usually contained in his emotions and muted in his enthusiasm for anything other than preparing his squad for debate tournaments, craned his head to the right and stood on his tiptoes. His normally demure face had broken into an excited smile. He, too, glowed with the thought of an impending closeness to the President of the United States.

"They're coming!" Margie Pendergrass yelled excitedly, as she turned and took a couple of steps toward the street corner to her right.

"Randy—across the street! Hurry!" Ira yelled.

Randy *did* want to snap pictures on the hill from that side of the motorcade. But he balked at the potential for debacle. Some of the cops in sporadic places on the roadside looked as though they had arrived in a time machine from Nazi Germany and straight from the *Gestapo*. This, after all, was the President of the United States—not a two-bit city councilman.

Maybe one of the policemen would shoot Randy.

So he froze.

Ira clasped his camera, as he wound the film and adjusted the focus. He saw Randy standing motionless, clutching his duffel bag at his side.

"What's the matter?" he asked impatiently.

Randy uttered in a cowardly voice, "You go across the street, Ira. I want to see things from this side."

Without much hesitation, Ira shrugged and took a step in the direction of the north side of Elm Street. *He* would climb the hill, move to the white barricade, and there snap pictures of the entire motorcade as it passed.

But Tommy Wright put out his hand and stopped Ira in his tracks. "Hold it, Ira! What's—what are you *doing*?"

He glared at Randy, his face contorting into a sinister entity, not just its usual, annoying cockiness. "*You* go over there, Randy! You want the pictures from that side, *you* take 'em!"

Randy frantically looked about, hoping to see Ira or one of the other teenagers from Long Beach already crossing to the other side of the street. But not one of them had moved or was about to go anywhere. They were all looking directly to their right, waiting for a glimpse of what everybody else down the block had been cheering.

Tommy Wright was not God. But especially since his encounter with Randy a few minutes ago, and the subsequent emotional drubbing Randy had received from Maria, Randy wasn't about to let Tommy get the better of him again. Who did this punk think he was, anyway?

Bullies on the debate team they did not need.

"You go, Tommy! You big diphead!" Randy goaded.

You go, Tommy! You big diphead!

That was the best Randy could come up with? *That* was his rendition of masculine opposition to adversity? *That* was going to cause Tommy Wright to cower in a dark corner and forget about ridiculing him ever again?

But after Randy's less than James Bond-style comeback, Tommy didn't laugh in his face. Shaking his head and sighing with a hint of pity, he scoffed at Randy, announcing loudly, "Jeez, Randall, you are such a chickenshit!"

And then maybe for reasons only Randy Whitman and a psycho-therapist could ever explain, an overwhelming sense of revulsion came over him: that Tommy Wright already had scoped out Maria Barquin; that Tommy wanted more from Maria than the new poverty statistics she had gathered from *Newsweek*; that Tommy, a tall, blonde boy with handsome, chiseled features—and a *senior*—fashioned some very serious designs on the sweetest, smartest, most beautiful creature on the face of the earth.

And to boot, Tommy had already publically humiliated him once—igniting Maria's anger toward Randy—and now he was about to do it again.

Tommy looked in the direction of the mounting, excited clamors in the distance and raised his voice volume so the others, especially Maria, might hear him, "Go over there and get your pictures, you chickenshit! A once in a lifetime experience, remember, you coward?" And then, causing even Ruther Gardner, standing far away and near the curb, to notice: "I dare you—you chickenshit!"

Okay, three *chickenshits* and one *coward*: enough!

Randy, after all, wanted those pictures. It wasn't as though Tommy had ordered him to clean a latrine with a toothbrush or dared him to go on top of the red brick building and jump off the Hertz Rent-a-Car sign. He had considered crossing the street, ever since Ira had convinced him of the possibility of a strategic pictorial advantage. But as the motorcade came closer, he had entertained second thoughts about rushing through the area in front of several Dallas policemen.

Randy imagined what it must have looked like to the others: that he now pleaded to *Ira* to run across Elm street, especially after Randy previously had signaled his apparent willingness to snap pictures from the other side—and then changed his mind. He envisioned how he would appear to Maria Barquin, if he again retreated from Tommy Wright's intimidations.

Randy harbored a quiet, seething resentment for Tommy. In a different time and a different place, he would have walked over to Tommy and served him a knuckle sandwich. And Mr. Lott would have found that satisfying, not disturbing. Tommy was ranked number six on the team competing at Southern Methodist. In Mr. Lott's eyes, Tommy's behavior had been deplorable, especially when his provocations often were aimed at the number one debater on the squad.

Randy reached for his camera, pulling it from his small duffel bag. He felt Maria's gaze but didn't know if this was just his imagination. Despite his reluctance to change his location on the parade route, he *would* have liked pictures of the first three cars following one another in the motorcade—and from a totally different angle and, perhaps, perspective.

After all, Ira had already staked out to snap pictures from the south side of the motorcade.

So like a streak of lightening, Randy shot across Elm Street, quickly reaching the grass on the other side. He passed two women —one who wore a bright red dress—and a man with a little boy. As he moved up the low grassy hill, Randy figured the cops weren't concerned enough to intervene. Not even one policeman had tried to stop him. The motorcade had not reached the corner, so perhaps it was still permissible for a spectator to move from one side of the street to the other.

Randy turned around and saw several policemen on motorcycles heading north on Houston Street, toward the corner on which the big Dallas Records Building and the red book building stood. Small American flags fluttered from the handlebars of those motorcycles. Randy Whitman knew that close behind them rode his hero, the President of the United States, John Fitzgerald Kennedy.

—CHAPTER 14—

Near the sixth floor window behind the cardboard boxes obscuring his presence, Hidell crouched against the lower wall. Only his eyes and the top of his head would be visible to anyone who may have looked up that far from the street below.

Two motorcycle cops led the way, followed by a series of black Lincoln Continental limousines. The large black car behind Kennedy housed members of the President's staff. The next large black car housed members of the American Secret Service, official looking men in suits, designated to protect the President. Hidell knew that earlier this morning all vehicles in the motorcade were covered by storm proof bubble tops. But the rain had stopped, and President Kennedy had asked specifically that the bubbles be removed from their Lincoln Continentals.

Hidell fretted. Although pleased that he could shoot the President from such a close distance, he still wondered if he would escape from behind the boxes in time to get down six flights of stairs, out the front door, and onto a bus before the police and Secret Service swarmed every room of every building in Dealey Plaza. Because the schoolbook company employed Hidell as an order filler, his attendance at the site would have probably gone unheeded. No one would stop him—let alone arrest him—for his presence in the Texas School Book Depository.

He would meet the others tonight at eight o'clock in New Orleans at the Cajun Bar and Grill. Confirmation of allegiance was required in person. If anything had gone wrong, it would be discussed and the details analyzed. Error would not—could not—figure into the equation. No matter what happened in the next few minutes, Hidell contemplated only a single concern: to be in New Orleans by eight o'clock. No other options existed for him. After shooting at the President of the United States, he could ill-afford for further events to unfold in any other way.

****

Panting from excitement and out of breath, Randy clutched his camera. Now in his clear view, the motorcade crawled slowly toward the busy corner of Elm and Houston, where it would make a sharp left turn, move past the Texas School Book Depository, and continue onto the Stemmons Freeway. At the Dallas Trade Mart, the President would address an assortment of rich investors and economists.

Having eyed the exact spot from which he wanted to take pictures, Randy turned again and this time headed to the top of the hill. At first grateful no one else seemed to be staked out in the vicinity, Randy now felt mildly spooked. Suddenly more conscious of an absence of surrounding spectators, he experienced a temporary sense of isolation, as though this current moment in his life was not real—perhaps a movie he had been watching on television.

He stood far enough from the street that he sensed some solitude. But then he remembered the significance of what was about to happen, of which he would become a part: he, with his trusty camera on this side of the street, and Ira Cushman, with his dependable camera on the other side of the street.

And then for just a few seconds, Randall Walter Whitman, suspended in time, entertained a surreal vision and a distortion of reality.

****

From the third floor of the Dallas Records Building, the tall man in the tattered electrical worker's clothes raised the rifle. He pulled the sight scope to his left eye, as he balanced the butt of the firing arm against his right shoulder. Each time he had practiced a dry firing of this weapon he shot it at grapefruits and pumpkins. He had made it comfortable and familiar. But now, as his famous target in the limousine approached, all that comfort and familiarity abandoned him. Irritated that it just didn't feel right, he was smart enough to understand that how it felt had nothing to do with the success or failure of his operation. He had been assigned to do a job—a mission that would rock the world. If the Tall Man died, he died. The world would not miss him. He had no children, no real family to speak of. For the first time in his life, the Tall Man had enlisted to be part of a team, a rugged group of men from two countries who would make the world better by working for one common, unifying goal.

As he saw the President smiling and waving to those who lined the streets, he wondered what it would feel like to be hit in the back of the head by a bullet fired from over a hundred yards away. As his head exploded into blood and brain matter, would he feel pain—if even for an instant?

The Tall Man's mind preoccupied, the President of the United States now turned his head to the right. For a split second, the Tall Man startled: *President Kennedy had seen him*! But, of course, irrational thoughts were fueled by gross apprehension, and the Tall Man raised his professionalism a notch, remembering the virtues of patience and calm. The Tall Man would wait for the President's car to make a left turn at the corner, and Kennedy would be at a prescribed spot in the street: in full view of one man exactly to his right; another man above him, slightly to his left; and the Tall Man himself, poised directly in back and from up high. In the crossfire of three rifles from these trained marksmen, President Kennedy certainly would not survive another day of his imperial Presidency.

With under a minute to go, the Tall Man removed the rifle from his shoulder, stared at the barrel, and shook his head. After his deed he would have less than five minutes to disassemble the gun and put it back in his electrical pails. Soon the police would be milling throughout the area. And a lone electrical worker, after having finished his innocent, simple repair job, would want only to escape the chaotic atmosphere and outrageous commotion that would surely take over the building.

****

One hobo was kneeling, shouldering a rifle, readying to point it across a concrete barrier atop the hill. The other hobo sat on his knees, looking behind him in the direction of the railroad tracks, his gaze seemingly fixed on nothing, yet seeing everything.

Randall knew immediately the incongruence of what he witnessed: men dressed like lousy renditions of tramps, one pointing a gun at a street toward a spot in the road that in less than thirty seconds from now would hold a car carrying the President of the United States.

Randy's thought processes choked, a flustered response to a scene he would never be able to clear from his memory.

He said nothing.

He did nothing.

Paralyzed with inaction brought about by shock and confusion, he let his camera slip from his hands and drop to the grass. He could have bent over and picked it up. It would have taken less than a second. But when the camera fell from his hands to a spot directly between his legs, he stiffened. One of the hobos —Randy would never be sure whether it was the rifleman or the railroad tracks watcher—snarled in a voice he eventually heard over and over in his nightmares, "*What the hell!*"

And then Randy made a hasty decision; it was a reflex that would haunt him, perhaps, forever: He left his camera on the ground—and *ran*.

But instead of running down the hill toward the street, he bolted to his right, sprinting toward the freeway overpass.

As he heard rapid popping noises behind him—three or four pops in all—he instinctively knew that shots were not being fired in his direction; that they probably did not come from the rifleman he saw behind the barricade. At least, he was fairly sure the man was not shooting at *him*.

But the gunshots terrified him, overwhelmed him, and he dove to the ground, seeking refuge in the dampness of the cool afternoon grass. He lay there, waiting, trembling. The concept of time eluded him, replaced by an unsettling, new quiet in his head. Unsure if he was dead or alive, injured or unscathed, he listened to the eerie silence.

Randy Whitman's young body shimmied from his runaway conceptions of the horrors being perpetrated all around him in Dealey Plaza and remained paralyzed for what seemed like an eternity.

—CHAPTER 15—

Shortly after 11:00 A.M. in California, Samuel J. Whitman, Randy's father, prepared to close his hardware store for an hour so he could enjoy a leisurely lunch with a long-time friend of his, Jarrod Kendall. For days, Samuel wanted to discuss business with Jarrod: a possibility Jarrod would buy into his shop.

Preparing to meet Jarrod at the Beefeater Restaurant, Samuel locked the cash register and pulled the blinds on one of the windows.

Just then, the telephone rang.

In the vicinity of the cash register, the phone, still vibrating as Samuel picked up the receiver, clanged with a disquieting urgency.

"Sam, it's me."

Samuel recognized his wife's voice, but its distressful tone was foreign to him.

"Mimi, I'm on my way to meet Jarrod. I'm late."

"Have you heard the news?"

This had better be important, Samuel thought to himself. "No, what?"

Her words hit him low in his abdomen, causing his legs to sag. "President Kennedy is dead."

At first Samuel didn't process the comment, so he bought himself some time by repeating it. "President Kennedy is dead?"

Her voice picked up speed. "It just happened, Samuel, in Dallas. Somebody shot him. In *Dallas*! That's where Randy and his debater friends are today. Randy might have seen it—been there! I don't know…"

"When? Did Randy call?"

"No, he hasn't called…I was watching *As the World Turns*, and Walter Cronkite broke in. I'm looking at him on the T.V. right now…He just announced—just now—that Kennedy died, and he started to cry."

Although President Kennedy was not a favorite of Samuel Whitman, he knew how much the President meant to his son. Now he worried about Randy and his actual location when this happened. For Randy, the distress of this assassination would have been awful enough. If Randy had been there and actually seen President Kennedy's murder, Samuel didn't wish to speculate how that could have traumatized his son.

"Wow…Okay, I'm going to close the store for the day and come home. Randy will call us; I know he will. We'll take it from there."

"Do you think they'll still have a debate tournament?" Mrs. Whitman asked her husband. "Because I want him to come home —now."

"There's no sense in his getting on a plane today and coming home," Mr. Whitman said with an even calm in his voice. "But I doubt they'll be holding a debate tournament."

Walter Cronkite had just cut to a live view of the Dallas Trade Mart, the destination for Kennedy's speech that afternoon. Television viewers saw dozens of people milling about a banquet room—most of them aimlessly—in a state of shock. Tears streamed down the faces of those in view, as others began the task of clearing the banquet tables and putting away utensils that would have been used during the luncheon. In the front of the room, stood a conspicuously empty wooden lectern with a microphone. The podium had been decorated with the seal of the President of the United States.

"Sam, I don't want Randy to stay in Dallas," Mrs. Whitman complained.

"He won't be in Dallas for long."

"I don't want him there at all."

"Well, he's already there," Samuel replied, reflecting briefly on the absurdity of their conversation. "Nothing's going to happen to him."

"It's just—this is so—upsetting."

"Think of how upsetting it's been for President Kennedy."

Mrs. Whitman did not brandish a macabre sense of humor. For her, this moment did not lend itself to even a bit of comedy.

"Anyway," Samuel said. "First I've got to meet Jarrod for lunch, and then I'll come home. By then, we'll probably hear from Randy. I imagine the phone lines have been jammed."

Samuel Whitman closed the store. He fulfilled his obligation to meet with Jarrod Kendall for lunch. But The Beefeater Restaurant had already been closed by the time he walked up to the front door of the upscale eating establishment. A few businessmen, trying to figure out what to do about their afternoon meal, were loitering in the parking lot, but there was no sign of Jarrod. So Samuel drove home, as he had promised his wife he would do.

When he walked up the front steps of their suburban house and greeted Mimi with news of the closure of the Beefeater Restaurant, she looked especially despondent. Her eyes were filled with worry. She told her husband Randy had not yet telephoned; that she had been sitting next to the phone for three quarters of an hour, but it had not rung even once.

Randy's parents had only sensed it, but their worries and fears about their son in Dallas were very well founded.

****

Earlier, at approximately 11:15 P.M. in Los Angeles and 1:15 P.M. in Dallas—and at about the very moment Samuel Whitman hung up the telephone after speaking with his wife—events of monumental significance were unfolding in Texas.

Hidell had shot two bullets from his Italian Mannlicher-Carcano at President Kennedy and missed his target both times. One bullet bounced off the curb, and another one thudded into the back of the governor of Texas, John Connolly, who had sat in a jump seat in front of Kennedy. Hidell then sprinted down five flights of stairs in the book building and attempted to camouflage his participation in the shooting by calmly drinking a Coca Cola while standing next to a vending machine on the first floor.

Several people had seen him, including a Dallas policeman who ran into the building with his gun drawn. Pointing the gun at

Hidell, the policeman yelled, "Hey!"

But the foreman of the depository, Roy Truly, reassured the policeman. "He's all right; he works here," Truly told the cop.

At which point the policeman, without inserting his revolver into the holster belted around his waist, made a hasty dash up the stairs of the Texas School Book Depository.

Hidell then calmly walked out the front door of the building, expertly blended into the confusion, and patiently boarded a bus. Unbeknownst to the other passengers—none of whom had the slightest idea what had occurred in their city only a few minutes before—one of the most infamous murderers in the history of the world sat among them.

After catching a taxi, Hidell returned to his boardinghouse in Oak Cliff, where he snatched a revolver and stuffed it into a jacket pocket. He then began walking to his destination, a bar in a mostly ignored Dallas neighborhood. There he would talk with the Hat Man, who the Grinning Man had liked and found valuable to the cause, mainly for the Hat Man's strategic Dallas location and his vital connections.

Hidell's confirmation with the Hat Man would be a first step in their post game operations. Other discussions of strategy would ensue in New Orleans later that night.

But the history of the world would be altered by what happened around 1:15 P.M. on November 22, 1963, just as Alex Hidell walked on a residential sidewalk toward his destination, the Oak Tree Bar.

A Dallas Police patrol car, traveling in the opposite direction of Hidell, crawled slowly along the street. As he stopped his car, the young police officer rolled down the window and called to the stranger on the sidewalk, "Excuse me—can I speak with you a second?"

Hidell briefly hesitated and then moved to the street. The passengers' side of the car was open, so Hidell peered at the Dallas policeman behind the steering wheel. "Yeah?"

"Where are you going?"

"Uh, the liquor store."

Perhaps Hidell looked rattled. Maybe his face portrayed his

words as lies. But the policeman opened the door on his side of the car—a mistake, one of many by the police that day—and got out to face Hidell. Instead of calling for backup or ordering Hidell to come around the car, which would have placed Hidell within arm's length of him, the policeman casually and inattentively removed himself from the vehicle, as he said, "I think I'll need an I.D. Do you have any identification…?"

Before the Dallas police officer could straighten and stand on the street, Hidell slipped his Smith-Wesson revolver from his coat pocket, aimed it point-blank at the policeman, and fired it at least five times into his torso.

The thirteen-year veteran of Dallas law enforcement died before he hit the pavement.

Several neighborhood onlookers raced to his side. One of them grabbed the police car's microphone to summon help.

His plans now in disarray, A. Hidell was on his way to a movie theater down the street, a dark sanctuary, a refuge, while the world outside reeled in fear, sadness, and confusion.

****

Randy hadn't called home, because he had no opportunity to call home.

Immediately after diving to the grass and hearing the sounds of popping firecrackers behind him, he rose from the ground blurry-eyed and frightened. He was barely cognizant of the action happening around him: men and women running down the grassy slope; a woman, bent over, sobbing; policemen jumping off their motorcycles, their guns drawn and scurrying into buildings lining the streets. But he heard sirens, so loud that he worried a vehicle was about to run up his back.

Barely conscious, but desirous of wanting to escape the grassy hill, Randy somehow had found his way back to his friends on the other side of the street. He was hazy but aware of Maria and Tommy and Mr. Lott. His eyes focused on Maria, who stood next to a weeping Ira. Maria stared into Ira's face. She showed a strong determination to be helpful, but Ira seemed inconsolable.

If Randy had been able, he would have observed the same frame of mind for practically everyone who still lingered on Elm Street. Confusion and fear permeated the scene, but for those who had settled down, an overwhelming state of grief rattled through the throngs who still huddled on the street side.

Before going to Randy, Maria continued to work on soothing Ira. But aware of her increasing trepidation over Randy's welfare, she hurried over to Randy, grabbed his shaking hands, and held them tightly.

"Are you okay?" she asked him, breathing unconvincingly to herself that she personally had weathered the storm.

Randy did not—could not—respond to anyone, his ashen face expressionless. His new debate partner tried to console him, help him. But unable to generate an antidote to his overwhelming numbness, Randy did not react to Maria. An abrupt detachment from the events that had just occurred disconnected the circuits in Randy's head. A once brilliant tool, his brain now was shredded with fear and shock and surprise, all thrust in his direction by pure coincidence and random unfolding of circumstances.

"Randy…"

Maria decided against raising more meaningless questions and folded her arms around his shaking torso, holding him close. Randy had never felt so cold and alone and terrified, but Maria's body now temporarily gave him the warmth and security he so desperately required.

If he could have looked around, Randy would have seen similar circumstances all about him: people comforting each other, holding each other, hugging each other in desperate, final attempts to confirm the world as they knew it still existed. They longed to verify that time, which suddenly had stood still, would soon spring forward once again, and the violence would not spread to them.

Human touch provided such havens.

—CHAPTER 16—

Immediately after he shot President Kennedy in his back from the third floor of the Dallas Records Building, the Tall Man, disguised as an electrician, unlocked the door of the small office and began to fidget randomly with wires, bulbs, and other equipment.

Fortunately for this assassin, the others in the building had been forced to steady their own sense of horror and confusion. The importance of checking on the safety of those in various offices mattered much less than defending themselves against stray bullets from the FBI or the police. If the perpetrators had taken refuge in the workers' vicinity, perhaps those in the building were in harms way. For many in the Dallas Records Building, ducking had become the highest virtue.

But the Tall Man was aware the authorities would soon infiltrate his nest. He needed to solidify his method for escaping the building unscathed and undetected. If even *one* of them was caught, their plan would be jeopardized, *all* of them eventually arrested for slaying the President of the United States.

Clutching his pail of tools, The Tall Man walked into the third floor corridor of the Dallas Records Building. Providing further decoy behavior as an electrician might allow him to leave the premises inconspicuously. He saw that several people strolled around the hallway, holding on to their looks of astonishment.

At the instant the Tall Man decided to flee the building, he ran into Judd, who had just emerged from his temporary office space. Looking colorless, Judd fixed his attention on the Tall Man, causing the Tall Man momentary concern he had been fingered as an assassin. But in the mixture of Judd's uncontrollable emotions, the Tall Man had become a stranger to him. When Judd finally recognized the electrician, he robotically said, "Everybody's going downstairs."

The Tall Man feigned ignorance. "What's going on?"

"You didn't see?"

"I—"

"You didn't hear it?"

"No…What happened? People were running all over the place down there."

How could he not have seen it? "Somebody's shot at the President! There were gunshots all over the place!"

"What?"

"I don't know what happened," Judd said confusedly. "I don't know. We should all go downstairs."

The police hadn't arrived. The Tall Man thought going downstairs—and out the door—was a good idea. Others were already headed in that direction. But if a cop stopped them, he couldn't have the murder weapon in his possession; that hadn't been part of the plan. The safest choice now would be to leave the firearm behind. By the time anyone searched the office and found the German Mauser, he would be well on his way to New Orleans.

But he still needed a cover. "Should I get the rest of my equipment?" he asked, hoping he already knew Judd's answer.

"Yes, yes. Just—hurry. We all need to go downstairs."

Provided with the answer the Tall Man did not want to hear, he frowned. "But what happened?"

"Let's just go!" Judd commanded. "I have a feeling we all should get the hell outta' here—and fast!"

At his assurance Judd and the others were headed down the corridor and on their way to the elevator, the Tall Man slipped back into Judd's office and finished packing his electrical equipment. He prayed that no one—especially a policeman—would stop him as he made his way downstairs with a concealed rifle.

****

"Hmm," Mr. Lott said, pouring over the debate tournament schedule with his assembled debaters, "it looks like we need to get over to Southern Methodist by three o'clock."

The Motel 6 guest room, replete with the bright and hopeful

just a few hours earlier, now crawled with the dark and dreary. Even as the sun radiated its brilliance outside, the closed drapes in Mr. Lott's room leered gloomily at the teenagers from Long Beach, daring them to go on with the debate tournament—and with life as usual.

Among these teenagers, who now wanted to debate at the Tournament of Champions? Randy sat in a corner by himself, a sedate, staid expression on his face. His detachment from the pending debate tournament could not have been more evident if he were a strange child who had wandered in from the street and randomly joined their group.

Margie Pendergrass, her eyes red from sobbing most of the afternoon, sniffled. "I can't believe that they would go on with the tournament."

Ira looked over at Randy but said to Mr. Lott, "I don't think any of us feel like competing."

Randy remained virtually motionless.

Tommy Wright selected this opportunity to express his ornery, contrary self: "Well, I don't feel like debating either, but I think we should. We came all this way and need to get our money's worth. Kennedy's dead, and there's nothing we can do about it now."

A small black and white television in the motel room flashed images of a young man with dark hair being led in handcuffs down a corridor at the Dallas Police headquarters. A reporter shoved a microphone in his face and asked him if he had shot the President of the United States. He politely mumbled something like, "No, I don't know anything about that…I would like, however, to see an attorney."

The contingency from Long Beach had been glued to the television for the past hour. They assembled in Mr. Lott's room in order to decide what to do about the rest of their stay in Dallas. Maria was clearly adamant about not showing up for the tournament. Her partner had been practically comatose for the past two hours, and the emotions she and Margie had expelled in their hotel room made it impractical for them to think straight.

Wouldn't this sort of hopelessness also be true for the other hundred or so high school debaters who had journeyed to Dallas for the Tournament of Champions?

Mr. Lott didn't wish to press the issue very far. He said, "Okay, here's my take on it. I'll say this once and then you decide: President Kennedy was killed today. We all saw it happen right before our eyes. But we came here for a purpose—something totally unrelated to President Kennedy or anything else that happened out there. And that something is still possible for us to achieve. It's up to you."

Mr. Lott shrugged. He knew he had not made a good argument for his side. He was conflicted. The idea of spending a couple thousands dollars to get here and then going home without competing in the tournament seemed at odds with what could be productive, showing up for their debates and trying to make the best out of a terrible situation.

And Mr. Lott secretly believed this would be his last Tournament of Champions.

Individually, they expressed their desire to compete or not to compete. By the time they turned to Randy for him to cast his vote —he was last—the answer to their quandary became obvious: By a vote of 4-2 (Mr. Lott and Tommy voted to compete; Randy remained silent.), the Long Beach High School debaters decided to withdraw from the Tournament of Champions.

Tournament entrants from other high schools had lined the parade route. But when the bullets were fired, none of those teens had been standing as close to President Kennedy's motorcade as the Long Beach group had stood.

The trauma faced by the Long Beach debaters could not be compared fairly to the pain of those who were not in Dealey Plaza. Maybe the tournament would carry on, but not with Long Beach's presence.

Mr. Lott looked at Randy, who huddled with a blanket on a cheap wooden chair. "Randy, you want to make it official? Are Tommy and I the only *go* votes?" he asked bleakly.

But Randy did not flinch.

He refused to care about a debate tournament.

Mr. Lott said, "You do understand that we can't fly home

until Monday? You do know that? We can't change our flight reservations; that would cost an enormous amount of money. What are we going to do?"

Ira lapsed into rapid blinking. He always did that after being hit by a sudden bout of stress. "We can just sit here in the room and watch television: all assassination coverage, all the time."

Tommy Wright scoffed, "Not funny, Ira. You're just not funny."

"Really?" Ira said sarcastically. "I didn't know that, Tommy!" He then pointed to Randy. "Look at him. That could have been you—or me!

It should have been me! Ira remembered that *he* had been poised for his romp across Elm Street about the time Tommy had taunted his way under Randy's skin.

Mr. Lott interrupted them. "We've all been told that that the Dallas Police will be speaking with each of us—they took our home addresses and phone numbers…Which leads me to another question: have you all called home? That's important."

They all nodded in the affirmative.

Except for Randy. He had not called home, yet. He had not spoken with parents who anxiously—even desperately—waited for his phone call from Dallas.

Even as Mr. Lott discussed the situation in Dallas, Mr. and Mrs. Whitman talked about the matter in California.

"Samuel, I'm calling the motel again. He's got to be there by now."

Mr. Whitman shrugged. "If he was there, he would have called us."

"No," she responded with anxiety and sadness, causing her voice to quiver. "He hasn't phoned. There's something wrong."

"He's at the debate tournament."

"No," she shook her head again. "He's not. I just know it. If I don't get an answer from his room again, I'm calling the Dallas Police."

Mr. Whitman offered a soft, sardonic chuckle. "Do you think the Dallas Police might be slightly busy this afternoon, Mimi? He's okay. Just give him time. I don't know where he was when this happened—but he's in Dallas for Chrissake! He's in the same city where the President was murdered! I'm sure there's a lot on his mind right now besides checking in with Mommy and Daddy! He'll call in due time, so *please* don't telephone the Dallas Police! Jeez!"

****

No one knew what occupied Randy's mind that afternoon, because they each had to deal in their own way with these horrors. They all assumed everyone else had been facing the same mental and emotional challenges.

Only this wasn't true.

Randy suffered in a state of shock. His condition stemmed not so much from being so close to President Kennedy when he was shot—or from his love and admiration of the President—but from his experience of having come face to face with the devil. He had dealt with those vital seconds with the hobos by fleeing the scene, tumbling to the ground, and, thus, obliterating his memory. In fact, even the actual events preceding his trip up the slope were foggy. Randy now lacked any capacity—at least, temporarily—to sort in his mind what had occurred that afternoon in Dealey Plaza.

At 4:30 P.M. as Randall Whitman lay in bed with his eyes fixed on the ceiling, Mr. Lott walked into his motel room. Ira answered Mr. Lott's knock; he'd been watching the television set with its additional reporting on the day's historic activities.

Mr. Lott looked over Ira's shoulder and saw his roommate. "Is he okay?"

"He won 't talk."

Mr. Lott frowned. "Has he said anything, yet?"

"I don't think he's uttered a word since just before he ran across the street with his camera. And that's another thing. I don't think he has his camera."

"The police took your camera, didn't they, Ira?"

"Yes, but I don't think they took Randy's. I think he lost it on the hill. I've asked him about the camera, and he keeps shaking his head. Maybe we should take him to a doctor."

"His mother called before and left a message at the desk, Mr. Lott said. "I'm going to call her back. I don't think Randy will."

"I don't think Randy *can*."

Mr. Lott picked up the receiver from the telephone next to Randy's bed. "I'll call his mother. If she wants me to, I'll put him on a plane tonight." Then he looked at Ira. "I guess you should fly back with him. Take care of him."

Ira grinned for the first time since the shooting. He turned in Randy's direction. "Hear that, Randy. If you'd like, you can go home tonight. Maybe, I'll go with you. Or maybe we can get Tommy Wright to go with you."

Without returning the smile, Randy shot a glance in Ira's direction. Ira figured his quip about Tommy Wright had jolted him from his trance. But Ira and Mr. Lott discovered that something else had awakened Randy from his state of semi-consciousness.

"No, Ira! No!"

Ira shot a look at Mr. Lott. And then back to Randy. "Randy, I was kidding, man. You okay?"

"I'm not going back home tonight! I don't care what my mother wants!"

Mr. Lott set the phone down. "Randy, there's no tournament. They cancelled it. I guess almost nobody decided to show up, and —"

"It's not about the stupid tournament!" Randy screamed, suddenly turning red in the face. "It's about the police!"

"What?" Mr. Lott asked.

"The police!" Randy repeated more softly, containing his emotions. He added words that came out painstakingly and haltingly, words he could not believe he had said. "I saw the people who did it. I *saw* them."

"Randy, are you all right?" Mr. Lott's voice rang with sympathy.

"I saw them," Randy maintained. He face was pasty white, haggard with dehydration. "I wasn't more than five feet from the men—behind the barrier up on the hill. That spot we talked about: the one in front of the parking lot and old box cars on the railroad tracks."

"Randy…" Ira came off as listless. He was exhausted.

"No, Ira—Mr. Lott, listen," Randy begged, but this time his tone of voice tinged with reasonability. "There were two men behind that wall up there. One of them had a rifle. The other one was standing guard, I guess. But he was on his knees. They were both dressed like bums, but something about them—if you saw them—told you that they weren't bums, just very bad bum impersonators. Did you see anybody like that?"

Neither Mr. Lott nor Ira could attest to what they had seen. Just as with so many other bystanders during that long, dramatic day, everything they had said, seen, or done had become a blur, a series of events coming in and out of their memory's focus.

Mr. Lott bent down and picked up a dirty T-shirt that lay on the floor. He flipped it to a chair behind him. "I didn't see anybody like that, Randy. It doesn't mean they weren't there, though. You probably saw something."

"I *know* what I saw!" Randy insisted. "It's been stuck in my mind. I just couldn't get it out—couldn't say it—before. I saw these two men, and one of them looked right at me. All I could see were his teeth. And he said to me, 'What the hell are you doing here!'—Or something like that—and I ran. I think that's when I dropped my camera. I dropped my camera and I ran. And then I fell. I was running away from these men and I heard shots…and then I…and then it was like the ground and the grass and the dirt came up and hit me right in the face!"

Who knew what to say? Mr. Lott didn't. Ira didn't.

Randy suddenly had become lucid—or was he hallucinating? Considering what had already transpired, nothing should have seemed shocking to anyone on the team.

Randy continued, "I need to tell someone what I saw."

"They've arrested a guy," Ira said. "Some young guy who worked in the building across the street—that red brick building."

Randy frowned. "They said a guy shot President Kennedy from that building?"

Ira nodded.

Mr. Lott added, "He also killed a policeman. That's what the people on television are saying."

Randy began to breathe more rapidly. "Does he—did he confess to it?"

Mr. Lott shook his head. "We don't know; I don't know."

Randy sat up in bed and propped the pillow behind him. "The killer didn't shoot from that building—not from the red brick building on the corner. Is that the one you're talking about?"

Randy leaned back, grimaced; his head hurt.

Ira observed, "Nobody knows too much, yet. Everything happened so fast. I heard those popping sounds…The cops took our phone numbers and addresses…and they took my camera."

Ira didn't want to talk about it anymore.

Randy asked, "Did they get my phone number and address?"

Ira nodded. " I gave it to them. You weren't talking."

Just then the phone next to Randy's bed rang, and both Ira and Mr. Lott almost popped through the ceiling. Randy, lost in his thoughts, made no attempt to answer it. Ira leaned over Randy and pulled the black receiver from its hook.

Checking on Randy's condition, Maria held the telephone on the other end of the line. Mr. Lott told Maria that Randy was up and coherent. He explained to her what they had decided about returning to California, and that they were going to call Randy's parents. Maria volunteered to accompany Randy home if Mr. Lott wanted her to do so.

But Randy was adamant about his need to speak with the Dallas Police. Although he should have been thinking about talking to the Secret Service or the FBI, he remembered seeing only Dallas policemen around Dealey Plaza. Only those images were fresh in his mind, and they sealed an obsessive compulsion in Randy Whitman to squeal to the police about the nightmarish scene he had witnessed on the grassy hill.

—CHAPTER 17—

Earlier that afternoon at a movie house in Dallas, Alex Hidell bought a ticket for the l:15 P.M. showing of Audie Murphy's World War II film, *War is Hell*.

The Texas Theater, a typical single-auditorium house, played a different first run feature beginning every Wednesday. Hidell wasn't familiar with the place. He had fled to it by chance, immediately after unloading his revolver into the body of a Dallas cop. The large marquee on the theater building had attracted his attention. The sign invited him into a dark asylum, until he could slip outside again and continue to his destination.

Hidell settled in the middle of the auditorium, unable and unwilling to concentrate on the film. He had, after all, shot at the President of the United States (and wounded the Governor of Texas) and then killed a Dallas patrol officer in full view of several strangers. Just how much safety the movie theater would provide him, Hidell didn't know.

Had anyone on the street seen him walk inside?

Further legwork by the Dallas Police Department answered that question. After speaking with witnesses to the shooting of the policeman, more than a few officers traced the cop killer—or someone who matched his appearance—to the box office of the Texas Theater. The attendant affirmed (Hidell) had bought a ticket. She then slithered inside the darkened auditorium and recognized the man. She returned immediately to the investigating officers and provided them their suspect's exact seat location.

In the full view of a smattering of people who were also viewing the matinee showing of the war movie, the policeman surrounded Hidell and told him he was under arrest.

Hidell yelled out, "It's over!"

He raised a hand in defiance and attempted with the other

hand to strike one of the policemen. Another policeman reacted quickly, planting his fist in Hidell's right eye—a patented shiner that would be with him during his subsequent appearances on television. In arresting Hidell to the floor, the force of the cops' movements struck his right cheekbone, also creating an obvious bruising effect. What some would allude to as an example of "typical police brutality" had been, in actuality, the result of defensive punches used against Hidell after he had attempted to clout a Dallas cop and possibly pull a firearm from his jacket.

Media speculation about what Hidell meant by, "It's over!" later dominated his almost every appearance in front of newspaper reporters and the broadcast media. He continued to cry out for an attorney, only a phone call away; but he was not allowed to make that call, at least, on Friday. He spoke behind closed doors with interrogators from the Dallas Police Department, the Secret Service, and the FBI, always denying any involvement in the killing of President Kennedy and—with much less enthusiasm— any direct participation in the murder of a Dallas policeman by the name of J.D. Tippit.

Since no fewer than five people confirmed they saw Hidell shoot Tippit, the country watched television with rabid curiosity, wondering how he might successfully disguise his participation in the Tippit killing. Perhaps time would offer details about Hidell's alibi, although most observers figured it would take an escape act comparable to a handcuffed Houdini getting out of a tank of water for Hidell to extricate himself from these sorry, incriminating circumstances. But throughout the media, rumors of a mistaken identification of the assailant in the Tippit murder began to surface. This meant a lot of different witnesses had made the same, exact *mistake* by implicating the man arrested in the theater.

When the police apprehended Hidell in the Texas Theater, he possessed identification labeling him as A. Hidell, a member of a committee called, "Fair Play For Cuba," and identifying A. Hidell as its president. Immediately recognized by Dallas and New Orleans reporters as the man who had recently given several radio interviews defending this organization and its pro-Cuban leanings, Hidell's face began to take on the media visage of a pro-Castro maniac in charge of a large group of Communist sympathizers. But, in fact, the committee boasted of only *one* official member: A. Hidell.

Identification of the suspect as A. Hidell presented the police with a web of confusion. The suspect in the Tippit murder worked as a book stacker on the sixth floor of the Texas School Book Depository. A Dallas policeman had found him drinking a Coke near a vending machine on the first floor of that building just seconds after the bullets were fired at Kennedy's motorcade. The suspect then slipped out of the building and was later positively identified by a cab driver who had provided him a with ride, and also by several people on a bus he had ridden in his flight from Dealey Plaza.

The mystery lay in the name on Hidell's driver's license: A. Hidell. The problem: the man who worked in the book building was named Lee Harvey Oswald. The employee identified himself to co-workers and his bosses as Lee Harvey Oswald. And when his wife went to the police station to visit her husband, without even the slightest hesitation she acknowledged the suspect was her husband, Lee Harvey Oswald.

The first question Marina Oswald asked Lee was, "Why did you leave your wedding ring and all that money on our dresser?"

Oswald blinked but said nothing.

—CHAPTER 18—

For almost five hours, Samuel Whitman sat in his living room watching the T.V. Each time the telephone rang, he jumped. Samuel hoped he would hear from his son, who, for all he knew, was competing in a debate tournament in Dallas, Texas. Randy, ever vigilant about appeasing his parents and assuaging their fears, would have called home if he had the time. Of this, Samuel was positive.

The thought of an illness, accident, or another sinister force precluding his son from checking in with his parents drove Randy's father crazy with anxiety. Relatives on the East Coast and a couple of nearby friends phoned to casually chat about events, but this served only to anger him. He bottled up resentment against those who had dared try to communicate with him, while his own son did not.

Or could not.

At approximately 5:10 in the evening, Samuel and the rest of the world watched in sadness as Air Force One, after its short flight from Dallas, touched down on the runway of Andrews Air Force Base in Washington D.C. The plane carried President Kennedy's body, Jacqueline Kennedy, and a beleaguered supporting cast unfortunate enough to have been in Dallas that day. Just as these sullen, weary travelers walked down the steep ladder from the plane, the phone rang again in the Whitman home.

This time, much to the relief of his parents, Randy's fatigued voice sounded on the other end of the line.

As soon as the preliminaries had passed, and Samuel felt secure his boy was alive and well, he scurried into what bothered him all afternoon: "Why didn't you call us, Randy? Your mother and I have been sick with worry here."

"I'm calling now," Randy answered.

"Calling now," Samuel echoed. His relief had tempered his previous anger. "Randy, we've been waiting over five hours for this phone call. Why didn't you call us to let us know you were all right?"

To his father's surprise, Randy replied, "Because I *wasn't* all right. I couldn't call."

"What happened?" his father's voice revealed concern. Mrs. Whitman, who stood by her husband as he spoke on the phone in the kitchen, suddenly felt her heart sink.

"We saw it," Randy answered, barely audible.

"You saw it?"

"Yes."

"What?" Mr. Whitman could hardly understand him. "You were there when the President was shot?"

"Yes," Randy replied again, but this time his father could not hear him at all. So he had to repeat himself. "I was there, Dad. I didn't..."

"You saw Kennedy get shot?"

"No, Dad, I didn't actually see it. But I saw who did it."

"You saw—what?"

"I saw who did it, and I need to speak with the police; so I can't come home—don't ask me to come home. I'm all right...I'll be home Monday."

Samuel Whitman could barely process the words his son had flung upon him. During his entire life—through attending college, investing in businesses, getting married, and now raising a family —nothing extreme, no other incident that shouted in tragic, bold letters had ever happened to him. But his only son had just told him that he saw a man who killed the President of the United States; that he had to stay in Dallas in order to talk to the police. And through his son's inferential tone, there had been so much *more* to reveal—but he could not do so in the short amount of time remaining on a public telephone with a four-way party line.

"What, Samuel? What?" Mrs. Whitman stammered.

Samuel shook his head, as he hung up the phone. "He'll be home Monday."

"Is he all right?" Randy's mother was on the verge of panic.

But her husband looked at her and shook his head. He added quietly, "No, Mimi, I don't think he is."

"What? Where is he?"

"I don't know. At the hotel, I guess. No speech tournament: cancelled, of course, just like I told you it would be."

"But—"

"I told you, Mimi, he's not okay. He was there. He was there when President Kennedy got shot. And he saw who did it. He *saw*."

Mrs. Whitman opened her mouth to scream.

But nothing came out.

—CHAPTER 19—

Mr. Lott issued orders to his debaters: Don't leave the motel grounds—under any circumstances. Keep the doors of your rooms locked. The girls (Maria and Margie) were not to go into the boys' rooms—and vice-versa—without getting prior permission from Mr. Lott. The boys were to stay out of the girls' rooms as well. Meals would be eaten together as a group.

Mr. Lott promised he would call the airlines in order to expedite the process of leaving Dallas, but he knew it would be a waste of time. The airport would be inordinately busy, flights would be juggled, and there would be no time for airport officials to redo the travel reservations of a bunch of teenagers who wanted to return to their parents in California.

So even though he had promised, Mr. Lott did not call the airlines. He simply reconciled himself with the situation: stuck with six teenagers at a Motel 6 in Dallas, and practically every store and restaurant in the state of Texas—the nation, for that matter—closed for the entire weekend. Until after Kennedy's Monday morning funeral, movie theaters would stay dark, all television channels geared to the same coverage, and sometimes the same feed, of assassination events as they unfolded.

As Mr. Lott, Ira, and Randy watched Dallas Police Chief Jessie Currie hold up a large rifle in front of T.V. cameras, Randy had a disconcerted feeling he wasn't looking at the same rifle he saw the hobo holding on the grassy hill. When the Chief explained that the rifle had been found hidden between some boxes on the sixth floor of the Texas School Book Depository, Randy knew it was the not the same rifle.

Which meant: in addition to the hobo on the hill, someone else had shot the President.

Later that evening Dallas law enforcement scheduled Lee

Harvey Oswald to conduct a televised midnight press conference. America wondered what this man, who allegedly had slain the most powerful, popular person in the free world (more popular than even Elvis Presley), would say—what sorts of answers he would give to the anguished nation he had brought to its collective tears.

Everyone wondered about Oswald; that is, everyone except for Randy.

Randy had practically burst with angst. Mr. Lott called the police for the purpose of offering him as a key witness to the assassination. After being put on hold for thirty minutes, a desk worker told Mr. Lott that that the police or FBI would eventually interview all those who were in Dealey Plaza.

When Mr. Lott relayed this news to Randy, the teenager fell into an uncharacteristic, convulsive anger. "What? But *I* have something to say! I saw something they don't know about! They need to know what I saw! They don't have it right!"

Mr. Lott said consolingly, "We don't know that, Randy. Others may have seen the same thing. They might have already arrested these, uh, hobos."

"No," Randy insisted. "They couldn't have, Mr. Lott! You don't see any of them on television. But they were there—behind that wall at the top of the hill. I'll bet they went back into those railroad cars after they shot President Kennedy. Have the police looked back *there*?"

"I don't know where they've looked."

"It might be too late," Randy said resolutely.

"There were many others on the grassy hill, Randy."

"But nobody went up as far as I did. Nobody else decided to get photos from behind the retaining wall or near the monument. And they counted on that—that there wouldn't be many people around that spot. And nobody would be dumb enough to walk up a hill *away* from the President…because right before and right after they killed Kennedy, they were nothing but a couple of hobos. That's what they counted on—and it worked, Mr. Lott."

Mr. Lott admired Randy's tenacity. But he thought he now suffered from tremendous, though unreasonable, guilt: he should have yelled out when he saw the hobos; he should have fought their guns away; he should have stood his ground; he should have immediately run to a cop—right after the shots were fired. All this was self-loathing in the form of Monday morning quarterbacking.

Could the quick thinking and courage of a sixteen year-old boy who just happened to be in the wrong place at the right time have rewritten this tragic part of history?

If Randy had done *something* to draw others' attention to the waiting assassins, or if he had distracted the assassins at the last minute, would it have been enough? At least one other man with a rifle had shot the President from the book building. Randy could not have done anything about *that*.

****

Randy received permission from Mr. Lott to take Maria for a short walk around the motel. Motel 6 did not have a substantial lobby area, and a dimly lit parking lot jammed with automobiles offered them their only venue for privacy apart from the confines of the indoor corridors of the motel. But Randy had begun to feel claustrophobic in his room. And even though he verbally agreed with Mr. Lott that walking around the parking area was hardly a wise move, out of desperation, he steered Maria in this direction anyway.

For such a crowded parking area, stillness gripped the night. The clock in the hotel's office displayed 7:50 P.M., but to Randy and Maria it may as well have been midnight. The day had already been long, and intense exhaustion riddled the bodies of both teenagers.

"When I was about ten, I got my tonsils out," he said to Maria, as they strolled without direction on the outskirts of the parking lot. "After the surgery my parents and sister came into the recovery room to see me, but I was still under the influence of the anesthesia. I mean, I could hear them talking about me—my father made some wisecrack about my looking like an angel when I was unconscious and a devil when I was awake—but I couldn't *say* anything. I couldn't answer them. They thought I was unconscious;

I wasn't. I tried to wiggle my big toe so they would know I was able to hear them, but I couldn't do that either. I *thought* I was moving my toe, but nobody could remember seeing anything resembling a moving toe. Well, I'm telling you this because that's how I felt this afternoon. I heard what was being talked about: that Kennedy was dead; that the police told us they would contact us eventually…I knew all that, but I couldn't move my mouth. My brain was trying to send signals to my mouth, but my mouth didn't seem to be working."

Then he smiled for the first time in many hours. "That would be very nice under normal conditions—my mouth not spouting off immediately after getting its very first signals from my brain!"

Maria didn't know whether to laugh or throw her arms around Randy and embrace him in a huge hug—for warmth, for comfort, for both.

So Maria chose the latter.

Without hesitation, Randy returned her affection; he hugged her—hard. He pulled Maria close and felt the firmness of her body under her denim coat. Strands of her long, brown hair gently tickled him as they fell on his neck. He had finally discovered a form of intimacy with Maria Barquin: if only for a moment, if only for the dire, awful circumstances that had brought them together in an embrace—in a dimly-lit parking lot of a Motel 6 in Dallas, Texas.

****

Mr. Lott had congregated his remaining troops for a meeting in his own motel room. No longer caring about decorum, Mr. Lott had strewn his clothes about the room. He had taken care to deposit only his dirty socks and underwear in his suitcase. Everyone's mood solemn, no one seemed to mind the mess.

Still oblivious to its origins, Mr. Lott also had been forced to deal with the disgusting, unpleasant—and rather odorous—ramifications of the Ex-Lax prank.

And nobody cared to inquire about his success or failure in that endeavor.

Mr. Lott sat on the edge of the bed; his debaters surrounded him. "Obviously, things haven't turned out like we hoped they would. Not getting to debate at a tournament is, of course, the least of our troubles. And naturally, nobody else in the entire nation gives a rat's ass about that right now."

"Nobody else in the entire nation gives a rat's ass about debate under the *best* of circumstances, Mr. Lott!" Tommy Wright interjected with his patented smirk.

Ruther took a cue from Mr. Lott's short pause. "Who cares? Really, Mr. Lott, none of us care right now. Not a bit."

Margie Pendergrass added, "This has been awful. Terrible. Who cares about *our* minor problems? I sure don't."

Ira chimed in. "I guess all we'd be doing right now if we were home is watching the T.V. stuff anyway. We might as well do that here—give each other some moral support while we're at it."

"Yeah," Margie agreed. "We all saw it happen. We—"

But before Margie could finish, Mr. Lott interrupted her. "Just exactly what *did* we see, Margie? What? Look, I wanted to talk to you without Randy here, because he seems most affected by this—at least, for now. He thinks he saw things nobody else saw. He says he actually saw the assassins; that he came face-to-face with them behind the fence at the top of the hill."

"Which is impossible," Ira said, "because the assassins were *behind* the President."

"We don't know that, Ira," Mr. Lott grumbled. "Nobody knows anything for sure right now. The point is, Randy has been traumatized, and we all need to help him get through this."

Of course, Tommy Wright took Mr. Lott's inadvertent cue: "Oh, please, Mr. Lott! Everybody knows that Randy was in *love* with President Kennedy! After all this stuff happened, he began hallucinating! He didn't see anything the rest of us didn't see!"

Ira shot back at Tommy, "What makes you think you know anything about Randy, Tommy? And you know what? If it hadn't been for *you*, Randy would have never crossed that street in the first place!"

Tommy stiffened. "That's bull, Ira! *You* were the one who said you should take pictures from different sides of the street!"

"Correct," Ira acknowledged, less antagonistic now than in his first comment to Tommy. "But Randy had second thoughts. You goaded him into doing something that he ultimately didn't want to do."

"You're so full of it, Cushman!"

"Great comeback, Wright."

"Ooh! A tough guy! A *Jewish* tough guy, no less!"

"Tougher than you."

"Hey, you wanna' mix it up and *see* who's tougher?"

"Right, Tommy! Who are you trying to impress right now? Maria's not here!"

Tommy made a move to spring from the bed. But before he and Ira could come to blows, Mr. Lott intervened. Mr. Lott knew if these two tangled, the mere sight of such a physical mismatch would disturb even the most stoic of people, ranking only second to observing the aftermath effects of the Ex-Lax stunt.

"Hey!" Mr. Lott raised his voice. "We need to stick together here—not go for each other's throats!"

Then he brought the issue into focus. "Just what *did* anybody see out there today? Actually see? Something you could—and would—testify to in a court of law. Because that's what it might come down to. If you want to know the truth, I didn't see anything. Nothing. It happened so fast. I heard firecrackers, looked all around the area, and by the time my eyes came back to President Kennedy, his car was already by us, heading to the freeway. So I'm wondering, exactly—I mean *exactly*—what did you guys see?"

No one spoke.

So Mr. Lott pushed the matter. "I told you what I saw. Did anybody else see anything different?"

Again, there was no immediate response. But after what seemed like an interminable length of time, Margie Pendergrass said softly, "When I heard the firecrackers, I was already looking to my left to see if one of us was taking pictures...I saw Ira snapping his camera—"

"I stopped when I heard the shots," Ira glumly confessed.

"But my eyes...uh, my eyes went right to the motorcade," Margie continued. "And I saw Kennedy hunched over like this..."

She bent forward, clasping her hands over the front of her throat.

"He was bent forward. And I had no idea what'd happened to him...and then I heard another firecracker...and the car just kept going—until it went faster. I saw a guy in a suit jump out of the car behind Kennedy's car, and he ran toward the limousine...I also think I saw Mrs. Kennedy—I know this sounds crazy—try to climb out of her car. But by that time people were yelling—a few were screaming—and a lot of people were moving down the grassy hill over by where Randy went. But Randy wasn't there anymore."

"Did you see Randy after that?" Mr. Lott asked.

"After—what?"

"After the shots—the firecracker sounds?"

Margie shrugged and said quietly, "I don't really remember seeing much of anything after that. I don't—I mean, maybe it will all come to me later, but there was—I don't remember very much. People were running around. Some of them were falling to the ground. Maybe that's why nobody noticed Randy fall. A whole lot of people were falling. Sirens in the streets started blaring, and everybody just looked dazed."

The others listened attentively, sympathetically. Only Margie had witnessed indications of President Kennedy's injury. Perhaps Maria had seen something, too. But so far she had said nothing, and since she now was walking around outside with Randy, she couldn't contribute to this conversation. Initially, Mr. Lott had thought only Randy could offer the police a viable, interesting recollection of events. Now Margie Pendergrass fit that bill, too.

Or did she? *Several* people standing in Dealey Plaza had watched the President grab at his throat. But according to reporters on television, John Kennedy had been shot in the head—*on the right side, near the temple area.* No one had witnessed that. No one in the group from Long Beach, California, could substantiate injuries on the right side of the President's head.

Randy, however, said he had come upon shooters at the top of the grassy hill. He could provide an eyewitness description of these men. And maybe others who saw them would validate Randy's descriptions with recollections of their own. Randy, now single-sighted and driven by his memory of the men behind the wall, would speak with the police soon. Right now, though, they were so tied up in their confusion and immersed in bureaucratic red tape, the Dallas cops had no time for the wide-eyed ranting of a sixteen year-old kid from the suburbs of Long Beach, California.

****

Like from a scene in a movie, Randy and Maria, gravitated toward a space in the Motel 6 parking lot from which they heard the romantic instrumental, "Theme From a Summer Place," by Percy Faith.

His radio running, a man sat cozily with his girlfriend in his 1957 Chevy. By 1963 this record had already become an oldie but still offered a favorite dreamy backdrop for young couples all over America. Randy and Maria had not thought of themselves as one of those young couples, but the music, coming immediately after their comforting embrace, certainly provided ambience. And the image of another twosome locked in love within a short distance from them filled the air with an electricity inconsistent with the appalling events of the day.

"What do you want to do?" Maria asked him. They stopped walking, now listening to the sounds of the music around them. "Do you want to go home tomorrow?"

"No, and even if I wanted to do that, there's no way to get out of here right now. The airport's a nightmare. I called them a little while ago. I mean, if I wanted to pay three times what my ticket cost…besides, why would I want to leave here now? What's the advantage to that?"

"Well, your parents are concerned about you."

"All of our parents are concerned about us."

"But you are the one who went into shock."

Randy flashed a slight grin. "Oh, is that what happened?"

"Randy," she said, "there are advantages for you to go home."

Maria's implication startled him. Guilt rushed through his body. She had subtly alluded to Carmen. He had not called Carmen since his arrival in Dallas; in fact, as Randy stood in the parking lot with Maria, it dawned on him that calling his girlfriend in California had never entered his mind during his entire stay in Dallas. "I'm not going home," Randy said half-heartedly. "Even if I wanted to, it would cost triple the price of the ticket to change it."

"I'm sorry," Maria said with such sincerity and sweetness, Randy had already forgotten what she was sorry about.

"That's okay. I need to speak with the police before I go. For me."

"Not about that," Maria corrected him softly. "I'm sorry about—everything. President Kennedy meant a lot to you. He meant a lot to most of us, but for you...this has been hardest on you—and people like you."

Randy silently wondered if Maria's "people like you" denoted a good thing or a bad thing. He hoped, coming from Maria, it served as a compliment.

"Yeah, well," Randy muttered before changing the subject, "I'm sorry about the tournament [he really wasn't]. I know how much you wanted it, and we were so prepared for it. I sincerely believe we would have kicked some ass. Sorry—"

"Randy, why are you apologizing?" Maria frowned. "Do you think that after all this I am feeling bad because they cancelled the debate tournament? Don't you think I have more depth than this?"

Randy *did* think Maria had more depth than this, but this was precisely the moment he was thinking about Carmen—and Carmen *didn't* have more depth than that. And the comparison of Maria and Carmen bothered him, especially now, in this time and this place and under these circumstances.

"Randy," Maria began again. When she lifted her left hand to gently touch his arm, a powerful emotion he had never felt before came over him. Singed with shame, but overwhelmed with admiration, Randy caught her eyes.

Maria explained, "I just want you to know that I really respect you for what happened today—for hurting so much emotionally. It shows that you care. A lot of boys do not. I know this, Randy, even though many people are giving you a hard time."

Randy looked down. Gazing into her eyes now would be too

distracting. "Nobody's giving me a hard time. Not really."

But he remembered Tommy Wright; Tommy always gave him a hard time.

Randy sighed, folded his arms, and felt his eyes tearing. For the first time today, he expected to cry. He knew he would be safe with Maria. "But how can you be proud of me? For being really, uh, *emotional*? That's such a good thing? Look, here's...here's why I'm dying inside right now. Here's the...Look, I'm glad you're proud of me, Maria, because of all the people in the world I'd want to be proud of me, you would be number one."

Should he have said that? Randy wondered.

"But the fact is, I think you're proud of me for the wrong reasons. The *real* reasons to be proud of me—the reasons you *could* have been proud of me—don't really exist, because I didn't do anything to be proud of. My face slamming into the grass was not that graceful or dignified."

Maria's eyes glistened. "You want to stay here to make sure the police get your story, no matter how unpleasant it is going to be to tell them. Well, Randy, to me this is showing a lot of courage."

"It doesn't take courage to talk to the police, Maria," Randy argued. For the first time that night, he strolled away from her, creating some physical distance between them. A part of Randy wanted to keep walking—forever. "*Courage*—if I had *courage*—I would have jumped on the man with the rifle and raised such a commotion all eyes would have been on that hill. Courage—I would have run into the street and yelled and yelled and yelled at the cops to stop the parade in its tracks. *Courage* would have been to scream at the top of my lungs, 'Help!' so the gunman wouldn't have made a straight shot."

Randy's mouth curved into a sarcastic smile. "Do you really think it's brave that I saw a man with a gun—*a man who is obviously going to shoot the President of the United States*—and ran away so fast that I landed flat on my face and then stayed on the ground? Come on, Maria. As much as I want you to think I'm a brave, wonderful boy—and I really do want you to think I'm a brave, wonderful boy—I'm not going to stand here tonight and allow you to call me brave, especially when you know and I know that if I had been even a *little* brave, things would have turned out a lot different."

Despite Maria's prior knowledge of Randy's innate ability to eloquently string words together, his monologue surprised—and impressed—her for its depth of clarity. Randy hurt because he thought he should have saved President Kennedy. As ridiculous as this notion may have seemed, Maria had to allow Randy to come to grips with the improbability of its reality, without undermining the pain his unreasonable perception of that reality had caused him.

She softly touched his arm near the same spot she had stroked him before. This time she riveted her eyes into his. "Randy, suppose you had not crossed that street to take pictures. Just suppose. Then what would have happened to President Kennedy?"

But Randy would have none of that. "But I *did* cross the street to take pictures. Maybe God had put me in that spot to save the President, and I blew it. Maybe God picked the wrong guy."

Randy could have added something, but he wisely fought it off. Maria's anger with him because of the manner he had handled the incident with Tommy Wright, and Tommy's subsequent provocations were the main reasons he felt compelled to accept Tommy's crazy dare, leading to the fateful dash across the street. He had felt compelled to restore his manliness in Maria's eyes.

"You think God would select a sixteen year-old high school debate weirdo to save the President of the United States? Is that what you think, Randy?" Maria teased, forcing a grin. She hoped for some levity.

Instead, Randy ignored her question. "I could have saved him, Maria. I could have done something other than *run away*! Come on! I ran like a Frenchman fleeing the Nazis! And to add insult to injury, I ate a mouthful of dirt! *Your hero!*"

Maria hinted a smile and tried another route. "Let us say, Randy, that you had tackled the bad guys and wrestled their guns away from them—and they never had a chance to shoot the President; and that during all the commotion, the police poured into the street, even though there were not that many police around to begin with. Let us say there was all this—this confusion. What about that man in the book building behind President Kennedy's car? Wouldn't he have still been able to shoot the President? He is in custody now. Obviously, somebody thinks he shot the President from way up *there*."

His eyes full of tears, but without sobbing, Randy repeated, "Maria, I could have done something; I didn't. I'm a coward."

Maria shook her head, falling into silence.

"So now I'm going to tell the police everything. If they already know about the hobos, and even if they've already arrested them, I can't leave here until I've done everything I can to make it better—even if it...*won't* make it better."

"See, you *are* brave."

"Spurred on by my embarrassment."

Then Maria surprised him. Even with Randy considerably taller than she, Maria put her arms around his waist and snuggled her head against his chest. Burying her virtually flawless face into his blue flannel shirt, she said, "Just hold me, Randy. Please..."

Randy Whitman enveloped Maria Barquin with his strong, rangy arms, now only half-hoping that all of this had been a dream.

—CHAPTER 20—

The Cajun Supreme Bar and Grill did not sit squarely in the center of the French Quarter.

Crime-ridden and desolate, the outskirts of New Orleans was even more deserted tonight. Fearing that the restaurant might close in deference to the assassination, each of the perpetrators had a contingency in the event their designated meeting place did not open its doors to them. The Tall Man, for example, planned to check into a Holiday Inn and wait for a phone call from one of the others. He communicated to them that whether or not they established formal contact in New Orleans, he would be staying at a Holiday Inn.

At precisely 9:00 P.M., the Tall Man's automobile drove up to the Cajun Supreme Bar and Grill. Unable to judge if the building was open, he crept up to the front door and, fearing the worst, slowly pulled the handle. The vast majority of the country, at the loss of its fallen leader, wallowed in self-pity. But the Cajun Supreme Bar and Grill remained true to its seedy, tawdry self. It gaily entertained a few men and women who had snuck inside for a quick drink and maybe a sandwich, and were either apathetic about the day's international headline-grabbing events, or completely oblivious to them. This crowd would not notice major historical developments like the assassination of a President, even if they had happened right under their noses (which, ironically, was now the case).

The sordid dive on 8th Place suited their agenda nicely.

Alex Hidell, now known to officials as Lee Harvey Oswald, would not be present. But the Tall Man noticed Howard, already seated, facing forward with drink in hand and sipping from his glass. The stubble on Howard's face had grown significantly in only the past several hours. It looked like the beginnings of a beard. Now dressed in nicely pressed plaid pants and a blue dress shirt—save for the growth on his face—Howard barely resembled the hobo he had poorly portrayed on the grassy hill in Dealey Plaza.

Ricardo soon joined Craig and Joey, large men who also had significant hair growth on their faces. They all took great strides to subvert the formality of their meeting: smoking accessories, continuous servings of food and snacks, even relaxed body posture while they sat. But a closer inspection of their faces would have alerted observant strangers to the seriousness of their interaction. Seated at a long, square table in a dark corner of the bar, and nurturing their drinks, the three men began to talk about the grim business that had brought them together.

Ricardo nodded with approval at the Tall Man. "I'm glad you made it. I was almost worried about you." And then he quickly downed what filled his shot glass.

The Tall Man leaned forward, his shoulders hunched. "I had to make some quick adjustments."

Conspicuously lowering his voice as a suggestion the others should follow suit, the Tall Man said, "I was able to get the rifle out of the building. But three or four policeman rushed by me with such determination—waving their guns—I was prepared to swallow."

The Tall Man referred to a cyanide capsule each man had possessed—just in case. The directions were to ingest the pill *before* interrogations commenced. Immediate death would result. No secrets would be spilled.

Howard whispered with the glee of a twelve year-old, "Imagine how this would have driven them crazy! Mission complete! Suspect dead and unable to talk! Ha!"

Ricardo shrugged, again with approval. "This is why our plans had to be so disciplined." And then his face turned sober. "But Hidell did not comply with the rules. He is sitting in a Dallas jail right now. Who knows what he is telling them."

"What the hell kind of name is *Lee Harvey Oswald*? He should have swallowed as soon as they picked him up in that movie theater!" the Tall Man injected. "Had he done that, we wouldn't be worrying about it now."

"Oh, we would still worry," Ricardo corrected him. "But at least our worries would not be about *him*. I am afraid we are forced to take action."

Ricardo then whispered even more covertly, "Our man in Dallas is not here tonight because I have alerted him to his new mission. He has to lay some foundations. But the good thing, he is a strip club owner, and many policemen frequent his establishment. He has inside contacts with the Dallas Police, who should grant him access when he needs it most."

Ricardo let out a chuckle. Before nurturing his drink, he said, "Just this afternoon, Jack showed up at police headquarters with fresh sandwiches and soft drinks and coffee. He sympathized with their long hours, necessitated by this very tragic occasion."

The others let out muffled, nervous laughs.

Until Hidell could be dispensed with, though, they were in great jeopardy. No one knew what—if anything—Hidell had told the authorities so far. But his thin, ashen face with the blackened left eye and bruised cheekbone, looked more pathetic each time he stood before the cameras on national television. His compatriots feared that he would crack under the strain from constant pressure applied by the Dallas Police, the FBI, and the Secret Service. And worse: he was just a few hours away from a nationally televised midnight press conference, scheduled to happen around midnight.

"He was an idiot!" Ricardo ranted. "How stupid of him to shoot a cop!"

The Tall Man lit up a Chesterfield and puffed away. "Even if that cop had arrested him, what could they have held him for? As of now…" He looked at his watch. "At almost 8:30, he's still not been charged with anything to do with Kennedy. They would have released him by now. The fool!"

Howard narrowed his pensive eyes on Ricardo "So he'll be taken care of?"

"Let us hope with all our loving hearts that it will not be too late," Ricardo replied. "Remember that we have trusted him for months. Gordon, we did not trust. That is why he was eliminated weeks ago. He was buckling. He opened his mouth once too often.

This became obvious to everyone. But now that the deed is done, there is no tolerance for anything resembling even the slightest weakness. Hidell will not break under pressure. Not yet. But for the *future*—for the long term—plans are being drawn up as we speak."

Vagueness didn't wear well with the others. But vagueness always came with the onset of this group's next move. The exhilaration of having succeeded in their first objective, the assassination, had been tempered by the worry of potentially failing to reach their immediate objective, not getting caught.

Indeed, Hidell had to be silenced.

Ricardo calmly pulled a cigar from his coat pocket. He rolled it as he spoke. "Kennedy died at Parkland Hospital about a half hour after you hit him. There were extensive attempts to revive him, but you obviously did good work."

Howard turned apprehensive. "Do they have any evidence where the shots came from?"

Puffing away, Ricardo replied in hushed tones, "Hidell left his rifle near the window of the book building. My guess would be his fingerprints are all over it. Paraffin tests on his hands will show gunpowder residue. Let us just assume that Hidell is finished. This is precisely why cyanide was a major part of the plan. As far as the Records Building…"

He steered his attention to the Tall Man. "Your ability to safely walk your implements out the building preserved your existence—at least, for the time being. Good work. They think all the shots came from the book building. I am depending on nothing being traced to the Records Building."

Howard twisted in his chair, downed another shot of whiskey. "And about us, Ricardo? I heard reports they think Kennedy was shot in the right temple. Obviously, that bullet was from us."

"Will they find evidence of that?" Ricardo held the cigar in his teeth and stretched his arms above his head. "Connally was also hit. He's in intensive care. Did you hit him?"

No," Howard somberly shook his head. "I got Kennedy. His head burst after I fired."

"You waited around to look?"

"No, not at all! Joey, Craig, and I strolled around the hill before and after, and we were asked some questions by a few cops. Just like we planned. We'd convinced them we lived in the boxcars on the railroad tracks. They weren't happy with that, but at least they didn't think we'd just shot Kennedy. No one smart would have thought something so stupid!"

He laughed at his own attempt at a joke; then, in the absence of a response, he clammed up.

"Did you remove the rifle?"

"Sure. As we'd planned, we stashed it in our suitcases in the box car."

Ricardo pulled off Howard's confident grin, flashed a smile of his own, while shaking his head in subdued bewilderment. "We depended on their incompetence; that they would not search. For the time being, you appear to be safe. Congratulations. The Boss will be happy."

Howard's smirk disappeared. "Just one thing: This kid…just a kid—maybe a teenager—came running back behind the barrier a few seconds before…and he saw us. But Joey scared the pants off him. He really did. The kid pissed in his shorts and dropped his camera."

Howard gestured with his head toward Joey, who produced a small 127-film camera from his coat pocket. Joey handed it to Howard who, in turn, passed it to Ricardo. "I have no idea what's on here."

"We will have the film developed. If things get dicey, we may have to find this boy. Perhaps this camera will help us out."

Joey, the most muscular and physically intimidating of the three so-called hobos, joked. "That kid ran so fast, I think he's still running—maybe in New Mexico by now."

Ricardo probed, "Did you look for him afterwards?"

Joey shrugged. "No. We were too busy imitating bums."

No one reacted to his nervous laughter.

"Doesn't sound like it should be too tough for you, Joey. Maybe you can make looking like a bum an avocation," Ricardo said.

"Hey!" Joey reacted, but he didn't know what *avocation* meant.

"Intriguing," Ricardo laughed. "It was difficult making the three of you look like you lived in a rundown freight train. You resembled successful business entrepreneurs putting on costumes for an old play. But you succeeded in your mission, and so far, that is what counts. Now we need to make it all go away."

Howard, wary—and weary—asked, "So you don't think we should worry about the boy?"

"I do not think worrying about the boy would do any good right now. We'll wait until we see where this is going." And Ricardo added with a long pull on his cigar. "Right now, we need to worry about Hidell."

****

"His name's Lee Harvey," Mrs. Whitman said to Melissa. Melissa came home from UCLA when her Friday afternoon classes had been cancelled after the assassination. In tears for most of the day, Melissa hadn't coped well. Worse, her anxiety over Randy's situation drove her into a deep state of emotional wreck. Melissa teetered on the verge of physical illness.

"Lee Harvey?" Melissa wrinkled her nose. "One man killed him? One?"

"We don't know, honey," Mrs. Whitman replied, putting a bowl of soup in front of her daughter.

Melissa had arrived home well after the dinner hour, but she craved some warm food. Her mother was famous for her chicken soup with steamed rice and noodles. The temperature, now having dipped to around 55 degrees in Southern California, had a cold, distressing effect on an already morose disposition. Hot soup miraculously cured even heightened emotional disorders.

"You said he's going to be on T.V. soon? When?" Melissa asked, testing her mother's soup.

"There's a—Harvey is doing a special press conference at midnight. Your father said that with the two hour time difference it should be ten o'clock here."

For the first time all day, Melissa smiled. She had just spooned some chicken soup into her mouth. "This is good, Mom!"

"I make it every Friday night. It's your father's favorite."

"Are you sure I've never eaten this kind before?" Melissa dipped into her bowl for a clump of rice. "It tastes familiar. It's like from Soup Chow Down or something."

"What?" her mother shot back with disapproval. "Soup Chow Down! That's a Chinese place your father and I don't even like! The last time we took you and Randy there, you were just kids. Maybe you were six or seven. And you didn't like anything about the place! So please don't compare the soup I've slaved over in the kitchen all afternoon to some cheap Chinese hole-in-the-wall that all of us can't stand!"

Melissa stopped and wondered for a moment if her mother was seriously upset—or just kidding around—with her comment about Soup Chow Down. Then she realized that her mother, having dealt with the emotional wear and tear of the day, had needed to vent. The death of the President didn't help. Unrelenting worry over Randy helped even less.

Melissa remained calm and said, "It's delicious. The best I've eaten."

"Better than Soup Chow Down?"

"Of course. I'm sorry, Mom."

Mrs. Whitman changed the subject. "How's school?"

"School's school. But today was bad."

"Where were you when—you heard?"

Melissa stopped spooning her soup into her mouth. "My history professor was talking about events just prior to Pearl Harbor, and then another teacher came in and whispered something in his ear. They both stepped outside the classroom for a minute, and when my teacher came back inside, he was crying. That's when he told us. Somebody in class turned on his transistor radio, and an announcer came on saying the President was dead..." Tears subdued her, but she continued, "Then they played *The Star Spangled Banner...The Star Spangled Banner*, Mom..."

And for the umpteenth time that day, Melissa Whitman cried. She cried hard, curling her body into a ball and allowing herself to drain away the physical remnants of her despair. Mrs. Whitman came around the side of the table and hugged her only daughter, weeping right along side her.

—CHAPTER 21—

Carmen Pedro tucked her three year-old brother into his bed, kissed him on the forehead, and told him good-night. She walked down the short hallway from his room to her own, where she had placed a pair of her flannel pajamas on the bed. Hesitating, she slowly lifted the pajamas and then let them fall back on the blankets. Eating away at her was an alarming realization that her boyfriend hadn't telephoned her in over forty-eight hours. She hadn't spoken with Randy since he had left for Dallas on Thursday morning.

Familiar with Randy's admiration for Kennedy, Carmen knew how much he must have been mourning him—even as she pondered Randy's absence. However, she thought Randy would have made some attempt to speak with her, if just to hear her voice for a few minutes, and so they might share their sadness together. Carmen hurt, too. She liked President Kennedy a lot—maybe not as much as Randy did—and she felt pain from his sudden demise at the hands of an assassin.

Carmen winced with the aggravation that came from not knowing the name of the hotel in which Randy was staying. She hadn't bothered to ask him, and he hadn't bothered to volunteer the information. For a moment she thought about calling Randy's parents, but she remembered how much she didn't like them, mainly because she knew she repulsed them.

She was, after all, Puerto Rican and simply not good enough for their son. Mr. and Mrs. Whitman had poisoned the waters around her. She was sure of it. Their constant nagging about inter-racial dating protocol (you simply did not do it), a narrow-minded society (of which they had been a major part), and her grades in school (a healthy 3.2 GPA), probably had driven a wedge between Randy and her. And it was beginning to show lately in the way

123

Randy treated Carmen.

Not that Randy had been cruel or abusive—Randy was incapable of such meanness—but she detected moroseness, a sullen mood that had not been there in the past. Randy always had a reason why they could not spend time together—or for spending less time—but she noticed a waning enthusiasm for her in his personality: his eyes drooped, he didn't open his mouth with as much precision when he spoke with her, he didn't look her in the eye, and he was listless. He seemed like a husband who had grown bored with his wife but stayed in the marriage purely from a sense of duty and responsibility.

When the telephone at the kitchen table rang at about 9:45 P.M., Carmen already had settled into gloomy reflections on her relationship with Randy Whitman.

Which is why when she heard Randy's voice on the other end of the line, her heart leaped through her shirt. "Hi," she heard him say.

Her goal: not to sound desperate. But she couldn't have been happier—and more relieved—now that he had called her. "Hi! Are you okay?"

Randy measured his words very carefully. "I'm okay. A lot's been happening."

"Yeah, it has. You're okay, though? Did they cancel the tournament?"

"Of course."

"What are you doing? I mean, now that…"

Randy's voice came back with a hint of impatience. "There's nothing to do anymore. But we have to stay here anyway—some of us were witnesses."

"Witnesses? What?"

"Witnesses to the assassination."

"What—Randy? Are you kidding?"

"No."

"You were there when he was killed?"

"Yes. I'm—I'm going to speak with the police or the FBI. I saw who did it."

Carmen felt overwhelmed. This was Randy on the other end

of the line. *Randy.* Her boyfriend now told her—calmly told her—about being *a witness to the assassination of President Kennedy*! That he saw who did it! Even though Randy stretched his credibility here, he had never damaged his integrity with Carmen before this, unless they counted his fabrication about not getting any help from his mother with the chocolate chip cookies he baked Carmen for her birthday.

"Randy, what happened?" she asked him.

"Look, I can't talk about it now on the phone—and I don't really *want* to talk about it now either. The reason I called is to find out how you are. So…how are you?"

"I'm fine," Carmen replied, not really thinking about how *she* was. Randy had divulged no information to her, but a feeling of apprehension, one that she couldn't describe, attacked her equilibrium. "Randy, when are you coming home?"

"Monday."

"Will you call me as soon as you get in?"

Her words walloped Randy, for they gave off an appalling suggestion. "I'll need to rest for a while. I'm so tired, and it's going to get a lot worse by Monday."

Randy's response provided another example to Carmen of his diminishing affection and desire to be with her. Now in emotional turmoil, wouldn't he need her more than ever? She thought so—and she certainly hoped so!

"Just call me as soon as you can, Randy," she said.

"Okay," he answered, barely audible.

At once, Randy Whitman realized that his role as Carmen Pedro's boyfriend had come to an end.

****

Around midnight, Lee Harvey Oswald was led in handcuffs from the interrogation room at the Dallas County Jail to a much larger room in the same building. Dozens of media reporters, perhaps as many as a hundred, congregated. Their job was to ask questions to the man accused of killing the President of the United States. At this point Oswald had not been officially charged with murdering Kennedy. He had been booked for murdering Tippit, the alleged reason for the press conference. But everyone knew the truth: the Kennedy assassination preoccupied everybody's agenda.

Oswald looked tired. A huge black and blue welt over his right eye bugged out at people in the television audience. He didn't seem nervous, just determined to let everyone know of his innocence; in fact, he radiated an arrogance that told others he was disgusted that they had gotten the wrong man.

"Oswald!" someone yelled. "Did you shoot the President?"

He leaned forward into a microphone. "No, I haven't been charged with that. When they brought me here, they told me I was under arrest for shooting a policeman."

"Did you kill the policeman?" Another question came from the confused crowd. Nobody pursued any sense of order. Nobody sat. The mood in the room parroted the rest of the day with its panic and confusion.

"No, I don't know anything about that."

Someone else directed a question at Oswald, but he didn't listen and ignored the reporter. "I haven't been offered counsel, yet. I would like to ask for counsel. I would like for somebody to represent me."

And with that, two policemen pulled Oswald away from the microphone, as if to say, "We don't wish for anybody to hear that this man has not been given a chance to obtain a lawyer." And they began to lead him away.

Just as Oswald turned to his left, someone shouted, "How did you get that bruise on your face?"

"A policeman hit me…" Oswald eagerly leaned his head to the right to show off his wound. But yanked away, he could barely finish his words.

"I'm just a patsy," he added clearly before disappearing into a corridor.

In the back of the room, hidden from Oswald but captured in several photographs of the press conference that night, sat a curious onlooker, a man who wore a gray business hat.

As they sat around their television set, the Whitman family, minus their son, shivered with anger. Samuel wanted to break the glass, reach inside, and strangle the leering little bastard. He had just murdered President Kennedy, the young, handsome leader of their country. How could one man commit such a reprehensible act? How could one man so upset the cosmos of the universe? How could one man bring such pain and suffering to so many people?

For most Americans, all of this had not registered as real. But with somewhat greater clarity than before the abbreviated, so-called midnight press conference with Lee—whoever—Oswald, people sat dazed in front of their televisions, hoping to make sense of a murder they still refused to believe actually happened.

The screen cut to replays of President Johnson's remarks at Andrews Air Force Base and substandard newsreel footage of a waving, smiling President Kennedy, unaware that these were the last few seconds of his life, but relishing the beginning of his re-election campaign at the corner of Elm and Houston in Dallas, Texas.

Samuel spoke over the broadcast. "I don't think he did it. No way. Not by himself. There's no way this twenty-three year-old good-for-nothing creep could have pulled this off all by himself. No way."

****

Ricardo had emptied his fourth shot glass by the time the abbreviated press conference concluded. The television in the bar and grill droned on in the background, but the men sitting at the back table no longer needed to watch it. With a sense of relief, they thought Oswald had handled himself well.

But he had spoken of a lawyer, and there was no telling what Oswald would say to an attorney. Would he tell him the truth? Attorneys sometimes demanded the whole truth before they agreed to represent people, especially in homicide cases, and particularly for a crime as enormous as this one. What would Oswald's lawyer demand of him?

But he hadn't yet been granted a lawyer. The police seemed hell-bent to keep him away from one. Ultimately, the state would have to provide counsel, though. The Constitution required it. Now that Oswald had publically complained about his conflict with the police and his lack of legal representation, thousands of attorneys would hound police headquarters. And the longer Oswald spoke with a lawyer, the more likely he would spill any remaining beans in the assassin's jar.

Ricardo narrowed his dark eyes on Howard. "We have to move quickly. There are too many loose ends to tighten."

Joey didn't understand. "What? We…except for the—"

Howard glared at him; Joey stopped stumbling and went into silent mode.

Ricardo used his eyes as daggers. "What? Except for what, Joey?"

Joey sighed and spoke to Howard. "It's not a big deal, Howard. We need to tell him. The fact that we didn't get arrested accounts for some good news here."

Ricardo grabbed his smoldering cigarette and actually thought about shoving the whole thing into his mouth. "You may recall what happened to Gordon. The slightest provocation and you will be silenced after Oswald. I swear this is true."

Howard easily caught his drift. "Ricardo, we went back to the boxcars right after the job. Craig had gone by then—taken the rifle. Everything was cool, until the cops began searching the train. They did it a lot sooner—they found it sooner—than we thought they would. We didn't have time to get outta' there."

"Continue…" Ricardo listened very attentively.

"Well, the police detained us this time…but never took us back to headquarters for questioning. They still thought that we were a couple of hobos and nothing else. They hardly paid any attention to us—it was so crazy around there. Just bums, that's all we were to them."

Looking down, Ricardo smiled slightly. "Yes, well, I, too, always thought that about you."

Howard's apprehension had already deflated his own sense of humor. He continued, "They didn't find the gun. They never asked for names. Some of the cops talked to us on the grass right afterwards, as—we were a couple of bums and that's all!"

He then added with a timidity that dwarfed his forced attempt at bravado, "But we were prepared to swallow."

Silence echoed in the near-empty restaurant. While Ricardo contemplated, the others could not understand the droning sounds of the mounted black and white T.V. set over the bar. The tension turned thick.

Finally, Ricardo extinguished the remains of his cigarette and nodded with apparent approval. "You did well. Things never go exactly according to plans. You proved your loyalty—and your intelligence—by how you reacted. You were never supposed to be detained or questioned. *Seen*, yes—that was part of the plan—but not detained, even for a minute. The fact that you escaped without even providing your phony names bodes well for your ability to withstand pressure. And I have no doubt that, if necessary, you would have swallowed."

Once again, the others could hear the television. They could breathe again.

"But with Hidell we have a different scenario," Ricardo continued. "He is not only in detention; he is in the international limelight. The world is focused on him, a young book crate worker who shot a policeman. People saw him do it. He broke from protocol. He made himself too obvious in the wrong places at the wrong time. Basically, he cannot any longer be trusted. If he went to trial, it would be a disaster.

Howard nodded. "What's going to happen?"

"Our friends in Dallas will take care of him."

Joey poked at his burger steak with his fork. "When?"

"For now," Ricardo sighed, "keep watching the television. Go home. Lie low. Our bosses will take care of the financial end of it, but you must wait. Do not get overly anxious."

And then he leaned forward, his brows furled. "This is very important. Your *own* survival depends on what I tell you. Do not make contact with each other—not in person, not by telephone, not by mail. You will be told when this ban will be lifted, though it may *never* be lifted. Never. But your social life does not revolve around these people you have worked with, does it?" His face laced into a grin. "You are not dependent upon each other for fun

129

and games, are you?"

The others remained expressionless.

"So stay apart. Lose each other until you are given further instructions. The financial compensation arrangements have been worked out, and you will be contacted."

The Tall Man sipped from his coffee mug and looked down. He then took a deep breath and said, "What if we never hear?"

"Hear about what?" Ricardo asked.

"Hear about the, uh, financial part?"

"You will."

"But what if we don't?"

"I said that you *will*."

"Yes, Ricardo, but you don't have control over this part, do you? They may have something else up their sleeve. So far, we've required blanket trust of each other; we still do. But what if we never hear? When it comes to the money, what if they just forget about us?"

"In that case," Ricadro said with a shrug, "you should consider yourselves extremely lucky. Because after something like this—what we accomplished today—no news is usually very good news. And the kind of contact you seek with our bosses may very well turn out to be shockingly, uh…*disturbing*."

—CHAPTER 22—

Sometimes the morning after a very bad day brings to one's life new vigor and vitality and optimism. But by Saturday morning, Randy's hotel room in Dallas conveyed anything but vigor, vitality, and optimism. The drapes were closed, and it was dark inside, with a small bed light providing minimum illumination.

At 6:30 in the morning, the T.V. screen showed international dignitaries carrying large umbrellas after getting out of chauffer driven limousines. A steady rain fell over Washington D.C. Average people lined the streets, hoping to get a glimpse of President Kennedy's casket being brought to the Rotunda of the Capitol Building. By the thousands they hoped to pay their last respects to their departed leader. For millions of Americans, the rains pouring from the sky symbolized teardrops draining from the eyes of men, women, and children all over the world, as they tried to come to grips with the grief that that had befallen them.

Randy watched a T.V. reporter stick a microphone in the face of a middle-age man who stood with his son on the sidewalk just outside the White House lawn on Pennsylvania Avenue. Randy thought the man holding the microphone had asked an incredibly stupid question to the dark-haired father, who tightly held the hand of his eight or nine year-old son. The well-dressed male reporter asked, "So on this rainy, dreary morning after the shocking assassination, how do you feel? And how is your little boy taking it?"

Randy wanted to leap from the bed and switch channels, rather than observe this poor man struggle with his words on national television. But to Randy's surprise, the boy's father waxed eloquently. Without hesitation, the man replied, "I'm thirty-eight years old, and I've never lived through anything this tragic. I was sixteen when Pearl Harbor happened. There was this terrible fear that we would be bombed on the mainland. I remember that well. But the sadness today, yeah, it matches the skies here in D.C."

He leaned toward his son, who had lowered his head, too timid or too sad to look at the camera. "As far as my boy here goes, he's doing about as well as can be expected. And I know he's not alone. We just thought we'd drive in from Baltimore…because we could. We wanted to pay our last respects.

"And if you look around at all these people here…I was just talking to a couple—a man and his wife—who'd been driving all night from Harrisburg. They're going to walk by the casket, kneel, and then drive all the way back home to Pennsylvania."

The man started to choke through his words. Randy pulled the blankets over his head, drowning him out, blocking both words and pictures. To Randy it seemed incongruous that just a few hours ago he was within just a few feet of a vibrant, smiling President, and now this same President lay dead in a coffin over fifteen hundred miles away in the nation's Capitol.

Ira came in the door and didn't see him blanketed in his bed. "Hey, Randy, you here?" Ira called.

"No!" Randy answered, flipping up the covers he had just draped over himself.

"Had a pretty good breakfast in the coffee shop downstairs. I know how you like crispy, almost burnt bacon. That's what they have down there today for breakfast: crispy, almost burnt bacon."

Randy knew about the bacon. He had already eaten a few strips in the coffee shop yesterday morning, which seemed like a millennium ago.

"Mr. Lott's down there…had a bad night on the, uh, toilet, I guess."

Randy didn't care to know about this. "*Ira, please!*"

"Maria's there, too."

Maria? Hmm…maybe some almost burnt bacon and eggs *would* start off his morning on the right track.

He moved his feet and left them dangling over the side of the bed that faced Ira, who had slipped into the wooden desk chair.

"How long have they been down there?" Randy wondered aloud.

"I don't know. They were all down there stuffing their faces when I got there. I ate with Ruther at a different table—and then left 'em there. Thought I would come and check on you, former debate partner."

Debate now seemed so irrelevant to real life.

Randy knew that as soon as he stepped into the coffee shop, the others would be gone. He could always see Maria later. Hunger pangs gnawed at him, especially after Ira's recounting of the crispy, almost burnt bacon. But he couldn't help being burdened by the nagging feeling of not having conversed with the police yet. They had so many people to speak with, to interview, to drill. Why would they turn their attention to a sixteen year-old kid who had done a header on the grassy hill?

"Ira, I've got to try the police again. They need to talk to me."

"Seems like you need to talk to *them*."

"Yeah, I have to tell them what I saw."

"You should. And eventually they'll get to you."

Randy sighed. "We're leaving on Monday morning."

"There's the telephone; it works."

"No, Ira, I want to talk to them in person."

"Okay, I'll support you on that," Ira nodded. "I'll stay with you in Dallas for as long as you need to be here. I'll go with you to the police station. We can camp out right in front until they listen."

"Thanks, Ira, you're a good friend." Then Randy paused and zeroed into Ira's brown eyes. "You believe me, don't you? About what happened on the hill?"

"Randy, I was the one who came up with the bright idea for you to run across the street, remember? Tommy dared you, but I'd thought of it first, remember? You never would have been there if not for me, Randy. I feel terrible about that."

"You didn't answer my question. Do you believe me?"

"I believe you're not lying. You saw what you thought you saw."

"I may have been hallucinating or something? Is that it? After I hit my head, maybe something happened to my brain?"

Ira grinned. "You said you went face down into the grass.

That might have rattled a few screws up there. Besides, what a sight that must have been! You should consider yourself lucky that you dove down right after the people heard the shots. They were distracted from looking at you, because they were looking in the other direction, at the grassy hill or the book building. Consider yourself very fortunate. They could have been looking right at you at the exact moment you hit the deck."

Ira's macabre humor bordered on the tasteless; it always did. But pathetically, everything he had just joked about was apparently true. Nobody paid any attention to Randy, because Randy had run in the opposite direction of the rapid firecracker sounds. If Randy had run to his left or down the hill, others would have seen him fall. Other people had stood on the streets or crumbled to the ground when they heard the gunshots, but in a defensive posture and right in their tracks. Randy, on the other hand, had blindly scurried away in a state of panic in order to escape the intimidation of a hobo with a rifle. He then lost his balance and plummeted hard to the ground, embedding his face into the earth.

"So," Randy went on. Several hours' sleep had cleared his head. "Do you believe that I saw two men hiding behind the embankment? And one of them had a rifle that he was about to use to shoot Kennedy?"

Ira hesitated. Whenever Ira framed this scene in his mind, he found it impossible to envision that his friend Randy Whitman had interrupted—startled—two men who were about to shoot the President of the United States. But almost equally difficult to digest was the idea that he and Randy, among so few others in the world, had stationed their bodies on *that* street, giving them a preferred position to view the assassination of John F. Kennedy.

"Yes, Randy, I totally believe you saw something; and if anyone thinks that guy Lee Oswald was the only one who shot the President, they're crazy. You can set them straight."

Ira leaned forward and set his elbow on the end table. "And I hope there are other people who can confirm your story. If not, you're going to have a hard time recovering from this. It's going to be a long year, pal—way too long for a square peg debater like you."

—CHAPTER 23—

There were too many mouths. Some of those mouths were now expendable; they needed to be closed.

As Craig lay on the sofa in his home, his wife and small child played in their backyard. It had taken Craig almost ten hours to drive from New Orleans to Nashville. He had driven all night, sensing an intense desire to return to his wife and four year-old daughter.

Craig had already spent desperate minutes alone in a boxcar behind the wooden fence. He hastily retrieved the rifle used by Joey and Howard behind the wall and afterwards scampered down the hill to join them. Questioned by the police while the rifle sat in the boxcar, all Craig could think about was the smiling face of his toddler, and yearning to see her once more.

Only a debilitating exhaustion that ravaged his body precluded his playing non-stop with his daughter.

Although he had fired no bullets, his participation in gun disposal and decoy was instrumental in the frontal fire on the motorcade. Immediately after questioning, Craig returned to the train car, retrieved the gun, slid it in the trunk of his car, and then stopped in an alley. Wiping the gun off with a rag, he then tossed it into a dumpster. Though unlikely anyone would ever find the rifle —on the slim chance they had—it would now be free from incriminating fingerprints.

Craig could not believe the cops or FBI had not run a thorough search of the empty boxcars on the track behind the picket fence. Of course, they were unbelievably busy—frazzled. Maybe that search would come later. But by that time, evidence they needed to build a case for apprehending the hobo imposters would have permanently disappeared.

The authorities had not arrested the hobos. They had not

confiscated a rifle. And they had not spotted Craig as he went back to the boxcar for a little house cleaning. These omissions in the initial part of the investigation became a trademark for the guffaws made in the early stages of response by those in law enforcement.

The afternoon had become mundane, just more of the same as the day wore on. Comments from famous people like Harry Truman, Dwight Eisenhower, and Martin Luther King flooded the T.V. screen. View after view of an endless line of mourners waiting to pass by the President's coffin soon became muddled and mundane. Watching these distraught people, however, highlighted the very ugly to Craig. He had been a large part of the reason the country now mourned— and why thousands waited in line in the cold rain for a chance to pass by a coffin holding the still body of the President of the United States.

But for Craig the money had trumped any sense of moral decency or political ideology. In the past he had been able and ready to take out members of crime rings who had clashed with his own long term goals and financial plans. Considered a professional —for the lack of a better way to describe someone who murders for profit and gain—he wanted to believe that the overriding motivation for his willingness to risk his life and hurt people came from an underlying desire to feed his family: at first, only his wife; and in subsequent years, his little daughter.

He, like the others, had been sworn to secrecy. The ultimate cash payout owed to him depended on his ability to keep his mouth shut. But what bothered him now—as he lay on the couch and drank from a bottle of beer—was the impending chance that one of his legion would talk, and the scary probability that Lee Harvey Oswald would be the first to do so.

Somewhat relieved Ricardo had indicated plans were being made to stifle Oswald, Craig relaxed a bit more. But that relaxation only served to produce more listlessness and fatigue.

So when a soft knock sounded at the door, he stumbled in a daze to answer it.

Glad that he did not have to alarm his wife, who thought he worked as an operative for the Central Intelligence Agency, Craig didn't share the concern of legitimate agency operatives. Secretly indifferent to others knowing his street address, he made no attempt to shield that information. Strange knocks at the door, however, were always a bit eerie. But by now, after all that Craig had been through, answering a knock at three o'clock in the afternoon settled in as a low priority on the list of things that frightened him.

The kid, maybe fifteen years old, held a catalogue in one hand and a briefcase in the other. His clean-cut good looks gave him away. Craig thought, just what I need right now! A Boy Scout magazine sale!

Craig's apprehension before and after his nefarious deed in Dallas had drained him of energy and confidence. With a lackluster smile, he asked the young man what he wanted. The Boy Scout told Craig that he was polling people in the neighborhood about their attitudes and feelings about the assassination of President Kennedy; that he worked for *The New Republic*, but his bosses told him the magazine would not put a conservative slant—or any kind of slant—on the opinions given to the pollsters.

"I have no opinion on that," Craig responded belligerently. The irony of this question, and his answer, fell upon him like a pot of boiling water.

And then he slammed the door in the teenager's face.

But someone knocked again, this time more persistently.

Damn-it! Craig thought. There used to be a time when a silly, door-to-door salesman—or pollster—would take "no" for an answer!

So this time he intended to chew the kid out.

Craig opened the door to do just that: chew the kid out.

He saw a revolver staring him in the face. He glimpsed the visage of the same sixteen year-old boy, who now appeared to be ten years older than he looked just a moment ago. Before Craig could object to inordinately rude treatment from a Boy Scout—of all people! —the lad at the door discharged one bullet into Craig's forehead.

Craig lurched back a step, and his legs gave way beneath him. He fell to the floor like the sacks filled with rocks he had gathered to throw at neighborhood bullies during his childhood. As he thudded hard on his back, blood poured from a small hole in the front of his head.

Because of the silencer on the gun, no one heard a sound; in fact, Craig's wife and daughter did not come back inside the house until fifteen minutes later. But by that time, he had already died next to a *Boy Scouts* magazine on the recently laid tile floor.

His little daughter found him first, thinking it such an odd place for her even her very tired daddy to fall asleep.

—CHAPTER 24—

On Saturday night debaters from another high school in Southern California invited the Long Beach High School debaters to their hotel.

The Magnifico Inn boasted of a heated, indoor swimming pool. The coach of Rolling Hills High School, a team staying at the Magnifico, called Mr. Lott and asked him if his team would like to join Rolling Hills for an afternoon of swimming.

Mr. Lott became jubilant. An apparent absence of places to go or things to do after the assassination had thwarted his priority of getting his students outside their motel rooms. Practically everything had been closed for the weekend—until Tuesday. President Kennedy's funeral would be on Monday, and every television and radio station in the free world planned live coverage of the casket's journey down Pennsylvania Avenue, from the White House to its final destination at Arlington National Cemetery.

Four of the six debaters leaped at the opportunity to swim in the heated pool at the Magnifico Inn, quite a step up from the joint without a pool in which they were currently holed up. The Motel 6 was not exactly the Ramada Inn—or the Magnifico Inn, for that matter!

"I just don't feel like swimming, Mr. Lott," Randy complained. "I won't be able to have a good time while I'm there."

"I'll stay here with Randy," Maria offered. "I'm not in the mood to swim either."

"We need to get out of here, guys," Mr. Lott said. "We've been sitting around this dump for almost two days now. How much more watching the same stuff on T.V. can you take?" And then he grinned. "Besides, it should be safe. I think I'm finally done using the bathroom now."

"Watching the television is all I care about doing, Mr. Lott,"

Randy confessed. And it was the truth. Other than sleeping and catching occasional glimpses of Maria, Randy cared about little else but assassination news.

"Well, the rest of us are dying to get out of here. The folks from Rolling Hills were nice enough to invite us over. But I can't in good conscience leave both of you here alone; after all, you, Maria, are a girl, and you, Randy, are a boy."

They simultaneously rolled their eyes.

"So," Mr. Lott finished, "you're both going swimming."

Reluctantly, Maria and Randy accompanied Mr. Lott and the other four debaters in their rented white station wagon to the Magnifico Inn. The hotel was located in the opposite direction of Dealey Plaza and afforded them an opportunity to drive around closed off sections of the city and through detours that would take them closer to their swimming rendezvous at the Magnifico.

The swimming pool, at ground level of the upscale hotel, lived up to its billing. Indoors, steam rose from the water, as the inviting, cleansing fragrance of chlorine tempted even Mr. Lott to put on his turquoise swimming trunks and join the rather subdued teenagers in the pool.

Fortunately, Mr. Lott thought better of swimming with the kids and remained fully clothed. He sat next to the elderly debate coach, Mr. Jardin, near the edge of the pool.

Not of Olympic size proportions, the swimming pool was certainly big enough for this rather sparse gathering: seven people from Long Beach, three from Rolling Hills, and three other hotel guests. Randy surmised that those other hotel guests were all over 110 years old.

Tommy Wright cannonballed into the deep end of the pool with a series of primal yelps, communicating the most joy and energy of anyone at the swimming pool. Randy and Maria sat on the deck wrapped in their dry towels and watched Tommy with apparent disdain. His exuberance here played as inappropriate, his toothy smile out of place. Tommy radiated health and vitality, while the others sagged in that department. With his shirt off, his muscles rippling, highlighted by remnants of a beach suntan even in the middle of November, Tommy appeared physically out of sync with everyone else.

The Rolling Hills entry to the now cancelled debate tournament consisted of only two students, both boys. But a teenage girl who had come to town with her parents for a custom car show made her way down to the pool by herself and followed Tommy Wright around as though he were the Pied Piper. Cute and giggly, the girl adored Tommy the moment she laid eyes on him. It seemed that the more immature his antics, the greater the intensity of her idolization.

Randy recoiled at this girl's attraction to his rival, but he did notice she looked alluring in her gray, two-piece bathing suit. All the while Maria, covered in a terrycloth towel, sat next to him. Despite Randy's despondency, his male nature took over, and his attention, if only for a few seconds, diverted to the unknown girl in the alluring two-piece swimwear.

For that reason, the childish behavior of Tommy Wright rattled him more than he ever would have admitted to anyone else —except for Maria: "Check out Tommy," Randy said to Maria, so quietly no one else could hear him.

Maria had been doing just that: checking out Tommy.

Tommy then splashed enough water to soak Mr. Lott and Mr. Jardin, who still sat and talked in lounge chairs near the edge of the swimming pool.

"He's such an idiot," Randy whispered to Maria.

Maria did not respond. She watched silently as Tommy prepared himself to drop his body with as much force as possible into the deep end. For a tense moment, Randy wondered to himself if Tommy's hopeless clowning impressed Maria, or she gawked at Tommy in the same stupefied horror as he did.

Tommy rolled off the edge of the pool. Sure enough, Mr. Lott and Mr. Jardin were sprayed. The teenage girl cackled with delight, insuring that Tommy would notice her approving laughter soon after he came to the surface of the water. Oddly, Mr. Lott refused to chastise Tommy, continuing in earnest to converse with an increasingly irritated Mr. Jardin.

"Tommy is such a jerk," Randy complained.

Maria quietly readjusted the towel to fully cover her exposed kneecaps.

Using her silence as his cue, Randy turned to her and said, "I suppose you think all that messing around and running and splashing is really cute or something."

Maria, suddenly taken aback, said nothing, so Randy figured he had to explain. "I mean, I know it's convenient to forget what happened here yesterday, and why we're sitting in this godforsaken hole in the middle of Dallas. But—hey—a guy like Tommy doesn't let it bother him all that much, so I suppose it's kind of alluring to you girls."

Maria looked at him inquisitively. "Randy—what? Are you talking to me?"

Randy watched Tommy throw his arms around Gray Two-Piece from behind, thus, augmenting his anger and decreasing his patience. "Sorry I was wrong to think you would actually pay attention to what I said."

Maria froze. She knew that she had better reply quickly, or an escalation of something amounting to very little would suddenly amount to a lot. "Randy, you were commenting on Tommy. What could I say to that? He was having fun. I don't see what is so wrong."

Maria sensed her comments would do more damage, so she added, "Really, Randy, this trip has been terrible. So what if Tommy has a little fun? I know you are my debate partner…"

Wrong to bring up the debate partner thing…

"But I don't have to agree with you on everything, do I?"

Maria's emotional strength overwhelmed Randy in a time of great weakness. "No, I guess you don't," he snapped back under his breath and rose from the lounge chair.

Walking briskly away from Maria at poolside, he felt her eyes on him, and then he sensed Mr. Lott's stare. He didn't know where he was headed. As a matter of fact, in the next few seconds he began to feel foolish. He circled the swimming pool aimlessly, first crossing in front of the two debate coaches and then winding up directly in the path of Tommy and his new babe in the gray two-piece.

Grinning from ear to ear, with his arms folded around Gray

Two-Piece's waist, Tommy heralded another chance to torment Randy. "Taking a little stroll, man? Know where you're going—even? Duh!"

Gray Two-Piece hooted. Steam bellowed from Randy's ears. He truly wanted to avoid a confrontation, but when he tried to move around his two hecklers, Tommy and Gray Two-Piece had intentionally moved to block his way. And when Randy jerked to the right, Tommy moved to the left, again cutting off Randy, and holding Gray Two-Piece in front of him like she was his shield.

Randy stopped, showing obvious frustration with his predicament. He now quickly assessed that the only direction for him to move was backwards, into the same spot he held before. This would have made him look ridiculous. The swimming pool sat to his immediate right, and during Randy's brief, contemplative hesitation, he had leaned slightly toward the pool. Tommy seized this opportunity to slightly push him—*splash!*—into the deep end!

By the time Randy had surfaced, Mr. Lott already had rushed to the scene. Gray Two-Piece laughed hysterically, but she was not under Mr. Lott's supervision, so Mr. Lott's immediate attention went to Tommy. Tommy recognized the ire in Mr. Lott's face. He remained silent, having finally released his new girlfriend from his behind-the-back, wrap-around hug.

Mr. Lott was worried that Randy would charge up the ladder of the pool and go directly for Tommy's jugular. It would not have been a pretty sight. Though Tommy was much bigger and stronger, Randy was faster and knew karate. He had to be fuming. Mr. Lott assumed Randy would emerge from the pool incensed. And after what he already had been through in the last couple of days, somebody was going to get hurt.

By this time Maria had moved around the pool to meet Randy at the top of the ladder. She wanted to prevent him from going berserk at Tommy, who was not listed at the top of Randy's greeting card list. Only Mr. Lott and Maria may have stood between Tommy and certain death.

Bedlam had never been more silent. Nobody yelled; nobody screamed. Gray Two-Piece had stopped laughing. Mr. Lott didn't say a word. All eyes watched Randy come up from the pool ladder, his clothes drenched, his stylishly short hair pasted by its dampness over his eyebrows.

What would Randy do?

Without looking at Tommy, Randy calmly asked Mr. Lott, "Could we go back to the motel? I need to change my clothes."

Mr. Lott nodded. "I think that would be a good idea."

"Thanks," Randy said politely, and he bent forward with a slight shiver.

He still had not glanced at Tommy.

Mr. Lott, while pointing at a lounge chair, positioned himself to look at Tommy Wright. "Tommy, you are to sit down on the chair over there—by yourself. There will be serious consequences for acting like an idiot. If Mr. Jardin tells me you've uttered so much as one more word to this girl, I'll see to it that you're suspended from school for defiance."

Mr. Lott fought hard to contain the full range of his anger. He surveyed Randy's drenched condition in his street clothes. He paused so Tommy would notice his revulsion and then returned his attention to Tommy. "You may think you're real tough. But really tough men don't kick other men while they're down. And Randy is down right now—or haven't you noticed?"

Mr. Lott switched to Gray Two-Piece, who'd also begun to quake from the settling dampness. The water temperature inside the swimming pool was higher than the air temperature outside the pool, even though inside a building. "As for you, honey…are you with a debate team?"

"What?"

"I guess not. Where are your parents?"

"Out. On business. I don't know where."

Mr. Lott wagged his finger at her. "I want you to stay away from my students. I'm going back to our motel with Randy here, the boy you stupidly helped throw in the swimming pool. Tommy is no angel—not by any stretch of the imagination—but you weren't helping much with your…"

Mr. Lott stopped short of telling her what he really thought of her, a very wise decision on his part.

****

Carmen Pedro's mother had migrated to the United States when she was only four years old. Settling in an apartment with her much older brother and his two children, Marisol needed to get a job by the time she was fifteen. Lying about her age, she began washing dishes in a local restaurant that specialized in what they called, "the handsomest cheeseburgers in town," although little Marisol had no idea what this really meant. She met Gustavo, a local high school student, in 1947, and a year later their first child was born. They named her Carmen, after Gustavo's great grandmother. Her long, dark eyelashes became a magnet for attention whenever the family visited.

It wasn't long until Marisol and Gustavo were married, much to the relief of the two families, embarrassed by their children's sexual indiscretions.

Gustavo never finished high school, but he found assembly worker jobs at a myriad of factories, while Marisol held down the fort as a mother of two children: Carmen, and a little boy, who came along a few years later. Both Pedro kids did well in school, and their teachers had no extraordinary problems with them.

As the whole extended Pedro family soon discovered, Carmen could be petulant and demanding. She grew into a beautiful teenage girl who was forced to reject boys—so *many* of them—who asked her for her address or phone number. Gustavo often fretted about Carmen's consistent selection of Caucasian boyfriends. But Gustavo would have preferred if his daughter had no boyfriends at all.

Gustavo did like Randy Whitman, a polite, extraordinarily intelligent boy, who did, after all, know karate well enough to protect his daughter.

But Randy could never be Puerto Rican.

One of Carmen's ex-boyfriends once described her as being "a bottle of poison." This may have been the consequence of having been dumped by Carmen after only three months of dating. It also may have been the result of Carmen's constant pressure on him to go places *she* wanted to go, meet with her at times *she* alone designated, and occupy his time while he had other commitments.

At one time, Carmen had enlisted her older, live-in cousin, Carlos, to frighten unwanted boys off her doorstep. Carlos was big, tough, mean, and maybe a little bit crazy. But even without him, Carmen Pedro had garnered a reputation for being extraordinarily difficult.

On Saturday night, November 23, 1963, reminders of any difficulties in Carmen and Randy's relationship had vacated the Pedro household. Carmen found herself in tears for most of the day. As she tried to collect herself—especially after her conversation on the telephone with Randy—she followed the assassination coverage on the T.V. set until her eyelids began to close. She fought it off, but sleep finally had begun to overtake her.

Marisol settled in beside her daughter on the red sofa. "Are you okay, honey?"

"Yes, Mama."

"Are you worried about Randy?"

"Yes, Mama."

"But he will be home Monday, no?"

"I think so, Mama."

"Then you can see him, no?"

That, of course, was Carmen's major concern. Randy did not seem so delighted with the prospect of seeing *her*. She wanted to see him immediately after he returned from Dallas, but he had complained about having to sleep. And he didn't know for how long. Carmen knew if *she* had been In Dallas and standing there when President Kennedy died, she wouldn't be able to wait to see her wonderful boyfriend—sleep or no sleep, traumatized or not traumatized.

"Maybe, Mama. Maybe I can see him when he gets home. I don't think he's the same anymore. I think something happened to him there. I don't know what he saw, but I know it was pretty awful."

"Then he is going to need you."

In all her distress, Carmen failed to realize that her mother temporarily had washed aside her blind prejudices toward her daughter's Caucasian boyfriend.

With one eye on the television—again running the comments by former President Eisenhower about the assassination—Carmen said, "I don't know, Mama. I think his debate friends have been there for him. I guess I haven't been very nice to Randy. Lots of times when he wanted to tell me things, I yelled at him. And I kept telling him that when we got married, we would move to Puerto Rico, even though his family is here. He got very sad about that. I would yell at him for nothing. Sometimes he came late to our house to take me somewhere—he would walk here because he doesn't drive a car—and I got mad at him for not being on time. I don't think I have been a very nice girlfriend."

Marisol pulled Carmen close to her and smiled, "Then you can show him now, when he needs you the most. You can show him what a good girlfriend you are. It will be your way of letting him know you made a mistake before—that you appreciate him now."

"I don't know, Mama," Carmen said, shaking her head sadly. "He has new friends now…and there's this girl, his speech contest partner. She's very pretty and…" Carmen managed a smile of her own. "She's a Mexican. I think Randy likes her. Randy likes the girls from South of the Border."

"You are prettier than this girl."

With her head reclining on her mother's shoulder, Carmen giggled, "I don't know about that, Mama."

"How could this not be true?"

"She is very pretty. And she's very, very smart. Their teacher put them together for the speeches in Dallas this weekend. They've been working together for a couple of months. But now that the speeches have been cancelled, they have a lot of time with nothing to do there."

"And this is what really has you worried." Her mother made a statement, displaying an understanding of her daughter's concern about Randy's claustrophobic predicament.

But Carmen said nothing more. She knew her mother was right. And afraid to reinforce the truth to even herself, she suddenly clammed up.

—CHAPTER 25—

They called him the Tall Man for good reason. Standing over six feet, four inches tall had lots of advantages, but it possessed its disadvantages, too; for example, shorter women usually did not find the Tall Man as attractive as taller women found him. And it took the Tall Man longer to get out of his car. His legs would often become trapped for a few seconds under the steering column. Seemingly unaware that this would become a problem, the Tall Man never thought about how his head stuck up higher in the air than a shorter man's head would have stuck.

On the night of November 23, 1963, the Tall Man, after seeking a case of beer, had just driven home from a street corner liquor store. The long weekend invited back his old bad habits. As he watched the assassination coverage unfold on television, *something* had to numb his brain.

During the short three-block jaunt by automobile back to his apartment complex in San Antonio, an uneasy feeling settled into his psyche. Somebody had followed him home. There was no doubt about that. Sometimes the headlights behind him were so close, they had practically blinded him. And while he drove his car to his space through the apartment's parking section, the car behind him had steered into the driveway, too. The driver finally cut the headlights, instigating a frightening darkness.

Unaware of the exact location of the anonymous automobile, the Tall Man sensed danger. A flashing irony encircled him: A little more than one day before, he had impersonated an electrician, imprisoned himself in a small office space, and murdered the President of the United States. Now at his own home, he was overcome with an apparently irrational sense of being in even greater danger than he had been in Dallas.

But he figured he could bolt from his car, run to the steel gate leading to the apartment units, and reach the entrance of his own home quickly enough to lock himself behind the door.

There he would grab his gun.

How frustrated he was that he had decided against keeping a concealed revolver in his glove compartment! For weeks, guns of all kinds had surrounded him. Today, the present unavailability of even the simplest form of gun may cost him his life.

Driving to his parking space very slowly, he geared up for a sprint to the gate. As soon as his 1961 white Impala eased into place, he turned the engine key, shutting off the motor. In the same motion, he jerked the keys from the ignition with his right hand and pushed open the driver's side door with his left hand.

But he had always been the Tall Man, and tall men do not emerge from automobiles as gracefully—or rapidly—as shorter guys. His panicky, wild turn to the left jammed his knees into the steering wheel just above his legs. As quickly as he realized he would have to shove his body back further, embedding it into the lower, rear portion of the driver's seat, his visceral awareness of his immediate surroundings switched to black and then—almost instantaneously—slipped into nothingness.

If the Tall Man had not become momentarily wedged under the steering column, he might have made it to safety. If he had not been as tall, the bullet that exploded his brain would have sailed harmlessly over the top of his head.

****

The Motel 6 had never looked as menacing. With the Long Beach debaters gone, Maria at the swimming pool of another hotel, and the deadness of night thick with hopelessness, Randy could not put himself into dry clothes fast enough. He longed to get out of that room and return to the swimming pool back at the Magnifico.

Slipping on a plain, white T-shirt, he politely said, "Thanks for bringing me back here, Mr. Lott."

"It wasn't your fault. Besides, you've gotta' stay warm."

"Yeah, thanks."

"I might point out, Randy, that I was quite impressed with your restraint by the pool."

"Yeah, I wanted to punch his lights out. That's what I really wanted to do, Mr. Lott."

"And you could have. I know that. No matter how big he is."

"He's *not* that big—and I'm not that small, Mr. Lott."

Mr. Lott concurred. "That's true. But you probably wanted to deck his little admirer, too. Your restraint was admirable."

"Thank you."

"And while we're away from the gathered throngs," Mr. Lott continued, "maybe we can talk about a couple of things? By the way, I thought we would all do some sighting seeing tomorrow. There might be a few things still open: the Old Red Museum, Dallas Stadium, *Southern Methodist University*," he added with emphasis.

"Southern Methodist?"

"Well, we never got over there for a tournament, and who really knows what's going to be next year! It's a beautiful campus, and you can walk around and gawk inside the classrooms and pretend that you're doing a debate round inside."

Did Mr. Lott really think that would be fun—or had he simply been under so much pressure lately that his noggin was beginning to take a beating (or some other malady had gotten to him, such as a reaction to the nefarious subterfuge of numerous chocolate laxatives dumped into his hot coca)?

Randy wondered about Mr. Lott's mildly sadistic sense of humor, but he said, "Sounds nice. I'd like to see the campus. Ira was actually talking about going to school there."

Would Southern Methodist be a wise choice for a nice Jewish boy?

Mr. Lott squared off. "Here's the deal, Randy: You need to speak with the police. That's it. You need to do this for them, your country, and yourself. After that, no matter what, you can rest."

Randy paused, looked into his hands.

"That's it, Randy," Mr. Lott said sternly. "No more thinking about what you might have done or could have done or should have done...*no more*, because you can't undo the past. You can only do what you plan to do now—and that's go to the police. Just why are you so sure you could have done *anything* to stop those bastards?

"Because I *could* have. I—"

Mr. Lott held up his hands. "No, Randy, you can rant about it for the rest of the weekend or until you tell the police your story. But after that…it's *over.*"

Randy decided against arguing with Mr. Lott. There was no point to it. Mr. Lott had made up his mind, and he also had chosen sides in Randy's conflict with Tommy Wright. Mr. Lott was a nice man, a conscientious man, an exceptional man. But he could not empathize with the hollowness in Randy's heart.

After waiting for him to reply, Mr. Lott accepted a silent, partial nod as Randy's response, and he said, "There's one other thing: You want to hear what it is?"

Randy shrugged. He felt defeated.

"I've noticed what's going on between you and Maria Barquin. And so has everyone else. It's tough to ignore."

Panic swept through Randy.

Mr. Lott continued, "I think you need to cool it."

Now Randy saw that his panic was justified. "We haven't done anything, Mr. Lott!" he contended.

"I'm not accusing you of *doing* anything. First of all, Randy, a weekend debate tournament, even guised under the romantic label of *tragedy*, does not give you license to do things you would not do at home under ordinary circumstances. Second of all, you two are a debate team. You'll eventually be among the top debate teams in the United States; if not this year, next year is an absolute certainty. And third of all…and it pains me to tell you this…I hate doing this to you when you're down, but my goal here is to save you a lot of grief…she doesn't like you in that way, Randy."

Randy's heart sank; his façade was transparent.

First: "What do I care?"

Then: "How do you know that, Mr. Lott?" Randy asked as though he were cross-examining Mr. Lott during a debate.

"Because she likes Tommy," Mr. Lott said softly.

"How do you know that?" Randy asked again, this time

barely allowing the words to escape.

"Because he told me. They've been friendlier with each other than you thought."

"*He told you that?*"

Mr. Lott nodded, "Yup, he brags. You know that, Randy. Maybe he thought he'd impress me, get on my good side."

"And do you *believe* him?"

"What did *you* see by the pool today, Randy?" He waited for his debater's reply, but the teenager hung his head.

"Three solid reasons to leave Maria as your debate colleague and nothing else. And besides, Randy, you have a girlfriend, don't you? That Carmen girl?"

That Carmen girl? Those few precious moments with Maria in the motel parking lot flashed before Randy's eyes. He and Maria had spoken so candidly with each other, and he believed they had connected. He then remembered his last phone conversation with Carmen and her invitation to visit her immediately after he got home from Dallas—and the sensation of motion sickness he felt as she had uttered those words.

How he now wished that while at poolside he had delivered a swift round-kick to the side of Tommy Wright's face!

—CHAPTER 26—

Oswald agreed with the police that for his own protection more security needed to be employed at the jail. Death threats by the tens of thousands had already poured into the Dallas Police Department and to media centers, especially newspapers. Although Oswald did not know of these thousands of threats, he suspected as much. After each encounter with unmolested, unsupervised men who had jammed frantically into every room and corridor the police had escorted him, Oswald felt a new sense of dread.

Oswald brought up concerns for his safety to a personally assigned guard, a cell-based policeman by the name of Horace Glouchin. Appearing jolly—and very large—in his fatigues, his clothes belied the man's personality and reputation. Glouchin had tussled and tangled with the worst of them, but his normally reserved manner and soft spoken voice gave others the impression he was nothing more than a gentle giant, always willing to give even the most heinous prisoners the benefit of the doubt.

Oswald had noted his courteous demeanor and wanted to use it to his advantage. "Horace, I think I need your help," Oswald whispered while Glouchin made one of his regular inspections of Oswald's cell.

At first, Glouchin didn't react. He was used to prisoners asking him for small favors—or even big favors. But Oswald was a different breed of prisoner. The man in this teeny cell had been charged with killing one of their own, a Dallas policeman. And he had just been booked for assassinating the President of the United States. So far this was the only person anyone had implicated in that spectacular crime.

"I can't help you, Lee," Glouchin said in a louder voice than that used by Oswald. "I have no power here, even if I wanted to help you—which I don't."

"They're gonna' kill me, Horace," Oswald whined.

"Whose gonna' kill you?"

"Did you see all those television and newspaper people at the press conference the other night? Every time you guys lead me through the hall, I have nowhere to move. I tell you, I'm going be killed."

"The T.V. people are going to kill you?" Glouchin asked bemusedly. "I don't think so, Lee."

"No, Horace, listen to me," Oswald pleaded, gripping the bars of his cell with both his hands. "People want me dead."

"I don't blame them. You killed JFK and a cop."

"No, Horace, I did not kill Kennedy. I swear to you: I did not kill Kennedy."

"Then who did?'

"Horace, I need an attorney. After I speak with an attorney, I'll know more. I'll talk more. But right now, I'm like a sitting duck in one of those arcade games where you shoot the tiny ball out of a toy gun."

"I love that little game!" Glouchin chuckled.

Oswald frowned. "I need your protection while they're moving me from here to there—and all over the place."

"Hmm…that could be dangerous for *me*. From what I hear, in a few hours you're going over to County. They'll hide you away then."

"And they're going smack me around, aren't they? They think they can get me to say stuff that isn't true by hammering me with their clubs, right Horace?"

Instead of showing his gentle grandfather-like personality, Glouchin began to twitch, his face a blend of involuntary muscle movements. "Now, they haven't done that yet, have they, Oswald? You know, Lee, I'd really like to come in there and smack you around myself. Lots of people would like to do that."

Oswald's body sagged; Glouchin continued, "I don't know whether you killed Kennedy or not. But I don't really care about that, if you want to know the truth. As far as I'm concerned, he was a no-good Communist anyway. So we might be better off without the likes of *him*. But what I do know—what everybody knows—is that you shot a poor cop in cold blood. You murdered Tippit; and, frankly, Lee, you son-of-a-bitch, I hope they use your head over there at County for soup!"

****

When Randy and Mr. Lott returned to the Magnifico Hotel, the only people left by the swimming pool were the two boys from Rolling Hills, their coach Mr. Jardin, and the five debaters from Long Beach. Probably fearful of Mr. Lott, Tommy's little lust object had abandoned him; the others went about their socializing.

Three of the Long Beach team swam with the Rolling Hills debaters, while Tommy Wright sat on the edge of the lounge chair Randy had previously occupied, engaged in a conversation with Maria Barquin.

The atmosphere was much more subdued than it had been an hour before, when the teens had experienced some gaiety. Mr. Lott thought twice about leaving Randy alone poolside and going over to talk with Mr. Jardin; he sensed more trouble. He saw Tommy and Maria locked in discourse. Knowing how Randy felt about Maria, and right after he had told Randy the new Maria guidelines, Mr. Lott considered it a probability he still would be needed for emergency intervention.

But to Mr. Lott's surprise, Tommy stood up from the lounge chair and peacefully approached Randy. Before stopping in front of the slighter boy, Tommy extended his right hand. "I'm sorry, Randy. I acted like a jerk. I *was* a jerk."

Randy automatically accepted his hand and shook it. He now felt worse about everything. Tommy had charmed even *him*. He couldn't imagine what his effect could be on Maria, especially in light of what Mr. Lott had told him. After the handshake, he felt a little dirty shaking hands with the enemy.

"Randy, I'm also sorry about what happened...out there yesterday at the motorcade. I never should have called you what I did. And I never should have dared you to run across the street. That was very juvenile on my part."

Randy nodded. His voice box had involuntarily locked up.

155

Mr. Lott saw that they were talking—at least Tommy was talking. He figured things were going well, especially since no one had yet thrown a punch or pushed the other boy into the pool. He noticed Maria carefully surveying the situation, and he wondered about which of the boys she now favored.

Randy watched Maria, too. From his perspective, Maria had been studying Tommy, not him or even both of them. As he and Tommy broke away, Maria flashed Randy a large, toothy smile, which he immediately recognized as pretentious. It was as though Maria had just told him through her smile, "See, wasn't that nice of me? I talked Tommy into apologizing."

Maria would not, of course, admit that she had coerced Tommy into taking the rap for earlier skirmishes and mishaps, but somehow Randy sensed the truth—and he didn't like it one bit.

"Fine, Tommy," Randy said half-heartedly, secretly wishing Mr. Lott would muster the courage to toss Tommy off the debate team.

Tommy debated well. He worked fairly hard. His personality didn't necessarily gel with everybody else's, but he fit in socially with most of the other debaters. But Randy surmised, for reasons touching on envy, Tommy couldn't stand him. He normally shrugged this sort of thing off. But now their conflict involved Maria: a mortifying dare in her presence to cross the street in Dealey Plaza, Mr. Lott's revelations about Maria's desire for Tommy's affections, and the humiliation he suffered in front of her after being shoved into a swimming pool.

"Hey, man, it's cool," Tommy raised his thumb and flashed a big, phony smile at Randy.

"Yeah—cool, Tommy."

"Cool," Tommy reiterated.

Did this idiot really not *get* it?

Mr. Lott looked around and said, "Maybe we should all go back to our motel. Have you all had enough swimming?"

Margie and Ruther emphatically nodded their heads. They shivered, not from the cold, but from the bitterness of a long, depressing weekend in Dallas. The others made no indication of their preferences, but Mr. Lott had already decided they would leave the Magnifico.

The Pilots from Long Beach High School slowly gathered their belongings and began their efforts to leave the swimming area, while Randy stood motionless and contemplated what he might do to Tommy Wright before the end of the school year.

—CHAPTER 27—

Lee Harvey Oswald had just finished a breakfast of pancakes, bacon, and orange juice in cell #12 of the Dallas City Jail. At approximately 10:27 A.M, John Young, one of the Chief's right-hand men, paid a visit to Oswald to inform him of his transfer to the city jail at around noon Central Standard Time.

Fifteen minutes later Jack Clayton, media liaison for the Dallas Police Department, announced to the world via network television that Lee Harvey Oswald's transportation would be an armored car, but some press and television reporters would be allowed to attend the transfer proceedings after bring provided security clearance at the jail.

The entire galaxy knew precisely when Oswald would again be paraded in front of masses of strangers.

And that information had not been lost on the Hat Man.

With Oswald tightly cuffed, the elevator moved slowly up to the first floor of the Dallas City Jail. The doors opened, and Oswald noticed an array of cameras held by people he did not know. Somewhat used to this scene, he relaxed a bit, figuring any trouble he might encounter would occur outside in the parking lot at the hands of jeering citizens who thought they knew the whole story. Still inside the building he had become familiar with the last couple of days, Oswald enjoyed a semblance of serenity.

Flanked by the Chief on his right and another officer he didn't know on his left side, the handcuffed prisoner emerged from the elevator, ready for his short jaunt down the sterile corridor. A little relieved from the stifling, stagnant air of the elevator and the stale atmosphere of his jail cell, Oswald took momentary pleasure in fresher surroundings; yet, the sea of humanity ahead of him did not bode favorably for his sense of security. He felt a wave of uneasiness as the cameras flashed and clicked. But even as he heard those familiar sounds, he grew increasingly uneasy as to their origins.

Oswald's eyes then moved to his left.

To many individuals who later would look at the tapes of this jail transfer—and perhaps, to those who had been there in person —Lee Harvey Oswald lived a brief instant of recognition: Off to his far left, but easily identifiable because of his gray business hat, Jack Ruby was visible and recognizable to Oswald.

After all, Oswald and Ruby knew each other.

The Guy In The Black T-shirt and the Man In The Gray Business Hat had brainstormed together, created together, and then plotted together to kill President Kennedy. Ruby and Oswald were not friends, but they had united out of a sense of urgency and justice. They were not comrades, but they had tolerated each other due to their mutual obligations, born of patriotism and nationalism.

After eyeing Ruby, Oswald fought the temptation to divulge the identity of the man he had conspired with for months; instead, he turned and faced forward, now experiencing bile in his throat.

And for good reason: Seemingly from nowhere, Jack Ruby stepped in front of Oswald and raised a gun, pointing it at him with a deadly accuracy others would later extol. Dozens of people in the corridor watched in frozen horror, as yet another chapter of history had been written, this time in less than two seconds. As Jack Ruby moved, he fired his revolver directly into Oswald's solar plexus, causing the younger man to grunt in pain, fold his right arm over the affected area, and pitch forward to the floor.

Several cameramen dropped their equipment to the ground. They and others in the corridor fell to the floor. For those in attendance, the scene was surreal. A few men who occupied space in that hallway experienced a furtherance of the horror they had come to know in Dealey Plaza—practically to the exact minute— two days before.

Simultaneously, scores of policemen rushed the shooter, pulling him backwards and dragging him out of sight.

Pandemonium.

Bedlam.

And the entire scene, from Oswald's leaving the elevator, to the crack of gunfire and the wild scene that followed, had been witnessed by hundreds of millions of T.V. viewers who now began to believe their living nightmare would never come to an end.

****

"Is he dead?" Mrs. Whitman asked her husband.

Coincidentally, just as Mrs. Whitman asked the question, her answer appeared on the television screen: *Lee Harvey Oswald died at 1:17 P.M. today.*

"Oh my God!" Mrs. Whitman said, cupping her mouth.

"Now we'll probably never know for sure what happened." Samuel joined in chorus.

"But why? Why did that man kill him?"

Above the fanfare on the tube, Mr. Whitman explained, "Probably because he doesn't want anyone to know what really happened. Maybe this guy Oswald wasn't the only assassin. Maybe he wasn't an assassin at all, and they had to shut him up."

****

All Randy wanted to do was sleep. He'd now slumbered for more than twelve straight hours, retiring late Saturday night and then awakening, blurry-eyed and barely conscious, at almost noon on Sunday.

Events from the past few days had been blotted from his mind, and he managed to navigate through the first ten minutes of his morning without dwelling on specifics: He still reeled from his encounters with Tommy. He felt vaguely nauseous knowing about Maria's affection for Tommy. The sadness of Mr. Lott's illness sat heavily in his heart. And he throbbed with an urgency to speak with the police. But at least for the first few minutes on Sunday, Randy had thrust all that behind him, too groggy to make sense of time and space.

Ira had vacated the room. Randy figured he'd gone down to breakfast and then stopped to talk with Mr. Lott or Ruther Gardner. Randy knew he hadn't been Mr. Chipper the past couple of days, so he didn't blame Ira for trying to evade him whenever he found the chance.

He briefly wondered where Maria had decided to hang out, but the thought was fleeting, and he shrugged it off. Remembering a music station he had enjoyed upon the group's arrival in Dallas (only a few days ago?), he switched on the radio by his bed, already set to that A.M. rock-in-roll music station. "Be My Baby," by the Ronettes, blared throughout the room. He then immediately adjusted the dial, lowering the volume.

Decidedly not hungry—but still weary—he climbed back into his bed and reclined on top of the covers. He closed his eyes and vaguely heard some of his favorites: "The End of the World" and "Sugar Shack." But he never fully returned to sleep. This early stage of dozing remained soothing until Ira, slamming the door behind him, rousted Randy from his drowsiness.

"You're still sleeping?" Ira asked with a mixture of incredulity and irritation.

"Not really. I'm just sort of lying here, waiting to die."

"Have you seen any T.V?"

"No," Randy replied with sudden uneasiness.

Ira sat down on his bed and folded his hands. "Oswald's dead."

At first the name *Oswald* did not ring a bell. But after a few seconds, Randy recalled that name and its grizzly associations. "What?"

"He was being taken to the county jail, and, uh, this guy— and I swear we all watched this happen on T.V. an hour ago—this guy walked right in front of him and shot him in the chest. He's dead."

Randy didn't know what to say.

"The whole thing was nothing short of bizarre," Ira added.

Randy, of course, could not have more emphatically agreed with Ira's observation. His throat went dry, but he managed to ask, "You saw this happen? On television?"

"Yeah, we were all sitting in Mr. Lott's room. Ruth and I were playing cards."

His mind wandering into places he wished it would not go, Randy wondered what Maria had been doing then.

And Tommy.

"And suddenly there was all this commotion on television. They keep showing it over and over. 'Somebody killed Oswald! Somebody killed Oswald!' Whew!"

"Well, I'm probably never going to talk to the Dallas Police or the FBI or anybody, not with all this commotion. Not now. We're flying back home tomorrow and then what? You think they're going to phone me at home as a courtesy? You think that?"

Ira shrugged. "I don't know."

"Maybe if I kept calling them—just made a hideous, raging nag of myself."

Ira sighed and began to crack his knuckles. Realizing it served only to irritate his friend, he ceased the cracking and said, "Randy, if you think you have something to tell the police, they're going to listen to you—just not today. They have so much to deal with now—and so many people to talk to."

"Yeah," Randy insisted, "but I should be one of their main people."

"Why, Randy?" Ira asked tiredly. "What can you tell them?"

"I can tell them about the guys on the grassy hill."

"You don't think they know about the guys on the grassy hill?"

"I haven't heard anything about them on T.V. Have you?"

"No," Ira replied, "but that doesn't mean they're not looking for them. They don't announce everything."

"But, Ira, the guy had a rifle. Why else would he have a rifle, if not to shoot somebody?"

"And you're sure of that, Randy?"

Randy initiated a response; then he stopped: *Was he sure the guy had a rifle?*

Was Ira kidding?

It suddenly occurred to Randy that his friend didn't fully believe him. It dawned on him that the others had been working to placate him, agreeing that he had been, yes, *stressed out* by the assassination, but had not *seen* something different from what anyone else had seen. Randy's well-publicized admiration for President Kennedy provided the catalyst for his hallucinations about assassins.

Randy lost his patience. "Are you kidding me, Ira?"

"What?" Ira asked feebly.

"You don't believe me, do you? My trusted *friend*."

"I believe you saw something."

"But you believe it's what *everybody* saw."

"Maybe you saw something else."

"Maybe?" Randy mocked.

"Maybe it was a Secret Service guy with a rifle."

"Jesus, Ira!"

"I can't vouch for what you saw. Frankly, only you know that—or maybe you don't know that either."

"You don't think I'm in my right mind, do you?"

"I do think you're in your right mind," Ira answered. "But for whatever reason, your right mind is focused on some things that may not have been—in your right mind at the time."

Randy didn't know whether to laugh or cry. "Do you realize that makes no sense whatsoever? Do you, Ira? I either saw those two men behind the concrete barrier, or I didn't. I either saw one of them pointing a rifle, or I didn't. And you think I didn't. Just say so."

Ira got off the bed. He didn't want to continue an endless, counter-productive bickering session. Anything was better than this, even sitting in Mr. Lott's room, reeking with the aftereffects of the Ex-Lax prank, or having to deal with Tommy Wright's insufferable boasting. "Randy, I'm going back to Mr. Lott's room to watch the coverage. All that—your stress and fatigue—can get things mixed up in your brain. But the good thing is somebody else must have seen it, too; that just makes sense."

Ira carefully watched his friend. Randy lowered his head and balled both his hands into fists.

Ira said, "But I still think you should talk to people in charge of the investigation. You probably have more to offer them than they think. To them, you're just some dippy teenager visiting their city for a few lousy days. They have no idea how bright you are;

that you're a great debater with an extraordinary vocabulary. They have no idea how honest you are and how much integrity you have. But they'll catch on, and maybe they'll listen to you. Maybe then you can get all of this off your chest."

Ira hesitated, now worried that the karate boy might spring from his bed, chew on him, and then spit him out.

But Randy unclenched his fists and raised his head to look Ira squarely in the eyes. "That's all I want, Ira: to move on. But until I tell them what I saw, I won't be able to move on. Do you understand?" His last question sounded pitiful and hopeless.

Ira affirmed him anyway. "You may recall that I was almost the guy who ran across the street. Me. If I'd seen what you, uh, saw, I would be feeling the same way—frustrated and impatient. It must be hard to keep all that inside, harder than anyone else could ever know."

This time Randy didn't answer him. At once he began asking himself whether or not he had, indeed, seen two hobos behind the concrete barrier just a few seconds before the assassination. He pondered whether or not a rifle really existed on that hill at all.

Maybe a gun came into his purview only *after* he heard those firecracker sounds, rose from the grass, and returned to the fearful, watchful eyes of his colleagues on the debate team.

—CHAPTER 28—

Now Joey knew precisely what Ricardo had meant when the Latin spoke of, "taking care of Oswald."

Lee Harvey Oswald lay in the morgue on Sunday, November 24, 1963. On that same day, Joey, the hobo who had teamed with Craig and Howard to kill the President of the United States, vomited his guts into the bathroom toilet.

Joey's vague nausea grew even more intense after he had carelessly broken a cardinal rule and communicated with another assassin: He called Craig at his home in Nashville.

Craig's wife answered the phone and tearfully told Joey that Craig had been brutally murdered in the doorway of their home on Saturday, and their little girl had discovered his body. She didn't have any idea what her husband had been involved in. But as a veteran C.I.A. agent's wife, she had been used to his pensive moods and the constant drama in his life.

She also thought that whatever good he had done for anyone else with his work could never compensate for his loss to her and their little girl.

She had no idea what Craig actually did: that he had been a covert operative involved in anti-Castro groups for three years; that he had conspired with organized crime bosses to kill John F. Kennedy, whose Attorney General brother had ruthlessly gone after the Mafia and other crime establishments in the United States.

The President also had failed to follow through in his efforts to get rid of Castro, thus blocking hundreds of millions of dollars in potential revenues from targeted Cuban casinos and other clandestine gambling operations.

Joey had told his wife good-bye on Monday morning; that he was off to a training operation in the Caribbean, but to return home on Saturday—of course, all a lie. He never could have divulged that he had conspired against his country's leader, planned to execute him on a city street, and then later collect a million dollars from crime bosses who didn't know even his first name.

After Joey spoke with Craig's wife, jittery fingers dialed the home of Howard, the triggerman at the top of the hill. Joey had stood there as Howard delivered a perfectly aimed shot into the right side of Kennedy's head, fanning blood and brain matter all over the back seat of the Lincoln limousine. Howard had then dropped the gun under the barricade and casually moseyed down along the grass with him, as if to check on all the commotion.

Meanwhile, Craig sneaked from the boxcar, retrieved the rifle, and the three of them later offered up the veneer of a trio of hobos. Their sudden, brief encounter with the police had been unexpected—though not shocking—so they used it as part of their front: *Hobos cleared of wrongdoing after police interrogation.* In essence, they had dodged a bullet heading in their direction.

Ricardo had forbidden them to contact each other, and now Joey broke that rule for the second time in the past ten minutes.

"Howard, Joey."

"What!" Howard practically screamed over the line.

"Are you watching television?" Joey asked, ignoring his emotions.

"Say nothing over the phone, Joey. Nothing."

"This thing is much bigger than we are, Howard. And pretty soon we're not going to have anywhere to hide."

"But you knew that."

"I didn't realize the danger would come from—*within.*" Joey complained.

"From breaking the rules!" Howard said with force.

"But—listen, Howard. I just called, uh…" And then he reconsidered what he was about to say, figuring he should not reveal names. So he slowly corrected himself, "My partner's wife answered the phone. One of our partners is dead, Howard. Somebody selling magazines for the Boy Scouts shot him in the head when he answered his front door!"

Silence had fallen on the other end of the line.

"Howard, are you there?"

"Yeah, yeah…"

After his pause, Howard said, "The *Boy Scouts*? Look, Joey, stay put. Don't answer the door or go anywhere for a few days. If they trust us, we have nothing to worry about. You're lucky your partner couldn't answer the phone when you tried to get him. You weren't supposed to do that. You were supposed to maintain your dependability."

"We're dust."

"No, not necessarily. They gave us the job. They trusted us."

"But too many mouths. That's what they're thinking now."

"Maybe, maybe not. That Boy Scout has a mouth, too. They can't take out everyone—just those who won't abide."

"Okay, Howard, I'll do what you say."

"Good."

"Yeah."

"And remember," Howard admonished him, "you're to call nobody—and keep your mouth *shut*. That's your life insurance."

"Yeah," Joey said contritely. "I get it."

"Good."

But when Joey hung up, Howard muttered to himself, "Poor bastard." He knew that Joey would be the next assassin to be silenced by the men who had once trusted him to help preserve their financial empire.

****

When Carmen spoke with Randy late Sunday afternoon, she noticed he sounded a lot friendlier. While he did not exactly communicate an overt joy or zest for living, at least he didn't convey contempt for her, as he had done in their previous phone conversation.

"Are you sleeping okay?" Carmen asked him.

"Yeah," Randy answered with a muffled laugh. "That's what I've been spending most of my time doing: sleeping. It keeps me from having to look at myself in the mirror. Ugh!"

"Your body needs it," Carmen analyzed for him. She had no idea what kind of trauma her boyfriend experienced in Dallas. She didn't know what he had done or seen, because he had not told her. But she observed that he'd been torn asunder emotionally, and she decided offering him some advice might get him to pick up on her compassion and concern.

"I guess so," Randy said. "How are things with you?"

"Fine. We've all been home watching everything on television. The funeral is tomorrow."

"Yeah, tomorrow. Right about the time we'll be on an airplane headed home."

"You'll probably see some film of the funeral. They're going to take him all the way up Pennsylvania Avenue to Arlington National Cemetery. That's what they said today."

"Yeah," Randy muttered sadly.

"Is there anything you need? Can I get you something from the store? There's still a drugstore open here—one right up the street. Do you need some Aspirin or anything? Maybe some gum or candy?"

"No, thanks," Randy replied. "Thank you for being so understanding, Carmen."

"You're welcome."

"And I'll definitely stop by right after I get home; I'd like to see you. I'll need a shower, of course—and maybe a nap. But then I guess I can come over, and we can just talk or listen to music or something."

"Anything," Carmen told him.

And for the first time in days, Carmen happily sensed that her relationship with Randall Whitman might not be coming to the sad conclusion she had dreaded.

****

Tommy Wright had valiantly tried to put the moves on Maria Barquin. She, after all, had responded to him, even eyeing him during those moments she believed his concentration was elsewhere. But Maria had eventually understood Tommy's obsession for attention, and she fought to revoke her habit of closely examining people she thought to be physically attractive.

She had become terribly embarrassed that others had noticed her wandering eye.

And though Maria thought Tommy was, indeed, handsome, she knew making him privy to this information would not be in anyone's best interests, especially her own.

Maria liked boys who were smart and hard working. Tommy fit both of these categories, but he was neither the smartest nor the hardest working kid on the debate team—not by a long shot. She also enjoyed boys who had a reputation for being honest, but here Tommy did not come close. Undeniably, though, Tommy Wright seduced girls with his rugged, blond, beach boy good looks.

Maria, however, eventually became furious with herself for being attracted to this quality, above all others, in a boy. She finally started to fight her gullible subservience to Tommy's magnetism.

At around six o'clock in the evening on Sunday, Mr. Lott commanded his flock to meet him in the parking lot. They were going to a steakhouse they had planned to visit after their first couple of rounds of debate on Friday. Now they faced their final chance to dine on superior beef before they left Dallas, and Mr. Lott insisted they take advantage of this last opportunity.

Maria emerged from her room with Margie Pendergrass. But Tommy swooped over and dragged Maria away, swiping her hand and pulling her down the hall.

Before Margie could object to Tommy's aggressive moves, Maria laughed nervously and informed her that it was all right. She had told Tommy they could walk to the parking lot together. They both wanted to finish a conversation they had been having about proposed changes in student government at Long Beach High School (they were both grade level representatives on student council).

Maria and Tommy lagged behind the others in a very slow walk that would bring them to the parking lot well after everyone else had arrived.

As they strolled together, Tommy and Maria began their conversation about student council affairs. But by the time they came to the edge of the adjacent parking area, Tommy had changed the topic. Out of the blue, he injected, "Randy is stuck on you."

Maria blanched. "Why do you say that?"

"It's quite obvious. And it's one of the reasons he hates my guts."

Maria actually felt her blood rush into her face. "I don't get it."

Tommy laughed—a mean laugh. "He thinks you like me, so he hates me, man!"

Maria denied nothing. She feigned, "I still don't get it."

"He's jealous."

"But why?" Maria laughed, trying unsuccessfully to hide her nervousness.

Tommy quieted. His face bore the grin of a Cheshire cat, but Maria did not notice that grin. By the time they had gotten to Mr. Lott's rented white station wagon, the other debaters were assembled and ready to leave for the steakhouse. This included Randy Whitman, who leaned back against the car, his head tilted upward, and the moonlight illuminating his face.

****

The long ride to the Dallas-Fort Worth Airport on Monday morning turned out to be especially gloomy. The Kennedy funeral arrangements progressed; the procession was imminent. The Long Beach High School debaters would be in the air during the actual funeral.

The streets of Dallas, bubbling with excitement only a few days before, were now desolate. Ruther commented about the litter on the street, blown about the ground by the wind, and how the scene reminded him of some popular science fiction movies depicting the evacuation of large cities prior to a nuclear attack or an invasion from Mars: the debris, the desolation, the deadness. This uncanny, unsettling atmosphere rushed the debaters to the airport with a greater urgency.

As their car made motored from the city, Randy spotted an advertisement on a large billboard for Hertz rental cars. His stomach churned, as he remembered seeing that same sign over Dealey Plaza on Friday. It still towered over a part of the city that had become a horror for most of the free world and a personally designated hell for Randy. Far away, but still close enough to see, Randy watched the billboard duck in and out of a few tall buildings, until it finally disappeared for good.

Meanwhile, televisions all over America brought home the tragic funeral of John Fitzgerald Kennedy: a horseless carriage; a sullen ride down Pennsylvania Avenue, from the Capitol Building to Arlington National Cemetery; a little boy standing next to his daddy's coffin, with his hand lifted to his forehead in a last gesture of reverence to his father and the President; a grieving widow draped completely in black; thousands of tearful mourners lining the street; a twenty-one gun salute; and, finally, an eternal flame flickering over a freshly dug grave.

Even when the military bugler blew taps at graveside, he faltered, causing a momentarily out-of-tune, yet, strangely appropriate farewell to the tragically fallen President of the United States.

The air terminal, unusually quiet and deserted, welcomed the California debaters as much-appreciated company on this lonely, despairing day. Normally, Dallas-Fort Worth International Airport, situated a long thirty minute freeway drive from downtown, was one of the busiest in the United States. But due to its geography, today it had become one of the most tranquil.

Dragging their luggage through the airport, the debate squad handed their bags to quiet curbside porters. They exchanged flight information with officials who would put their suitcases and briefcases on the airplane. Hardly anybody spoke, though occasionally, they could hear someone laughing in the distance. Other incongruous sounds, such as the clanking of dishes from nearby restaurants, the announcements giving flight information over the public address system, and the squeaking of wheels on baggage carts interrupted their silence—and distracted them from the droning of television sets that brought the Kennedy funeral, live, into the airport.

Around the time the group arrived at their gate designation, Randy looked over at his coach. Mr. Lott was panting, out of breath, his face lacking color. Randy knew Mr. Lott not only had to

171

deal with the assassination horrors, as did all Americans; he also faced the further responsibilities of chaperoning six teenagers on a trip far from home, while managing the disappointment they felt because of a cancelled major debate tournament.

And Randy remembered what Mr. Lott had told Maria and him about his leukemia. Thursday night now seemed like such a long time ago.

Mr. Lott, holding his briefcase on his lap, and sitting next to an elderly lady on one of the benches near Gate 7, noticed Randy watching him.

So Randy asked, "Are you okay?"

Mr. Lott just nodded, not wishing to draw attention from the other debaters. But Maria recognized the situation for what it was and said quietly to Randy, "He doesn't look too good."

Randy battled his inclination to remain aloof and went with his desire to be nice to Maria. "He's exhausted. We all are. But you're sweet for being concerned."

"Well, you know, he's sick."

"Shhh!" Randy whispered, although no one had been paying enough attention to them to hear their comments about Mr. Lott's health. "He'll be all right. He promised to see a doctor and begin his treatments as soon as he gets home. It's quite curable."

Not a bit of authenticity echoed in Randy's voice. Faced with the mounting perils of Mr. Lott, Maria, and Kennedy, his life had plunged into an abyss of hopelessness. He wanted only to hear some good news. But it appeared this would not be the case, either: The loudspeaker sent a message throughout the airport terminal that their flight to Los Angeles would be delayed for two hours.

—CHAPTER 29—

In a small office in a large building in the heart of New Orleans, Ricardo spoke with The Boss. They both smoked as though each puff would be their last. They began to build a mound of tobacco waste in several ashtrays, as they considered what had already transpired, and what still needed to be done to complete their mission safely and securely.

They spoke in a deserted building, while the rest of the world glued their mournful eyes on the funeral of the President Ricardo and The Boss had persuaded others to kill.

As Ricardo snuffed out his cigarette, he leaned back in his padded chair at the desk of a man who would want him dead, if he somehow screwed up his assignment.

"The cigars are definitely better," he told The Boss. "But sometimes I need a change."

The Boss kept his cigarette lit. "We all do."

The Boss possessed no sense of humor. He was known for his brazenness. The seriousness and complexity of their situation had only magnified his intensity and augmented his desire to begin closure to this major enterprise, the murder of a President.

Ricardo continued, swerving his thoughts from the previous topic. "Ruby served us well. You were right to have a man in Dallas of his fortitude."

The Boss scowled. "But now we have to be careful about what he says. Every bone in my body says that we can trust him, but we need only one screw-up to poison the operation."

"There will be a trial." Ricardo warned.

"And Jack Ruby will know what to say. We're hiring the best defense attorney in the country, a lawyer by the name of Melvin Bellae. Jack will feed Bellae the bait, and Bellae will take it. Good story: hated to see Kennedy's murderer alive, figured he could spare Jackie and the family the pain of watching—even testifying —at the President's murderer's trial. All special stuff—all based on sadness and tragedy. And all, of course, a bunch of bullshit."

"But it will work." Ricardo nodded.

" Hidell wasn't supposed to be caught."

"No, he was not. One of my operatives called me yesterday. He found out about Craig. He was very sad about that. And scared."

"Then we need to eliminate that asshole, too. Can't trust him either."

Ricardo laughed. "He was already on the list."

"And what about Howard?" The Boss leaned forward. "Is he on your list?"

"I knew you would ask about that," Ricardo sighed. "The CIA does not have infallibility in their operations skill, or in reliability of character. If you must know, we believe it was Howard who fired the fatal bullet from atop the knoll: the one that hit Kennedy in the temple. Hidell hit Connally—an accident. Our man in the Records Building got the President first—in the back. So this leads me to the conclusion that Kennedy would still be alive if not for Howard. But it's more than that. He can still be used for other operations in and out of the Cuban mainland. I like his courage, and I like his style. I also like his politics."

The Boss twisted uncomfortably in his seat. "Strength comes in numbers: the fewer, the better."

"Then it would be better if we were all dead."

For the first time the hint of a smile showed on The Boss's face. "Everyone except for me."

"Only you…with all that money."

"Ah! The money!"

"For Hidell politics played a big part. Such an idiot! He will be the only shooter: a lone assassin—a miserable twenty-three year-old, pro-Castro psycho who wished to have his worthless, little name go down in the history books."

"But we'll need witnesses," The Boss said. "And some witnesses will need to be discredited…or eliminated."

"Already this has happened—no?" Ricardo grinned.

"We knew that by setting up Hidell he would take the rap for all of it. But he shouldn't have been caught. If that cop hadn't stopped him, he would've eluded escape. And we would still have our patsy, but one without lawyers and courtrooms."

"And he knew it!" Ricardo chuckled. "You saw him on television: 'I'm just a patsy!'"

Both men laughed. Ricardo, though, laughed a lot harder than The Boss.

The Boss said, "When there is an investigation—and you can be sure there will be an investigation like no other in history— there have to be many theories. If all theories seem to have equal credibility, they'll all be dismissed with an equal amount of deference. Who do you believe? I mean, they all sound so good— or so terrible. You see what I'm saying? When men begin to talk— and they will talk—you can be sure each time their honesty will come into question. Only those who were actually there will have the details to expound and explain. And by that time, they'll be dead, too."

"Howard?"

The Boss nodded, but his nod was not an affirmation. "I'll leave that up to you."

Ricardo appreciated The Boss's candor. And he respected his toughness. It was amazing how they got along so tensely, yet could sit across a table from one another, discussing one of the most astonishing, impacting events of the Twentieth Century thus far.

An episode for history *they* had designed.

Just like a couple of old school chums chewing the fat at a class reunion, they went on about their families, their foibles, and their futures. Being dead or in prison in the next ten years did not lie in their plans, and they would do everything in their power to make certain two decades from now they would be alive: two men, polar opposites, playfully reminiscing with each other about November 22, 1963.

****

Randy ached.

Randy ached for the slain President he had adored. He ached for his former, naive relationship with Maria Barquin. He ached for some good news about Mr. Lott's grave health condition.

Mr. Lott took off from his teaching job on Wednesday in order to visit his doctor and make arrangements for some long overdo blood transfusions.

The excitement over returning to school offered Randy a semblance of routine, gave him some relief, and for the first time in a while, brought contentment. He still could not sleep soundly. He still had very little appetite. But he focused on getting back to his studies and beginning preparation for the next debate tournament, an invitational over Thanksgiving weekend, at UCLA. He also planned to attend his karate classes on Wednesday night. More normality.

When he called Carmen, he figured he could delay seeing her for a few days. Exhaustion poured through his system. And his heart still yearned for Maria, although he would never admit this to anyone else. Still in the role of her boyfriend, his seeing Carmen meant taxing his patience, and that first required some rest.

Randy's courage quotient had been overtaxed already.

She was still energized by their last telephone conversation when Randy called from Dallas, and she thought he still loved her and missed her. So she decided she would visit him. This way he could not ward her off. She didn't ask him to leave his house. He had been resting all day. Certainly he had no viable excuse for refusing to let her come over with his favorite cookies.

"They have walnuts in them," Carmen smiled, as he opened the bag of chocolate cookies. A fresh aroma filled Randy's bedroom, and again, if only momentarily, he appreciated Carmen Pedro's presence in his life.

"Thank you," he said, realizing his voice sounded smarter and healthier than it had for days.

Carmen wanted to kiss him as he poked through the bag of cookies. He put one in his mouth and began to chew. Leaning over, she did deposit a kiss on his cheek and said, "Welcome home, tough guy," with authentic sweetness.

Randy, distracted by the cookies, hardly noticed the kiss

Carmen had just planted on him.

"I miss you, Randy."

Setting the bag aside, he said, "I missed being home. Those few days were like living out a nightmare."

Carmen hesitated. She didn't want to mire herself in an *analytical* Randall Whitman. She liked Randy least when he over-analyzed people or events and was into one of his debater modes. She adored him when he acted passive, hurt, almost like a puppy craving a good neck scratching. When she dominated, acting as her stronger self, she felt more confidence around Randy and found him to be much more appealing.

"Well, you are home now," she assured him, "and hopefully you can put all that behind you."

Even though Randy knew she would eventually utter something shallow—and, perhaps, inappropriate—he hadn't yet geared himself up to deal with her callous side. Only with openness could he handle Carmen, her spooky cousin, his own parents, his sister, his teachers, his friends—and anybody else who occasionally stuck under his craw, whether they meant to end up there or not.

"What does that mean?" he inquired with restraint. "'Put all that behind you.'"

"Well, it means, you had such an awful time with your debater friends—and it wasn't your fault. Now that you're home, you can forget about all the bad stuff that's happened."

"Can *you* forget about the assassination?"

"I can. I mean, I still think about it every now and then, but it doesn't possess me, Randy."

With her last comment, she slipped into a thick accent reflecting her Puerto Rican roots, settling into an irritating, sassy Carmen.

He said, "You weren't in Dallas."

"I know."

"In Dealey Plaza."

"What's that?"

"Dealey Plaza is where President Kennedy got killed!" he practically shouted at her.

"Of course, I wasn't there, Randy. Is that going to be it from now on? Every time you get sad or do not get your way, you are going to cry, 'I saw President Kennedy get shot! Boohoo!'"

Randy preferred to ignore her taunt. "I didn't see Kennedy get shot," he said tautly. "I saw the person who shot him."

"You saw the person who shot him?" Carmen sounded incredulous.

"Yes."

"Who? That guy who got shot, too—that guy on T.V.?"

"No," Randy replied, now eerily calm, "not that man. I saw the man who shot him from the grassy hill. There were two men there."

"What grassy hill?" Carmen began to feel stupid.

Randy didn't have the patience to explain. He wanted Carmen to know everything *already*. And even if she didn't know, she should just understand anyway. He didn't want the old Carmen. He couldn't deal with her right now.

"Carmen, I was there, and I saw the men who shot the President—maybe not all of them, but I saw two of them. And the men I saw weren't on T.V—they shot a rifle from a place nobody's talking about."

Carmen obligated herself to a defensive posture. "So why didn't you just tell the police?"

"I've tried. Nobody wants to talk with me."

"That's impossible, Randy. If you saw the men who did it, they will talk to you."

"Why don't you just call them up now and tell them that!" Randy barked sarcastically.

"You have to be aggressive, *hombre*!"

" I've tried. They won't speak with me."

"But they will."

"I suppose—maybe," he relented, his shoulders sagging.

"You are not aggressive enough," she reiterated, playing with a strand of curly hair that hung over her left eye.

How he wished he had not been so polite in the past and had actually let her know how much that playing with her hair thing annoyed him!

"Did you see these men before they shot their guns?" she asked.

"Yes, just before. One of them—one of them had a rifle and was about to shoot."

"And you just stood there? And you didn't do anything or say anything?

Randy grimaced as though she had hit him below the belt.

"You know, in my culture," she went on slowly, about to drop a bomb on herself. "If a man is what he says he is, if a man is right, he does what he has to do. And he keeps trying until he no longer needs to try, because he has succeeded. That's a Puerto Rican man! Do you think if a Puerto Rican man saw the person who killed Kennedy, he would not go to the proper authorities and *demand* to be heard? He would stand on a rooftop and shout, if he had to! He would do whatever he must do to be honorable."

What a crock! Randy thought to himself. He said, "Maybe you haven't noticed, but I'm not in Puerto Rican culture, Carmen. The Dallas Police Department is not in Puerto Rico; neither is the FBI! I mean, it's not enough to tell you that I've already done what I can do to be heard by the police? Now I have to remind you that I'm not of Puerto Rican culture? I'm an American, for God's sake, Carmen!"

Again, fiddling with her hair: "Well, Randall, I am an American, too. But after we get married and move to Puerto Rico, you will have the opportunity to pick up some culture that will actually turn you into a man."

"I'm not going to Puerto Rico," Randy replied through his teeth. "And every time you mention it, I want to go less and less."

"It is my dream to return to my roots."

"Yes, well, go."

Unashamedly, she looked hurt. "How can I go without my husband?"

"You can't," Randy admitted. "So I guess you'll have to find a husband who wants to return to your Puerto Rican roots—preferably, a Puerto Rican."

Randy noticed her lip beginning to quiver. She moved off the bed and went in the direction of her warm, beige coat, which she had hung at the foot of Randy's bed. "Maybe you are not the man I thought you were, Randy!" she stormed.

Amazingly, Randy remained calm on the outside. "You may be right, Carmen. But I'm not sure what kind of a man you thought I was. I mean, I'm sixteen—and I don't have roots in Puerto Rico."

"You would do it for your woman!"

"That's interesting," Randy shrugged, "because your father didn't do it for *his* woman. And besides, your roots aren't in Puerto Rico. They're here in California. Your whole family is here in California. Who do you have in Puerto Rico? I mean, Carmen, that's just weird!"

Now holding her coat, Carmen took a deep breath. "Dallas changed you. I could hear it in your voice the first time you called me from there. And it took you days to call me, so I think Dallas changed you, Randy."

"Maybe. Then again, why should it have changed me in the slightest? Because I saw the President of the United States get his head blown off? *That* meaningless, little event?"

"No, Randy. It is not that—oh, maybe a little of that—"

He didn't want to hear her anymore.

But she went on. "It is Maria—what's her name? You spent three days with Maria. You probably did things there you would not dare to do here."

A big part of Randy wished Carmen was right about that. But, of course, she was wrong, and Randy fumed that she had accused *him*! Or did it anger him that her insinuation about a tryst with Maria was about something that had not panned out?

Despite everything, he managed serenity in his voice. "Maria and I hardly talked. There was no debate tournament, remember? We had very little opportunity to speak with one another."

"Yeah, Randy. I'm not talking about *debate partners*."

"That's what *I'm* talking about, Carmen!" Randy was suddenly feeling foolish about his lingering, needless explanations. "We hardly spoke with each other."

And then Randy added words he wished he could have taken back, although he knew he spoke the truth, a truth that cut through his heart like a butter knife slowly struggling to slice up a porterhouse steak: "Besides, she's not interested in me. She likes another boy on the debate team."

"Yes? Who is that?"

"His name's Tommy Wright."

Carmen had heard of Tommy from school gossip sessions, and Randy had spoken of Tommy in disparaging words and tones before this. She said, "Too bad, huh?"

"What?"

"Too bad she likes Tommy and not you. He is a debater, too, *and* very handsome and athletic."

Randy grimaced, could not speak.

"Look, Randy," Carmen said, now putting on her coat. "You need to be honest with me. I don't want a boyfriend who doesn't love me, too. I deserve better than that. There are lots of boys who think I'm swell—who would like to go steady with me—and I can pretty much have my pick."

She then squinted in concentration, as though she had an epiphany. "Come to think of it, I don't know why I picked *you*."

"Maybe because I'm easily manipulated," Randy retorted caustically. He realized this wasn't very far from the truth.

"If you wish to go steady with Maria, you can," Carmen continued, ignoring Randy's quip. "I'm freeing you to do what you want. Maybe I should date only Puerto Rican boys. I know that's what my parents would like."

Randy suddenly felt very alone. He'd always had Carmen— her pushiness and clinginess aside—to rely on, to count on, and to obliterate his loneliness. Now he suddenly had no one. "I'm not dumping you, Carmen," he said less emphatically than he wanted to sound.

"No, but maybe I'm dumping you. I need to think about this. While you were gone, I couldn't stand the thought of being without you. Now that you're back—the way you are acting all soft and girlie about Kennedy—I'm not so sure I want to put up with you anymore."

Randy sizzled in the irony: *she put up with him*? The tables abruptly had been turned. He found himself suddenly regretting his behavior. He detected a sense of panic inside him and thought about begging her to reconsider. But groveling was not his style; it never would be his style. Considering all that happened to him lately, he didn't care what went down now. He only felt desolation and abandonment: by Maria, by the police—and now by *Carmen*. He had always thought Carmen would ax him someday, especially when he refused to marry her and go to Puerto Rico to live. But he didn't think she would kick him out of her life *now*.

"Why don't you just go home now, Carmen," he politely commanded. "I'll be all right. I want to be alone with my thoughts anyway."

As his eyes filled, he saw a hint of moisture in Carmen's eyes, too. Randy Whitman had been taught by his father to save his tears for times that truly mattered—and, considering the intense emotion and morose confusion building up inside him, he silently prognosticated that his huge cry would be coming very soon.

—CHAPTER 30—

The dumbest thing anyone at school said to Randy Whitman came from a short, corpulent boy named Eddie Evans.

While most of his schoolmates quietly respected Randy's privacy—and that of the other debaters trapped in Dallas—a few students at Long Beach High School were curious enough to ask questions: A cute blond by the name of Susie McCormick asked Randy how close he had been to Kennedy when the shots were fired. (Twenty yards or so, Randy guessed. But he didn't admit to Susie McCormick that he'd been running wildly in the opposite direction from the shots as they were being fired.) Another girl, Priscilla Clinton, wondered if Randy could see any of the shooters in the window of the book building. (Being honest, Randy noticed no shooters in the *book building*. As for giving further detail about what he actually saw, he didn't want anyone else to think he had simply flipped his lid.)

Eddie Evans, however, pushed the envelope when he asked Randy if he had been close enough to Kennedy to get "splatted" by some blood. (Randy thought about answering him this way: "Not as close as I'll be to you, Eddie, when I get *splatted* by *your* blood." But he didn't say that. Randy merely shook his head, took a deep breath, and moved away from the ill-mannered Eddie Evans.)

****

On Friday, November 29, exactly one week after the assassination, sixteen debaters (eight debate teams) from Long Beach traveled to the University of California at Los Angeles for the UCLA Autumn Debate Classic.

After observing that they had been scheduled first to debate a local team, two boys from West Covina, Maria and Randy relaxed. They didn't discuss any issues, strategize, or do any last minute preparation for that debate.

Carrying their heavily packed brief cases to their assigned classroom proved to be more exhausting than either of them had calculated. Since they hadn't yet debated in a tournament this year, they were out of shape. And it now showed.

In addition to the trauma of the previous week, both Maria and Randy worried about Mr. Lott. He had begun his transfusions on Wednesday, but still insisted on attending the debate tournament Friday morning. For reasons of his own, Mr. Lott had elected to keep his illness a secret from all but Randy and Maria, strongly imploring them to "win one for The Gipper," even though no one had ever referred to Mr. Lott as "The Gipper" before.

Disaster struck early.

Unable to unglue her lips, Maria delivered a first affirmative speech dotted with *ums* and *uhs*, and she blanked out a few seconds during West Covina's first cross-examination period. Unable to quickly answer a question by quantifying the number of people on a new welfare program called Aid to Families With Dependent Children, she told her questioning adversary that her partner (Randy) would present those statistics in his next speech. She did, however, already know that they had not been able to find this particular statistic during their research.

Randy cringed at his seat. As Maria sat down after the cross-examination period, the judge overheard Randy, in a loud whisper, admonishing Maria. A fundamental sin in high school debate, and a sure sign of amateurism, was chewing out a partner or somehow signaling to a judge that a partner had made a mistake. Randy's clumsy behavior, along with his flustered inability to deliver the promised statistics—with Maria's growing nervousness due to her partner's surprising intimidation—prompted the judge to vote for West Covina High School as the winner of round one.

Since each debate team would compete in six preliminary rounds, only one loss was not enough to eliminate them from the competition. But even without definite knowledge of their judge voting against them (competitors did not receive their results until much later), Randy and Maria were livid with each other.

Sitting outside a row of classrooms that housed the headquarters of the tournament, Mr. Lott was holding a discussion with another one of his teams. But he altered his attention as Maria and Randy rushed toward him, each projecting an equal amount of anger and frustration.

"Mr. Lott," Randy fumed, "you won't believe what Maria did!"

"What *I* did?" Maria blurted, short of breath. "How about what *you* did!"

"*I* didn't promise the other team information that I clearly knew we did not have! God—that is such a freshman mistake!"

"I am not a freshman, Randall!"

"You might as well be!"

Bracing himself and struggling for balm, Mr. Lott turned to Randy. "Quietly, Randy—because people are watching—tell me what happened."

Maria tapped her foot with anger and impatience. But as Randy spoke to Mr. Lott, she reluctantly noticed that he really did look impressive in his black, lightly pinstriped suit and a thin, black and white tie.

"Okay," Randy said, barely able to contain himself, wondering why he felt so compelled to use a hatchet on his new debate partner. In the scheme of things, she had made fewer mistakes in the debate round than he had. "It's like this, Mr. Lott: We've been having a hard time gathering statistics on the total numbers of people on certain welfare programs, because they've been fluctuating so much recently—*and* the last census in 1960 didn't bother to count them all. I knew that; the other team knew that. *And Maria knew that.* Still, when the guy asked her for the total number of men, women, and children on AFDC, she said that *I* would present that in my next speech! Of course, I just ignored it, and during cross-x the guy from West Covina nailed me—made us look like we were incompetent or lying. Everybody knows you aren't supposed to guarantee evidence for the next speech! Jeez!"

Mr. Lott had waited patiently. "Are you done?"

"Yeah."

"What?"

"Yes, Mr. Lott."

"You're sure?"

"Yes, I'm sure."

Randy breathed heavily as he finished his dissertation. By this time a couple of others, including Tommy Wright, had gathered around their coach. Maria stood silently, as Mr. Lott cued her with a nod of his head.

Maria failed to take off with a head of steam. She calmly explained the situation as she saw it: "I shouldn't have promised evidence in Randy's speech. That was a mistake. I was nervous. This was our first debate in competition. It was the first round. I gave a terrible first affirmative. I could barely talk. So I blew it. But Randy *yelled* at me in front of the judge and the other team the minute I sat down. It was so embarrassing."

"Is that true?" Mr. Lott asked Randy. "You yelled at her?"

"Well, if a loud whisper can be interpreted as a yell, then, yes, I yelled." Randy, now more subdued, lowered his head.

Ira and Margie moved into the circle, both eager to share their first round with their coach. But Mr. Lott needed to quell the uprising on his number one team who, by all accounts of the debate, had begun the tournament by (unofficially) losing to a mediocre team from West Covina.

The rest of the weekend went without much fanfare. Despite the largeness of their entry, Long Beach High School placed only one team in the elimination rounds. Ira and Margie compiled Long Beach's best record (5-1, before their elimination loss to Oklahoma City). No other Pilot team went better than 4-2. Struggling along like an old clunker automobile, Randy and Maria finished with three wins and three losses, finally edging out a couple of terrible debaters from Pasadena High School in the sixth and final round of the UCLA Fall Debate Classic.

Randy and Maria had barely spoken with each other between rounds of the tournament. But afterwards they didn't speak with each other at all. Maria went home in a car driven by Tommy Wright's mother, and Randy heard they were stopping for pizza. Images of any possible joy experienced by the group in Mrs.

Wright's car, along with the despondency of his own group (in Mr. Lott's car), drove Randy to the brink of irreversible depression. Or so he thought. Conflicts and challenges and self-doubts surged inside of him.

Randy's mother and father greeted him as soon as he walked in the front door. Their faces were tired—and grim. Randy dejectedly asked himself what more bad news could possibly be pushed his way. His father then said, "The FBI called. They want to talk to you."

All at once: fear, excitement…and relief.

"When?" Randy wanted to know.

"Monday morning."

"They're going to call?"

"No, they're sending someone here."

"Good," Randy sighed, and even though the interview had not yet occurred, the news immediately pulled a huge load off his shoulders.

"The man said they're talking to witnesses," Mrs. Whitman told her son. "They're getting to you early, because you called *them*."

"It's not so early. They should have talked to me in Dallas," Randy grumbled, throwing his two briefcases by a leather couch in the corner of the living room. "It would have saved them a trip."

"I don't think they care about that," Samuel said. "The man who called said that Sunday messed things up for them. Oswald's killing was a huge distraction. It probably took them this long to begin unscrambling things."

Randy knew this to be the case, and he merely sighed.

"I don't know if you've been following recent events, Randy," Samuel said, moving closer to his son. He wanted to hug him but did not. "Yesterday—Friday—President Johnson named a commission to investigate the assassination. The Chief Justice of the Supreme Court is the leader of the commission."

Randy knew a little about the Chief Justice. His name was Earl Warren. He was an extremely progressive judge (although a Republican), who had drawn criticism in recent years for his outspokenness—and his liberal positions. The Court had also taken controversial stances on issues revolving around pornography, free speech, and criminal investigation procedures. Many people argued that this liberal Supreme Court favored the perpetrators. And in the cases they ruled on, the true victims wound up the losers.

But Randy liked Earl Warren. And his immediate assessment was that they will get to the bottom of this. They will determine who assassinated President Kennedy and why. They had already planned to send an FBI investigator to speak with him. From this decision alone, it was clear that they finally knew what they were doing.

—CHAPTER 31—

In 1947 Jack Rubenstein and his brothers changed their name to Ruby. Already vested in several business escapades, they did not want to risk losing money because people identified them as Jews.

Jack Ruby was fifty-two years old when he murdered Lee Harvey Oswald at the Dallas City Jail.

A nightclub owner, Ruby knew several Dallas policemen by name. And they also knew him by name. He would take the police sandwiches, cookies, and offer to help them locate people they were investigating. The police took Ruby seriously, especially since he had been kind enough to let them into his strip club, The Carousel, free of charge on numerous occasions. He even set up policemen on dates with his most popular employees. Ruby treated his girls well, and although he had not married or produced any children of his own, several of his employees looked up to Jack as a father figure.

Ruby acquainted himself—and had a fleeting relationship—with fellow restaurateurs, Sam Giacani and Joseph Campisi, both suspected members of the Italian Mafia. Joseph Civello, however, headed Mafia operations in Dallas, and Ruby also had met with him on several occasions. Ruby wrapped up his depth and breath as a *man* in his associations, his contacts, and his connections—his ability to know people who were *somebody.*

FBI officer Alger Polk sat with Jack Ruby for dozens of hours during the week of Monday, November 25. While scores of others from the Secret Service, the Dallas Police Department, and other members of the Federal Bureau of Investigation came and went, Polk glued himself to Ruby like the other half of Siamese twins. He believed Ruby held the key to the mystery behind the assassination of President Kennedy.

Jack Ruby's pudgy cheeks, punctuated by beady brown eyes,

stayed with Alger Polk when he went home to his wife. Even as he made love to her, images of Jack Ruby, his gray business hat and the crackling of a snubbed-nose Colt Cobra 38 being fired into the body of Lee Harvey Oswald, stole from him his peace of mind and robbed his beautiful wife of the sexual attention she deserved from her husband.

"Why did you do it, Jack?" Polk wanted to know for the umpteenth time.

Ruby, growing accustomed to the same questions from this man—and other men not nearly as cordial—relaxed into the wooden interrogation chair at the Dallas County Jail. In due time he would be flown to Washington D.C. But the city of Dallas and the state of Texas had an investigation of their own to conduct, so Ruby replied, "I couldn't stand the little creep. I wanted him dead."

"Why?"

And then Ruby, as though on cue, dropped a few tears. "He killed my President. He didn't deserve to live anymore."

"Is that it?"

"And," Jack shrugged, "if Oswald went to trial, Mrs. Kennedy would have to testify. I didn't want to see that. I wanted to spare her that."

"Just exactly when did you make the decision to kill him?"

"The moment I did it. It was impulsive."

"But you brought a gun into the basement of the jail."

"I always carried a gun. I had a gun the night of the press conference, too. I obviously didn't use it then. I could have, but I didn't."

"So you just shot him—like that?"

"Just like that, Polk."

"But—"

"I saw him walking towards me, and my instinct was to use the gun. I didn't think about it. I just did it."

Polk, a physically imposing man with blond hair and blue eyes and crew cut hair, had already been down this road several times with Jack Ruby. Only thirty-seven but already a seasoned veteran of interrogating mass murderers, kidnappers, and serial killers, Polk knew that the best way to succeed in this process was to befriend the suspect and earn his trust. He had to press, but not destroy. Once he had destroyed, all the kings' horses and all the kings' men couldn't put the suspect back together again.

He sought another path. "The cops liked you?"

Ruby shrugged again. "Sure. I helped them out."

"You like to help people out."

"I do. That's why I wanted to help Mrs. Kennedy—and all of America, for that matter."

"So you could get into the press conference and even the basement of the city jail during the big transfer without anyone checking your credentials?"

"Sure," Ruby replied proudly. "It was always, 'Hey, Jack!' Or, 'Morning, Jack!' I didn't need to flash a card at anyone. If a cop didn't know me, he just asked another guy. Somebody'd vouch for me."

Polk decided to use new information he had recently received. "Several years ago you were arrested and implicated in the shooting of Teamster's boss Leon Cooke. Is that correct?"

Ruby stiffened. "If you know about that, Polk, you also know that the charges were dropped. I was exonerated."

Polk nodded. "Yes, I do know that."

"And you should also know that I changed my middle name to *Leon* in honor of Leon Cooke. Did you know *that*?"

Polk shook his head. "No, I didn't. I know that your middle name is Leon, but I never put the two together." Recognizing that Ruby had just spat some anger, he tried to mollify him. "There are probably lots of good things about you, too, Jack. I just don't know about them yet."

"Well, that Cooke thing is behind me. Innocent until proven guilty—right, Alger? Isn't that the way it is in this country?"

Polk thought about the irony of Ruby's statement. If he, indeed, cherished the concept of innocent until proven guilty, did he not see that he had disqualified Lee Harvey Oswald from the real blessings of that philosophy? Technically, Oswald had not killed *anyone*, not the President, not the cop who had died in the streets of a Dallas suburb. Technically, Lee Harvey Oswald was innocent.

In a court of law, he had not been convicted of a crime; and because of Jack Ruby, convicting Oswald in a court of law now had become an absolute impossibility.

—CHAPTER 32—

Randy had spent the weekend with Maria Barquin, but only in a capacity as her assigned debate partner. Together, they had lost half of their debates, bickered endlessly, pouted like little children, and gone home from the U.C.L.A. tournament in separate automobiles. Despite this, Randy called Maria at her home late Sunday night. Being contacted by the FBI qualified for the good news category, and he burned to share this good news with somebody. Although Ira Cushman should have been Randy's obvious outlet, he gravitated towards Maria Barquin on Sunday night—for reasons he did not quite understand, and also for reasons that would stay inexplicable for only another five minutes.

As he finished dialing her phone number, a rush of panic assaulted him. What if Maria hadn't arrived home yet? It was almost eleven o'clock at night—before a school day—but what if, after pizza, Maria had decided to go somewhere with only Tommy Wright?

The endless possibilities and the ugliness of it all seared around him like the flames of a forest fire. But when Maria's mother answered the phone in a calm, controlled voice, Randy knew Maria had come home safely.

When Maria spoke, Randy detected distinct irritation in her voice.

She said, "I am almost ready for bed. It's late."

"I'll be quick. Will you talk to me?" Randy asked, trying to sound perky.

"I don't know why. You had the whole weekend to talk to me, but you chose to ignore me instead."

Randy wanted to chastise her. He wanted to remind her that it had been *she* who had run off several times for secretive, covert discussions with Tommy, probably none of which had anything to do with debate strategy or the growing plight of America's poor people. But *he* had called *her*, and fairness implored Randy to remain civil.

"I'm sorry," he apologized. "I guess everything finally got to me. And, yeah, I was really disappointed in how we performed, not to mention the results. The whole squad did crappy—except for Ira and Margie—and we could feel it was happening the whole time. But there didn't seem to be anything we could do about it."

She apparently accepted his apology. "Randy, I am only a sophomore. I've been to a total of ten debate tournaments my whole life. You are the star of the team. You are the man. For whatever reason, Mr. Lott put me with you. There has been so much pressure on me—way too much pressure. And with everything that has been going on—and maybe even without everything that has been going on—the pressure finally got to me. I was bound to make some sophomore mistakes."

She longed to tell him more, but she didn't need to. Randy immediately picked up on the point she fell short of making. "And I'm the veteran—*the man* as you put it. It was my responsibility to help you, to be patient, to remind you not to do certain things, and then be kind to you even after you still did them. It was my responsibility, and I wasn't any of those things. I was an ass. I'm so sorry, Maria."

"Thank you, Randy," she told him with a familiar sweetness in her voice.

He wanted to melt (and he wanted her to deny his contention that he was an ass). His heart popped up about five inches, and he grabbed it with his throat, caressing it there until he managed to again journey through their conversation.

She continued, "Do you think Mr. Lott is going to break us up now?"

He wanted to say, *over my dead body*! Instead, he said, "He might, but Mr. Lott listens to me. He doesn't always do what I ask —despite what some people might think—but at least he's reasonable. I'll talk with him tomorrow."

And then Randy remembered what was on tap for him tomorrow, the reason he had called Maria so late at night in the first place. "Look, Maria. The reason I called…I just wanted to tell you some good news—at least, I *think* it's good news. While we were at the tournament, the FBI called. They told my dad that they want to talk to me. Finally. They want to talk to me, and they're flying out here tomorrow. I mean, they're probably out here by now, because they're coming to my house in the morning."

"Tomorrow?"

"Monday, yeah. So, obviously, I won't be at school tomorrow, and—for some reason—I just thought you should know."

Maria immediately understood why she, "should know." At the moment, though, Randy didn't see it. He wasn't in tune with Maria's perceptions. But Maria got it, and she wanted to keep talking. "Good luck with them, Randy. You will do fine."

"Yeah," Randy laughed nervously. "But it's not really a performance. I just have to get it off my chest."

"Yes, you do. I have known this since it happened. I really have."

"Then you believe me—what I saw there?"

"Now I do," Maria replied evenly. "At the time you were traumatized. You were in shock. I didn't trust your reactions then: your concepts of time or space or even images of what you saw. But now I do, Randy. You have had time to reflect, to calm down. I know you saw what you said, and I think you will be very helpful to the FBI—to our country."

"I'm not nervous, you know; I'm excited."

"You have nothing to be nervous about. You should be proud."

"Well…" Randy started and then paused. He prepared himself to reveal to Maria a fear he had been confronting ever since Dallas. Horrifying Randy, and weighing on his mind since lucidity had returned to him, he dared not discuss these thoughts with anyone else until now.

"Maria, I'm terrified."

"I know."

"I dropped my camera. They probably picked it up. There're all kinds of family stuff on it. And if they can find me, they might do to me what that guy Ruby did to Oswald. Or they might kill my whole family. It won't matter at all whether or not I tell anybody about what I saw. They're still going to *think* I'm telling the authorities about what I saw."

"Randy, nobody would be able to track you," Maria tried to reassure him. "How would they get your name or address or anything personal about you? They only saw you for a split second, right?"

"Yes, except for something that scares the heck out of me..."

He paused. His silence spooked Maria. Randy was never one to spare words or even to think through matters before he spoke up about them. His self-assurance always precluded his having to agonize about what he planned to reveal. His unusual display of quiet ruffled Maria's feathers. He said, "One of the pictures we took was in front of my house. It was a family portrait right at the end of the summer, after we'd come home from the beach."

"Nobody would figure out where that is from, Randy."

"We were standing on the porch, facing the driveway, where my Uncle Bernie took the picture from. There's a good possibility that our street address was photographed. It's right on one of the porch posts."

Maria shuddered. "But they—no one—could figure out what state—let alone what city—the picture was taken."

"Other pictures on the roll of film were taken at Balboa Beach. There are signs all over the place, like the Balboa Ferry sign. If smart people wanted to put two and two together, they could."

"They would really, really have to want to, Randy."

"And," Randy continued with his *as if this weren't enough* voice. "It would not take a genius to find out who that small group of high school kids on Elm Street was—and where they came from. Once I'm tracked to Southern California, if they have the street address, I'm a goner, Maria."

To Maria, Randy's prognostication came off as melodramatic. But she knew he was right about one thing: if the people who now possessed Randy's camera really wanted to track him down, with some effort they could do so. "Randy, it's two weeks later. If these people had wanted you dead, you would be dead by now. They probably figured you didn't have valuable enough information—or it was too late because you already told everyone everything you knew. Either way, you appear to be safe."

"This nagging feeling like someone is going to pop out of the bushes and kill me is a weird thing, Maria. I may have it for the rest of my life. And the rest of my life might not be that long."

Sleepiness began to overtake Randy. Despite his excitement, his physical limitations had conquered him. He went to bed that night in higher spirits than any other night of the past week. Both his belief that he and Maria were on friendly terms once again, and his pending communication with the Federal Bureau of Investigation served to alleviate some of his deepening depression.

Finally exhausted, Randall Walter Whitman, with a look of contentment and a half-smile on his face, dozed off into a deep sleep.

But two hours later, he dreamed that when his father started up his Plymouth Fury the next morning, the car exploded into searing metal fragments, blending his father and the surrounding landscape into indistinguishable, little particles.

—CHAPTER 33—

How he hated cats! He loathed the tenuous, almost sinister way that they slithered about. But his roommate loved cats, so they had begged their landlord to allow them one; they would keep it inside and quiet. It was of the shorthaired variety, entirely black, except for its white-tipped claws.

The cat leaped from his bed and hit the floor with a resounding, authoritative thump. How he hated when his roommate wasn't home at night! More often than not, the undesirable feline jumped on his bed and curled up along side him, not in an endearing way, but in defiance of his need for sanity.

Startled awake by the cat's sudden movements, he opened his eyes wide in the still darkness of the room. The door of the bedroom was cracked slightly open to allow a modicum of light to enter, and it provided the cat an outlet to slide into other rooms of the apartment. Perplexed, but not totally mindful of the cat's unusual behavior, he relaxed his body and thought about turning over and hiding his head in the pillows.

He hadn't been able to sleep very well since the project had been completed; in fact, looking back, insomnia had taunted him well before the project began. He knew if he didn't get some rest, he wouldn't be able to think straight, to keep his mind clear enough to avoid any of dangers that may come his way.

And now the loud crash of something falling to the floor had sent him into an upright position on the bed.

Why, he thought, would the cat knock something—whatever it was—over? The cat knew their apartment well. It had never turned anything over before. But now...

Reclining in his bed in a defenseless, compromising position, he was no match for his assailant. Even if the blonde-haired attacker had not been so large, he probably would have been able to subdue and overpower him anyway.

And the blonde-haired attacker was huge.

Possessing the muscles of a bodybuilder, the attacker had learned long ago how to utilize this greatest asset. He propelled himself forward with a sudden burst of speed that could have come from a talented fullback.

The blonde-haired attacker hurled his body against him on his bed, rolling both of them onto the hardwood floor. He: surprised, taken off-guard in the most painful and horrifying of all compromising circumstances; the blonde-haired attacker: single-minded, calculated, and determined to complete his assignment without an inordinate amount of noise.

He never knew the size of his attacker. He never knew of his attacker's golden blonde hair. He never knew his attacker had an assignment of the highest order, one that could effect the writing of American history.

But here is what he did know: His back had hit the hard floor with a force that pushed air from his lungs and may have bruised his kidneys. A hand the size of a large hockey glove attached to the bottom of his chin and thrust his head back with such power he thought he heard his tendons ripping away from his neck and shoulders.

It happened quickly; Joey didn't stand a chance.

When the steel blade of the knife cut deeply through the flesh of his vulnerable, exposed throat, the darkness that finally came to him was a blessing.

Joey would never know about the cat's retreat from the lamp it had toppled over, or how the feline had leaped through the open window of his apartment. The cat, too, had been terrorized by the blonde-haired attacker. He never liked that cat anyway, so the fact that it had ditched him in a time of his greatest peril would not have been a surprise to Joey.

And had Joey survived this assault, he would have been thrilled that the cat never came home again.

—CHAPTER 34—

The man from the FBI who visited Randy on Monday morning did not fit a stereotype. Fairly small in stature, not tall, and with a slender build, he sported a well-trimmed mustache. His soft brown hair, cut short around his head, profiled neatness and cleanliness. His voice did not sound badgering or intimidating, and he smiled much more than the FBI men in the movies or on that television program about Eliot Ness, called *The FBI*.

Randy's mother offered the agent a Coke, but he declined. Randy also refused a Coke, an uncommon rejection that surprised Mrs. Whitman.

Randy's sister, proclaiming to be terrified of government workers, especially the FBI, left early for school and said she would not return until well after dinnertime. Samuel offered to remain at home in case his son needed him, but Randy thought that to be a bad idea. He needed to represent maturity for the agent's visit—not act like some ditsy kid who nervously depended upon his father to cue his every word and facial expression.

After the preliminary niceties, the FBI man took out a small reel-to-reel tape recorder. Most tape recorders in 1963 were large and bulky, but this one, though similar in style to the enormous, intimidating types, appeared miniature by comparison. When the agent pressed the record button, the reels turned smoothly, almost effortlessly, in an eerie silence. Randy liked the quietness of the machine. Thankfully, he could now ignore the daunting dynamic of being tape-recorded.

"My name is Agent Stephen Balcomb, number TRDSI7368. Today's date is Monday, December 2, 1963. The location: Long Beach, California. The subject's name is Randall Whitman, age sixteen."

Balcomb leaned in, turned up the volume on the recording device, and said, "Speaking with the subject: Last Friday President Johnson ordered an investigation into the murder of President Kennedy. Are you aware of that, son?"

"Yes, sir," Randy replied, a wave of relief traveling through his body. He officially had said something to the FBI! Finally!

"These interviews are being conducted by various law enforcement agencies, including the Secret Service, the Justice Department, and the FBI, and may be used to do assessments by the Commission assigned to investigate the assassination of President Kennedy. Are you aware what that means?"

"Yes," Randy nodded.

"Finally," Balcomb cleared his throat. "Based on information given by you during this process, you could be asked to testify before the Commission headed by the Chief Justice of the United States Supreme Court. Is that clear, son?"

Randy had not seriously considered that possibility, but when the agent mentioned it to him, he instantly, with some trepidation, relished the idea. He bravely nodded again. "Yes, sir. I understand."

"Good," Balcomb responded without facial expression. "What's your full name, son?"

"Randall Walter Whitman," Randy replied.

Balcomb then surprised Randy. He pressed the stop button on the recorder. When Randy looked up, he saw an entirely different man than the one who had asked him formal questions with the tape recorder running. Balcomb became, once again, the more amiable chap who had chatted informally with him and his mother upon his arrival.

Balcomb grinned. "Are you kidding me? *Walter Whitman?* When I was in college, I majored in English. I took a whole semester course on the poetry of Walt Whitman. There's never been another American poet who could match Whitman for his empathy, his ability to feel for others. He's my hero. Of course, there's hardly any practical use for somebody with a degree in English, so I got into law enforcement. But I just wanted to let you know that I'm a great fan of your namesake."

Amused, but genuinely flattered, Randy smiled. Not even members of his extended family had ever made similar comments about his name. Most people hadn't the faintest clue about his so-called namesake, or they chalked it up to some weird name given to him by his eccentric parents—and they felt sorry for Randy. He immediately liked Stephen Balcomb. He was glad this particular agent had been assigned to conduct his interview. Being an English major, perhaps Balcomb would be impressed with his debating skills and achievements. Maybe they would relate to each other on that level, too. Randy certainly could use a friend in the FBI!

But when Balcomb again clicked on the recorder, they circled back to the drudgery of their dreary formalities. Balcomb asked, "And what's your address?"

Randy provided his street address, city, and state in a firm, clear voice.

"How old are you?"

"Sixteen."

"Your birth date?"

"December 5, 1947."

Again, the agent flipped off the machine.

"Happy birthday," he smiled.

"Thank you," Randy replied.

"Uh, Thursday?" Balcomb calculated.

"Yes, sir."

"Got any plans?"

"Just want to be alive," Randy replied nonchalantly and saw that Balcomb winced at his wisecrack.

He put the jets back on and continued, "What grade are you in, Randy?"

"I'm in the eleventh grade."

"How are your grades in school?"

"I get mostly A's."

"Are you an athlete?"

"Yes, sir, I'm enrolled in karate. No school sports, though. I don't have time for those. I'm actively involved in the school's debate program."

"You compete in debate?"

"Yes."

"Okay, Randy, you were in Dallas, Texas, on November 22, 1963. Correct?"

"Yes."

"And what brought you to Dallas?"

"I was there to participate in a debate tournament: the Tournament of Champions at Southern Methodist University. It was supposed to start late Friday afternoon and continue through until Sunday night. If we were lucky—doing well—we would be debating in the elimination rounds throughout the day Sunday."

"Who's the *we*?"

"The *we*? Oh, that's our debate squad. I was there with our debate squad, which consisted of six debaters, including me, and our debate coach Richard Lott."

"So, counting everybody, seven of you made the trip to Dallas for the debate tournament? Seven of you from Long Beach High School?"

"Yes, sir."

Balcomb kept the questions coming without hesitation. This would be the style of this interrogation; he was good at it. "Were all seven of you in Dealey Plaza on November 22?"

Randy nodded. Balcomb waited for something audible, and when Randy realized the recorder could not pick up his non-verbal affirmation, he added quickly, "Yes, sir—all seven of us were in Dealey Plaza…on November 22."

A sensation of tremendous relief flowed through Randy. Knowing he was about to rehash his personal story for someone in an official capacity, his excitement was palpable Ever since he had awakened from his state of shock on that Friday afternoon, Randy felt most of the time as though his mouth hung open, empty, while his words were trapped forever in his brain.

And without an outlet, they were just rotting there.

"How did you find out about the Presidential motorcade?" Balcomb asked him.

"I heard a commentator on the radio—Thursday."

"On—that's November 21?"

"Yes, sir."

"You were already in Dallas?"

"Yes."

"You were excited about seeing the President?"

"Absolutely. He was my hero." Randy's last few words were tainted with sadness.

"Were the others in your group as excited about seeing the President as you were?"

"Probably not, but they were excited."

"But you were more excited?"

"Yes."

"Exuberant?"

"Uh, huh."

"Off the charts exuberant?"

Randy wondered what that question meant, why Balcomb had pressed it so hard, and even how to measure his answer. But he replied, "Yes, sir."

"How did you get to Dealey Plaza?"

"Mr. Lott rented a station wagon."

"Mr. Lott—your debate teacher?"

"Yes, sir."

"What time did you arrive in the Plaza?"

"We wanted to get there early, because we figured there might not be any room later. The parade route was long, so when we found a spot where hardly anybody was standing, we were totally shocked. But it was the end of the route—Dealey Plaza— just before they would get on the freeway."

Randy didn't realize he had ignored Balcomb's question, so, again, the agent patiently asked, "What time did you arrive at Dealey Plaza?"

"Uh, around 10:30 in the morning."

"So you had a long wait."

"Yes, sir."

"What did those in your group do during the time you were waiting for the President to pass by?"

"Talked. Goofed around. Maybe a couple of the kids were going over debate cases. At the time there was still a tournament scheduled."

"What time were you supposed to be at Southern Methodist?

"Four in the afternoon."

"Okay, Randy, were you all standing on the north side or on the south side of Elm Street?"

Balcomb surmised that Randy had learned his exact location down to the minutia. And he was right: Randy answered without hesitation, "We were on the south side."

"So you were across the street from the red brick building, the schoolbook building?"

"Yes."

"And across the street—across Elm Street—from the grassy knoll?"

The first time Randy heard that exact term used to describe the grassy hill area, he nodded, "Yes, sir."

"During the time you were waiting at this location, did you ever cross Elm Street? Did you ever go to the other side of the street—the north side?"

Randy wallowed in some anxiety for the first time during the interrogation. "Yes, sir, I did."

"Why did you decide to cross the street?"

It helped to make Randy relax when he thought of the answer he really *wanted* to give to the agent: *Why did the debater cross the street? To get to the other side*!

But the tape recorder stared him in the face, and he immediately relinquished this lame idea.

Randy answered, "I wanted to take some pictures from that angle. My best friend said he would snap pictures from—uh, the south side—this side, and he thought I should cross the street, go up the grassy hill, and take some pictures there. But we decided to wait until the President arrived. I didn't want to cross the street and stand on the hill by myself or with a bunch of strangers."

But if Randy Whitman *had* crossed the street and gone up the hill just *five minutes earlier*…

At this point Randy wound up, ready to detail his change of mind about crossing Elm Street, his conflict with Tommy Wright, the dare—even though all of those incidents now seemed so irrelevant. Besides, he just wanted to get to the main point of the interview: what he had witnessed on the grassy hill behind the concrete barrier.

Balcomb snuffed the recording device again. "Randy, all your friends who were there will be contacted by the Bureau. Eventually, we'll speak with every individual who was in Dealey Plaza that day. Most of those interviews will be conducted by telephone. Basically, everyone saw and heard the same thing. [Conflicting reports later proved this observation by Balcomb to be laughable.] Reportedly, you contacted the Dallas police twice in order to give them information. That's why we have come here in person. Ostensibly, you have something different to add to the report—something relevant to this investigation."

Balcomb stopped. Had Randy just been asked a question? He didn't know.

Balcomb went on with the formal interview, after putting the tape spools into motion once again.

"What time did you cross Elm Street?"

"Well, I can only estimate the time by corresponding my movements with the arrival of the motorcade. But I would say that I walked across the street around 12:28 P.M."

"Were you carrying anything with you?"

Randy sighed. From the beginning he had dreaded this question. "Yes, sir."

"What?"

"My camera."

"A film camera?"

"Yes."

"Still picture?"

"Yes."

"Color?"

"No, sir. Black and white."

"Do you still have this camera in your possession?"

"No, sir."

"Where is it?"

"I don't know."

Balcomb remembered that law enforcement had confiscated cameras from people in Dealey Plaza, and the Dallas Police had put out requests for movie cameras or still picture film cameras from anyone who had taken photos of the assassination. Randy's confession about his camera suddenly piqued Balcomb's interest.

"You don't know where the camera is now?" he persisted.

"No, sir."

"When did you lose contact with your camera?"

"After I dropped it."

"Do you know where you dropped it?"

"Yes, sir, I dropped it on the grassy hill in Dealey Plaza. Would you like me to explain?"

"Later. We'll pursue that later, Randy. Let's get back to the timeline here. So you crossed the street at approximately 12:28. Could you see any of the motorcade at this point?"

"Yes, sir. I was able to see the lead motorcycle officers. Eventually I saw the first cars—that I later found out were carrying members of the press, Secret Service, and so on."

"Approximately how many other people were on the hill when you arrived?"

"The lower part of the hill?"

Balcomb thought this to be a strange clarification, but he nodded to Randy.

"Well," Randy replied, "maybe a dozen or more. I'm hazy about that. I don't know about that." He felt himself getting flustered. "If you're talking about the people around me when I first crossed the street—not that many. Which was surprising, because it was the President and all—and there were so many people downtown..." And then he added some bitter irony, "We were lucky to get such a good spot to see the President."

"So," Balcomb continued, "you get across the street. Are you still holding your camera at this point?"

"Yeah."

"Please respond clearly."

"Yes—yes, sir."

"Did you continue to move up the hill, or did you take a stationary position?

"Since my goal was to take pictures from near the top of the small hill, I moved up the hill to the wooden fence area—with the concrete structure in front of it."

"You moved quickly?"

"Somewhat—yes. The President was about to pass by."

Finally.

Randy held his breath.

For Agent Stephen Balcomb, however, this would be just another question. Balcomb asked, "When you finally arrived at the spot where you planned to take pictures, did you observe anything strange or out of the ordinary?"

"I think it was strange and out of the ordinary, yes."

"What did you see, Randy?"

"I saw two men behind the concrete barrier."

"Two men? Behind the fence at the top of the hill?"

"No, sir, not behind the fence. The fence is further back. Behind the fence are railroad tracks. In front of the brown fence is a monument, and from that monument, extends a low, concrete barrier. I went behind that barrier—or just slightly to its right side."

"And you saw two men." Balcomb repeated Randy's statement.

"Yes."

"Were they standing?"

"No, sir. One was crouching, and the other one was on his knees."

"From what you observed, what were they doing?"

"They were getting ready to assassinate the President."

In a flash, Balcomb turned off the recorder. "Randy, just answer the questions I ask you. So far, you've been doing terrific at this—better than most people three times your age. But you shouldn't jump to conclusions, unless you're asked to jump to conclusions. Okay?"

But Randy's adrenalin was pumping so fast, he barely heard Balcomb's rather polite admonition. He nodded and slurred, "Yeah."

"Good," Balcomb tried to force a smile. He, too, was being drawn into the drama of Randy's recounting. He pushed the record button again and settled into his objective questioner mode. "Again, Randy, what were these men doing?"

"One of them, the one crouching, was holding a rifle—I got the impression at that time...I think I saw him after he had just finished..."

Randy gulped. He wanted to follow Balcomb's rules. "The man was holding a rifle. I saw him with a rifle. The other man was kneeling by a suitcase type of garment or something like that. I got the distinct impression he was doing lookout—you know, making sure nobody was around."

"Do you know what kind of a rifle he was holding?"

"Absolutely not."

"Do you think either, or both, of the men had seen you approaching?"

"Maybe—yes. But I came across the street pretty fast, so a cop wouldn't stop me—and I continued up the hill. It's not too far up that hill. It's a very small area of land, and I sort of looped over toward them from what would have been...their right side."

"Go on."

"Well, I, uh, still think I took them by surprise, because by the time they saw me, I was pretty much already there."

"How were these men dressed?"

"Like bums. Like hobos. Street people."

Balcomb experienced a sensation of being kicked in his testicles. He remembered sketchy references to bums, hobos, who were interviewed by the Dallas Police. But they had no identification or addresses. Apparently, they had been living in empty boxcars stationed on the tracks behind the Texas School Book Depository and atop the grassy knoll.

Had this teenager been inspired, prompted by vague reports about hobos he may have seen on television? Balcomb wondered.

"It's strange," Randy reflected. "I remember being startled by them—especially seeing the rifle and all—and I also remember noticing that these guys had unshaven faces and sloppy hats. But their jackets were too nice for them to be real bums. It just looked very weird."

Balcomb vaguely remembered hearing the same comments from somewhere else. He would have to check that aspect out.

He asked Randy, "Did these men say anything to you?"

"Yes, sir, one of them did."

"What did he say?"

"One of them said, 'Get the hell outta here!' Or 'Where the hell did *you* come from!' Or something like that."

"Which one said that? The guy crouching with the rifle, or the one kneeling on the grass?"

"I don't recall, sir."

"At that moment, how did you respond?"

"I think I dropped my camera and ran."

"You *think* you dropped your camera?"

"I'm not sure. I know I didn't have my camera with me later, but I had it when I walked up the hill."

"Did you say anything to these men?"

"No."

"Did you scream?"

"Nope."

"What?"

"*No.*"

"Which way did you run: further up the hill, down the hill, or to either side?"

Verbal paralysis had set in. Randy opened his mouth to answer but could not speak.

But then, for the very first time since the event had occurred, his brain discovered some clarity. The images were no longer hazy, confusing, and meshed together with other scenes from Randy's young life. His mind now focused so vividly, he began to relive those precise moments on November 22, 1963.

Balcomb saw Randy suddenly struggling to speak; he shut off the recorder. "Want to take a break?"

Randy shook his head and managed to utter, "No."

"Because this must be difficult."

"This part, yeah."

"We can take a break," Balcomb urged politely.

But Randy shook his head. He fought to control his body spasms. "No, please. I want to get it out. I want to get it over with. Please."

"You want some water?"

"Mr. Balcomb, I've been waiting for over ten days to talk to you. Please. I need to get it out."

"I'm listening, Randy. That's why I'm here."

"Yeah,, but I've got to convince me, too."

"Of what?"

"That I'm not crazy. That this all actually happened. Because I gotta' say, as I sit here talking to you, I'm struggling to believe my own story. But I *know* it happened. I do."

Balcomb waited, examining his subject. To Balcomb, Randy Whitman's words rang with sincerity and a mature veracity. But what he would say next would cloud Balcomb's belief that Randy accounted with alacrity his experiences on that fateful day last November.

"Okay, Randy," Balcomb submitted and pushed the gray record button for the umpteenth time. "Again, Randy: You said that you ran. In which direction did you run?"

"I ran to my right, which would be west. I wanted to get off the grass."

"Looking back, do you have an idea why you chose to go in that direction?"

Randy shook his head. "No, sir. I just wanted to get away from them, and I guess my momentum must have pulled me that way."

"That was toward the overpass, correct?"

"Yes, sir. In retrospect, perhaps I mistakenly thought that overpass would give me some shelter from them—or something. I don't know."

"Do you have any idea why you didn't run back *down* the hill?"

Randy knew that this particular question would yank his heart from his body and ring it out, like when his mother had readied a soaking washcloth for drying on the clothesline. But his strength prevailed. "Going down the hill would have been in the direction of the street, and I knew the motorcade was coming. My feeble brain—at that instant—told me…told me that…it would be wrong to disrupt the motorcade. Maybe I figured if I ran into the street, a policeman or a Secret Serviceman would shoot me. And I wasn't sure…so like a wild, insane animal, I just ran blind—to the right—away from the men behind the concrete barrier. Frankly, Mr. Balcomb, that's the best I can do. I'll never know why I did what I did—why I ran like that."

"Did you have any specific concerns at that moment?"

What a stupid question! Randy thought.

But he answered, "I guess I might have been worried they would shoot me in the back or chase after me. Of course, now that I think about it, that wasn't rational. They weren't going to chase me or shoot me."

"You ran. Then what happened?"

"I heard the shots."

"As you were running?"

"Yes."

"Immediately?"

"Yes—almost."

"Did they sound like they were shooting at you?"

"No, sir. They seemed far away—sort of like someone had set off some firecrackers behind me in the distance."

"In the distance. But not right behind you?"

"No."

"So you didn't think someone was shooting at you?"

"No…" Randy found himself dazed and a bit confounded.

"What's the matter, Randy?"

"Well, sir, right now, I'm not sure whether or not I heard those firecracker sounds before I fell—or after I fell."

"You fell?"

"Well, sir, I dove—fell to the ground, flat on my face."

Randy checked to see if Balcomb was laughing at him, but the FBI agent remained ever serious.

"Why does this confuse you now? Had you been sure of the sequence of events before now?"

"I thought I was sure. But now that I'm talking to you—and I want to get this just right—I remember hearing two firecracker pops that *did* sound like they went off right behind me, directly behind me. For the last one—the last pop—I think I was already lying on the grass."

"So let's get this straight, Randy. You see these men who look like hobos. One of them says something like, 'Where the hell did you come from?' And then you run to your right. You hear popping sounds, like firecrackers. They don't make you think the men are shooting at you, because they seem too far away. You fall on your face. While you are lying there, you hear another popping noise. This time, it scares you, because it seems right behind you on the grass. Is that right?"

Amazed by Agent Balcomb's ability to synthesize his reporting on the sequence of events, Randy replied, "All of that is true. What I am saying now is I'm not exactly sure whether or not I heard the first popping sounds before I fell or after I fell to the grass. It would seem logical that I heard them while I was running, because maybe it startled me, and it's what caused me to lose my footing—or duck. I don't know."

"As you were running, did you think somebody was shooting at the President?"

"I don't remember."

"What did you think it was that you heard?"

"Gunshots. I'd just seen a man with a rifle."

"But you didn't think he was shooting at you?'

"No. I don't know. Maybe I did."

"But not at the President?"

"No."

"You're sure of that?"

"No. I don't remember! I swear, Balcomb, I don't remember anything I was thinking about the President then!"

"After that loud popping noise and while you were lying on the ground, what did you hear?" Balcomb asked, leaking some irritation in his voice.

"Screaming. I heard screams, shouts. I heard police sirens immediately—and the sounds of motorcycles whizzing by me."

"This was while you were on the ground?"

"Yes, sir," Randy replied softly.

"How long were you lying face-first on the grass?"

Randy had lost his confidence. The last couple of minutes

had rekindled his experiences, drained him of his emotions, and pulsated his conscience with guilt. "Too long," Randy answered. "I was on the ground too long. It was like being in a nightmare, and you're trying to call out for your mother to come to your room, but nothing comes out of your mouth, because your body is paralyzed by fear. That's what happened to me, Mr. Balcomb. I was literally frozen on the ground in fear. I couldn't move; I couldn't get up."

Growing increasingly dubious about the teenager's recollections, Balcomb knew he had to keep it moving. "Can you estimate how long you were on the ground?"

"No, sir."

"More than two minutes?"

"Maybe."

"More than five minutes?"

"No."

"Randy, as you were lying there on the ground, did you feel any physical pain from the fall?"

"No, sir, which surprised me, because I knew that I'd fallen pretty hard. I went straight down."

"Any bruises or cuts on your body?"

"No."

"Did you—were you aware of what was happening around you?"

"That someone had just shot President Kennedy?"

"Yes, Randy. Did you think that might have happened?"

"At this point...I thought that he'd been shot at. I didn't know if he'd been hit. I knew—yes, I knew that. I was well-aware of that—yes."

Balcomb mentally filed Randy's contradiction: at first Randy said he wasn't sure if the President had been shot; now, he changed his account and said he was well-aware the President had been hit.

Balcomb asked, "When you got up from the grass, what did you first observe?"

Randy closed his eyes to get a mental picture. Images from that part of his experience were tucked away in his brain. "I saw... people—other people—who were still lying on the ground. At first I thought they might have been shot, too. I remember cops running around. Some of them—and other people, too—were racing up the grassy hill toward the embankment. People were in the street. Commotion was all around me—all kinds of commotion. I figured Kennedy had been shot, but I didn't see it. These people had seen it, and they were crying and hugging and mostly hysterical."

"Did you go to a policeman?"

"No."

"Did you try to find someone in authority to tell them what you'd seen?"

"No, sir, I couldn't. I was out of it."

"Where did you go first?"

Randy sighed. They had come to the part of the interrogation he had been most dreading. For not only were faces and events still hazy, but here he would confess his weakness, his cowardice. If he had talked to a policeman and pointed him in the direction of the concrete barrier, the cop would have run up the hill, checked behind the monument, and possibly located a rifle. Maybe he would have gone behind the brown fence and found the bums, the hobos Randy had seen only moments before. Perhaps a cop would have looked in the boxcars and discovered the men cowering there, hiding from their imminent apprehension.

But Randy had slid into shock that afternoon. And the moments after rising from the hill were worse than a blur, his recollections non-existent. Somehow he had found his way across Elm Street again. He had returned to the other members of his debate team. He couldn't remember. He drew a blank whenever he tried to focus on the immediate aftermath of his rising from the grass. In truth, he couldn't remember when he had begun again to process his thoughts—when he first emerged from the shock that had crippled him for several hours. And whenever he attempted to go beyond this stumbling block, this impediment to his memory, his head ached. The throbbing pain presented a deterrent to further attempts for recalling his thwarted memories.

Did it really matter, anyway? After Randy had risen from the ground, the dastardly deed had already been done. His unbridled fear explained his memory loss after that point, and his cowardice until that point. Amazingly, he still managed to recall the specifics of what he had seen and donated valuable information to the investigation. This, after all, was the least he could do. His nagging —perhaps irrational, unreasonable, and illogical—belief that he could have done more to prevent the assassination of President Kennedy probably never would abandon him completely. But at least for now, he had temporarily satisfied his massive yearning to tell all that he knew to someone who had official reasons to care.

After Agent Stephen Balcomb left his home, Randy went to his bedroom, shut the door behind him, and threw himself on his bed. Until he finally fell asleep, he sobbed with an intense, powerful abandonment he had never experienced before.

—CHAPTER 35—

Randy's birthday came and went with the speed of light. His mother baked him his favorite cake, moist chocolate with dark, creamy icing. Ira threw him a small party, inviting over only a few of Randy's friends. Randy planned to go over to Carmen's house after the party.

Carmen called Randy at home to remind him about his birthday celebration at her house. Ever since Carmen had angrily attacked Randy a few nights before, they were not communicating much with each other. Carmen's birthday gesture reassured Randy that she was still his friend. Her overtures seemingly erased any hostility caused by their most recent rift.

Soon after Randy had applied that last dab of Bryl Cream to his wavy brown hair and a final spray of Old Spice to his freshly shaven face, his father cornered him in their living room. About to leave for Ira's, and eventually Carmen's, Randy was already running late.

"Have a good time at Ira's," Mr. Whitman advised.

"Thanks, Dad," Randy replied. But he knew his father had more on his mind.

"Good cake—your birthday cake—your mother made." Mr. Whitman said awkwardly.

"Very good," Randy acknowledged.

"Are you feeling better, son?"

"Yeah, since the FBI, I feel a lot better."

Randy had chosen not to divulge to the family his fears over the lost camera. Worrying them about the possibility of someone coming to their home and blowing them all away did not sit high on his priority list of things he wished to do.

"Randy," Samuel said, now blocking the doorway exit, "we love you very much—your mother and I. You know that."

"I know that."

Just let me outta here!

"And maybe this isn't the time, but you're going to a party tonight, and I know there might be some drinking—"

After all that I've been through, you're worried about me having a beer?

"No way, Dad! It's a *debate* party! None of us drink. We sit around and listen to music! We do the Twist to Chubby Checker! Maybe some of us dance a little after the cute girls get there, but it's a *debate* party for God's sake!"

Randy prayed his father could see the humor in his apprehensions. But Mr. Whitman had not yet shared his greatest trepidation.

"That's the point, Randy," he said softly. "I know you won't do anything with the girls you would regret later. At least, I was always sure of that before. But now, well, it's your birthday…and you know and I know—we all know—you haven't been yourself since, uh…you know what I mean? Sometimes when I see you, Randy, you don't look like the old Randy. You know what I mean?"

Huh?

"Yes, Dad. Don't worry." And then Randy laughed and lied, "I'm not interested in the girls on the debate team—not in that way. And Carmen barely kisses me on the lips, let alone what *you're* thinking!" Again, he sheltered himself with a twitch of nervous laughter.

But Mr. Whitman failed to find the humor. His major concern about Randy had not yet been addressed. "Randy, you're very vulnerable right now. You're obsessing, maybe hallucinating, and I'm worried you're going to look for comfort in all the wrong places."

Randy could have taken this intrusion in one of two ways: on the one hand, he could have been insulted, angered by his father's lack of trust in him and disregard for his usual mature judgment. But on the other hand, he could have been flattered, grateful for his father's outpouring of love and concern for his immediate well-being and, ultimately, his future.

At this moment Randy found himself drawn to the latter; it was safer. Without a word he walked over to his dad and draped his arms around him. He grasped his father in a hug filled with genuine gratitude. He held the older man close, saying nothing, but returning his father's tenderness.

Mr. Whitman, so overcome by the sudden outpouring of his son, decided against discussing with Randy the most disturbing aspect of his concern, the actual reason he had temporarily blocked the door before Randy could pay another visit to the home of Carmen Pedro. That unpleasant business could wait until later.

****

The muffled voice exasperated him.

He had thought Howard was loyal, trustworthy—and now he began to worry about being wrong in his assessment. Still, he needed Howard. Eliminating him offered no tangible benefits.

Howard called him with concerns he should have discarded weeks ago. The unusual rasping in his voice bordered on the comical. "What about the camera—the film—the boy dropped at the top of the knoll?" Howard asked Ricardo.

"It has been taken care of."

"What does that *mean*, Ricardo?"

"It means it is no longer your concern! And there is nothing on that film."

"The boy can describe me."

"And he most assuredly already has done so."

"I was hoping you'd taken care of that by now, Ricardo."

Ricardo's voice came back as cool as a cucumber. "This boy probably spoke with the police two minutes after we accomplished our mission. And all that exists on his camera are pictures of his nice, little family—parents, probably his sisters or girlfriends—and lots of shots of a beach. We have no idea who he is, or where he lives."

"That's not very comforting, Ricardo. He saw me fifteen seconds before I fired."

"He has no idea who you are."

"Find out about him. He might be testifying before the Warren Commission. Can't we prevent that?"

After a pause on the other end, Ricardo lowered his voice to almost inaudible levels. "We will take a look at those pictures again…and, Howard: Joey is gone; Frank is gone. Craig is gone; Hidell is gone. Do you know what I am saying?"

Howard always found dumb questions disquieting. "Yes," he answered anyway.

"Then the next time we talk—no matter when that may be— it is because I call you, or because The Boss calls you. Do not risk making your already short stay on earth even shorter by becoming paranoid. The Warren people have gone into their hearings based on the premise that Oswald was the lone assassin, and that is the way they ultimately will report it."

"How can you be so sure of that? We have no idea what the Commission has been told—or what they'll be told. Someone else must have seen me on the knoll. Our disguises have been too well publicized."

"Yes, but the authorities questioned you and let you go."

"But the boy…"

"He will be taken care of."

"But—"

"Good-bye, Howard," Ricardo teased.

And Ricardo quietly hung up the phone.

****

Randy had an uninspiring, unexciting birthday party with the other debaters.

Later he dipped back into his doldrums by spending a couple of hours at Carmen's house. Randy and Carmen listened to Carmen's favorite music, did not feel much like dancing, and discussed topics of trivial importance—ignoring Dallas—for fear of cascading into an argument. It seemed to Randy as though their unpleasant interaction a couple of nights before never happened. Although he didn't think it healthy to rehash old conflicts, Carmen's present aloofness, especially after the awful things she had said in anger to Randy, bothered him. He wanted peace and harmony, too. But with Carmen in his life, perhaps these were unattainable. Carmen's repeated reminders about living in Puerto Rico, her outward disdain for his debate obsession, and her overt displays of superiority around anyone not as pretty as she was had taken their toll on Randy. Yes, removing Carmen from his life would amplify his loneliness. But having her in his life highlighted severe challenges that she brought with her to their relationship.

Despite these reservations, Randy visited Carmen after his birthday party. Her parents, now somewhat ambivalent about him, congratulated Randy upon his birthday. As a present, Carmen gave him a framed picture of both of them at Balboa Beach. In a rare color photo, Carmen stood with her left arm around Randy's waist. He wore a pair of green swimming trunks, his slender frame appearing a little tanner and more muscular in the photograph than it was in reality. She, of course, stood out in her orange bikini, her already chocolate body charred even darker by the summer sun.

As Randy looked at this picture for the first time, he thought about how tantalizing it would be for any other boy to gawk at Carmen's beach shore photo, while conjuring up thoughts and feelings that were better not discussed in mixed company. But in just a few short months, Randy had come to a place in which Carmen's sex appeal had been trumped by her incompatible, wholly self-centered personality.

At Randy's birthday party earlier in the evening, Maria had barely spoken to him. She did talk a lot with Tommy, though. They didn't seem particularly chummy, but any kind of contact between Tommy and Maria drove Randy crazy. Mr. Lott's haunting words in the Dallas motel room flew back into his head—over and over again.

Now late at night, Randy drove numbly through the streets of Long Beach before he suddenly realized his car was crawling toward the curb in front of Maria's house. Her small, white stucco home bore familiarity, especially when dimly lit by a single, small bulb on the front porch. Although at first the scene did not register in Randy's mind, what had been invisible to him soon became a blur; then what had been a blur finally settled into full focus: Both

Tommy Wright and Maria Barquin, arched slightly away from the light, stood on the porch. She appeared to have both her hands resting on his upper arms. His hands lightly caressed her waist. Looking into each other's eyes, they spoke muted words. She had tilted her head slightly upward in order to neutralize his extreme height advantage. They were not in an embrace; but they didn't appear to be a couple of debaters discussing their opponents' cases, either.

Feeling a wave of nausea coming over him, Randy punched hard on the gas pedal with his right foot. Tires screeching, he pulled into full gear and fled the scene as quickly as he could. He prayed that neither Tommy nor Maria recognized his car or otherwise figured out the identity of the crackpot who had spied on them.

—CHAPTER 36—

The debate season had catapulted to a disappointing start for Randy. Already in the middle of December, Randy and Maria had been to only two tournaments: one cancelled and the other one a debacle. They judged at a local novice tournament but, of course, they had been unable to compete at the level set just for beginners. Randy was determined to make the next competition a success and scheduled three consecutive evenings of work with Maria. He also nagged Mr. Lott about hearing them practice a couple of times, as practice debates were excellent vehicles for coaches to render their expertise and offer valuable strategic pointers.

But Mr. Lott told his debaters that he was scheduled for a week of medical therapy and would not be at school. After this peculiar proclamation, the cat hopped out of the bag. Students throughout the school grew skeptical about Mr. Lott's health, and with his absences beginning to accumulate, they were certain his health had gone awry.

Maria clammed up; Randy did not. He revealed Mr. Lott's ailment to Ira. Ira then called a general meeting for the whole team and informed the twenty debaters who showed that Mr. Lott now battled leukemia. "The prognosis is uncertain, but Mr. Lott is a fighter," he disclosed tearfully.

Stunned, the Long beach debaters hastily made plans to get together with their individual partners, held one general case briefing meeting, and arranged transportation for the coming combat at Loyola University in Los Angeles. The high school's principal Mr. O'Shannon offered encouragement and assistance to Mr. Lott's students.

Exactly a week before the Loyola Invitational, Randy met with Maria for the first time since their disastrous performance at UCLA. But before they delved into the particulars of their case discussions and evidence research, they fell into the trap of debating off the topic. Which, in the context of a competitive debate round, usually resulted in a loss. In real life it often resulted in rampant frustration.

Materials were spread throughout the den in Maria's house. And in the front of the room, a television with the volume turned down displayed invisible personalities. Maria and Randy were set up to work.

"We need Mr. Lott," Maria commented, as they surveyed the cluttered scene around them.

Randy agreed, but he would not do so outwardly. "Not really. We're going to brief the cases we hit at UCLA. We don 't need him for that."

"But we *need* him. He is a stabilizing force in our lives."

"Mr. Lott?"

"Yes."

"He's a taskmaster."

"But he keeps us *on* task. And we win."

"We didn't win at UCLA," Randy observed sardonically.

"You may remember, Randy, we were not exactly on task there. You may remember that a week before, our attention was slightly diverted from debate."

"Mr. Lott couldn't get us back on task then."

"Neither could you," Maria chirped.

"It wasn't my job."

"To pull yourself together?"

Randy rose from the leather chair he had chosen to be his own. Kicking off a pile of blank 4 by 6 cards, he moved without purpose toward the front of the room. Releasing some frustration would feel good, however.

"I seem to remember the first team we debated—that awful team from West Covina—asked us about AFDC. You told them I would bring up statistics in my speech—stats you knew we didn't have—"

"Are we going to rehash this *again*?" Maria interrupted. "Because if we are, I have homework I could be doing right now."

"Or you could be pulling yourself together."

"What?" a baffled Maria asked.

"Getting back on *task*?"

Randy's innuendos left Maria blank.

"It does seem to me, Maria, that it's you who've been off task lately."

"Me, Randy? I've been off task?"

"Let's just say that your attention hasn't been on the debate team. Scratch that," he quickly added. "It's not been on the *team*, but it *has* been on a single debater—and he's not your debate partner."

Maria felt herself blush, but she didn't know why she blushed. She hadn't done anything to be embarrassed.

"Tell it straight, Randy," she insisted.

"Look, if you have this thing going with Tommy, why are you guys keeping it such a secret?"

Maria's mouth fell open. She didn't know how to respond. Randy accused her of having a "thing" with Tommy, but she hadn't done anything to indicate that. The fact that she found him handsome shouldn't insinuate she had been involved with him intimately, and Maria resented Randy's remarks.

"Go home," she commanded, but somewhat subdued.

Startled by Maria's order, Randy swooped down to lift his evidence boxes and briefcase. The surprising weight of the second tin box proved to be more than he could handle, causing his body to jerk forward. The other box fell to the carpet, and the cards spilled everywhere. They were no longer neatly filed by category.

"I said *go*!" Maria repeated more strongly, after Randy had paused and then bent over to retrieve the cards.

"But I need to get these," he said.

"Go home, Randy. Just leave your stuff. I'll take care of it." Maria's voice sounded a little less angry but still quivered with emotion.

Randy straightened and darted out the door without saying another word.

The next night they tried it again. Encumbered by files of evidence cards and long, yellow legal pads, Randy and Maria fully intended to progress in their tournament preparation. Maria had encountered the additional problem of a new assignment by her English teacher, a research report due on the last day before the Christmas break. Inordinate stress reigned in her young life.

Maria and Randy had not spoken since the blowup the night before. He hoped to keep them on task. But with her accusation that Randy could not discipline himself and attain the requisite amount of focus on debate, she had impugned his masculinity.

He handed her a flow sheet, a record of the arguments from the first round, a loss, at UCLA. "West Covina had some good inherency points. They were mediocre debaters, but they had some good arguments about expanding current welfare programs."

"We should have carried inherency," Maria reflected. "Welfare programs are racist. Racism is inherent in America. These programs cannot be expanded without a massive federal entitlement such as a guaranteed annual income for *all*."

"Is that what you want to say?" Randy asked her, slightly irked.

"It is good affirmative inherency. Look, the structure of the *status quo* is such that millions of Americans cannot eat. Why can't they eat? Racism: racist attitudes, racist proposals that bypass the people who need help the most, corrupt state officials who divert federal matching funds and use the money for other state programs —or for personal reasons—instead of getting it to the poor. There are tons of evidence on this Randy. But unlike a lot of arguments we present in a debate round, *these* are the truth."

Randy shook his head and made a pronouncement he immediately regretted: "Your folks seem to have done all right. What's the problem, Maria?"

Maria reeled. "My parents have worked hard, taken chances, made sacrifices, done whatever they've been ordered to do by the establishment. That is why we've done all right. Not all Mexicans in America are as fortunate."

"I think you sell yourself short, Maria," Randy commented, while busily scanning a phony brief, nothing more than a page of old notes from debate class. "That's what it's all about: those things you just said. If you work hard, take chances, and make sacrifices, you can really succeed in America, much less need welfare or a guaranteed annual income."

"It is not that easy, Randy," Maria argued between her teeth. "Not everybody is as lucky as we have been."

"Maria, you just listed those things your family has done to become successful. It didn't have to do with luck. It had to do with hard work and taking chances. You just said so yourself."

Maria put down her flow sheet. "But racism is rampant."

"If people can overcome it, what difference does it make?"

"It is very difficult."

"But *difficult*, Maria, is not inherency in a debate round. Inherency implies structural barriers. We don't need a guaranteed federal income program to circumvent those racism barriers you've mentioned. We don't."

"Randy, we are on the *affirmative*, now. We are thinking *inherency* on the affirmative, now."

"Well, Maria, maybe I'm not thinking debate at all right now. Maybe *I'm* thinking the real world. Wouldn't that be an interesting concept: debate and the *real world*?"

Maria bristled. "What is the matter with you, Randy? I am the one who just got insulted here—with all this talk about 'how did *you people* make it'? And all this nonsense about no racist barriers to the poor getting help."

"There aren't, Maria."

"That is not what Kennedy said. Is it, Randy?"

Randy's eyes flooded with tears. He choked; his voice failed him. In the absence of being able to speak, he wanted to rush to Maria, throw his arms around her, pull her tight, and tell her that she was right: that when Kennedy passed, the poor had lost one of their greatest champions; that when Kennedy died, a huge segment of America—with all their hopes—had had died with him. And Randy was hurting inside, the pain excruciating.

But he did not run into Maria's arms; instead, he stormed from her home and into the night. The next time they even spoke to each other was when the Long Beach High School debate team met the school bus at 6:30 in the morning on December 16.

Round one was less than two hours away.

—CHAPTER 37—

On December 16 several American newspapers posted information they had received regarding the assassination.

The Boston Herald indicated in a *Front Section* story that Lee Harvey Oswald had been a member—in fact, the president—of a pro-Castro organization called Fair Play For Cuba. This committee believed that John Kennedy had been hostile to Fidel Castro and, in fact, had directed the Central Intelligence Agency to make several assassination attempts on Castro, including the use of exploding cigars. Oswald was the only member of Fair Play For Cuba.

The Washington Post reported the bullet that struck President Kennedy also wounded Governor John Connally, who ultimately had survived the attack. That bullet, unidentified sources speculated, first went through Kennedy's back, exited his throat, traveled through Connally's back (Connally sat directly in front of Kennedy), exited his ribs, penetrated his left wrist, and then lodged in his left thigh. The columnist surmised that one assassin from the sixth floor window of the Texas School Book Depository, Lee Harvey Oswald, had fired this bullet.

But a small, obscure story in *The New York Times* told of witnesses who thought they heard shots fired from what the writer referred to as "the grassy knoll," a hilly area north of Elm street, bordered on the backside by a parking lot, a brown picket fence, a large monument, and a white concrete barrier. Immediately after the shots were fired, several policemen, their guns drawn, had run *up* the grassy hill. Although none of the witnesses would corroborate the sighting of an assassin, the police had stopped several people on the hill for questioning, including *three men who made their temporary home in a boxcar on the railroad tracks, behind a large parking lot and a brown picket fence.*

Randy's eyes bulged from their sockets. Reading the school's copy of the *New York Times* on the bus while going to the debate tournament, turned out to be an extraordinary distraction from everything else on his mind. At last, *some* confirmation of his personal experiences in Dallas! Others, too, thought shots were fired from the grassy hill! The police had questioned three men resembling those he had witnessed behind the barrier. This was especially important to Randy, because almost a month after the assassination, he had begun to doubt himself: to doubt what he saw; to doubt what he heard; to doubt that he had even walked up that hill in the first place.

After still another blood treatment, Mr. Lott languished in a hospital. Mr. Palladin, a well-respected, popular history teacher at Long Beach High, escorted the debaters to the tournament. Mr. Palladin sported a bushy mustache and had a balding head, quite a departure from the conservative, conventional appeal of the team's debate coach. He offered to take on judging assignments and mediate disputes that may arise among the debaters.

He gave some helpful hints as far as content and information on the debate topic were concerned, but he was clueless about debate strategy. The debaters thought Mr. Palladin's strategy suggestions were a bit bizarre and silently dismissed those strategy tips he had tried to impart to them. And they did so with a bit of humor, because they were wary about hurting Mr. Palladin's feelings.

By the time Randy and Maria arrived at their room for round one, Randy was bursting with excitement. Feelings of validation prevailed—finally! No longer did he suspect he was the only person in the world who thought assassins crouched covertly behind a barrier at the top of the knoll. Truth in numbers: wasn't that the way the world saw current events—the way it saw history? For once, the numbers on his side were mounting.

Despite these energizing distractions, a debate round loomed.

As the first speaker on the negative side, Maria would begin the debate for her team, speaking immediately after Randy's cross-examination of the first affirmative debater (the speaker who opens the contest).

Their draw of opponents for the first round of the tournament could have been worse. And it could have been better. Well-dressed and adorned with glasses, two boys from Hilltop High

School in San Diego made a positive first impression on the judge —even on Randy and Maria. Randy's questions were mediocre, taking his team nowhere, setting up nothing substantial to argue later in the debate.

By the time Maria got up to speak, her knees shook. But the judge, an amiable, older male coach from a high school in Utah, reacted positively to Maria's arguments, to her presentation. He occasionally nodded his head as he wrote something down, and he smiled when he perceived Maria had cracked a joke. But the truth was, Maria felt inadequate. She had not rehearsed any of her best arguments against Hilltop's particular approach and had not briefed a case focused primarily on the needs of Americans with inadequate diets.

She had no research, no evidence, directly refuting this case.

And then she made one of the worst maneuvers imaginable while debating on the negative side: Inexplicably, after stammering point by point through the affirmative's case, Maria decided to run *topicality* issues; this means, she argued the affirmative team was not debating within the parameters of the debate resolution. Because the affirmative argued for the federal government to give *food resources* to Americans, instead of cash, Maria contended that this was not what the debate topic mandated: *a guaranteed annual* ("cash," she specified) *income.*

Hilltop responded by suggesting the debate resolution did not require *cash* as the guaranteed income. Maria—and now Randy by virtue of being her partner—had to struggle to defend her topicality position.

Maria had made an amateurish error and fretted silently about it for the entire hour it took the debate to conclude, further mangling her ability to present cohesive arguments in a persuasive, charming manner. Maria knew Randy would pounce on her— deservedly so—and he would doubt that she met the necessary standards for being his partner.

But Randy surprised Maria. Immediately after packing their materials away, they dragged their briefcases to tournament headquarters in the large cafeteria, a room in which the participants congregated between their debate rounds. Maria and Randy discussed nothing about their disastrous debate. Nothing. Shortly after stepping inside the cafeteria, Randy walked casually over to the snack bar and bought a sandwich. Maria plopped down on a bench and sat silently by herself, communicating with no one else.

Tommy Wright, dressed in a white blazer and dark slacks, his shiny black shoes covering his feet, paraded up to her and set down his briefcases. He looked exasperated about something— probably from his own debate round—but before he complained about his own situation, he first checked with Maria. "How'd it go?" he asked her.

"Not well," she answered, not wanting to say anything more.

"Tough draw?" Tommy questioned, unsure if Maria had heard him because of the excited, clamorous chatter all around them. Debaters comparing notes, relating stories, and complaining to coaches can work up frenzied conversations.

"Not really," Maria shrugged.

"Who?"

"A team from San Diego."

Tommy asked about a respected team from Grossmont, a school also in the San Diego area, but it wasn't that one. "No, Hilltop," Maria said.

"Good?"

Maria shrugged again. "We should have beaten them, and we probably did not."

Noting Tommy's surprise with her assessment, Maria added, "I made a stupid mistake."

To Maria's chagrin, Tommy laughed, "What'd you do?"

At about that moment, Randy returned with his grilled cheese sandwich on stale wheat bread. He had arrived on the scene just as Maria answered, "I attacked topicality at the *end* of the first negative speech. I first argued their case, and *then* I threw up topicality. I didn't even run it very well. I just sort of put it out there as an afterthought."

Tommy looked at Randy and made a stupid face, implicitly mocking Maria's intelligence. He then twirled his forefinger up over his left ear and made several cuckoo sounds in an annoying high-pitched voice.

Maria silently lowered her head.

Randy, however, sizzled. "What's that supposed to mean, Tommy?"

"Topicality at the end of the first negative?"

Again, he made a dumb face.

"Maria did fine," Randy interceded. "I'll bet if I asked Ruther about *your* stupid antics, he'd have some stories to tell."

"Ask him, man," Tommy said, trying unsuccessfully to sound nonchalant. He pointed to the snack bar. "He's over there getting a burger."

Tommy then grinned demonically at Maria, visibly fighting to hide her mortification. He ridiculed, "*You* do dumb, *you* no get no burger—and you no get no other meat, either!"

Randy suddenly lost his perspective—or maybe he gained one: *His* girl had been insulted; *his* girl had been on the brink of crying; *his* girl needed a strong guy to defend her. Despite his belief that a time and a place existed for everything—and this was neither the time nor the place for what he was about to do—Randy went with his heart, instead of his brain.

With one powerful push of his karate-trained arm, Randy jammed his right hand flush into the side of an unsuspecting Tommy's shoulder, accelerating him sideways into a spin, and causing him to stagger. His feet tangled and, thus, unable to maintain his equilibrium, Tommy toppled to the floor on top of a pair of ox boxes belonging to another high school. Upset by the crashing weight of a six-foot, two hundred pound football player, the enormous briefcases spilled open, leaving the six-foot, two hundred pound *debater* lying in a clutter of evidence cards, legal pads, and a large bag of Cheese Puffs.

Margie Pendergrass screamed, and so did another girl from a high school Long Beach frequently debated. Maria sat bug-eyed and watched this amazing scene unfold. Ira Cushman, who had just come into the room, hurried to Randy, figuring Tommy had attacked him, and Randy needed his help.

All eyes were drawn to Tommy Wright, who had righted himself after his sprawl. With ferocious determination, Tommy, red-face and angry, barreled towards Randy like a bull charging a matador. Intending to crash into Randy with the full weight of his rock-solid body, thereby taking both of them to the floor, Tommy's mad rush in the other boy's direction was short and powerful. But Randy's countless hours perfecting his karate moves as he moved closer to his Brown Belt gave him a decisive advantage, shortening the length of the altercation: At the exact moment Tommy intended to make contact, Randy quickly stepped aside and shot his right fist into Tommy Wright's nose. The combination of Tommy's speed and the straightness of Randy's crisp, well-trained, well-aimed punch sent Tommy to the floor like a sack of potatoes falling from a flat bed truck: straight down Tommy went.

A collective gasp filled the air.

At first Maria worried about Tommy's condition, for he had landed on the back of his head, hitting the floor with an ugly thud. Several students from other schools ran to the scene. A teacher from Portland, Oregon yelled, "Everybody, back!" And she looked around for assistance—medical or authoritative. A young male debate coach from Bronx High School of Science grounded a place between the fallen Tommy and the now sitting and gazing Randy. The teacher's job was to quell tempers and prevent further violence. Nobody dared to mess with this debate coach from New York; his size was prohibitive.

By this time chaos had enveloped the cafeteria. Dozens of teachers and students gathered around the Long Beach team. Some of them apparently thought a debater had experienced a seizure. Pandemonium went on outside. A few people hollered about a riot inside the cafeteria.

Tommy Wright had suffered a broken nose, Randy Whitman and Maria Barquin were ejected from the tournament, and Mr. Palladin swore he would never again accompany the Long Beach High School debaters to another tournament.

Randy and Maria later found out that, inexplicably, they had defeated Hilltop High School in the first round. Despite Maria's boneheaded ploy of arguing topicality at the very end of her first negative speech, the elderly judge from Utah had disregarded this breach of protocol and voted for Randy and her anyway.

****

Mr. O'Shannon banned the entire debate squad from the next competition, a tournament at the University of Redlands. And the principal suspended Randy from school for five days. Tommy Wright, who received no disciplinary action from anyone, nursed his broken nose while he lay in bed watching *I Love Lucy* and *Leave It To Beaver* on T.V. Maria decided to spend more time with her family, since they suddenly breathed the greatest amount of sanity into her young life.

Randy, sullen and remorseful about unleashing his anger — very much unlike him— contended with a few other problems that came from the pummeling of Tommy Wright at Loyola: First, word of the violence got around, and when the brass at the karate studio heard about the fight, they dismissed Randy from the premises and cancelled his membership; second, Mr. Lott, mortified, especially for Mr. Palladin, made the decision to suspend Randy from competing at tournaments for one month; and third (and foremost to Randy), Maria's father, apprehensive about Randy's propensity to turn his temper into fits of rage, forbade Maria from working with Randy as a debate colleague.

All of this, Randy thought, was just too much for him to take. He thought it impossible after his experience in Dallas, but Randy now sank into an even deeper depression than he had found himself after the assassination.

His only consolation now came in his visits to Carmen Pedro's house and their sharing of an occasional movie or cheeseburger on a Friday night. He tried to take solace in his music, but familiar ballads reminded him of Maria. So most music made him feel a lot worse.

And just when he thought he'd hit rock bottom, a suspicious telephone call on January 2, 1964, convinced him that an even deeper bottom awaited him.

"Randy, this is Agent Balcomb of the FBI. May we speak with each other for a moment?"

Randy panicked. It surely *sounded* like Agent Balcomb. He *thought* it was Agent Balcomb. He *wanted* it to be Agent Balcomb.

But how could he be sure? What if the hobos who picked up his camera on the knoll had located him and obtained his telephone number? Would they pay him a visit? And what would they do to him when they got there?

"Agent Balcomb?" Randy inquired nervously. He felt perspiration dripping off his hands.

"Yes, Randy, it's Stephen Balcomb."

"I hope this doesn't offend you, Mr. Balcomb—but how do I know it's really you, sir?"

"We spoke with each other on December 2, 1963. I sat in your living room with you for almost an hour. And I made it a point to comment about Walt Whitman—that I'd been an English major in college—and how much I enjoyed Walt Whitman. Also, we talked briefly about your camera—the one you dropped on the grassy knoll—and I told you we would get back to that later. We never did that; we never got back to that later."

Randy relaxed. Hearing Balcomb's words soothed him. Only Stephen Balcomb could have known about those things. He would oblige the agent in a discussion. "Thank you, Mr. Balcomb. I feel better."

But Balcomb didn't miss a beat. "About that camera: I assume you haven't seen it again—and that you don't know who picked it up."

"I have no idea what happened to the camera, sir."

"It could have been the men you saw, and it could have been officials going over the hilly area with a fine-tooth comb after the assassination. You've already thought about this a dozen times or more, Randy, but I need to get some information from you. Was there anything on your camera that could lead to your identification, your home address, your school, your place of work, or your phone number?"

"Yes, sir," Randy replied. "I think there might be a few things."

"Such as?"

"Many of the pictures were taken at the beach—Balboa Beach—a very popular spot for young people here in Southern California. In one photo the sign *Balboa Beach Ferry* is clearly visible as at a beach resort. Someone could easily figure out the location as Southern California."

"All right," Balcomb sighed. "But that still leaves a lot of territory and several million people."

"Except for something else I'm really worried about," Randy advised. "In a couple of pictures that we took of my family in front of our house, our street address is glued to a post on the front porch and probably shows in the picture."

"If you're right about all that, Randy, if anybody really wanted you, they could find your house—at least theoretically," Balcomb warned. "But without the name of the street, it would be like finding a needle in a haystack."

Randy gulped that he already knew this.

"What kind of a camera was it?"

"A Kodak 127. Very cheap but took pretty good pictures."

"Well, the good news is," Balcomb said more reassuringly, "anything the people who found your camera wanted from you, they probably would have already taken by now."

"That's what I keep thinking, Mr. Balcomb," Randy squeaked with more confidence.

And then Balcomb hit him with this: "But we can't be sure of that, Randy. Look, chances are that no one involved in the attack took your camera. And if they did, there's no guarantee they would have looked at it or found anything of interest. Even then, they would have to put two and two together. And anything urgent these guys would have tended to by now."

"Right."

"*However*, Randy, watch your back. Keep your doors closed at night and warn your parents of the possible dangers. I'm sure you've already done this a million times." He laughed. "Probably over-doing it, right?"

Randy forced a laugh in return. "Yeah," he chortled. But the truth was he *hadn't* spoken a word of this to his family. He didn't want to worry them or draw more attention to his clumsiness with his Kodak camera—or to his ultimate clumsiness, a face-first splat into the ground on the grassy knoll.

After his phone conversation with Agent Balcomb, Randy

convinced himself not to breathe another word about the camera to anyone, especially to his parents. Raising a vital issue that may never surface didn't seem fair to anybody.

And it probably wasn't going to be a problem anyway.

Probably.

—CHAPTER 38—

On January 5, Maria visited Tommy for the first time since Randy's pummeling of his nose.

More than a week after the incident, Maria still wasn't quite sure how she should have reacted. On the one hand, Tommy had ridiculed her in front of several people, including Randy. But on the other hand, Randy had practically blind-sided Tommy with a strong push that had toppled him to the floor. True, at this point Randy had not inflicted any physical damage on Tommy. But for a boy like Tommy, being shoved into a bunch of file boxes and briefcases in front of a crowd of wimpy debaters had sent him to the very top of the humiliation scale.

Maria believed that Tommy deserved the embarrassment he suffered after Randy pushed him. He had been relentlessly teasing her. She did make a stupid mistake in the debate round; but public disgrace, especially in front of dozens of debaters from other schools around the nation, seemed like an unfair, unjust punishment for her error.

Tommy's behavior was a different story. Hadn't Tommy humiliated Randy in Dallas? After Tommy knocked Randy into the swimming pool, Randy reacted in a calm, reasonable manner, one of restraint and dignity. Yes, Randy had finally allowed his temper to flair but only in her defense, a chivalrous act—rare in the today's world, indeed!

Then Randy had used his karate techniques to break the larger boy's nose.

In truth, Tommy first had charged Randy. Clearly, this presented a threat of bodily harm. Randy had been protecting himself from Tommy. But Maria could not get over the fact that Randy was the first to use physical violence (with the push) and then used much more force with his punch to Tommy's nose. In other words, Maria asked herself, was Tommy's making snippy comments and mocking faces to embarrass her worthy of having his nose broken? Randy had appraised Tommy's behavior as deserving of forceful retaliation, but Maria could not quite agree with the impulsive, angry actions of her debate partner—or, since her father's ominous proclamation, her *former* debate partner.

When she finally saw Tommy, Maria thought he looked much smaller and meeker than he had looked only a week before. In red, flannel pajamas at three o'clock in the afternoon, Tommy no longer resembled a bruiser somebody didn't wish to cross in a dark alley.

Maria sat at the kitchen table with Tommy, while he munched on a chicken sandwich. "How long before you can take the cast off?" she asked him.

"About another week. Man, this thing makes it hard to breathe! And it's itchy."

He touched the cast covering his nose from the top of the bridge down and winced.

Maria smiled. "You look like you just went a couple of rounds with Sonny Liston."

"It wasn't fair. He came out of nowhere!"

"You ran at *him*, Tommy," Maria reminded him.

Tommy shrugged and bit into his sandwich, a small bite for such a big, growing boy. "No, I didn't. Not at first. He pushed me down. I didn't even see it coming. That chickenshit would never get into a ring and fight me fair and square, man to man."

"He might. But then he would use his karate moves on you, and you wouldn't stand a chance."

Tommy bristled. "That karate is a bunch of sissy crap! Boys who can't fight the *real* way are nothing but queers!"

Maria wondered if Tommy knew how ludicrous he sounded. She hoped that he did. "He was defending me, you know. You do know that, don't you, Tommy?"

Tommy remained silent.

"If you weren't trying to show everybody in a cafeteria full of debate geeks how stupid I was, Randy never would have pushed you. He didn't even retaliate in Dallas when you embarrassed him

239

by pushing him into a swimming pool. But he finally reached his limit with you, when you made fun of me in front of everybody."

The more Maria said, the clearer her own analysis convinced herself: she was sitting next to the wrong guy. Just because he'd been the most severely injured party—or the *only* injured party—it didn't entitle him to her compassion and forgiveness.

Suddenly everything became clear.

"You know, Tommy, I think I am going home."

"What? You just got here."

"Yes, but you're not a very nice boy."

"What are you talking about?"

"I mean, I was always nice to you—partly because you always felt inferior to Randy. I usually felt sorry for you."

"I didn't feel inferior to Randy!" Tommy stormed, dropping his sandwich.

"Yes, you did—you still do. Especially now, after what happened at Loyola."

"You're crazy, Maria!" he yelled. "You think you're so superior to everyone, just like Randy does. You think you're smarter than anyone on the debate team! And you're the one who keeps screwing things up!"

Maria fit herself into her long, black coat, her soft hair dropping past her shoulders. Taller and slimmer than Tommy remembered her, she looked especially exquisite in the imprecise kitchen lighting. She also appeared older than a sophomore in high school. "I may mess up in the debates," she said, "but at least I am always nice to people."

"You're not being nice to me. I'm the one who got hurt."

"I fully intended to be nice to you, Tommy. You do not deserve it, though."

"I thought you liked me."

"What do you mean?"

"You know."

Maria scrunched her face. "Not like that. I just tried to give you the benefit of the doubt."

"What about the other night when we talked for hours about our lives and—and—you know—our hopes and dreams? How we held hands on your front porch."

"We did not hold hands, Tommy!"

"Come again?"

"Well, you were obviously beguiling me."

"What?" Tommy winced. "I don't even know what the hell that means!"

Ignorance was not a turn-on to Maria Barquin.

"Look, Tommy, do you know what you could do to redeem yourself—at least, *somewhat*?"

"What?" Tommy asked, and then he figured he should add, "Redeem myself for what?"

"For the way you treated me at Loyola; for the way you have always treated Randy, even though he did not deserve it."

"*He* didn't deserve it?" squealed Tommy.

"Well, you deserved *something* in that cafeteria, Tommy."

"He broke my nose!"

"He didn't touch you after you tripped him into the pool. He was down and out and really hurting, but he still didn't lay a finger on you."

Tommy laughed.

"And he could have kicked your butt right then—and you really would have deserved it. At Loyola he finally got fed up with you."

"My parents are thinking about suing his parents," Tommy bragged. "They're seeing an attorney."

Maria shook her head. "Boy, you are going to look like such a chickenshit!"

The way she said that word, a rarely present, heavy Mexican accent almost made even Tommy laugh again; plus, he knew what Maria said was true: he *would* look like a chickenshit if his parents filed a lawsuit over the Loyola skirmish.

Tommy desperately grasped for any straws he could find. Nothing helpful came his way. So he sighed and asked, "Then how can I redeem myself, Maria? In your eyes, because that's all I care about."

"Tommy, everybody thinks you act like a jerk," Maria insisted. "Being good-looking doesn't compensate for that—not in the eyes of a nice girl. That girl by the pool in Dallas was not nice. You were not acting nice together."

Tommy had had about enough. "Okay, what do you want me to do, Maria?"

She looked at him squarely. "Quit the debate team."

"Huh?" Tommy reeled.

"Call Mr. Lott—or, if you are man enough, go over and see him in person and then quit the debate team."

"But—why?"

"Because you are not an asset."

"I'm a senior!"

Maria chuckled and threw her head back. "That does not make you an asset. And the truth be told, you are a liability. People feel uncomfortable around you. You embarrass the other squad members. And you have given me a bad reputation."

"Me?"

"Yes."

"How did I give you a bad reputation?"

"You pester me a lot. You get me alone whenever you can. I think other people see this—even Randy. And somebody—it wasn't me—told Randy that I liked you; that I was trying to get you to go steady. I just know that somebody told Randy this. I can tell from his behavior, his attitude. It is not that he likes me so much; it is that he dislikes you so much."

Tommy stared agape.

"So just quit the debate team, Tommy. Ruther will find a new partner. You guys have not been doing that well anyway. Have you even broken a five hundred record? No. Just quit the squad, Tommy."

For a personal distraction, Tommy began accumulating breadcrumbs on the table. Maria had come after him directly, point-blank, and he now needed to weave away from her blitz.

"Well," Tommy said in a voice wreathed with self-pity. "Here I was, expecting you to bring me flowers or something. And you came here to throw poison ivy in my face."

"I did not come here expecting to do this, Tommy. I didn't. I did expect to shower you with sympathy. But then I remembered why you wound up with a broken nose, and I heard you say things that were vile and mean. Randy deserves a lot more sympathy from me than you do. The problem is because of my father's restrictions on Randy, I cannot do that anymore. I can't even help him to get better."

"Help *him* to get better?"

"You haven't the faintest clue what Randy went through in Dallas. As usual, you have been so self-absorbed, so wrapped up in yourself, you don't—you can't even *begin* to relate. It was terrible —and it still is for Randy. Not only is he consumed by the notion that he should have done something to save President Kennedy— that he was the one person who *could* have done something—he is scared to death right now that somebody is going to come here and kill him."

"He told you that?"

"Yes, he did," Maria nodded. "And I know for Randy to admit something like this to me, it must really bother him. Besides, he lost his camera that day, and Randy is terrified that somebody is going use the camera to find him and hurt his family. And he probably will be afraid of this for the rest of his life."

Gazing at her, Tommy said nothing.

"And that debate round—you called me stupid? We won that round, Tommy. I *was* stupid, but we won. The judge voted for us anyway. Maybe the judge was the stupid one. Funny, huh?"

—CHAPTER 39—

During the first week of January, the *Chicago Tribune* published a front-page story detailing John F. Kennedy's difficulties in dealing with Cuba. With the U.S. base at Guantanamo, problems had arisen about territorial rights, American soldiers moving about the Cuban mainland, and the secrecy of weapons facilities. In addition, alleged assassination attempts by blundering members of the Central Intelligence Agency did not exactly endear the Kennedy administration to the likes of Fidel Castro and his cronies. The failed Bay of Pigs invasion and the subsequent slaughter of invading Cuban nationals because of inadequate U.S. air support were now old news, but a tangible bitterness lingered. No matter which side of the ledger, both those who stood for and those who stood against Castro and Cuba had railed against Kennedy and loathed the various agencies he had anointed, authorized, and augmented in order to fight Communism.

The next day the *Dallas Morning News* broadcast a reminder that the route of the Presidential motorcade had been published in its newspaper on Tuesday. The likes of an Oswald, therefore, would have known for a few days about the President and Vice-President of the United States, along with the Governor of Texas, passing within a few feet of the Texas Book Depository building, Oswald's place of employment.

The paper suggested that others could have known about the motorcade and its route even days—perhaps a couple of weeks— before Tuesday, November 19. The local Dallas paper also expounded on what previously had been only a rumor to most of America: that on the morning of the twenty-second, it had rained. Kennedy's aids ordered the rainproof—not bulletproof—bubble top be used in order to shield the President from the inclement weather, a healthy, wise demand that would have made a successful assassination on November twenty-second a little less likely, but not altogether impossible. After the skies had cleared, Kennedy asked that the top be removed. He desired more intimacy with the people who had come to cheer him.

Randy slowly read the front page of the *Dallas Morning News* to Mr. Lott, as he lay on the couch in his living room. Newspapers and dirty clothes were strewn about. Mr. Lott had never been known to keep a clean house, although he had a reputation for running a tight ship when it came to overseeing his debate squad.

Maria sat in a corner of the room, her briefcase still unopened, and at her feet. Though Randy also occupied the room, Maria rationalized his forbidden presence: Mr. Lott sat there, too. And it was, after all, his house. Her father could not possibly be angered or worried about her. Besides, tonight she planned to plead with her father to reconsider the expulsion of Randy from her life.

"You need to get a maid, Mr. Lott," she giggled in a way that always tickled Randy's heart.

"A maid cost mullah," Mr. Lott said.

"Don't be so cheap," she teased.

Randy took a position, too. "We have a maid do our house once a week. She charges fifteen dollars and usually brings her sister with her. They're good. They take about four hours. You can eat food off the kitchen floor after they leave."

"Are they Mexican nationals?" Mr. Lott wondered.

"You mean, illegal aliens—isn't that what white people call them?" Maria asked, raising a brow.

"Lots of people want into this country," Mr. Lott responded. "We can't possibly let them all in. We don't have enough jobs, and our welfare programs are already lagging…as you debaters have so aptly discovered."

Maria was sorry that she had raised the issue. She despised discussions about Mexican nationals and immigration. She heard that a team from Alhambra High School framed their whole affirmative case around the need to pay for social services for the children of undocumented adults who smuggled their children across the border or bore their children here, which automatically made these kids natural American citizens. Maria quaked over the idea of having to take a stand against letting Mexicans without proper papers immigrate to America, since her own mother had done that very thing: bred a couple of generations of successful, productive citizens, both natural and naturalized, in the aftermath of much human hiding and subterfuge.

She changed the subject to its proper place, where it should have been already. "How are you feeling, Mr. Lott? Do you have more treatments scheduled?"

"I'm better," Mr. Lott nodded without much conviction in his voice. "I've got a transfusion scheduled for early March, and, depending upon lab results, only one or two follow-ups after that. I'm hopeful. To answer your question directly, Maria: I'm feeling tired, very tired. It's an effort to get out of bed, even if I sleep through to eleven or twelve o'clock. Driving is difficult, but I have some neighbors who help out with groceries and other necessities. Plus, the good thing: the doctor hinted that I would gradually get my strength back. We'll see."

"You can always call me if you need anything, Mr. Lott," Maria promised with total sincerity. "Or Randy—he'll be glad to help, too. His father drives him anywhere he wants to go."

"My father's a trooper!" Randy added enthusiastically. *But had Mr. Lott not been a white man, Samuel Whitman would not be such a trooper*, Randy mused to himself.

Both teenagers had already agreed that Mr. Lott would have made a wonderful husband and a terrific father. Life sometimes didn't work out the way it should, the absence of fairness in a universe full of injustices

"Thank you, Randall," Mr. Lott winked. Mr. Lott called him Randall during moments he was feeling particularly fond of Randy.

Maria looked around. "Why is everyone else so late?"

"They're not late," Mr. Lott corrected. "After I called the meeting for tonight, I gave you and Randy a starting time an hour earlier than the one I gave to everyone else."

A bit flabbergasted and—without knowing exactly why—feeling slightly honored, Randy asked, "Why is that? Did you need us for something, Mr. Lott?"

"Exactly," Mr. Lott answered. He threw the clipboard on his lap to the floor, an apparent, "Let's get serious!" gesture.

"Look, I want you both to know that I jumped the gun after the Loyola tournament. Randy, I felt really guilty. I wanted so much to accompany my teams to Loyola and Redlands. I wanted to coach my teams. I was useless in the coaching department. I knew that; I still know it. This is our first session together since—I can't even remember…"

"It's not your fault, Mr. Lott," Randy tried to pacify him.

"It doesn't matter. I still felt terrible. I also felt guilty about asking Mr. Palladin to take you to Loyola, especially after the, uh, fiasco that happened there."

He clapped his hands together. "So I have reconsidered my decision to split you two up. I've decided to keep my *still* number one debate team in tact."

Randy was elated inside but wondered why, after their mediocre showings, he and Maria would still be considered number one. Maria immediately came back at Mr. Lott. "I can't debate with Randy, Mr. Lott. My father has forbidden me to see Randy—anywhere."

Mr. Lott smiled. "Well, that was before I spoke with him this morning, while you were at school."

"What!" Maria interjected, sounding almost horrified.

"I called him at work. Nice man."

"Mr. Lott…"

"Maria, your father only wanted to protect his daughter. He's a good father. He figured Randy couldn't be trusted because he's violent. It took me more than fifteen minutes, but by the time we were finished talking, he knew that couldn't be any further from the truth. I convinced him that it was in your best interest to debate with Randy—that you and he have the most potential. And I told him about some major scholarships, especially if you stay together next year, too. Maria, your father didn't know—he didn't realize— that what Randy did at Loyola was to *protect* you, not to hurt you. When I explained to him exactly what went down, he agreed that Randy had done a courageous thing; that knowing karate is actually an attribute. And Randy used karate the way it's meant to

247

be used: in self-defense, or in defense of the defenseless."

Randy snickered, "Try telling that to my karate teachers!"

"Done-did that. I spoke with Mr. Kinota this morning, too. I explained to him that you never threw the first punch—or kick. And when you did punch, it was because a two hundred-pound football linebacker was rushing at you full throttle. It was either punch…or *die*!"

"But I pushed him first."

Mr. Lott waved his hand. "Ah, you pushed! Big deal! You could have decked him then; you didn't. And if you *had*, we would be talking about something a heck of a lot more serious than what we're talking about now: Then we might be discussing expulsion from school and a law suit from Mr. and Mrs. Wright."

"I think they've started one."

Again Mr. Lott shrugged it off. "Don't worry about it. Won't happen."

Randy suddenly felt a surge of excitement about debate once again.

But Maria didn't know what to think. Silently weighing the probabilities, she concluded that neither Mr. Lott nor Randy knew about her recent lambasting of Tommy—or her instructions to him that he should quit the debate team.

Coincidental to her thoughts, Mr. Lott said, "I'm demoting Tommy Wright. He's going to partner up with someone who's not as good as he is. Sometimes there are reasons other than the obvious for forming debate partnerships."

Lance Richards was a six-foot, two-inch, 230-pound senior. He played varsity basketball and debated only as a lark. Last year he had a huge crush on one of the female debaters on the team and inducted himself into the program because of her. The net result: he earned himself a girlfriend and learned a lot about competitive debate participation that looked good on college applications.

He would, however, never grow to meet the criteria for placement on the traveling squads, a launching pad for attending special tournaments. Lance accepted his obvious limitations in the debate arena. In three tournaments this year, he and his two partners had compiled a record of six wins and twelve losses. This was not particularly impressive, but expected, since Mr. Lott deemed Lance to be the better debater on each of those teams.

Lance Richards seemed the perfect fit for Tommy Wright. Mr. Lott figured if Tommy gave Lance any trouble, Tommy would end up with a second broken nose. Lance was a nice kid, but everyone knew he didn't have patience for teenagers who were aggressive, loud, obnoxious, and impudent. Tommy's personality sometimes carried a banner for all four of those qualities.

Lance also had a chivalrous streak in him. If he had been at Loyola at the time of Tommy Wright's taunting of a disheartened, forlorn Maria, Tommy would have wound up with a lot worse than just a broken nose.

Mr. Lott had now informed Maria and Randy that they could stay paired as a team. While both teens outwardly displayed some pleasure at this pronouncement, Randy strained to contain his elation. It meant continued closeness to Maria: a girl he adored; a girl he wanted for his own; but a girl whose parents, along with his parents (and Maria herself?), were determined he would never have.

Maria still considered herself an inadequate debate partner. So far she had displayed little to warrant Mr. Lott's placement on his number one debate team. And with Randy's personal traumas from Dallas, she had considered the possibility that the honor of being designated *number one* would never again be legitimately bestowed on Randy Whitman or anyone else who partnered with him.

Maria and Randy both agreed in *principle* to this new decree by Mr. Lott. And by the time the other fourteen debate students arrived at Mr. Lott's home for their first meeting in several weeks, Maria surmised they both had also agreed with Mr. Lott's decision in *fact*.

Tommy Wright showed up at the forum with a huge white band-aid covering the entire bridge of his nose. Along with barely being able to mask her desire to break out in uproarious, uncontrolled laughter—as a couple of others did—when she saw Tommy walk into the room, Maria was sure she had not hidden the disdain showing on her face. Obviously, Tommy Wright had not heeded her advice about quitting the team.

The meeting droned on for about two hours. Afterwards, Maria and Randy stood and chatted for a few minutes outside Mr. Lott's house, as they waited for their respective rides home. Alone, Tommy waited on Mr. Lott's porch for his mother. Tommy casually accepted his appointment to be Lance Richards' partner as a measure of consolation, for he believed that he had once faced the grim possibility of being tossed off the squad altogether.

Lance, however, beamed. Tommy was certainly a step up from the two girls who had been holding him down this year; at least, Lance *thought* they had been holding him down. Tommy also represented the only other boy on the debate team who enjoyed a reputation as an athlete. The other kids at school deemed most debaters to be squares. Both Tommy and Lance were big, strapping, and imposing—clearly not "squares." They presented a formidable physical presence—despite that stupid-looking Band-Aid right now on Tommy's nose—in front of a meek debate judge!

Randy and Maria were discussing this new pairing of Lance and Tommy, when Randy saw his father's white Fury rolling slowly in their direction from down the street.

Just as Mr. Whitman drove his car to the curb, Randy made another hasty decision, one sending into motion a chain of events persuading Randy Whitman that, yes, he *had*, in fact, been abandoned by good fortune, blessed karma, and maybe by even God Himself.

—CHAPTER 40—

About two miles represented the distance between the homes of Randall Whitman and Maria Barquin. Randy had already walked this trek of residential streets with inadequate lighting a few times. If he carried only a briefcase or two, Randy touted the experience as good exercise, and he spared his father the burden of having to take him to and from Maria's house. He also saved himself from the embarrassment of having to be seen in his daddy's tow.

But that had been before Dallas. No longer did these familiar neighborhoods beam with safety and familiarity. Randy thought somebody—anybody—could attack without warning, and before he knew what hit him.

Tonight, however, events had materialized that lifted Randy's spirits. Mr. Lott's confidence in him factored in his suddenly brighter outlook. He also had decided that Maria didn't hate his guts. And maybe her fling—if there had ever been such a thing—with Tommy Wright had cooled. Even his debate career looked more promising. Maria would join him again as his partner, with her potential for success unrivaled. And he would be the beneficiary.

As he had departed with his father, Randy watched Maria, who waited on the sidewalk for her own father to pick her up at Mr. Lott's house. Looking back before settling into the passenger's side of the Fury, he impulsively shouted to her, "I'll be by your house in an hour! I've got some really bitchin' records I want you to hear!"

And an instant before he slammed his door, he blurted, "No debate stuff tonight!"

Maria heard his message and had no chance to complain, even if she had wanted to complain, which she did not.

She now expected Randy to pay her a social visit at about 10:00 P.M. on a *Friday night.*

Randy, clad in a moderately warm, dark blue windbreaker, pranced through the neighborhood with more spring than he'd shown in several weeks. Down the semi-lit residential streets he sauntered, oblivious to the congregating storm clouds, the near-freezing temperatures, and the eyes that spied on him.

****

In New Orleans, the boss had just finished a very late and a very long meeting with a man named David.

David had every reason to hate President Kennedy, to want him dead. The botched Bay of Pigs invasion sent rumbles of confusion and roars of anger throughout the community in which David lived. John F. Kennedy's failure in directing the murder of Fidel Castro shattered what little faith men like David originally had placed in the President. Inept, at best, corrupt, at worst—John F. Kennedy needed to die.

He had stayed connected to men who were employed by the Central Intelligence Agency. He possessed a commercial airplane license and could fly almost any plane in existence. He amplified his communication with friendly operatives in America's largest covert intelligence agency. And in September of 1963, Ricardo contacted him with an intriguing offer: aid anti-Castro Cubans to murder the President of the United States.

David would pilot a get-away aircraft.

Already teeming with animosity toward Kennedy for what he believed were his pro-Communist leanings, David bought into the dim-witted notion that he could provide transportation for a team of assassins—and possibly their organizers—to another country or a remote island. Excited about the project, he cajoled his friends (who shared his obsessive anti-communism) about their impotency. They could not, after all, *do* anything to make matters better. *He*, on the other hand, had a few surprises up his sleeve.

But David's dreams were crushed in mid-October when he received a phone call from Ricardo, disqualifying him from their mission.

"It's not that you are not worthy of participation, or that you would fail to meet the standards required for the job we had considered you to perform," Ricardo carefully explained. "It is that we have decided, after much consideration, that we do not need a pilot for this mission."

Ricardo didn't specify details about the change of plans. But in his earlier discussions with David, he had not gone into any particulars about their original tactics. Ricardo cautioned him to be mute. His life depended on his willingness to do so. Besides, Ricardo tantalized him, his services probably would be required later. Nonetheless, David's self-worth, once higher on the scale of self-worth than it had ever been, had lost its stock faster than his own father did when the Crash hit in 1929.

On November 22, 1963, David sat home watching the coverage of the assassination on television, as all other Americans had been doing. He was somewhat surprised by the events, and wondered how long it would take before someone tried to shut him up; after all, he knew too much.

In the ensuing months after the assassination, no one had tried to contact him. Already jittery about the potential for an unannounced knock at his door or a sudden explosion under the hood of his car, David decided to take matters into his own hands. He first called Ricardo, who snarled a warning at him never to call again. Ricardo pointed out to David that others who demonstrated they could not be trusted already had been eradicated.

David, of course, wanted Ricardo's reassurance that he was safe and not a potential target for elimination. Although Ricardo did not offer a vote of confidence in the terms David would have preferred, Ricardo did remind him that he was still alive; and if they had wanted him dead, it probably would have happened already. He did, after all, have secret knowledge about the group that had conspired to kill Kennedy.

David, however, possessed special talents that would prove useful at a later time. Ricardo maintained that his potential value, luckily for him, precluded his immediate demise.

But then David did something he would later regret: He

called Ricardo and informed him that he had placed an important package in a bank vault. The package specified in detail what he knew about the plot to kill President Kennedy. David claimed he had left names, dates, and contact numbers. He alluded to what his role in the assassination would have been had he not been cut from the details in the last couple of months, and his knowledge about others' participation in what he labeled, "a major conspiracy involving rogue CIA men [he was one of them] and powerful individuals at the very top of labor unions and organized crime syndicates."

In the event of his untimely death in the next twenty years, this information would be transmitted to federal law enforcement. But as long as he remained alive, the material would stay in his secret possession at an unnamed bank. Bank authorities had been ordered to contact the FBI and present them with this informative package, if David died before January, 1984.

Ricardo immediately called The Boss. Needless to say, The Boss did not take kindly to David's threats. He almost ordered David killed for being so impudent, so out of control. Leveler heads prevailed, and The Boss developed a scheme to solidify David's involvement in the assassination plot, while offering him massive incentives to immediately remove the package from his bank locker.

Big money was involved, a huge payout. The immediacy of this reward possessed powerful ramifications and presumably kept David entrenched in the post assassination cover-up until the day he would die from natural causes. The Boss's operatives created a design for making David's death an unqualified hindrance, assuring him that he was worth much, much more to the team alive than dead, thus solidifying in everyone's mind that his life should be spared.

So on this cold night in late January, The Boss spoke for a couple of hours with David, telling him what he wanted and *needed* to hear: that his life was worth a premium in the assassination cover up; and his useful skills as an airplane pilot, especially when it came to skillfully navigating private planes, would later come in handy.

David could fly unceremoniously, unarmed, and undetected almost anywhere in continental America. And he was eager to destroy those who presented obstacles to maintaining the silence the team required for their own anonymity and safety.

****

Randy thought about the song playing behind them as they sat in Maria's father's den, "Little Town Flirt," by Del Shannon. And he doubted its appropriateness. Gazing at Maria in the dim lamplight of her father's workroom, Randy mused to himself how Maria, unlike so many other girls he knew in high school, had never really flirted with him. She hadn't been anything but kind and sweet and decent and helpful, and the onus was always on him to reciprocate. But Randy's bitterness about Dallas, nervousness over debate, resentment toward his parents, jealousy of Tommy Wright, and embarrassment about losing his head at Loyola seemed to preclude much reciprocity on his part.

Until now. The old Randy had gotten a break tonight, and the new Randy, set to glide into action, would be taking over.

They listened to "Blue Velvet," by Bobby Vinton; "Sugar Shack," by Jimmy Gilmer; "Donna the Prima Donna," by Dion; and the music played on. Sometimes they were aware of a song—maybe even commented about it—but most often they were locked in conversation, quietly sharing their passions and dreams. Always before they had been immersed only in the language of high school debate. Tonight, however, had already been different.

And then came a point in the evening that lacquered the artistry of what was being created between the two of them: Maria casually mentioned, "I'm so sorry about all that stuff with Tommy Wright. I mean, he is such a jerk. But I suppose I like to believe the best in people."

They sat about two feet apart on the sofa, their hands resting close.

Randy welcomed her pejorative reference to Tommy. "Oh, I'm sorry, too," he said. "I was being a jerk about it. I can't stand the guy. He's self-centered, obnoxious—"

255

"I asked him to quit the team," Maria confessed.

"You did?" Randy gasped, grateful for her courage.

"Yes, I did. But as you saw tonight, he didn't listen to me."

"I think being partnered with Lance will be good for him. Lance is a tough guy, but he's nice. And he won't put up with any of Tommy's crap. If Tommy had knocked Lance into the pool that night, Tommy would be in Springview Cemetery right now."

"Yes," Maria smiled warmly, "and I appreciate your putting up with him as long as you have. He had me totally bamboozled."

Randy looked amused. "That's a great word, Maria. Not *tricked* or *fooled*. But you use a totally boss word like *bamboozled*. Which, of course, is one of the main reasons I love having you for a debate partner!"

"It applies perfectly in this situation, Randy. I was stupid. And I'm sorry you had to watch it."

"It was especially tough after hearing what Mr. Lott had to say about it."

Maria raised a brow. "Oh?"

"Yes," Randy yammered. "After he told me what Tommy said about you and him, I thought I would go nuts!"

Mara looked nonplused. "What did Tommy say?"

"That you had this big crush on him and thought he was swell and wanted him to ask you to go steady. Stuff like that. Once Mr. Lott got going, I really couldn't stand to hear any more."

Maria' shake of her head related clearly to Randy her intense irritation and growing disdain for Tommy Wright. "I never told him anything of the kind, Randy. Never. It was not true. When did Mr. Lott tell you this?"

"When he took me back to the motel to change clothes [how he hated repeating this!], after Tommy pushed me in the swimming pool."

"Why would Mr. Lott tell you something like that?"

"Because he was trying to save me from being hurt even more. And maybe he wanted to keep his number one debate team in tact. Mr. Lott thought it would be in my best interest to think I could never have you as my girl. If you were after Tommy Wright, it would be strictly debate business between the two of us. I think it's as simple as that."

While they paused, they heard the Angels chime, "My Boyfriend's Back." The song blended in a timely manner with the subject of their conversation.

She said, "Randy, I never would have told Tommy this. I didn't really know him very well. Of course, now he does nothing but repulse me! I mean, yes, I would look at him, because purely from the standpoint of *looking* at a boy, Tommy is a nice physical specimen. But that is all. It takes much more than this for me to like a boy. My mother fell for a man who was not handsome, and she is still with him after years and years. I want to do the same when I meet the man I am going to marry."

Relieved—and a bit shocked—Randy grinned, "To pursue non-handsome boys, you're going to have to stop hanging around members of our debate team. What, with the likes of Ira and Ruth and, of course, *me*."

"Well, I would put you in a different category from Ira and Ruther."

"Really? How is that?"

Maria now grinned broadly. "I could have some fun with you right now, you know."

"That would be fine."

"But I know you are very fragile."

"Ah, but that was *yesterday*. After the nice things that happened to me tonight—and I think you know what I mean—my fragility has all but disappeared. I've been hardened, baby!" And with that, he flexed a bicep, while shoving his arm in Maria's direction.

Maria could see nothing, as his muscle lay hidden under his thick layer of shirts. She commented, "I don't know if your muscles are your greatest attribute, Randy."

"Oh, yeah? What's—then—my greatest attribute?"

"Your heart."

"Is that good?"

"You have a wonderful heart. You truly *feel* when so many other boys do not. When you love someone, I imagine you love with your whole heart and soul—and that is a wonderful attribute. I can tell this about you already, and I hardly even know you."

"I hardly even know me either, Maria," Randy reflected. "Sometimes the things I do surprise even me. Dallas—the way I *ran*." Then he lapsed into a sheepish grin. "Tommy Wright—the way I *hit*."

She laughed. "But these acts—both impulsive—were from your *heart*."

"Yeah, well, maybe I should try and use my brain a little more. That's what I think. Yeah. My brain."

"And you do have a wonderful brain, Randy. That is what most people know you for. You stand out for your brain."

"And my mouth."

"Absolutely."

"And, well, let's not forget my physique."

With much less concurrence in her voice: "Yes, that, too."

"I'm blushing."

"No reason for you to blush. You are amazingly brilliant—and very talented with words."

"But the thing is, Maria…"

Randy didn't finish. He didn't finish, because her penetrating brown eyes froze him. Just enough light from under the lampshade outlined Maria's silhouette, but her soft, friendly eyes bore through him in a way he had not yet experienced in his young life. Even if she said nothing else, Maria had already proven to him everything was now going to be okay.

"You are not speaking," she said, tilting her pretty head slightly to the side.

"Amazing, huh?"

She gently clasped her hand over his.

Had he rested his hand so close to hers, hoping she would make such a move?

"If I do say so myself, you are sweet. And you have run out of words for the first time since I met you," she teased.

"Well, we're not talking about a guaranteed annual income tonight, so I guess I just plum ran out of things to say."

"Then talk no more," she urged.

And he took the hint.

Leaning towards her, he lightly laid his lips on hers. He had wanted this since Mr. Lott mentioned her name as a possible debate partner back in early September. Or maybe he had thought about it even sooner. But he hadn't known of her own designs and was led astray by Tommy Wright's lies and innuendos, relayed to him with the best of intentions by a man he trusted more than any other man in the world—even his own father—Mr. Lott.

Now the warmth of her soft kiss taught him he had never cared this much for anyone else; that all he imagined, even fantasized, could finally be realized. The soft, quixotic words of "You Belong to Me," by the Duprees, floated softly from the radio, catching Randy in a rapturous moment he would never surrender, no matter what his future brought him.

****

Randy's walk home was not nearly as pleasurable. The journey to Maria's house had only hurried his anticipation; the departure from her house had brought sadness. Though jubilant over the turn of events, his speedy trot home was spurred by the inordinate, increasingly cold temperatures (hovering in the high thirties).

Then the extreme of possibilities, always the case with boys who had neurotic personalities like Randy's, began to gnaw: What if this meant a lot more to him than it did to her? While he had dreamed of these moments for months, could their kiss have been a fleeting, passing incident she will have forgotten about by Monday morning?

Walking harder, determined to stave off negative thoughts and to accentuate the positive, he propelled himself into his new world, a universe in which Maria was now a major part.

Then almost simultaneous with his mind switching over to bothersome thoughts of a forlorn Carmen Pedro, Randy heard the screeching of tires. The sudden noise first reminded him of a car about to peel out at the beginning of a drag race. He always hated that sound; he despised any form of speeding.

But this car did had not arrived prepared for a drag race. This car came only to throw more terror into the life of Randy Whitman.

****

The fiasco in Dallas had wound up draining more life out of Mr. Lott than he cared to admit to anyone else: for one thing, his decision to postpone medical treatment until after the tournament was, though a selfless one, not a very wise one. For another thing, the undue stress and heartache he dealt with in Texas had sucked the essence from his immune system.

Hundreds of scientists gallantly battled the scourge known as leukemia. Tremendous medical advancements were being made on the children front. But for adult men and women, having leukemia remained a virtual death sentence.

On Friday, January 10, 1964, Mr. Lott went to see Dr. Carl Hendrick. They would schedule another transfusion and any other treatments his doctor deemed imperative in their fight to save Mr. Lott's life.

But Dr. Hendrick informed Mr. Lott that his disease had progressed, rejuvenated itself, and future blood transfusions would serve only to exacerbate the evolution of the cancer. He suggested using a couple of experimental drugs during regular treatments, but said that some of these drugs were in their initial stages of development and the probability of failure was very high.

"What will happen to me?" Mr. Lott asked Dr. Hendrick.

"Eventually, your immune system will fail, and you'll get pneumonia or contract a fatal infection."

"Don't beat around the bush, Doc."

"You wanted to know; I'm not pulling any punches with you, Richard."

"How long?"

"There's no way of knowing for sure. The new drugs may have an immediate effect; they may take longer. They may have no effect at all. The goal is to minimize your white cell count and then take it from there."

"If we don't?"

"Three months. Maybe a little longer, but let's hope and pray for the best, Richard."

That morning Mr. Lott had gone home and made some telephone calls. He first phoned Maria's father to straighten out the mess Randy had created by sticking up for Mr. Barquin's daughter and defending her from the verbal assault of Tommy Wright. And then he called Randy's karate studio to reassure his teachers that Randy had used karate only in the circumstances they had taught him to use it. Finally, he telephoned his favorite relative, an aged aunt in Bismarck, and announced he would be visiting her during Easter Vacation.

He told her it would be the last time he would ever be in Bismarck.

****

The sounds of screeching tires startled Randy.

His instincts drove him into a gallop, an illogical reaction, indeed. He mistakenly convinced himself that if an automobile came after him, he could outrun it. So when the car slowed and pulled up to his immediate left along the curb, he was already out of breath.

He stopped. Now in a slow walk, he refused to glance over at the driver of the automobile. Maybe if he did not look, the guy would just go away.

With the passenger's window turned down, the driver yelled across the front seat of his car, "Hey, punk!"

Initially seduced by a vague familiarity in the guy's voice, Randy decided that not looking at the driver might prove to be a fatal error. If the driver had a weapon, deliberately ignoring him— to disregard the weapon—would not somehow cause the weapon to disappear.

He turned his head and saw the outline of a bulky man, a baseball cap pulled down on his forehead, at the steering column of the car. While his vehicle crawled slowly along the road, and as he gripped the steering wheel with both his hands, the driver shouted in a loud voice. "Watch your back!"

Then he repeated himself in an even louder voice, "Punk!"

Randy quickly assessed that it would make no difference if he asked the man to clarify the meaning of his message, and he hastened his already rapid walk. A street corner lay ahead. Randy would turn right. He prayed the guy in the car had already gotten his jollies and would head on a straight course—into the twinkling lights of metropolitan Long Beach.

"You know too much!" the man barked.

Which sent a flourish of fear throughout Randy's body.

"You're dead!" he added angrily.

As the stranger in the car and Randy simultaneously approached the corner, Randy halted. His abrupt stop would signal some ambiguity to the driver: turn left or go straight? But if the man stopped, too, Randy had to choose a definite direction and make a run for it.

Certainly, his karate lessons had convinced him he could outrun a 1952 Dodge Sedan!

Just when Randy saw his many potential tomorrows passing him by forever, the driver floored the gas pedal, and his car shot across the poorly lit intersection, barely missing a street signal lamppost.

Did this mean Randy was out of the woods?

How could he be out of the woods with a maniac running around the streets threatening his life?

And why did the man merely *threaten* him? No one else had been in the area. If the goon had a gun and wanted to kill him, Randy would have lain dead for hours on the sidewalk before someone discovered his body. Why all the mystery and this guy's cloak and dagger approach?

The energy, the fear, propelled Randy forward. He made it home in less than half the time it took him to get that far coming from the opposite direction.

****

Early the next morning after a long night of tossing and turning, amorous thoughts of Maria, cutting immediately to images of a creepy silhouette in the driver's seat of a Dodge Sedan, laced through Randy's brain. His stalker's sinister voice had sounded so disguised, so phony. But still feeling menaced, Randy marched directly to the telephone and placed a call to FBI Agent Stephen Balcomb.

Since it was a Saturday morning, though, Randy expected no answer from the FBI headquarters.

And he received no answer.

When he later described for his parents the incident of the night before, they—without knowing he had already done so—ordered Randy to call Agent Balcomb. And for the first time he gleaned a sense that his parents were slightly apprehensive about his vulnerability to violent retribution from Dallas.

"What was on your camera, Randy?" his father asked.

"Just pictures," Randy replied, trying to manage a casual shrug of his shoulders. "Not much, really."

"Of course, pictures!" Mr. Whitman growled. "But who was in them?"

"The entire family was in them."

Randy's sister Melissa put down a magazine she had been reading at the kitchen table. Mrs. Whitman, her mission to serve a scrumptious Saturday morning breakfast to her family, laid down a dishtowel and paused.

"We were all in those pictures!" Melissa squealed. "Who has them now?"

Randy quickly recognized the necessity of quelling any fears his family now realized by learning of the intimidating driver in the Dodge. But he wasn't quite sure quite how to do that; after all, those exact worries haunted him more today than they had right after the assassination.

"Try to calm down," Randy said, fighting to stay composed himself. Except for a slight quiver in his lower lip, he did splendidly. "Anyone with the film wouldn't even know who they were looking at or where the pictures were taken."

"But Randall," his mother said evenly, "someone threatened you last night. It could be tied to Dallas."

Of course, it *could* be, Randy thought. But the likelihood

didn't pose strong enough odds for him to bet on it. However, lingering doubts, manufactured fears, and memories of the ugly past crashed down on him this morning with resounding force.

"Yeah, Mom, that's a possibility," Randy acknowledged. "But if this guy had been somebody who was after me, doesn't it make more sense for him to kill me than to mouth off at me? Why would they send a guy here just to scare me? What good would that do?" Randy's arguments began to convince even him.

His mother shook her head. "Maybe they plan to come over here and…" Her mouth open, her words hung in the air.

"Mom," Randy forced a grin, "nobody's coming over here!"

"Then why did you tell us about this, Randy?"

Good question: Randy now wished he hadn't told them. The plan had been to advise them, just in case this turned out to be a serious matter. Now he realized they were too impotent to solve the problem—and too afraid to handle the situation coherently.

So Randy took another route. "Look, I wanted to make you guys aware. You need to be cautious for a while. But just think about this: if anybody wanted to harm us, they would have done it by now. And another thing: The guy driving that car last night—I mean, I could barely see him. But he did seem really young, way too young to be sent here by a bunch of thugs behind the assassination."

Melissa chimed in. "You're sure there's no way they can trace you to the camera?"

"Yes," Randy lied. "I mean, if they knew what city we lived in, they could come here and start to match faces. But they don't know about the debate team, the school, or what part of the country I'm from."

Mr. Whitman then offered a bit of analysis that frightened Randy almost to the brink of heaving up his pizza from the night before. "Randy, they don't know what state you live in. You're right. They don't know your name; that's right. But there is one man who knows *exactly* all that, and except for some telephone calls and his one visit here, we have very little assurance about his identity."

"Agent Balcomb?" Randy whimpered.

His father breathed angst. "Or whatever his name is."

"He showed us his card," Randy pleaded.

Realizing the triteness of his point, he quickly added, "And when I called the number he gave me, the FBI answered. They transferred me to Balcomb's office."

Randy only wished this were true.

Mrs. Whitman perked up. "Maybe we can call the FBI at another phone number. Where's his office?"

Randy didn't know, but he remembered Balcomb had flown to California from Washington D.C. He truly did not fit the mold of a stereotypical FBI agent, but he seemed patient and thorough.

Mr. Whitman promised to investigate on Monday.

But Randy had already panicked. Nothing was for sure, positive or negative, about Agent Balcomb. Still, his new wariness about the FBI, along with his frightening experience the night before, had put him on alert. Some comfort sprang from the mere fact that whoever had taunted him last night did *not* hurt him, especially when he'd had every opportunity to do so.

****

The week flew by.

For a few days, Randy mentioned the frightful incident on the street to no one else, not even to Maria. At the risk of coming off as even a bigger lunatic than before, he decided to clam up about everything for a while. He had probably unnecessarily alarmed his parents and sister.

His father checked with the FBI, and no agent by the name of Balcomb, at least, in the Washington D.C. office, answered to his probe. Refusing to be tormented by this chaos any longer, Randy promised his family that after the debate tournament this weekend he again would telephone—and connect with—Agent Balcomb.

Randy worked closely with Maria for the remainder of the week. They kept their relationship specific to their debate preparation and did not discuss their romantic interlude of last Friday night. Bothered slightly by Maria's seeming indifference to him, Randy chalked up this particular round of silence to her professionalism and to his paranoia. Though younger than he by more than a year, she was obviously the more mature of the two.

The league tournament at Millikan High School proved to be much easier than anticipated. The bulk of the debate squad's preparation had been for Southern Methodist, one of the highest quality tournaments in the country. Compared to the competition they had expected in Dallas, the teams in the local debate league paled.

Ira and Margie soared through their competition, not losing a round, and eventually winning First Place. This meant that Ira and Margie had gone to the coveted elimination rounds for their fourth consecutive tournament—and this time all the way. Three other Long Beach teams ended up undefeated, winning all five of their debates. Randy and Maria, one of those undefeated teams, wound up taking Second. Long Beach High School captured the top five spots in the tourney. Even the Pilot teams not placing had a combined total of more wins than losses. An exceptional performance overall, almost every competitor from Long Beach High School attributed their energy spurt to the renewed spirit they experienced with Mr. Lott's presence at the competition.

Tommy and Lance, on the other hand, won only one debate. They barely had spoken with each other all week and then hardly communicated at the tournament. Tommy believed that Lance— and his limited skills—was to blame for their demise. But Tommy would never have said this to Lance's face and would not dare risk commenting behind his back, fearing that Lance's ears would catch on fire. Angering Lance would not bode well for the lifespan of his new partner.

After exiting the bus back at their own school, Randy helped Maria put some of the debate materials in her father's car. He felt her father's gaze taking him apart, so he looked up and waved pleasantly to the man who, with one ephemeral decision, could destroy the tenuous fibers that held Randy's life together. He whispered to Maria, "See you tonight?"

She whispered back, "Only if you see Carmen first."

And then she slid into the front seat next to her father, too close for Randy to comment further without being overheard by the patriarch of Maria's family. Randy, however, understood what she had told him and what it meant: *Talk to your girlfriend. Level with her. If you don't do this, the status of our relationship must remain...only debate partners.*

Randy dreaded facing Carmen Pedro. His thoughts about an inevitable showdown had been weighing him down, paralyzing his social life for far too long.

—CHAPTER 41—

The following week the *Sacramento Bee* published a story with comments from a few individuals who claimed to be witnesses to the assassination. Two men who stood on the grassy knoll were certain they had heard shots from behind them on the small hill. A young mother who attended the motorcade with her six year-old son and had fallen to the curb on the north side of Elm Street, swore that bullets flew over their heads from directly behind them on the grassy hill. A man who had anchored himself on the steppingstones leading up to a monument on the hill told police he immediately ran *up* the steps after he heard gunshots. He saw but a few people milling around the grassy knoll. Two individuals had lain prone on the grass, apparently too frightened to get up for several seconds. And Jean Hill, a schoolteacher who stood on the south side of Elm Street, declared that she saw a puff of smoke coming from behind a white concrete barrier on top of the knoll.

The most amazing story related to the assassination, however, appeared in *Life Magazine*: Apparently, an elderly tailor, Abraham Zapruder, had been taking home movie pictures of the motorcade and captured most of the assassination on film. He stood at the foot of the grassy knoll with his secretary, his Bell and Howell movie camera whizzing away—frame by frame—preserving for history the exact moments the President and the governor were punctured by assassins' bullets.

Zapruder sold his film to *Life Magazine* for ten thousand dollars. His original pictures appeared there first. Soon periodicals from all over the world promised to pay untold amounts of money for the rights to publish Zapruder's film. In all likelihood, the Warren Commission would use the movie camera film in its investigation.

The film showed a smiling, waving President Kennedy. As

his limousine made its left turn on Elm Street, he was still smiling, his right hand in the air, and turned toward a thick line of people (not seen in the film) standing in front of the Texas School Book Depository. After slowly emerging from behind a tree that temporarily blocked Zapruder's line of vision, Kennedy's face had soured; both of his hands now clasped his throat. Jacqueline, obviously concerned, had turned and quizzically examined her husband. The film then displayed an explosion of red on the front, right side of Kennedy's head. A huge chunk of his skull disappeared. Mrs. Kennedy crawled out from her seat in the back of the limousine to a spot on top of the Lincoln's trunk. She was then pushed back into the car, and protectively covered by the body of a Secret Service agent who had run to her from the Lincoln directly behind the President's car.

The film also showed Governor Connally, who sat in front of the President. Immediately after the President grabbed his throat, the governor, holding a big Stetson hat in his right hand, suddenly dropped the hat. His face contorted in obvious pain, as his body slumped down and out of sight.

Randy could not believe his eyes! The first visual evidence of the assassination released to the public seemed to substantiate what he already knew: At least one of the bullets fired at President Kennedy came from the right—somewhere on the grassy hill.

Judging from the home movie of Abraham Zapruder, Randy should consider himself lucky: He had, after all, fallen to the ground and did not witness the splattering of brain matter from the head of the man he so deeply idolized.

****

Cushman and Pendergrass had become one of the hottest teams on the debate circuit. The next weekend at the Claremont Invitational, they won first place again. But this time their accomplishment had earned them a bit of prestige. Not by any means the most glamorous tournament of the year, the Claremont Invitational still garnished the respect of high schools throughout California and attracted some of the toughest teams in the Western

United States for three days of grueling debates.

In the final round, Ira and Margie had their hands full: Last year's State Champions, Weller and Berens, two girls from Beverly Hills High School and the winners of both Loyola and Redlands, had barreled their way into the final round again. As always, they had demolished all their competition along the way. Margie and Ira were aware they needed to be at their best—and then some—to squash the Beverly Hills girls in the final round.

In one of the most memorable high school debates in years, and with a room full of spectators—mostly comprised of debaters who had already been eliminated from the tournament—Long Beach and Beverly Hills battled toe-to-toe.

When Ira stood to render the last affirmative rebuttal, a four-minute speech that concludes the debate, his knees shook beneath the podium. Somehow, though, he managed to zero in on key issues, such as structural barriers to welfare jobs and ineffective employment training. He pounded his arguments home with a ferocity he normally reserved to bad-mouth Tommy Wright behind his back.

In the end, the five judges' ballots favored the affirmative team by a 3-2 decision. Long Beach High School had their greatest victory in years. And as the rest of the young squad looked on—including Randy and Maria, and, yes, Tommy—Margie and Ira accepted their First Place trophies.

In jubilation, Mr. Lott wrapped his big, gruff arms around Ira's waist and effortlessly hoisted him above the ground. He then tried the same maneuver on Margie Pendergrass, but fell backwards under her weight and landed against a wall of the cafeteria, after toppling over a trashcan full of garbage.

But the Long Beach folks didn't seem to care. They were off and running! The team of Ira Cushman and Margie Pendergrass had just reached an elimination round in their fifth consecutive tournament, cowering to no one and bending to nothing, after their second straight First Place finish. They had defeated, arguably, the most celebrated high school debate team in the United States.

Maria and Randy also had debated effectively, but a Sunny Hills team throttled them in the quarterfinal round. They landed in a tie for Fourth Place (all losers in the quarterfinals finish Fourth).

No other Long Beach debaters broke into the top eight. Tommy and Lance went a respectable 3-3 in the preliminary rounds, but that wasn't good enough to compete in the elimination part of the contest, which required at least a 4-2-prelim record.

Although Randy and Maria were not yet ready to hold hands in public—most of the time they used both their hands to haul debate evidence around—they couldn't hide their mutually admiring facial expressions. Maria, however, still insisted that Randy speak with Carmen about his and Carmen's relationship, so they all could reach an understanding of Randy's availability.

Even though Randy reassured Maria that his availability was entirely up to him, Maria reminded him that this was not the case —that Randy's relationship with Carmen was linked to Maria's willingness to accept him. Maria refrained from accepting Randy as a steady boyfriend until she was absolutely sure he had spoken to Carmen, huddled with her about the impracticality of furthering their relationship, and clarified for her that even without the presence of Maria in his life, their boyfriend/girlfriend thing had been destined to crumble.

Unless Carmen understood her relationship with Randy was over, Maria would not go forward as Randy's steady. Maria knew the inappropriateness of sneaking behind Carmen's back. Randy was sweet, attractive, brilliant, and talented. But *no one* was worth committing acts of disrepute, disrespect, and dishonesty, especially as Maria maintained ambitions of aspiring to a plateau of higher values.

Before her father picked her up at the school bus stop, she said to Randy, "Tonight, Randy. I want you to speak with Carmen tonight."

"Should I call you when I get home after I talk to her?"

"No, I can wait until Monday. I have a lot of homework to catch up on this weekend, and I am very tired."

"Okay," Randy said awkwardly. A good excuse to call or see Maria had just been frittered away.

"But be careful," she teased him. "Do not walk to her house. Have your father drive you. You don't need anymore maniacs chasing you around the streets of Long Beach."

Although it had been his beloved Maria who uttered the wisecrack, Randy did not find her little comment the least bit funny.

—CHAPTER 42—

David flew to Miami for a special convention.

The meeting with The Boss took place in one afternoon and about seven cups of hot coffee—black.

He then flew his private plane to Shreveport, Oklahoma City, Austin, Houston, and Dallas.

By the time he arrived in Dallas, exhaustion had taken over. Five cities in three days, with missions to accomplish in each city, would have taken its toll on anybody. David was sturdy. He breathed ruggedness into his work—a commercial airplane pilot, after all—but the monotony of his operations, combined with their pure unpleasantness, served only to exhaust him. Together they summoned him to a place in his body and soul that only a small, comfortable hotel room and a hot, steaming bath would be able to soothe.

He selected the Twin Palms Hotel. Up close, this appeared to be the kind of place he was looking for. One more mission to accomplish—at least for this month—he dragged his large suitcase into his assigned room. Plopping it on the bed, he thought a second time before opening it. While he wanted nothing more than to drop on the quilted bedspread and fall asleep for about ten hours, he reconsidered his options. He would need to look over his instructions one last time. Although his itinerary had been carefully drawn out for him, in none of the other four recent missions had he needed to use such a strange weapon—or had they required such tenacious preparation and exact application. But David's mechanical skills—not to mention his aeronautical talents—had kept him alive. A continuation of these highly impressive skills dominated the agendas of the men who had masterminded the murder of John F. Kennedy.

Digging through his suitcase, he unearthed a small folder

with braided white legal paper. The paper contained information that would ultimately lead him to his prey, along with advice about how to accomplish a feat hardly anybody else in America would have been able to pull off. David thought to himself: *Well, guy, you've been designated as rather special. You missed out on the main course, but here's your chance to partake of the dessert.*

Figuring this would be his final sampling of dessert, he set his jaw squarely, determined that he would not be caught with his hand in the cookie jar.

Carefully setting the notes and folder on a bedside table, David smiled to himself. He could sleep for about six hours before he set the rest of their plan into motion, finished the job, and then returned to New Orleans for a bowl of jambalaya at his favorite restaurant.

Ricardo would be pleased with him.

And so would The Boss.

****

Carmen, as usual, dressed really pretty. The Pedro family normally designated Sunday as the day the whole family lounged around the house, watching television, reading, playing board games, and practicing musical instruments—Carmen could play the piano on par with any other teen at her school.

So when Randy arrived early in the evening to take Carmen out for a short drive and a burger, he realized instantly that she had dressed in a dark blue pants suit just for him. Considering what Randy needed to discuss with Carmen, guilt pangs whacked away at his conscience. All these months they had been going steady she had nagged him, badgered him, and threatened him. She chipped away at his masculinity, trying to drain him of what she routinely referred to as his "male superiority bit."

But she had recently changed. She was now supportive of Randy's debate work—the time he spent away from her—and she understood his need to be alone during the weekends. She had relinquished her position as the bigger nagger of the two, showing an abundance of flexibility in her acceptance of Randy for being

Randy. She had stood by his side after he returned from Dallas, and even after their unpleasant altercation, she came back to him. She defended him against his detractors after Tommy's broken nose fiasco. Although Randy had not fought in *her* honor, Carmen looked at Randy's protection of Maria as a chivalrous defense of young women everywhere—at least, that is what she told everybody.

All of these perceptible changes in Carmen elevated Randy's guilt levels to proportions extraordinarily difficult for his rather crippled conscience. Randy needed to clear the air and free himself from the emotional bondage of Carmen Pedro.

For an hour or so, they chatted about minutia: school, debate tournaments, mutual friends who were dealing with problems of their own, Carmen's brother, her troublesome cousin, and movies they wanted to see together (Carmen encouraged him to take her out to a drive-in theater).

Dallas had not come up in their discussion. Randy's apprehension about being silenced by sinister forces associated with Kennedy's murder had not come up, either. And Maria Barquin's name had not come up, even in the context of discussing recent debate accomplishments. Randy did seem a bit envious of Ira Cushman's successes, but Carmen was determined to make their little cheeseburger jaunt a pleasant experience and refused to criticize Randy for his flagrant jealousy of Ira.

After almost eighty minutes of what he considered reverberating nonsense, Randy finally directed the subject to its requisite place in their conversation. He wished Carmen had finished her cheeseburger sooner. He didn't want her to choke after he began talking.

"So, I think we need to talk," he sighed suddenly.

"We are talking," she giggled. Sitting in their favorite burger diner, she took the eating experience to heart, chewing vigorously and lapping up her large Coke with a thick straw.

Randy's food sat in front of him. He hadn't touched it. "No, I mean—really talk."

"Having nightmares again about evil people trying to run you over with their car?" she asked, sipping from her glass.

"No—I mean, yes—but that's not what I want to talk about. Look, I think there's a way I can push most of this behind me. I mean, I'm always going to worry about the camera and some contract killer knowing who I am, but certain conditions would make my life more comfortable and a heck of a lot easier."

Randy didn't say, *getting you out of my life would give me some breathing room, and bringing Maria Barquin into my life would give me some real joy*, but he wanted to. This, after all, was the truthful answer. He had promised himself he would be honest, but restrictions on this promise existed. And these restrictions needed to be honored.

Naturally, Carmen *had* to ask, "So what can I do to help you with that? You hardly ever see me anymore. It's sort of hard to be helpful to you these days, but I will, if I can."

At first Randy waffled. "You've been very nice to me, especially since I came home from Dallas. Thank you."

"That was horrible—what you went through."

"Thank you. Not that I worked hard to accomplish anything, though. What I went through was a combination of stupid choices and dumb luck."

"You know what I mean."

"Of course."

Randy hesitated. He then attempted to underplay a clearing of his throat, but didn't succeed: The throat clearing became his sign posting for bad news. "Carmen," he said quietly, "I don't think we're compatible."

He waited, hoping he would have to go no further—a ridiculous form of hoping, for sure. But then she responded almost inaudibly, "I know."

Randy went on as though being forced to make his case now, or forever hold it in. "It's ridiculous, us trying to keep something together that was never...together. And we know it will never come together."

All those *togethers*, but presumably she understood.

Then silence sliced the air.

Who should speak next?

He tried. "I think we should be friends, though."

"Why?" she asked unexpectedly.

"Because you're a nice person," he lied.

"So what? There are a lot of nice people in the world—nicer than me. Should they all be your friends?"

"If I knew them," he answered feebly.

"Randy," she said with sugarcoated hostility. She put down the burger she had been holding since they began talking seriously. "I guess I was knocked out of the race. I figured this would happen."

Randy understood her unstated point, but he stupidly asked, "What do you mean?"

"Don't make me say it, Randy."

Carmen's face twitched. Her big, brown eyes suddenly became bigger. Randy figured it was just her way of fighting back tears. He confused her anger for sadness.

"What, Carmen?" Randy, like a fool, persisted.

"I lost out to another Hispanic. At least, I can say *that*."

Randy's table dominance withered in his silence.

"And she probably doesn't want to drag you to Mexico and her extended family after you marry her, does she?"

"Not hardly," Randy used a rare (for him) double negative.

"Your parents never would have accepted me anyway, Randy," she inserted, not mentioning that *her* parents would have never accepted *him*—or that his parents would never accept Maria, either.

And then she added abruptly, "You haven't been very nice to me. And I know why: that little Mexican girl has you by your balls and is holding on a lot harder than I ever did. Only you don't know it yet."

Despite Carmen's last comment about his balls, Randy finally had an experience that ended up better than he had thought it would! Guilt pangs ruled, however: Surely, Carmen wasn't as bad as *some* girls were to their boyfriends. She never had treated him *that* horribly. There were moments when she would come off too aggressively, too obnoxiously, too thoughtlessly, too cruelly. But he had stayed with her, a steady boyfriend for all these months.

Randy then consummated a few thoughts, almost pulling

him off his chair and dropping him on the freshly waxed blue floor of the burger joint: He had agreed to remain Carmen's boyfriend only because he had no other prospects; that her physical beauty kept him around far longer than he should have stayed; that his parents' aversion to Carmen Pedro had been based in their own racist beliefs about culture and skin color, rather than goodness and character. He fought his parents by trying to shock them with the revulsion of their ways and by rebelling against the repulsive idcologies they had used to try and separate him from Carmen in the first place.

To have left Carmen would have been a win for his bigoted parents and, as a result, a victory for racism.

By walking into his life, Maria Barquin had rendered obsolete these justifications for Randy's courting of Carmen Pedro.

Sometimes he thought about how well he treated Carmen: he spent money on food and movies; he opened car doors and always walked up to her porch to greet her; he carried her books to, and around, school; he defended unpleasant aspects of her character and personality; he never forced himself upon her, even when she didn't wish to kiss him—and she usually didn't. Randy had protected Carmen's reputation. By complying with her wishes not to engage in sexual activity or public displays of affection, he had been her guardian, and, he thought, knight in shining armor. They had both benefited from their boyfriend-girlfriend match up, and now the time had finally come to move on.

As Randy later bade Carmen goodnight, he took her hand in his own, gently squeezed it, and told her she would have absolutely no problem finding another boy to love her and take care of her (and kiss her feet).

Which Carmen knew was the absolute truth.

But Carmen Pedro, finally shunned by a boy she had always before been able to govern, to dominate, to manipulate, went home that night a very, *very* unhappy camper.

Carmen's jealousy of Maria Barquin and anger over Randy's indifference to her had been festering inside her for weeks. Her seemingly affable discussion that night with Randy would do absolutely nothing to quell that anger or to minimize the wrath of a young woman who had been burned by a boy.

****

On February 7, Randy received a telephone call from the *Long Beach Press Telegram*. The reporter requested an exclusive interview about his experiences in Dallas. Randy asked the reporter how he had found out—and, in fact, what he already knew—about his personal encounters on November twenty-second in Dealey Plaza. But the local newspaperman, committed to journalism's honor code about protecting sources, refused to answer any of Randy's probes.

Since he had already spoken to—supposedly—the FBI, and since he currently felt that his life might be in danger, Randy refused to talk with the reporter. But he couldn't get out of his head that someone had contacted a newspaper and shared information that apparently made him an interesting story. Yes, Randy believed he *was* an interesting story, but only if he told the truth. Most people either didn't believe his accounts or thought he had been hallucinating.

But no matter: while busily preparing for the State Qualifier debate tournament, he harbored no desire to detail to the whole world how he had fallen flat on his kisser just seconds after coming face-to-face with a would-be Presidential assassin in Dallas, Texas.

—CHAPTER 43—

Later that week Mr. Lott asked his debaters to come to his home for a squad meeting. He popped popcorn, provided soda, and put out a few old jazz records he wanted the kids to hear. He planned to play good music, provide tasty pizza, and promote, for a while, a party atmosphere. And then he would hit the kids with some pretty serious stuff.

As the last of Mr. Lott's twenty debaters drifted into his living room, the meeting had already taken on somber tones. The music failed to help; in fact, a solemn ambiance created by the sounds of a saxophone on the coach's hi-fidelity system donated a certain amount of untimely morbidity to the atmosphere.

Most of the students immediately noticed a change in Mr. Lott's home. The living room, usually strewn with clutter, looked flawlessly clean. Pictures that hung from the walls were straight, and no extraneous pen and pencil markings marred the walls. Later they would find out that Mr. Lott was far too weak to do any cleaning. He simply had hired a maid service to come in twice a week—to do very little work.

"Well, let's get started," Mr. Lott announced. He didn't have to order his students to quiet down. Everyone seemed prepared for a formal meeting, a congregation of youthful exuberance asked too often to deal with adult challenges. Mr. Lott had valiantly attempted to invoke a party-like climate, but his debaters wanted to get down to business. Since Mr. Lott had already told them not to bring their debate files and briefs, they knew "business" meant something more foreboding than going over opponents' cases and arguments.

One of the boys piped up, "When do we eat?"

Which caused everyone to laugh, since most of them had been stuffing themselves with food for over half an hour.

With a fleeting grin, Mr. Lott acknowledged the kid and then quickly waxed serious. "The goals of the meeting here tonight are to set our schedule for the rest of the season, determine who will be going where, and what our options will be for next year, based on what happens now."

Huh? Most of the teens didn't quite understand all of that, especially the last part.

Stillness filled the room. It was so quiet, they could hear a running washing machine from the depths of the basement.

Mr. Lott swallowed and continued, "I actually have some good news tonight, but I'm going with the bad news first: My cancer has returned. Despite the treatments and temporary remission, the doctors have told me that there's not much they can do. They've administered some experimental drugs, but so far they haven't taken effect. Maybe they will later. Maybe they won't."

As Randy looked at Mr. Lott, he saw a man who was transforming right before his eyes. Even as Mr. Lott spoke, his face became more haggard, his body thinner than Randy had ever seen it. He shivered with a sudden premonition. He now realized what bothered him so much about Mr. Lott's house: that very evening, the moment he had walked in the door, Randy had caught the scent of death.

As Mr. Lott spoke, he often hesitated and coughed. He willed himself to speak, hiding his physical pain. The emotional pain, though, was rather conspicuous. "I'm not going to lie to you guys and tell you that I think I'm going to recover from this, because the prognosis isn't good."

He gestured with his head toward the food table. "But as long as I keep a full supply of Cheetos around the house, and every so often some of you bring over a few Hershey's, I'm probably going to live a heck of a lot longer than you think! Almonds in those Hershey's, please!"

No one laughed at Mr. Lott's meager attempts at humor.

"Next," he said, clearing his throat, "Starting tomorrow, I'm taking an indefinite leave of absence from school. Mr. Covey, an able substitute teacher from Chapman College, my alma mater, will cover my English classes—and your debate class. I've known

Stan for years. He'll be great. I'll send you messages through him, arrange meetings through him, but we'll still practice and brief cases here at this house. But Mr. Covey won't work with you on debate; Mr. Palladin has volunteered to renew his commitment by risking his life and reputation in taking you to debate tournaments. That's the good news."

He waited for nods, grimaces—something. He saw tears, however, from a few of the girls. He heard some sniffles, perhaps, from a few of the boys.

He went on, his posture rigid, his face stern. "My major goal this year has been somewhat altered. I'm not going to tell you that this isn't selfish; it is. But by my reaching my goal, some of you will reach yours as well. First of all, I want us to capture all three spots for State; this means, we will have to place One, Two, and Three at the State Qualifier in a few weeks. Second of all, I want one of these qualifying teams to win the State Championship in Fullerton next month."

Mr. Lott paused. And then: "Okay? Is that clear?"

Tommy Wright spoke up. His voice cracked with resentment. "What about Nationals—the National Tournament?"

Mr. Lott replied, "One way to get to Nationals is by winning State."

"Yeah, but don't you care how we actually *do* at Nationals?"

"As with any of this," Mr. Lott explained, "it's the flight that creates the beauty, not landing on top of the mountain. The National Tournament is quirky. More people—especially those in the know—have more reverence for the California State Championships than they do for Nationals. So do I; so should you. We didn't get to the Tournament of Champions this year…and next year is sort of, shall we say, up in the air. So let's set our sites on this one goal. The cool thing is—maybe you guys say *boss* now— the really *boss* thing is that you can achieve these goals by working hard, fighting fair…and never losing your integrity. I want you to bring your debate arguments into the *real world*."

Mr. Lott forced a grin. His debaters could tell it hurt him to smile. "The traumatic events of this year have taught you what the real world is like. Do not confuse the truth in life with the bullshit that goes into trying to win a meaningless debate round. Very often they're not the same thing."

One of the freshmen girls, Susan Hager, spoke out next. Mr. Lott didn't know too much about her, although he had heard through the grapevine that Hager was a hard worker and possessed a voracious appetite for learning debate. In the few times Mr. Lott heard her speak, her innate talent impressed him: her brain was sharp, and her laid back, amiable personality defined her likability. "Is there are plan for those of us who are just learning? Cheryl and I are going to the State Qualifier. Everybody knows we don't have much of a chance of finishing First, Second, or Third. So what should be *our* goals?"

"Good question," Mr. Lott fumbled, embarrassed that he had temporarily forgotten the girl's name. "Your goal is to win as many debates as you can along the way. Beat some teams that you shouldn't beat. Work for some upsets. Win the debate at hand. Achieve that goal and then our whole squad moves up a rung. But achieve that goal with *truth*."

Tommy Wright moved next to Maria. His positioning had become noticeable only to her—and Randy. "Well, Mr. Lott," he snickered. "The *truth* is, it sounds like you've pretty much put the ultimate value of your life in our hands."

A few debaters groaned. Mr. Lott watched Tommy unflinchingly.

Tommy said, "Because if the value of your life comes down to a few teenage geeks beating a few other teenage geeks in some meaningless debates, then that puts the pressure on *us*, doesn't it Mr. Lott?"

Tommy turned his head towards Maria and flashed a phony smile. "Don't you think so, Maria? Doesn't that put way too much pressure on little girls like you? After all, he expects you to *win*— you and Mrs. Kennedy here."

That last reference, of course, was to Randy.

Randy clenched his fists at his side. The self-discipline of his karate training would have to come in handy here; he had to rely on that. He knew nothing else would give him the strength not to break Tommy's nose again.

Incredibly, despite the verbal unrest in the form of murmurs and whispers behind him, Tommy gloated. "I mean, if your life— the *one* life you have and have dedicated completely to geeks— comes down to winning First Place at State, then those *geeks* have some big pressure on them to make it happen, don't they?"

Where Tommy planned to go with this, Mr. Lott didn't have a clue. But he had heard enough. "Tommy," he said in a quiet, stern voice they had all come to know and were now thankful to hear once again, "I think you should leave."

But Tommy didn't flinch. "What—Mr. Lott? You said so yourself. These debates are meaningless. Who gives a damn? In your *real world*, Mr. Lott, who cares about some dumb debates?"

"Mr. Lott asked you to leave, Tommy," Randy interjected, as he stepped forward.

By this time the others were holding their collective breaths.

"What's this?" Tommy scoffed. "Sir Galahad coming to the rescue of another damsel in distress?"

Randy thought twice about moving a muscle or saying anything more. He stood, frozen, half-hoping that Tommy would just leave, as Mr. Lott had instructed, and half-hoping he would stay, so he could mangle him.

Then Mr. Lott shocked everybody in the room. Leukemia or no leukemia, he took a few steps in Tommy's direction and squared his shoulders. Even though a head taller than Mr. Lott, Tommy balked. His smirk disappeared.

"Tommy," Mr. Lott said calmly but between clenched teeth, "you have less than five seconds to leave."

But Tommy wasn't backing down. "I'll leave, Richard— *Dick*. I'll gladly get the hell off this so-called squad, after you admit that you only give a shit about two people on this whole debate squad!"

The others watched him, waiting for Mr. Lott to respond to his challenge.

Tommy went on. "Admit that your miserable little life as a man who will never get married—never-*ever* get married—won't be complete until these two people win some damn debates! And, pathetically, now you're going to die! Admit it, Mr. Lott!"

Tommy's face seethed red, a resentment of years unfulfilled.

The next logical step would have been for Mr. Lott to poke Tommy in the mouth. But he couldn't do that. Despite Tommy's completely inappropriate, outrageous outburst, he still wore the label of *student*—and Mr. Lott carried the banner of *teacher*. A teacher's options in these situations were limited. Mr. Lott entertained the idea of calling the police. And he would have done that, except Lance Richards stepped forward, his large body emerging from the smaller masses. Tommy was big and strong, but his debate partner's height and bulk dwarfed him.

"Tommy, back off!" Lance barked.

"Huh?" Tommy turned; he was surprised to see Lance standing next to him.

Lance's face did not project much congeniality. "I said to back off! Get out of Mr. Lott's face, Tommy!"

Everyone knew what separated Tommy Wright and his certain demise: about twenty seconds.

Tommy's body relaxed; Lance's did not. Lance was not finished. "You get the hell outta' my life, Tommy! You're a jerk! Just a jerk, man!"

Tommy did not know how to react. Remaining cool under this immense pressure—and an outraged Lance Richards epitomized immense pressure—seemed like the wisest choice. He said to Lance, "This teacher's screwin' you, too, Lance."

"Yeah, he put me with *you*." Lance retorted.

Tommy flailed, "Just so he could give *me* the screw, Lance!"

Which was probably the truth, but not the best thing for Tommy to have said at the moment.

Lance leaned forward and grabbed Tommy from the front. Pulling him close, he squeezed Tommy's body against his own, his enormous arms smothering Tommy's face into his bulky chest. Tommy sensed he was about to be crushed.

Mr. Lott thought about calling out, "Stop!" But he didn't. This was all far too interesting; Tommy had once again met more than his match.

As the amassed looked on, Lance pulled Tommy tight to him and locked his arms down at their elbows with his massive hands.

Tommy figured he had very few options here. He was able to free one arm and punched Lance repeatedly in his left side. Lance grunted each time Tommy's fist dug into his body, but this only incensed Lance even more, motivating him to increase the intensity of his devastating hold—not to lessen it. Tommy desperately maneuvered to defend himself but wound up helpless. Unless he could get Lance to release his suffocating hug, he would pass out. He banged on Lance's side even harder, but to no avail.

Mr. Lott, only somewhat grateful that Lance had not used his enormous fists on Tommy, finally jumped into the fray with the intent of pulling Lance off the smaller boy. But just before Tommy succumbed to imminent unconsciousness caused by his lack of oxygen and the potent toxicity of Lance's body odor, Tommy brought his teeth down and sank them deep into Lance's shoulder.

At first peril, Tommy had toyed with the idea of biting Lance, but even in the direst straights, he considered how awful that would appear to the others, especially to Maria Barquin. Biting could not be an option here, he *thought*. But desperate times called for desperate measures: Tommy chopped down hard into the deltoid muscle on Lance's right shoulder and expected Lance to free him.

Lance did free him. He violently pushed Tommy away, causing him to stumble backwards into Mr. Lott, who had quickly tried to saddle off in another direction. But impacted by Tommy's out of control body, Mr. Lott tumbled to the carpet. Girls screamed. Furniture toppled. A couple of kids fled the room, content to escape from the noise and carnage.

Helpless to prevent further destruction, Mr. Lott watched from the floor. He saw Tommy turn and try to escape, but Ira Cushman had inadvertently blocked the doorway. Barreling through Ira normally wouldn't have been much of a problem for Tommy, but now even the tiniest obstacle foiled his frantic attempt to avoid Lance, whose wrath had been quadrupled by the vicious bite.

This time, however, Lance did not resume his suffocating hug. After Tommy's wretched bite, Lance intended to inflict some serious damage. Stepping forward—with Tommy's back facing him—Lance drove his right fist as hard as he could into Tommy's kidney area. The result of the punch, akin to being struck by a powerful piston, dropped Tommy straight to the floor. Mr. Lott's next-door neighbor swore later that she heard Tommy Wright's agonizing grunt all the way from the back of her kitchen. She thought Mr. Lott had brought home a strange animal that made weird wailing noises.

Tommy crashed to the floor and onto his back. He had now stopped making noises; in fact, he had stopped moving altogether. Several witnesses thought Tommy Wright was dead. Others feared for their own lives, since Lance's temper had not fully simmered.

An ambulance took Tommy to the emergency room of the hospital. He spent three days in an intensive care unit, while doctors treated his punctured kidney.

The police arrested Lance. They filed assault charges, and he spent the night in a Long Beach, California, jail cell with hardened adult criminals.

Mr. Lott swore he would never invite anyone, especially high school kids, to his house ever again.

—CHAPTER 44—

The next weekend the Long Beach debaters—minus the team of Tommy and Lance, who were no longer students at Long Beach High School—scored heavily at the Spring Varsity league debate tournament. Against a pool of teams they would also face at the State Qualifier, Ira and Margie won First Place. Ruther and a junior named Chad Loney tied with a team from Sunny Hills High School for Third Place. Once again disappointed, Maria and Randy lost a controversial 2-1 decision in the quarter-finals to an inferior team, two boys from Excelsior High School in Norwalk, another suburb of Los Angeles. (Excelsior would lose in the finals to Ira and Margie.)

Randy thought one of the female judges, who was about fifty pounds overweight and heavily pimpled, had been quietly jealous of Maria's flawless beauty. "Perhaps she was jealous," Mr. Lott conceded. "But how do you account for the male judge who voted for Excelsior?"

Randy smiled and answered, "Maybe that guy was jealous of *my* beauty."

Maria laughed; Mr. Lott did not.

After the tournament, Mr. Lott invited Randy and Maria to dinner. They enjoyed scrumptious Italian cuisine at a place they tried on a whim. Happily gorging themselves with spaghetti and lasagna in a dimly lit dining room did not seem appropriate to Randy. This was an occasion for a fast food place, not one of the most expensive Italian restaurants in Southern California. Randy didn't seem outwardly bothered by another subpar debate performance. And Maria relaxed after the competition, discarding discouraging events and bad memories of the tournament from her mind, as she usually did.

But near the end of their dinner, Mr. Lott indicated he had

more on his mind than rewarding his team for a mediocre Fourth Place finish at a rather easy debate tournament.

"Now it's time to get serious, Whitman," Mr. Lott told them, putting down his fork.

Randy grimaced. "Oh-oh. Tommy's back."

"Oh, no," Mr. Lott waved. "He's gone. He's off the team and outta' the school. So is Lance—which is sad. He got involved only because he wanted to protect me."

"Then why didn't you defend him? Why didn't you confront Mr. O'Shannon about his decision to expel Lance?" Maria wanted to know.

"Because what he ultimately wound up protecting me from were stupid remarks—not offensive enough to try and squeeze the life out of someone or ram a first through his back."

"But Tommy would have assaulted you, Mr. Lott. It was coming to that."

"But it *didn't* come to that. Look, Lance is a nice kid, but on a debate squad he's like a fish out of water."

"He's smart," Maria said, forking the last of her meatballs.

"Obviously not smart enough," Mr. Lott modified.

"Maybe," she concurred.

Randy looked at her adoringly. They'd been seeing each other a lot lately, mostly to prepare for debate tournaments. They also shared romantic music together, a typical backdrop for a boyfriend and girlfriend. And Randy intended to give Maria a "going steady" ring right after the debate season concluded. He wanted her to wear it on a chain around her neck.

"Anyway," Mr. Lott said slowly, "I've been thinking…" He coughed. His colds had become more frequent. Lately he'd been bothered by intense aching, throbbing pain, mostly in the upper part of his back.

"Uh, oh," Randy guessed. "You're splitting the two of us up, aren't you?"

Mr. Lott shook his head. "Nope, not yet."

"Then—what?"

"It might be for the best, Mr. Lott," Maria suggested. "This is Randy's chance—and considering your goal, maybe you should pair him with Ira."

"Maria," Mr. Lott smiled, "don't jump the gun—please."

"Jump the gun?" Maria repeated softly. "It's already March, Mr. Lott."

"That's not what I mean."

"I want Maria on my team, Mr. Lott."

Mr. Lott threw open his arms. "For God's sake, guys! I just told you: I'm not breaking up this team!" And then he dead-eyed Maria. "Maria, I wouldn't have Ira debate with Randy. *You* are not the reason you two aren't living up to expectations. It's not *you*."

Randy wrinkled his forehead and gazed around at nothing. "Then *I've* been blowing it—right?"

Mr. Lott decided evenness was the best route. "You may not even realize this Randy—what I'm about to tell you. You think I'm sick, and maybe I am sick—obviously I am. You, though, you're sicker than I am. But not in your body. Your soul died out there on the grassy hill that day, and I'm doing what I can to salvage the part that's left."

Mr. Lott looked at Maria. "Maria, I've known Randy two years longer than you've known him. I remember the old Randy. You didn't debate with Randy last year. You weren't that close to him. But you observed him in practices; you studied him, because he was our second best role model at the time. You might recall the energy, the clarity, the sense of humor, the roll-with-the-punches attitude he would exhibit during debates. Of course, *then* Randy never had more on his mind than a chocolate shake he might be looking forward to after practice. But, Maria, Randy can't match that attitude, clarity, and sense of humor anymore. They're gone."

It peeved Randy that Mr. Lott referred to him in the third person, even though he was sitting right there.

A waitress with her order pad strolled over and wrote down their dessert requests. When she left, Randy steered them back to business. "So what do you want me to do about that, Mr. Lott?" he asked somewhat snidely.

"About your, uh, sense of humor and your clarity and your energy?"

"Yeah."

"Get them back."

Randy scoffed, but as he did so, he recognized Mr. Lott was dead serious.

"Because if you don't," Mr. Lott warned, "Maria will be debating with Ira Cushman at the State Qualifier, and you will be debating with Lance Richards."

Randy didn't bother to remind him that Lance Richards had been expelled from school. "Isn't that up to Maria?"

"No, it's up to me."

Randy's eyes went down to his empty plate.

Maria spoke next. "He's doing better than you think, Mr. Lott. We've had some bad breaks."

"You've had some bad breaks. All teams do. Ira and Margie have managed to overcome theirs so far."

"Who will you pair me with? Seriously." Randy asked, now sounding desolate, tired.

Mr. Lott pondered for a few seconds, but he already knew the answer. "No matter who I put you with, Randy, you'll be the one holding down your team. You. So it wouldn't be someone in the top ten."

"Are you kidding?"

"Just don't let it happen."

Maria took Randy's hand. She held it gently, reassuringly, supportively. Mr. Lott looked on, but he refused to be the bad guy here. He had decisions to make. He'd been so patient—maybe to a fault. He hoped Randy and Maria understood that his seeming callousness was not about debate results; it was about Randy's health and well-being.

He mainly wished to help Randy Whitman become a human being again.

Randy shook his head helplessly. "I don't know what to do, Mr. Lott. What are you asking me to *do*?"

"For starters, get some professional help. I've taken the liberty to find the name of a good psychologist, an adolescent therapist. Not an adolescent himself, obviously—but one who specializes in helping young people. Clear it with your parents and then go see him."

On cue, Mr. Lott handed Randy a small business card.

"I'll bet this man never worked with the likes of me," Randy said.

"Probably not," Mr. Lott forced a smile.

"He won't believe me."

"It's not his job to believe or disbelieve you; it's his job to help you get through this."

"What if my parents don't agree and won't pay for it? Don't these guys charge twenty bucks an hour?"

"Don't worry about that, Randy. I've already paid for the first two hours."

"But—"

"And by the way, it's a *she*: Dr. Mason. She was also a Kennedy loyalist. She said that she saw Kennedy when he spoke at UCLA a couple of months ago."

"Mr. Lott…"

Both of his elbows resting on the table, Mr. Lott waited until the waitress put their desserts in front of them. Apparently, none of the three was ready to eat, so Mr. Lott focused in on the core, the cadre of the issue. "Randy—Randy look at me. *Look into my eyes*: that's what I'm asking you to do right now."

Randy forced himself, and he did as Mr. Lott had requested: he looked into his wide-eyed gaze

"Randy," Mr. Lott said slowly, and as he spoke, Maria tighten her grip on Randy's hand. "Randy, you didn't kill President Kennedy. And there was nothing you could have done to prevent it. *Nothing*, Randy. If we had never gone in Dallas that weekend, Kennedy still would have died. And no matter where you were, what you saw, which direction you ran—Randy, listen to me carefully—there was *nothing you could have done to save him*. That's it. It's over. And if what's happening to you with debate is a predictor of what's going happen to you for the rest of your life, you're done, Randy. Over. Finished. Do you hear me? *You didn't kill President Kennedy.*"

By now Randy's tired eyes had filled with tears. On the verge of sobbing, he said to Mr. Lott, "Of all the people in the world, Mr. Lott, *I* was standing closer to the person who killed him. And what did I do? I ran! *I ran away, Mr. Lott.*"

Lowering his head in his hands, Randy sobbed. He cried longer and harder than he had cried during his entire life.

Restraining herself from smothering him with her own body was brutally difficult for Maria. Finally, she gently put one arm around Randy, as he rested his head back into its crevice. She then covered him with both her arms, and the floodgates of her own tears opened up as well. They bawled together, as Mr. Lott helplessly looked on. Randy and Maria cried even as the waitress returned with their dinner check—and Mr. Lott thanked her for the dandy meal.

Mr. Lott said, "Randall, it's okay to let it go. Just let it go, sport."

But as Mr. Lott advised Randy, he, too, began to weep. He cried, not for Randy, but for himself—his sudden, terrific sense of remorse: never getting married, no children, abandonment by family, not making special friends, over-indulgence in the amount of time he spent with high school kids in an activity that meant so very little in the totality of the universe.

And for a life that would be over much too soon.

—CHAPTER 45—

Time Magazine's feature about the Dallas Police Department brought about some intense water cooler gossip.

Reported connections between certain members of the department who were under investigation for alleged connections with organized crime figures dominated the content of the story.

Life Magazine, in an ongoing series of investigative articles about the assassination, confirmed much of the coverage reported in *Time*. According to these, and other journalistic accounts, unnamed police officers had been linked to Mafia figures harboring vendettas against the Kennedys. Bobby Kennedy, the late President's brother and Attorney General, carried out grueling, explosive investigations into organized crime—mostly related to gambling laws, casino investments, tax evasion, and nefarious business enterprises. One column, by Rene Ritter of the *St. Louis Dispatch*, alleged a puzzling rapport between Jack Ruby and several Dallas policemen, contending Ruby had befriended more than a dozen officers in the department. Ruby purportedly had provided them favors connected to his strip club, and, inexplicably, had brought them soup and sandwiches while they worked on the job.

The wheels in the minds of many thinking Americans began to turn: What affiliations, if any, did Ruby have to organized crime figures? And what motives, if any, prompted Ruby to kill Oswald? Did organized crime, in fact, play a part in the Kennedy assassination—and what was Lee Harvey Oswald's link to the crime syndicate?

These were mere speculations—questions, actually—that planted seeds in the assassination conspiracy gardens of average American citizens. Most of these average American citizens assumed these seeds were also being planted in the investigative minds of the professionally qualified individuals who officiated on the Warren Commission.

****

Randy left Maria's house shortly after 10:00 P.M. on the Wednesday before the State Qualifier. Mostly, they had filed briefs and looked through magazines and book sources for evidence on expenditure limitations. Randy's visits to Maria's home always went without any fanfare. They worked with the door open in her father's office. Her parents stayed out of their way.

On the other hand, when Maria came to Randy's house, Mr. and Mrs. Whitman were intrusive. They didn't like the idea of the two teenagers chatting—or filing—privately in his bedroom, but compromised their position when Randy promised to leave the door open at all times. Mrs. Whitman constantly stopped by to ask questions about—whatever—and Mr. Whitman moseyed over to their workroom to chat.

Randy's parents clearly did not like Maria's presence in his life, and they sensed more chemistry between them than they thought necessary for a healthy debate colleagueship. They became compulsive about learning the specifics of their relationship. But what incensed Randy: his parents judged Maria Barquin in her totality by her cultural heritage, and they judged her cultural heritage by an ignorant formulation of a stereotype.

Randy was never going to change his parents, and he wished they would just leave him alone. Their bigotry would never become his bigotry. When he and Maria got married, his parents would have to find a way to be more accepting, more tolerant, if they ever wanted to visit their half-breed grandchildren.

So when Randy's father picked him up in the Plymouth Fury with enormous fins at Maria's on Wednesday night, he felt more secure about everything in his life—everything but his parents. The Kennedy experience, of course, constantly intercepted his thoughts. But he'd become so accustomed to this unsettling emotional rollercoaster, he managed to navigate through his days, despite this seemingly permanent handicap. And the serious discussion in the Italian restaurant with Mr. Lott had worked to alter the direction of his self-loathing and helped him to become more focused on people and events over which he had more control.

As Samuel Whitman made a left turn onto their block, he noticed in his rear-view mirror that a car had pulled up extremely close to his own car's rear bumper. Suddenly, the vehicle's lights flashed to excessively bright, then back to their normal brightness, and finally to excessively bright again.

Blinded by the brilliance of the headlamps, Samuel slowed to a crawl, as he drove down the familiar streets.

And then the car got even closer, closer—and—*smack*! The automobile behind Samuel and Randy bumped them forward, creating a resounding thump.

"Oh, boy!" complained Mr. Whitman, who decided to step on the gas. Accelerating, he pulled away from the car that followed them.

Samuel didn't like the idea of stopping in their driveway, giving away their address—possibly opening the gate to an altercation in their front yard.

So Randy watched his father zoom by their own house. And without looking at their home, Mr. Whitman careened around the corner and headed directly for the Long Beach Police Station, about three miles from their property. But they never got that far. Their trailing assailant veered in another direction as soon as they came to a major intersection.

Randy saw that his father was panting, and beads of perspiration, despite the coolness of the night air, had formed on his forehead. Randy wondered why he wasn't as frightened as his father. But he quickly remembered that he had been immersed in some harrowing situations in the past few months—predicaments so alarming and threatening—that being followed by some idiot flashing his headlights could not scare him nearly as much as sitting in a diner, trying to find the right words to break up with Carmen Pedro.

As soon as Randy and his father steamed into the driveway of their home, they saw their front lawn had been littered with dozens of paper bags and rolled up newspapers. The newspapers, upon closer inspection, were soggy: a kind of liquid, probably urine, had saturated them. The paper bags had been filled with—possibly human—feces.

Barging into their house, Randy marched directly to his bedroom and slammed the door behind him. Mr. Whitman, before he could be intercepted by his wife and forced to indulge in conversation, went right to the telephone and dialed the Long Beach Police Department.

The Whitman family teetered on the brink of panic. They had no idea how close they may have come to tangling with real thugs, evil men who were capable of doing heinous, horrible things to other people.

But for all they knew, they may have been circumstantial victims of a rude, obnoxious practical joke.

****

Minutes before he shot Lee Harvey Oswald, Jack Ruby had walked into a Western Union telegraph office and wired money to one of his employees, a stripper, to help her pay medical expenses for her ailing mother. Ruby then walked up a street, down the ramp of a large parking structure adjacent to the Dallas City Jail, and mingled with police, reporters, and other acquaintances. A few minutes later, he carefully removed a revolver from his coat pocket and pumped one fatal bullet into the abdomen of the man who had been charged with assassinating the President of the United States.

Melvin Bellae, a nationally prominent defense attorney, primed Ruby for his potential criminal trial. Because the crime was a capital offense, Ruby would receive the death penalty—the electric chair—if convicted of murdering Oswald.

Bellae put it as succinctly as he could to Ruby: "If you know anything more than what you're saying, tell me. America is angry with the state of Texas. And the world hates Texas, especially Dallas. They'll fry you, Jack. But we could plea bargain and save your life."

But Jack Ruby maintained a steadfast position: He, and he

alone, had wandered into the Dallas jail—his idea, *only* his. He had known something about Oswald's transfer, rumors of the precise time it would happen. He hoped to get a glimpse of the man he had come to loathe in only forty-eight hours more than he hated any other human being on the planet. In an impulsive act spurred by his desire to spare Jackie Kennedy the ordeal of participating in a trial —and America the pain of following the trial of a man who probably had murdered their dearly loved President—Jack Ruby had shot Lee Harvey Oswald dead.

According to Ruby, it was no more, and no less, than this.

But The Boss in Louisiana knew better. There had never been a contingency for a trial of Jack Ruby. While Ruby was— without a doubt—far more reliable and trustworthy than the renegade Oswald would have been, seeds of doubt began to grow, especially as Ruby's testimony before the Warren Commission became imminent. Ruby might talk: in his criminal trial; in his testimony before the Warren Commission; in a police, Secret Service, or FBI interrogation.

Short of blowing up the building that housed him, The Boss knew no way of silencing Jack Ruby—at least, not yet.

****

The FBI, an agency of impeccably bad timing, called Randy Whitman only two days before the big State Qualifier debate tournament. His mind, though, was preoccupied on the competition, on Maria, on the deteriorating health of Mr. Lott, on his parents' intolerance, on threats made against his life, on property damage done to his home, on his inability to control his temper in combustible circumstances. Randy's concentration now wavered from the business of being interviewed by the government.

Which was quite a change. One recent night he dreamed of being chased on foot by three policemen, their guns drawn, hollering at him to stop. He breathlessly ran down a street in his neighborhood through bags of urine and human feces, until a young man in a slowing black Buick accosted him, verbally attacking him with slurs about his ethnicity (a white guy) and a fallaciously identified sexual persuasion (a homosexual guy).

In his dream, the FBI accused *him* of assassinating President Kennedy. *He* held the key to unlocking the conspiracy. They wanted to know what *he* could tell them about Oswald and Ruby and unnamed men who worked with him to murder the President. They wanted Randy to divulge how he had crossed Elm Street, scampered up the grassy hill, hidden behind the monument in front of the brown picket fence, and fired a rifle at John F. Kennedy, a man he claimed to love and admire.

But when the real FBI called on Friday, his heart sank. He didn't need any distractions from the important tournament ahead.

Even more alarming to Randy: the man from the FBI who called this time was not Agent Stephen Balcomb.

Agent Gordon Siegel wanted to "touch bases" with Randy about that day in Dallas (which immediately led to this question: Why hasn't the FBI contacted any of the other teenagers from Long Beach who stood on the parade route in Dealey Plaza)? But Randy could not be sure what Agent Siegel meant by, "touch bases"; nor did he know what happened to Agent Balcomb.

All at once fear whooshed through Randy's body. He told the man (who claimed to be Agent Siegel of the FBI) on the phone, "Look, I've already spoken to you guys a couple of times, and I've told you all I know. If you want me to go over stuff again, that's all right. But I'm only going to do that with Agent Balcomb."

Agent Siegel said that he didn't know an Agent Balcomb, which did not necessarily mean that an Agent Balcomb didn't exist; it just meant that certain elements of the federal investigative body were not communicating or coordinating very effectively. But Agent Siegel would respect Randy's reservations and pursue Agent Balcomb himself.

Randy wanted to ask Agent Siegel what it meant if he could not find Agent Balcomb—or if Stephen Balcomb did not officially work for the FBI—but he was far too frightened to delve into that aspect of the intrigue.

After getting off the phone with the FBI man, Randy prayed that Stephen Balcomb would be calling him soon. Since neither his parents nor Agent Siegel could locate Balcomb, another question, no less alarming, remained in Randy's mind: *Just who was that man who came to my house in December and asked me so many questions about the assassination?*

—CHAPTER 46—

At San Gabriel High School, a steady, cold rain drenched the State Qualifier.

The Long Beach debaters showed up in the school's parking lot on Friday with briefcases and ox boxes full of briefs, index cards, files, books, and magazines. The steady moisture soaked these materials well before the debaters could secure them in dry classrooms. And Ira Cushman quipped, "We're all in the same boat —so to speak."

The first round commenced on schedule, despite the inclement weather. Mr. Lott sheltered himself in the faculty lounge, which doubled as the relaxation headquarters for adults and results tabulation. Throughout the debates on Friday, Mr. Lott found himself fighting the chills, his teeth chattering noticeably, while he sat in the same chair for hours.

Several other coaches checked intermittently on Mr. Lott. In familiar fashion, he waved them off, brazenly pooh-poohing their concerns. But Mr. Lott silently suspected he was running a very high fever, a condition he had already weathered on numerous other occasions.

By the time the bus arrived to pick up the Long Beach debaters on Saturday morning for the second day of the State Qualifier, the skies were clear. The temperature had promised to rise fifteen degrees over yesterday's peak.

But now there was no Mr. Lott.

Instead, Mr. Palladin, dressed in protective headgear and wearing a pair of black boxing gloves, greeted the anxious Long Beach debaters. Their over-riding concern for Mr. Lott's health condition had eliminated their appreciation for Mr. Palladin's sense of humor, so the debaters didn't laugh too much at Mr. Palladin's attempt to make the best out of a bad situation through some creative costuming.

The only time that morning anyone cracked even a hint of a smile was when Ira wisecracked on the bus, "Hey, Mr. Palladin, I thought you said after Loyola you were never going to take us to a debate tournament again!"

To which Mr. Palladin responded wittily, "Yeah, well."

On this second day, Long Beach really started their ball rolling. Randy managed to shed the baggage from Dallas, at least long enough for Maria and him to advance to the final round. Mr. Lott's passionate discourse with his number one team in the Italian restaurant had had a positive effect.

Surprisingly, Susan Hager and her freshman partner Cheryl Gallardo cruised into the semi-finals and then won a 2-1 decision over West Covina. Mr. Lott and a few of the debaters had predicted Susan would come to realize tremendous success in debate, but not this soon and not, of all places, at the State Qualifier.

What's more, by virtue of a tiebreaker, Hager and Gallardo had secured a Third Place finish and thwarted West Covina's chances to compete at State. The Long Beach freshmen relegated West Covina to Fourth Place, a catastrophic spot to wind up at this particular contest.

Only the *three* top-ranked teams would make it to Cal State Fullerton and secure a position at the State Championships. Ira Cushman and Margie Pendergrass once again rolled over everyone else and zoomed into the final round (along with the team of Whitman and Barquin). Since teams from the same school, according to the bylaws, were not allowed to debate each other, the preferential point system would once again take effect. Cushman and Pendergrass clearly out-pointed the other Long Beach debaters and was crowned the top team in the league for 1964. They qualified for State and would be seeded second only to—a team from a different debate league—Beverly Hills High School.

On Sunday Mr. Lott called to congratulate each of his debaters. He reassured Randy that he and Maria still occupied the number one spot on his debate squad. The notion, ludicrous in its proclamation, had become an unstated joke around the Long Beach Pilots' debate office. But Randy didn't care. Without performing their absolute best, he and Maria had made it to State. Now they would have a chance of winning the State Championships. They would debate at State in the manner their much-loved coach had taught them.

Mr. Lott told Randy that he would not be at school all week. With the impending National Qualifier, a tournament now far less important to him than State, Mr. Lott told Randy that he couldn't help them to get ready. He reflected upon how sorry he was for the past few months—sorry that he could not have been much more supportive of Randy as a debater and as a young man dealing with an unwarranted amount of stress in his life.

Randy said, "Mr. Lott, you've been my coach—but more than that—you've been my inspiration for the past three years. Without you, Maria and I wouldn't know debate from, uh, da-fish, let alone have qualified for State! You've gotten Maria and me ready, and now we just have to do our thing. Stay home this weekend—that's fine. You've already done all you can. But *State*, Mr. Lott: By *that* tournament you'll be helping us kick some ass again. It'll seem just like old times!"

After he spoke these words, Randy held the telephone receiver further from his ear so Mr. Lott could not hear the soft whimpers he unsuccessfully tried to hide.

Randy would not see Mr. Lott for the rest of the week. He wanted to talk to him in person before the tournament, but Mr. Lott served up a steady stream of excuses. Randy spoke with Maria about it, and she confirmed with Mr. Palladin what she had already thought to be the case: Mr. Lott didn't want anyone to see him now. Not like this. His sickness had overtaken his body, and he wished for his troops to remember him the way he had looked under different circumstances in better times.

The tournament would begin on Friday. Maria visited Randy Thursday evening, but she and Randy didn't figure to qualify for Nationals. Ira and Margie, despite Mr. Lott's insistence otherwise, had to be odds-on-favorites to land First Place—and only *First Place* would be eligible for the National High School Speech Tournament in Cincinnati, in June. Randy knew Mr. Lott always frowned heavily on intra-squad rivalries, and with only the top spot winning the coveted prize, abusive and divisive behaviors among the Long Beach Pilots were certain to come. Randy's plan all along had been to go into this tournament with a somewhat cavalier attitude, looking for ways to elevate the status of other debate teams from his school.

Randy had set his sights on State—not the National Qualifier —as a means of getting to Nationals.

Ira wanted to win this tournament much more than Randy did. And Ira deserved it, too. His and Margie's record already indicated a clear superiority over Randy and Maria's, no matter what happened the rest of the year.

But State would be his, Randy insisted in his own mind. He had already promised himself that only one goal this year would be realized, that only one tournament mattered—and it was a mutual goal formed with Mr. Lott: *Randy and Maria would win State.*

Ira and Margie could have the National Qualifier.

****

At around 9:30 P.M, just as Randy and Maria put the finishing touches on their briefs and began to store their materials away, Mrs. Whitman called from downstairs to Randy and asked him to take a telephone call.

Figuring Ira was checking up on the transportation situation for tomorrow's tournament, Randy casually slipped down to the kitchen area. In the back of his mind, he held some uncertainty about having a substitute coach for the National Qualifier. Yesterday, Mr. Lott had gone back in the hospital for treatments, and Mr. Palladin had consented to run the show again, as long as Randy promised to contain his karate moves in pubic. Mr. Palladin was getting more proficient with his debate lingo, and his knowledge of national social issues helped the squad members enough to make a tangible difference in their argumentation. The substitution of Mr. Palladin provided to be a benefit, instead of a liability.

Still, Mr. Lott's presence was already sorely missed. During the tournaments he had personally attended, his debaters performed more effectively. They had picked up on little things, nuances, giving them a slight edge when they needed it the most.

"Hello," Randy said, cradling the receiver to his ear.

His mother stood beside him. She usually didn't hover while Randy spoke on the kitchen telephone.

As soon as Randy heard Mr. Palladin's voice, he enveloped the sullenness of the moment. Sadder words he probably would never hear again. "Randy, this is Mr. Palladin."

"Oh, hi," Randy said, hoping against hope that Mr. Palladin had called him only to verify transportation and a pickup schedule for tomorrow.

"Randy, Mr. Lott died today."

Randy blotted out the next several words, though he kept the receiver welded to his ear.

"After school today I went to the hospital to see him, and his room was already empty, cleaned out when I got there…"

Randy began to shake, alarming his mother, who stood by helplessly.

"…I found the doctor on duty—not his doctor—and he told me that Mr. Lott died from an infection…or pneumonia. He's not sure yet, but that's what he said."

Mr. Palladin clear his throat. "I'm so sorry to have to tell you this. He was my friend, and I liked him a lot. His students in his English classes…"

"Mr. Lott died," Randy finally said to his mother. But she already knew. Mr. Palladin had informed her when she answered the phone.

Mr. Palladin stopped telling Randy about Mr. Lott when he heard him switch his attention to his mother.

"Randy," Mr. Palladin continued, "with the two debate teams competing tomorrow at the National Qualifier…uh, we still need to make arrangements. Mr. Lott has an aunt who already consented to pay for the funeral. I think he always opted for cremation…"

But Randy had already handed the phone to his mother and said, "Mom, can you take care of this, please?"

In a trance he stalked up the stairs to give Maria the sad news. Two of the most important men in Randy's life had died within the last five months, and he now grappled with the effects of both of these deaths.

As soon as she saw him, she knew. He opened his mouth to speak, but nothing came out. Maria then went to him, cradled him in the loving warmth of her soothing arms. They staggered to the bed together, and she patted his back as though he were a baby.

When Mrs. Whitman came to the door, she found Maria and her son locked in grief. She carefully shut the door and let them release their sorrow on each other—both of them entwined with the commonality of the debate world, the warmth of their personal relationship, the death of a President, and the love of a wonderful man and teacher.

****

On Friday, March 30, Ricardo reached David on the phone. The pilot relaxed with a pipe and a vodka gimlet, his feet up, and his eyes fixed on a spring college basketball game on the television set. He marveled at the personal touch of watching sports on T.V. and no longer felt compelled to shell out a top dollar for special seats at the arenas. He could enjoy, up close and personal, the exploits of his favorite players.

When the phone rang, David answered it with one ear glued to the sportscaster. But when he recognized Ricardo's voice, the negligible formalities, and the seriousness of his demeanor, his full attention fell on the needs of this crazy Cuban exile.

"David, you are to stand by," Ricardo told him.

"Okay," David responded haltingly. He wondered what that meant but didn't want to risk appearing stupid—not to Ricardo.

Fortunately, Ricardo provided him more details. "The Boss said to wait. But he is not sure for what or how long. The Commission is interrogating folks like they are passing through an assembly line at a factory. And some of those we did not get to have already completed their testimony. There may be a need to eradicate later—much later, perhaps. And for that you are invaluable to us. Do you understand, David? Have I related The Boss's wishes to you—so very *clearly*?"

306

David swallowed and nodded, but the silence on the other end reminded him that the telephone was an auditory device that required an oral response. "Yeah, I get it," he finally answered.

He didn't, though—not completely. Had Ricardo told him he could now stop killing people? If so, that was good enough for him. The last one, the taxi driver who had taken Oswald home and later was scheduled to testify before the Commission, turned out to be a challenge. Fixing the brakes of his cab in order to make it look like an accident required a rare skill. But David had fared extremely well in that mission. His bosses were proud of him, satisfied with his work, and searched for ways of utilizing him in the future. Now he could expect a long life ahead of him.

Couldn't he?

"One thing more, David," Ricardo said, toning down the seriousness of his voice. "As these unfortunate accidents mount up, the authorities will undoubtedly become more suspicious. You are to speak with no one about this, not even those queer-types you hang around with and call your *friends*. Do you understand?"

"Yes," David answered weakly. He wondered how Ricardo *knew*.

Without Ricardo's permission, he wouldn't talk to anyone else anyway. Why did they have to be so adamant about letting him know what to do and not to do? It was already obvious. Hadn't he already performed flawlessly? Why did his bosses not yet trust him and believe in him with the kind of abandonment he had shown to them?

"Stay prepared, David. Things are brewing in California: a teenager who may have seen way too much. We may require your services at least once more."

David wasn't sure what that meant either. But he proudly suspected that, sooner or later, he would have more unpleasant work to accomplish.

—CHAPTER 47—

A warm, sunny California morning in late March brought an incongruous atmosphere among the student population at Long Beach High School.

Those who did not know the teacher very well, not in comparison to his dedicated debaters, had occupied Mr. Lott's four English classes. Word had not spread about Mr. Lott's death. But when the substitute teacher, Mr. Covey, walked into Mr. Lott's first period English class of thirty eleventh graders and announced that Mr. Lott had died the night before, the bad news jutted through the school like a forest fire in arborous terrain.

Word had leaked throughout the debate squad, and around midnight Ira Cushman called Randy and informed him of his decision to withdraw from that weekend's National Qualifier.

Randy already had considered this option but wasn't ready to discuss it with anyone. Now the final hours crept upon them, and decisions needed to be made.

"Maybe Mr. Lott would have wanted you to debate, Ira—not to drop out. You are the clear favorites to win this weekend."

"I don't care, Randy. I don't have the heart."

"You'll win; I'm sure of it."

"Randy? So what?"

"I'm glad you said that, Ira. I don't have the heart either; neither does Maria."

Once again paralyzed by the grief brought out by the death of someone who mattered so much to them, the debaters from Long Beach opted out of another tournament, *the* tournament that decided which team would compete in the National Finals. It was a coveted honor, but this competitive event—or any other debate tournament—paled in significance next to the untimely death of Long Beach High School's beloved coach.

Mr. Lott was buried in Forest Lawn Cemetery on Thursday. Over two hundred people, mostly students and faculty, attended. A Protestant minister Mr. Lott had never met presided over the proceedings, telling stories he had gathered from others about Mr. Lott. The mourners in attendance, those who had come to pay their respects, simultaneously laughed and cried.

For Randy and the rest of the Long Beach debate team, the most difficult part of the funeral came when the Reverend spoke of Mr. Lott's devotion to his students and his passion for teaching. He rhapsodized about Mr. Lott's commitment to his championship debate team, one he had molded in the style of integrity, honesty, and truth—values Mr. Lott had hoped to pass along as his greatest legacy. The debate teacher believed that living by these ideals was much more important than receiving the big trophy that came from a preferential nod on a judge's ballot.

****

On Friday at the end of lunch, Randy visited his book locker. There he found a piece of scuffed white paper haphazardly pasted with Scotch Tape to the outside of the locker door. While hurrying to his next class, he quickly read what appeared to be a note addressed to him: *Randy...we know where you go to school. If your* [sic] *asked to testify, you will die.*

In addition to the incorrect spelling of the word *you're*, that which truly warmed the cockles of Randy's heart was the amateurism of the entire incident. Randy now confirmed what he had already suspected: All three unexplained episodes in which unknown, mysterious culprits had threatened him were slipshod and unprofessional.

Which meant they were unrelated to the assassination.

When he later spoke to Maria about the note, approaching her with refined seriousness, she began to giggle. She thought someone had been playing a silly game with Randy. And now this last threat proved to be the tackiest, most ludicrous of all.

"Why are you laughing?" he beamed, as he grabbed her armful of books and strode alongside her through the long corridor of book lockers.

She looked at him and tilted her head slightly to the side, an endearing gesture he inhaled as the essence of life itself. When he saw her move her head like that and wrinkle her adorable button nose, reinforcement flew at him from all corners of the universe: In Randy's case, perhaps He had been temporarily napping. But now, *Yes! There is a God*!

She smiled, displaying her magnificent dimples. "Well, these just do not sound like people who have the moxie it took to shoot the President of the United States."

This time in a lower key, she laughed again—adorably!

"Maybe not the shooters, but *hired* by the shooters?" Randy stumbled.

They approached the door at the end of the hall where they would veer in opposite directions, so they stopped and stood facing one another. Finally serious, Maria asked, "What did Mr. Lott say to you about your dwelling on this, Randy? What?"

Suddenly Randy felt again as though heavy lumber lay on his shoulders: the recent death of Mr. Lott had consumed him all morning. Then the bizarre note Maria had tried to minimize nagged at his sense of safety.

Randy bowed his head. Grief returned in a rush. "Yeah, I need to give this up. I need to fight it, not join it. Yeah."

"And what did your therapist say?"

"She's worthless."

"Did she believe you?"

"No, but she held out her hand for forty dollars after our two hour session. And I think she cut me short by ten minutes—thank God!"

Without another word, she gave him a peck on his cheek, tenderly squeezed his arm, turned, and then disappeared through an open classroom door.

Randy had confirmed to himself why he was not heading off in thirty minutes to debate at the National Qualifier. He stopped and allowed himself to bask in the sunlight of gratitude for all that he possessed: his family, his life, his Maria, and the wisdom to know that he should put things in their proper perspective.

Mr. Lott's life, though too short and too unappreciated even by Mr. Lott himself, had been a Godsend for Randy—and probably countless others. Now Randy would honor Mr. Lott in ways he could exercise more control: listening to his advice about the whole Kennedy ordeal; peacefully co-existing with his parents; protecting Maria from harm—and two months from now, kicking some very serious debater ass at the California State Speech Championships.

****

By the end of April, the *San Antonio Register* in a Page One feature story concluded that four shots had been fired at the Presidential motorcade. The meticulously researched article, compiled by three staff writers, indicated that three bullets, two from behind, and one that apparently had been fired from the front and to the right, had struck President Kennedy. The bullet that plowed into his brain had produced the fatal result.

Various media sources, receiving leaks from officials close to the autopsy on Kennedy's body, suggested that doctors at Parkland Hospital who first tried to save the President's life in the emergency room believed Kennedy had been struck in the rear, possibly in his back, with the bullet exiting through his throat.

This contradicted earlier reports of a bullet's path through the President's throat from a gun fired *at the front* of Kennedy's location. In other words, medical experts speculated that President Kennedy had been hit by at least one bullet from *behind* and *above* the motorcade. This theory, however, did not account for a bullet, also probably from in back of the motorcade, that hit Governor Connally.

Questions materialized; rumors buzzed: Did one bullet strike both President Kennedy *and* Governor Connally? Doubts over the plausibility of this happening began circulating. And what of another shooter or shooters—those sounds described by witnesses as coming from the hilly area to the right of the motorcade? The veracity of these witnesses' comments to authorities was always in question, but those recounting the shots as having come from

311

behind and above—albeit a majority of the witnesses—received the highest praise from government and police officials.

****

By April, Randy had received from local newspapers and other publications no fewer than seven requests for interviews. He declined all of them; yet, he ached with frustration because the accounts he had already given to the FBI had received no serious attention from, well, *anyone*. And in the meantime, media sources were creating a circus-like atmosphere around the investigation of the assassination.

One nut case had accumulated seven interviews and two television appearances for his so-called eyewitness report of a man *swinging on a rope* from the records building behind the motorcade, through Dealey Plaza, and with a gun blazing the whole time. According to this eyewitness, the man disappeared under a manhole cover on Elm Street, pulling his rifle behind him.

Randy did not wish to garner this kind of embarrassing, demeaning publicity along with his—many would see it as such—sensational account of having a brief, fleeting encounter with two hobos behind the concrete barrier at the top of the grassy hill.

But what of his interview with the FBI? Why hadn't any substantive information from this interview with Agent Balcomb been reported by reliable media sources? Or, if the FBI had thought this information was serious enough to keep undercover, why hadn't anyone contacted Randy in the past few months for a follow-up interview? And whatever happened to Agent Balcomb? No one at the Bureau returned Randy's phone calls.

The lack of contact, the silence, reminded him of his nauseating discomfort during the week following the assassination, while he waited for someone—anyone—to call him or interview him about what he had seen. It *fried*—much less perplexed—Randy that none of the other five debaters (or Mr. Lott) had been called on by the FBI or Secret Service. The police in Dealey Plaza had taken their names, addresses, and telephone numbers, promising—or warning—them that they would be contacted in the future by at least one of the investigative agencies.

Through April, no one called them.

Randy's memory of Agent Stephen Balcomb had not faded, but he figured that unless Balcomb had fallen off a cliff or been hit by a freight train, the agent who had come to see him early in December pulled the weight of only a tiny feather when it came to possessing power and influence at the FBI. Either that, or Balcomb had chosen not to believe Randy. Too many kooks and nuts permeated the assassination circles these days. Alas, Randy had said or promised nothing that would prove him to be any different from those kooks and nuts.

Good news—in a different venue—came to Randy three nights before he would be going to Fullerton State for the California Debate Championships. Randy had been on pins and needles, scared out of his wits, by the potential for someone involved with the assassination to locate him in California and then kill him. The more time passed, the less likely this was going to happen. But each incident—the mysterious car, the excrement in the paper bags on his lawn, the note on his locker—struck him in the face with grim reminders of the dangers facing him.

But then there was that last episode of the three—the haphazard, clumsy note left on his book locker. After that third attempt to scare him, Randy decided he might be able to relax a bit. Professional killers, he concluded, do not come to high schools and use Scotch Tape to stick to book lockers warning notes scrawled in pencil on old, crinkled, notebook paper.

Which, of course, led him and several others to one obvious conclusion: Someone in the school pulled a demonic prank on him, someone with no empathy for his sensitivities and fears, someone privy to hypersensitive knowledge about Randy Whitman.

He and Maria put their heads together for about five minutes before they fingered their most obvious suspect.

Tommy Wright was mean, capable of caustic flame throwing and digging, hurtful taunts. But for him to have been that vile, his motives needed to be compelling. His attraction to Maria and then her subsequent rebuke of him, her blanket impugning of his masculinity, all rendered aspersions cast in Tommy's direction as viable. He also knew that Tommy's physical pain, caused directly or indirectly by Randy's hands, gave Tommy enough of a motive to assault Randy's sense of safety.

Randy brought the note to the school's discipline principal, who did a comparison with samples of Tommy's handwriting. Even if there was no link to Tommy Wright's penmanship, Randy and Maria thought Tommy might have had someone else write the note for him and had employed yet another person to drive the scary black Buick along the street that night in January. This same individual would later deposit bags of feces on the Whitman's front lawn.

Tommy's expulsion after the violent fracas at Mr. Lott's house made his physical presence at school impossible. If Tommy Wright's penmanship did not match the writing on the note, it would have been of little surprise.

But what the assistant principal, Mr. Mauer, did tell Randy startled him. "This isn't Tommy Wright's handwriting. I can ask him about it, but I can't accuse him of this. Obviously, he's had a very, shall we say, unlucky year."

Randy geared up to offer his boss his theory about the paid note-writer.

But then Assistant Principal Mauer, an older, balding man who always wore a bowtie and a pin-stripped suit, said, "Besides, Randy, this isn't the handwriting of a boy…"

Randy blotted out the rest of what Mr. Mauer said. When his A.P. implied a *girl* had written this note, he barely heard him. His mind had already immediately raced to an image of his former girlfriend—chidden, stymied, and dumped—Carmen Pedro.

—CHAPTER 48—

Two nights after Mr. Mauer's insistence about female input in the infamous locker note incident, Melissa listened quietly while Randy discussed with their parents the Carmen Pedro revelation. Melissa watched her father, clad in a maroon bathrobe, and her mother, still dressed in black pants and a white blouse, which she had now worn for the past ten hours.

Randy finished his summary of events. He watched his father, after a full day without shaving, rub the stubble on his chin. "So she allowed her live-in, juvenile delinquent cousin to do the dirty work: the slow car that scared me outta' my life and," he finished with a wry grin, "those little presents they left us on our front lawn."

Mr. Whitman, however, didn't smile. "Let me get this straight," he frowned. "This girl, your girlfriend—your *former* girlfriend—Carmen tried to get back at you? Is that it? So she exploited your emotions, your fears?"

Randy felt sadder, rather than madder, about this. "Yup."

Mrs. Whitman chimed in. "She hired people to scare you?" she asked aghast.

"Not exactly hired. It was her cousin. He did it out of family loyalty, beginning with the car thing while I was walking home from Maria's. I mean, Carmen didn't know about that at first. But I guess after I dumped her, she thought it was a pretty good way of getting me back. And so her cousin went ahead and messed up our front lawn, too. He did it all. Except for the note on my locker— her cousin didn't have access to my locker. But Carmen did. She put it there. She was so stupid. I mean, I knew Carmen wasn't the brightest bulb on the tree, but I didn't realize how massively stupid she was."

"Or evil," Mrs. Whitman added.

"Oh, I had an inkling," Randy sighed. "She is beautiful, of course. But she's one of the most manipulative, controlling people I've ever met."

"We should call the police and press charges—all the harassment," Mr. Whitman suggested.

Randy was already ahead of them. "Except for the damage they did to our property—and there really wasn't any lasting damage—there's not a whole lot there, Dad. The school suspended her for harassment for the locker stuff. And—yes—the police have already been notified about the urine and feces drops."

"Oh?" Mr. Whitman raised a brow. He had headed in the direction of the phone and then stopped.

"I told you about Carmen's being stupid. Well, here's the height of it: It seems that Carmen told Tommy Wright—the boy whose nose I broke—*everything*. They'd secretly been seeing each other for a couple of weeks. Didn't take her long, did it? Anyway, the police summoned Tommy to the school and asked him about the locker note, even though we knew he didn't actually write the note. Of course, he denied it. But then he totally spilled the beans. He even knew the first name of Carmen's cousin."

"Wow," Mr. Whitman whistled, "what luck! This Tommy Wright character seems to be behind all the miserable things that have happened to you this year."

"Yeah, well, this time the bum actually helped me out."

"And against his own girlfriend!" Mrs. Whitman exclaimed.

"Not exactly," Randy smiled. "Another stroke of good luck: Carmen had already dumped him. Last Saturday night. Good thing, too, because he hates her guts now."

Mr. Whitman put an arm around his son's shoulder, pulled him close and almost spilled Pepsi Cola from a glass he'd been holding. "Well, just consider yourself lucky to have that girl out of your life. I told you from the beginning she was bad news; so did your mother."

He looked over at his wife and winked triumphantly. "And now you see what their families are capable of doing. Everything with these people is blind loyalty, even when it's evil. They protect bad people in their family, even when they know they're bad."

Randy slithered away from his father's friendly caress. How he despised it when this man spread his racist wings and flew his ignorant, prejudice views about people! Since Maria also came from a brown culture, Randy knew that his father had the same feelings about her and her family as he did about Carmen and her clan. And casting aspersions on wonderful people such as those in Maria's family reeked of ignorance. He hated him for it, and at once knew why he could never be close to his father—not like he had been with Mr. Lott, and not like he was becoming with Mr. Palladin.

"I was on your side, Dad, until you made such a stupid comment. How do you explain Maria's wonderful character and the pride and dignity of *her* beautiful family? How? Aren't they also from that *ilk*?"

"I don't know anything about Maria and her family."

"Well, that's the whole point, isn't it? You don't know anything about them, although you know they're Mexican—and very American. How do you explain it?"

"Randy, I don't have to explain anything."

Mr. Whitman's revulsion about arguing with his son, especially as he had been sinking in the swamps of despair during the past few months, tugged on his heartstrings. He now regretted his insensitive, careless remarks, although he still believed them to be the truth.

"But you do, Dad; you do need to explain yourself."

Mr. Whitman gritted his teeth. "But I don't, Randy."

"No, Dad, here's why you do: I can't love a father whose bigotry flies in the face of decency. I can't love you, because I can't respect you. I want to. I really want to, and I've given you every opportunity. But I know if, and when, Maria and I decide to have a wedding, you won't want to come. And if you do come, you won't be supportive. You'd be there out of some blind obligation to your *family*—which is ridiculous, and the exact weaknesses that you spouted off about Carmen's family. But that's because of her family's lack of character, not because of their Hispanic culture."

Randy, observing his mother agape, shot a dagger look in her direction. "Which, Mom, is so incredibly ridiculous and sad and disgusting that I even have to tell you this stuff in the first place. *You* are supposed to be the adults here."

Mr. Whitman's bottom lip dripped moisture. His voice trembled. "Randy, you need to leave the room."

"Without dinner, go to my room? Huh? Is that it?"

"Get out!" Mr. Whitman barked.

"If you throw him out, I'm out of here, too," Melissa piped up. "He's so right about this—and you're both so wrong."

Looking hurt, Mrs. Whitman put her hand over her heart. "I didn't even say anything."

"And that is exactly the point, Mother," Melissa accused. She then gestured toward her father. "If you'd speak up every once and a while, stand up for yourself and tell this man off, maybe you both could move forward into the 20th century."

Her mother looked so wounded, Melissa turned away from her. She couldn't stand seeing the pain on her mother's face.

Melissa allowed Randy to continue the mugging. "Maybe you don't understand much, Dad. Maybe you're still living by the old-fashioned, outdated, retrograde values of your father and his father, and—and John Wilkes Booth! But the truth is that I can't respect a man who thinks the people of any race are all alike—all *bad*. I can't respect you, Dad—especially when I know better than you do, and I'm only nineteen."

Mrs. Whitman put a sympathetic hand on her husband's arm, but he threw it off. "Randy," he said calmly, as though reason would now prevail because of his age and maturity, "I understand how emotionally vested you've become in two girls who you think belie all what your mother and I have told you. And, yes, I do think that Maria is a nice girl. But the end result of relationships like these is almost always the same. Look at what happened to Carmen and you. See how her Puerto Rican family almost ruined your life. They tried to wreck our house, just because Carmen thought you had let her down. You think *that's* right? You think *that's* fair?"

"Dad?" Randy paused, now grinning through his own brand of pain.

"Dad?" he said, waiting for his father to say something but not expecting his father to answer his call.

"Dad…you think *that* is what I'm saying? You think I'm saying that it was okay for a bunch of thugs to stalk me, threaten my life, crash into our car, and try to wreck our house? Is that what you think?"

Mr. Whitman, too far immersed in the marsh of family divisiveness, blindly plodded forward. "Yes, Randy, that's what I think. These Puerto Ricans and Mexicans and Cubans and what not —they all have this blind loyalty to family and culture, above and beyond any gauge of morality. And with this, they're capable of doing *anything*. Why did Carmen want you to move with her to Puerto Rico, after you—God help you—married her? And, frankly, Mexicans are far worse that Puerto Ricans about this sort of thing."

"*All* Mexicans aren't *anything*, Dad!"

"Not all. But the odds are good."

"Do all Negroes commit crimes in the street?"

"Yes!" And then thinking better of his provoked outburst, Mr. Whitman corrected himself. "Not all, but many—most!"

Shaking his head, Randy started to leave the room. He thought he was about to have another emotional meltdown. "I give up. Really. Why am I arguing with you? It's hopeless."

"Ask Maria's parents what they think of you, Randy," he called after his son.

"I already have!" Randy turned around and squared himself. Of course, he *hadn't* asked Maria's parents intimate questions such as these. But he didn't have to. Maria's parents' vibes, unlike Carmen's parents' vibes, offered him respect and peace.

For an instant, a slight nausea rose up within him. What kind of vibes did Maria receive from *him* about issues like these? They rarely discussed delicate matters pertaining to race and culture, but he knew from working with her on the debate topic that Maria touted those who valued others mainly for their constancy of integrity and their quality of character. She thought it crucial to evaluate other people as *individuals*, not as groups to which all people in that group must conform in their actions and beliefs. Culture mattered, but it was not paramount.

As Randy hurried up the stairs to his bedroom, he heard his sister still chastising their father for his untimely, unseemly display of bigotry. Melissa's college teachers, she scolded, would never tolerate views such as those held by her own parents.

At least for the time being, Melissa's professors had done her a world of good.

—CHAPTER 49—

Unfettered by the murkiness of the investigation, and no longer daunted by the refusal, unwillingness, or pure incompetence of the FBI to follow up on their interrogation of him, Randy consigned himself to a new chapter in his life. After the fiascos with Carmen Pedro and Tommy Wright, both now expelled from the school district, Randy implored himself to take charge over that which he could control by himself.

The time finally arrived. Randy and Maria plunged into the State Championship with bugged eyes, clawed hands, and fanged teeth. Their mission was to take no prisoners, and to view their competition with a kind of competitive disdain that would lead them to just the right amount of confidence for a full course of constructive arrogance.

Mr. Palladin could not keep up with their determination, insisting his time would be better-spent coaching Ira, Margie, Cheryl, and Susan. Even in the few practice debates he had conducted, Mr. Palladin came to terms with his limited grasp of debate theory, the many coded terminologies, and the depths of complexity into which debaters delved while discussing the resolution. Mr. Palladin, a government/history teacher with great insight and knowledge of his subject matter, understood the basics of what the debaters spoke and could be trusted to judge other debates with accuracy, fairness, and aplomb. But no one expected him to raise the debaters to the next level of topic analysis—within the previously set debate boundaries—the way Mr. Lott had done.

The weather in Fullerton during the first weekend of May could not have been better. The sun blazed that Friday afternoon so bright and warm, it seemed a pity the teenagers would have to scamper indoors at 3:00 P.M, instead of slapping on their bathing suits, throwing together a picnic lunch, and heading to the beach.

Unlike other tournaments, the State Finals were double-elimination; that is, a team could afford one loss. Upon a second loss, however, they would be dropped from the contest.

Random pairings were drawn for the first two rounds, with teams from different leagues facing off against each other. In total, forty-eight debate teams had qualified for this very esteemed event; and by the end of Saturday, only a few of them would be left for the remainder of the competition on Sunday.

Susan brushed up against Randy as they fought others to get a quick view of the postings, the early round pairings taped to a wall in the college's student union building. She said in a cavalier way, "I'm not that nervous. We have nothing on the line."

"It's a tournament; that's all. You have the right idea."

"And Mr. Lott wasn't counting on me and Cheryl."

Randy could do no less than clench his jaw almost to the point of grinding his teeth into his gums. Susan was right. But this wasn't just for Mr. Lott or Maria's confidence or to get into a good college or to stick it to Tommy or to shun his parents or to make a name for himself amidst the geeks on the debate circuit. Randall Whitman had to win this for Randall Whitman: to prove to himself that the realness and coldness of the universe could be assuaged by fine-tuned intellectual gymnastics carried out inside white-walled classrooms—and it all could be accomplished in a meaningful and productive weekend.

In round one Randy and Maria, on the negative side, debated against a team from Clovis High School from the Northern part of the state. Long Beach proceeded to methodically throttle Clovis with the precision of a well-trained battalion of soldiers on a mission they'd been planning for a year. Two boys from the Northern school, a team of reputable quality, fled the room looking as though they had just thrashed about in the bowels of the Titanic.

Susan Hager, with Cheryl Gallardo in tow, slithered up to Randy after her first round. A look of consternation on her face, Susan delighted in kibitzing with Randy, whom she found to be extraordinarily bright, occasionally funny, and mildly cute. For a freshman girl on a new team of *anything*, the elements at work here could prove to be intriguing.

"You look confident!" she observed. She leaned over to Maria, who was seated at a lunch table behind him, and smiled. "He didn't let you down, did he?"

Maria shrugged. "I think we got it."

"Who'd you hit?"

"Clovis."

"Who?"

"They're from up North."

"They any good?"

"Very good," she grinned. "Randy was in true form! Very thorough."

"Sounds good."

Randy added, "I'll take my chances with *three* judges any time."

Maria asked the petite freshman, a budding star and a potential circuit cutie pie, "How about you two?"

"Oh, we got kicked around pretty good," Susan answered flippantly.

Surprised, Maria asked, "Who did you debate?"

"Head Royce. I guess they're a private boys school or something. We got chewed up and spit out."

By this time Cheryl thought it appropriate to add, "I freaked. I went up for my first negative and totally blanked out. Susan tried her best to pull us out of the quicksand, but…"

"But I wasn't any good either," Susan supplemented her partner's appraisal. "Really. We did *terrible*."

"Really bad," Cheryl sighed. "The main reason I think I blanked out during my first speech was that the two boys from Head Royce were so handsome! I wanna' kick myself!"

Carrying their ridiculously enormous number of briefcases and ox boxes, Margie and Ira circuited the room and found the rest of their squad. Letting their materials slip onto the floor, Ira and Margie—especially Margie—looked concerned. Ira lifted his face to the ceiling, jabbed his hands in his slacks under his suit coat, and shook his head.

Maria asked Margie, "What happened?"

"I ate it," Margie confessed.

"What did you do?"

"I messed up! I dropped all the plan disadvantages in my first affirmative rebuttal."

"How could you do that?" Randy asked her.

"How?" Margie deprecated. "How? I ran out of time! They spread the poop out of us, and I didn't get to everything. Guess that's the rumor mill now. How to beat Long Beach—at least Pendergrass and Cushman: talk as fast as you can, spread them with so many arguments, they won't have time to cover them in rebuttals!"

"It worked," Ira glumly added.

"What team?"

"Thousand Oaks. Two boys," Ira replied. "I've never seen them before. But they already had our case briefed and spoke as fast as they could. What a way to do this! It was so tacky."

"The judges won't buy it," Randy offered. He knew that Ira was cynical and almost always underestimated his successes; he probably won the round.

"We'll see," Ira said, as he looked off to his left and saw Mr. Palladin coming through the door.

Mr. Palladin held his judging ballot from the first round. He wore a smirk of confidence on his face, as though he had just judged a couple of teams he knew all three of *his* teams could destroy. Debaters and their coaches recognized in a heartbeat this universal debate teacher haughtiness.

By the end of Friday, the Pilot teams had mixed feelings about their performances: When the pairings for round 3, which would begin on Saturday morning, were posted, the team of Hager and Gallardo was conspicuously absent. They had not made the cut, losing both of their rounds on Friday. The freshman team, a surprising qualification to begin with, would not continue in the tournament.

Susan found consolation, even in defeat: "We're just chalking this up to getting good experience. Wait 'til next year!" And figuring that Randy would continue on in the tournament for a while, she pledged to watch him and support him in future rounds.

"I want to watch you do it all the way!" she told Randy.

Cheryl elbowed her. "What does *that* mean, Susan?"

"Stop it!" Susan squealed and elbowed her back, with both girls now behaving a lot more like freshman in high school than a debate team qualified to compete at the State Championships.

Meanwhile, Mr. Palladin had really gotten into it. All the way home in the car he chortled nonstop about the two debates he judged—the pros and cons of the styles he witnessed. With much verbosity he scrutinized these debaters' arguments and vowed to brief a Long Beach team who might clash the next day with one of the teams and their cases he had already judged.

It didn't take long. The very first thing on Saturday morning, Randy and Maria were paired against one of those teams, a powerful entry from Redlands High School. Rumor had it that the two boys from Redlands rode on a string of seventeen straight wins. And Mr. Palladin had already voted for them, extending the streak to at least eighteen.

"They run racism," Mr. Palladin said excitedly, huddling with his team five minutes before the round. "Their main inherency point [it sounded funny, and oddly sad, hearing Mr. Palladin talk about inherency] is the lack of protective civil rights laws on income distribution. Their whole point is that society is inherently racist, and the result is people don't get jobs and don't eat because of racial discrimination."

Maria despised these racism cases, which seemed to be thriving as the year went on. She silently cursed their unlucky assignment, having to go negative against this team from Redlands with the racism case.

"But here's the kicker," Mr. Palladin explained. "Their main point of inherency comes from the death of President Kennedy. Since it was Kennedy's intent to pass massive, sweeping civil rights legislation, they argue that his death also killed any intent Congress had of getting through that legislation."

Randy exclaimed, "They're right! What do we say about that? Kennedy was all about equality and helping the poor and justice for all. If that's their inherency, what do we do?"

Mr. Palladin then reached into his briefcase and pulled out a copy of the latest edition of *Newsweek*; in fact, the magazine's timeliness shouted through the printed emblem of *next* Monday's date on the cover! Inside was a major story about President Johnson, his first several months in office, and his plans for the nation's future. Several quotations, comments from officials in the administration, spoke of paying tribute to the late President Kennedy by forging ahead and doing what was right: outlawing racial discrimination, investing in tolerance programs, restructuring the welfare society, and declaring—of all things—a *war on poverty*!

What great inherency material! If the present system of philosophies, laws, programs, and legislative bodies actively sought cures and solutions *today*—then, of course, no need existed to adopt a federally guaranteed income for all Americans. The affirmative resolution, as a result of these crumbling barriers, should not be voted for, allowing the negative side to triumph in the debate.

Randy wanted to pull Mr. Palladin close and kiss him—but *later*. Right now he and Maria needed to scamper over to their assigned room and organize their materials, preparing to use *Newsweek* and Mr. Palladin's arguments to crush Redlands High School's racism case.

As the gangly, acne-faced first affirmative speaker delivered his speech, Randy calmly highlighted evidence from *Newsweek*. Maria would read much of it to support her newly formed— courtesy of Mr. Palladin—arguments in her first negative speech. Capable of thinking of, and structuring her own arguments, Maria required Randy's assistance in accommodating her only with the new evidence against this racism case.

The three female judges smiled pleasantly all throughout Maria's first negative. One of the judges, the older of the three, stopped note-taking entirely, grinning and nodding at almost every point flowing from Maria's mouth. Maria sank Redlands with inherency evidence on current laws, the flexibility of existing programs, pending laws, and—most impressive of all—President Lyndon Johnson's commitment to the legacy of President Kennedy. The new President had pledged binding, record-breaking civil rights legislation, steamrolled through Congress and passed into law by *the end of 1964.*

If people went hungry in the United States of America because of institutionalized racism, government intervention by the guarantee of money was not the best answer. The best answers: speak out against racism, make it illegal to be a racist, and punish those who do not conform to the letter and intent of the law. The cash, goods, and services would get to those who have the most problems without having to restructure for *everybody* American tax codes, welfare, and local distribution agencies.

The second affirmative speaker quivered when he spoke, and a debater in the throes of seventeen consecutive victories does not quiver in a big round, especially when he debates on his own ground, his personalized affirmative case.

Redlands' second speaker driveled hackneyed analysis about racism among lawmakers, argued that Long Beach High School did not understand the concept of inherency, and desperately fished for answers to *Newsweek.* But he delivered the very same arguments offered by his partner, albeit reworded in a more persuasive, eloquent manner. Since his dark features and broad shoulders gave this boy more visual appeal, he simply bludgeoned through his speech, emphasizing a method of debating that reaches for an intimidation factor: make his judges *afraid* to vote against him.

But it didn't matter. Maria and Randy, courtesy of Mr. Palladin, had already created the framework for drilling numerous holes in Redlands' case, and the boys would never recover. Updated evidence and extended analysis by Long Beach had decimated them. Although none of the debaters knew it at the time, Long Beach had won a 3-0 decision in round three, handing Redlands their first loss of the double-elimination tournament.

Later the second affirmative speaker caught Randy in the mess hall and said to him, "We knew about that *Newsweek*, man! It just came out yesterday! We were praying no one else would see it —or read it—this soon."

Randy shrugged, still not knowing the judges' decision. "We'll see it if did any good," he said modestly.

"Just do us a favor, man—"

"Yes, don't worry," Randy reassured him. "It would be very classless for us to share any of this with debaters from other schools. But one of *our* teams is still in the tournament."

"That's cool. I'm cool with that," the good-looking Redlands debater agreed.

"Swell," Randy signaled.

Rankled by their apparent defeat, Redlands debated horribly the next round but eked out a 2-1 win over Bishop Amat High School. Having faced elimination, they had barely avoided the authoring of the first major surprise of the State Tournament.

For the next several hours, both remaining Long Beach High School teams debated round after round. And Mr. Palladin, dizzy with excitement, came back from his judging experiences always eager to share what he had learned, "As Mr. Lott would have done," he always carefully added.

By the end of round 6, only nine teams remained in the tournament: two from Long Beach High School, two from Head Royce, one from Excelsior, one from Redlands, one from Beverly Hills, one from Bellarmine High School, and a team from Grossmont.

In order for the pairings of the subsequent round to work, eight teams would debate. And one team would draw a bye, receiving an automatic win, thus, advancing to the next debate. Tension ran high while the teams sought to know who had drawn the coveted bye. A bye always guaranteed more debates and would be chosen at random from a list of *undefeated* teams. Everyone knew that getting a bye meant a team had not lost even one round.

Maria sat at the cafeteria table munching on an apple as the postings went up. Although a mad scramble to see them occurred, by now only a fraction of the crowd that had hovered around the posting wall earlier in the tournament remained. After witnessing several cheers, a few sighs, and a couple of earsplitting screeches, Randy returned to Maria with much buoyancy and a look of confidence on his face. Just as Maria expected Randy to inform her of their opponent for the next round, Randy quipped barely loud enough for her to hear through all the noise, "We got the bye."

And for the first time in her debate career, Maria Barquin felt as though she had arrived. She had debated with an energy and alacrity she never demonstrated before. Her confidence, spawned by Mr. Palladin's magic briefcase, had generated enthusiasm and highlighted the positives in an already radiant personality. What before had been a tentative, small taste of her potential, now soared to heretofore-unreal heights in her perception of her abilities. She no longer felt like the partner who was holding Randy down. If anything, she had lifted him from a morass of depression and ennui he may have never overcome by himself.

"What about Ira and Margie?" Maria asked him, barely able to control her glee.

"They're getting Head Royce. Ira's on the affirmative."

Mr. Palladin had a round off from judging. As dinnertime approached, he invited the idle Maria and Randy to join him for a sandwich. They drove to a Yummy Burger stand, while Susan and Cheryl went with Ira and Margie to lend them moral support. This Head Royce team had already clobbered the freshmen girls in this tournament, and now the freshmen couldn't wait to see their hometown heroes return the favor, resurrecting the girls' honor and reclaiming their school's pride.

****

Mr. Palladin called a powwow at Yummy Burger. His debaters sat around him, both of them munching furiously on scrumptious cheeseburgers. He confessed, "I never thought I would like this so much. Never. I guess I'm hooked."

"It is even more fun when your teams are winning," Maria giggled, suddenly hoping she hadn't jinxed them.

"Our teams always win," Mr. Palladin gloated. "Either that, or we punch each other around and distract our opponents."

"Good point, Mr. Palladin," Maria played along. "After these debaters and judges saw what Randy did to Tommy, they would not want to anger him. This also helps us to win."

"We haven't won anything, yet," Randy interjected.

Mr. Palladin wrinkled his face, emphasizing his crow's feet, developed by age and sun, around his eyes. "It's looking pretty good," Mr. Palladin speculated, dipping his French fries into the ketchup he'd spread on his paper napkin. "Looking *mighty* good, as a matter of fact. And, Randy, you haven't even karate chopped anyone today!"

Randy nervously shook his head, looking away from Mr. Palladin. Maria saw him from the corner of her eye and reached down to his lap. She clasped his left hand, squeezing it with sensations of confidence mixed in with prickles of tension.

"What is it, Randy? Why are you so pessimistic about this? You two—and maybe our other team—are probably in the best shape of anyone in the tournament right now. Why are you so downcast?"

Randy said deliberately, "I guess I'm thinking about Mr. Lott right now. I mean, Mr. Palladin, don't get me wrong because you have really, really, really come through for us—especially today—I mean, it was amazing how you helped with *Newsweek* and all. But it's just not the same around here…around the debate squad room, or even at school. It's not."

"And this is the one that Mr. Lott wanted you to get?"

"Yes," Randy replied. "This is the tournament he wanted one of our teams to get, and right to the end he figured we had the best shot. I know that's pretty weird, because Ira and Margie have been much more consistent, more successful the whole year. But I figure Mr. Lott would also smile down from heaven if Ira and Margie won."

"Yes, Randy, I'm sure he would have a huge smile on his face if Ira and Margie won."

"But by winning the right way. Just winning isn't—wasn't—enough for Mr. Lott."

"Maybe Mr. Lott totally understood the reason you've been having a hard time, Randy."

"He did," Randy nodded, putting down his burger. "And that's one of the reasons I loved him so much. He knew the truth. I don't want for us to let him down—any of us. A Long Beach High School team is going to be the debate champions of California by this time tomorrow, and that's just the way it has to be!"

With that comment Maria enthusiastically nodded her head,

Mr. Palladin smiled amiably, and the three of them enjoyed each other's company, encumbered by crowds of hungry patrons vying for famous thirty-nine cent cheeseburgers and twenty-nine cent chocolate malts.

—CHAPTER 50—

FBI agent Stephen Balcomb served as an officer in the homicide division of the Chicago Police Department from 1955 until 1959. During his tenure, their mother's shack-up boyfriend slaughtered four small children on the South Side of Chicago. The boyfriend repeatedly stabbed the two older children, five and seven, while they slept. He then suffocated her other two kids, little boys under the age of four, with pillows from their own beds.

Balcomb's investigation into these horrendous murders marked the closing stages of his career in investigating the murder of children. Having two kids of his own, both of them under the age of four, Balcomb's sensibilities were rattled by discovering the mangled, lifeless bodies of those little kids in Chicago. He immediately sought transfer to another part of the Chicago department, a liaison between the local police and the FBI, and received a warm welcome and instant respect from those who already worked there.

It didn't take long before Stephen Balcomb labored to meet the qualifications for becoming a full-fledged member of the Federal Bureau of Investigation. He eventually passed all tests with exemplary results on the very first try.

Balcomb reacted with humility when a Bureau Chief chose him to aid in the investigation of the assassination of President Kennedy; he considered it an honor. His objective outlook, professional demeanor, and youthful vitality made him an obvious choice for the job. But the FBI and the Justice Department demanded that standard operating procedures be followed, and it took a while for those so-called standard operating procedures to be delineated, given the enormity of the crime and its implications for the entire world.

Balcomb's patient, steady personality received praise from

his superiors, and now he was entrenched in a position—along with a specific assignment—requiring all the patience and steadiness federal law enforcement could muster.

Before Agent Balcomb even heard of Randall Walter Whitman in Long Beach, California, he had been painstakingly glued to elements of the investigation already assigned to him by top brass in the department. In fact, Agents interviewed hundreds of eyewitnesses, talked to Lee Harvey Oswald's friends and family, and contacted self-proclaimed evidentiary experts in the murder of Kennedy.

In early May of 1964, Stephen Balcomb opened dozens of manila folders containing files of individuals he and his team had personally interviewed. His assistant, Roger Calhoun Crandell, wrote supplementary notes in the files as both men plodded through them, discerning who needed to be contacted for follow-up interrogations.

People were brought before the Warren Commission as the FBI scrutinized potential witnesses. The Bureau carefully researched those they would recommend to testify. They assigned a rating between one and five to each recommendation. A *one* meant an individual could be of possible interest, especially in a particular area of expertise, such as a weapons or paraffin analyst; a *five* meant the Bureau thought this individual possessed a valuable opportunity for the Commission to gather vital, perhaps unique, information regarding the attack on the motorcade in Dallas.

In the early evening on Friday, just about the moment Randall Whitman, three thousand miles away, had thrown himself into the throes of the State Tournament for high school debaters, Agent Balcomb pulled Whitman's envelope from an elastic accordion file. Reminding himself of Whitman's story, and then muttering to Crandell that he hadn't picked up this file for several busy months, Agent Balcomb scanned it peripherally. His subjective notes, doodled in printed abbreviations, suggested the following: *nice kid, very intelligent, articulate, seemed sincere, often nervous, passionate about Kennedy, debate trip, Walt Whitman's empathy*…and the list went on for dozens of entries.

But the notes he had circled almost immediately on the way home from California leaped off the page with the sort of power that made personal reactions automatic. The words darted deep into Balcomb's brain, and embedded themselves: *saw two men behind wall on knoll, saw rifle, ran, fell, lost memory, dropped camera*…but then…*delusional, too nervous, seemed personally involved, motivated by fantasy, admits blanking out for hours, can't remember much from during blackout, contradictions*…and finally, in capital letters, circled in red pencil: PROBABLY NOT WORTH THE FLIGHT TIME.

Crandell, too, did a cursory glance at the file, and said, "No one else we've talked to saw anything like this kid."

"Which is why what he claimed to see probably wasn't there."

"It's not for us to decide what was there, Stephen."

"But it's our decision as to whom we recommend to testify before the Commission. Our credibility is on the line."

"He said he had seen something. It could be significant."

"Based on the delusional tendencies of a *child*—and can't be confirmed by anyone, not even another child. He was a nice kid, apparently very smart. But his affinity for Kennedy and his proximity to the crime really left him vulnerable. Being at the site totally messed this poor kid up. I liked him. We had a good rapport. He had me going for a while. But nobody else can substantiate his claims. Nobody. Named after Walter Whitman, the poet. A crack up."

"The police interviewed some strange-looking hobos that day."

"Yes—and they were harmless."

"They could have been behind the fence with a rifle."

"No rifle was found. No hobos were seen there."

"Except by this kid."

"He saw hobos after the T.V. reported there were hobos."

"Are you sure of that, Stephen? Maybe you should recheck the time line with the kid on his hobo identification. *He* knows when he first thought of these guys as hobos."

"No one else has claimed to see hobos. Now why is that?"

"Nobody else has claimed to have gone behind the barrier either."

"And why is *that*?"

"Because they didn't. If they had, maybe they would have seen hobos with a gun, too. We don't know. The kid knows. The police and Secret Service botched this one, Stephen. Big time. It took them so long to regroup at the Plaza that day—which they probably never did. Why didn't they go through those trains with a magnifying glass and a microscope? The right ass cheek didn't know what the left ass cheek was doing."

Balcomb grinned. "And they still don't."

"This kid may have witnessed something big."

"You didn't talk to him, Roger. I went to his home. I thought he was very charming—just a little neurotic and very paranoid."

"No one else saw a man with a rifle crouched behind the retaining wall, Stephen."

"All right, all right," Agent Balcomb agreed with resigned irritation. "But he's a *one*. If other investigators get hot and heavy about knoll witnesses and want to go with more than the five dozen we've already recommended with a *three* rating or higher, they'll dig down into the *ones* and *twos*."

"Including this kid, who—Balcomb—said he saw assassins. This is the only witness who saw an assassin on the knoll."

"Yeah, exactly: the only witness," Agent Balcomb nodded. "And then he blacked out, said nothing for hours, talked to no one about it for days. He can't remember some critical moments. Other than that, he'd make a powerful witness!"

With his sardonic quip, Agent Stephen Balcomb took the folder from Crandell, checked it to confirm they had officially evaluated the material, marked the cover with a *one*, and set the pages inside, where Balcomb mistakenly believed it would collect dust in crepe-edge files for the next fifty years.

****

Four high school debate teams remained. One of them would reign as State Champion: Beverly Hills, Redlands, and two teams from Long Beach. Randy knew he could not debate Ira and Margie; he also knew he could not debate Redlands—not yet—since they had already faced Redlands earlier in the tournament. So this made the pairings for the semi-final round obvious: Randy and Maria would go against Beverly Hills, while Ira and Margie would duke it out with Redlands. They were still on the double-elimination track, without knowing who had already lost one debate, except for Redlands' loss to Randy and Maria. Mr. Lott had had enough coaching seniority to sneak inside the tally room and take a peak at results. But Mr. Palladin didn't even know how to locate the tally room—or what to look for, even if he found it.

So the Pilots were in the dark about their results so far.

Randy and Maria drew the affirmative side against Beverly Hills.

And what happened next culminated a dark period in Randall Whitman's young life and promised either to improve the quality of his future—or threatened to seal the ugliness of his fate.

—CHAPTER 51—

Karen Weller and Lori Berens immediately dug into them. The girls from Beverly Hills had not lost a single debate since they'd fallen to Long Beach at a comparatively inconsequential tournament in Claremont, and they refused to kowtow a second time to a Pilot team. Ready for action—and well-prepped on Long Beach's affirmative case—Lori Berens, her curly red hair and freckles ablaze, began her cross-examination of Maria (after Maria's first affirmative speech) in front of the now five-judge panel, the number of judges reserved for elimination rounds at State:

"How many poor people are there?"

"Over 17 million."

"That's according to the U.S. Chamber of Commerce?"

"No, that is according to the Humphrey Report."

"You know, of course, that even Hubert Humphrey admitted they had over-estimated the number of poor by setting a too-low poverty line at $4000 for a family of four?"

"I disagree with Senator Humphrey. His initial estimates were correct. *You* try feeding a family of four on less than $4000 a year."

"But even your own experts have questioned the findings of the Humphrey Report, right?"

"It doesn't matter. We have other estimates, as well."

"Fewer or more than 17 million people?"

Pause.

"Fewer than," Maria admitted.

"Okay," Berens trudged forward with the speed of light. "Just why are these people poor?"

"They do not have jobs."

"They don't *want*, or they can't *find*?"

"Probably both. But mostly, cannot find."

"In the last year, has the unemployment rate been up or down?"

"Down," Maria confessed too quietly.

"Down? Is that what you said?"

"Yes."

"Could existing jobs be filled by people who really wanted them?"

"Not if these jobs do not exist. Come on, Lori!"

"But if they did exist—hypothetically—if they did exist, there are enough people who would actually take them?"

"I assume if you are hungry, you will work at almost any job to feed yourself and your children."

"You assume."

"Yes. Only terrible parents would watch their kids starve."

"You would take that job. I would. Would everybody?"

"Of course not *everybody*. Don't be ridiculous, Lori."

"So," Berens extended her claws, stood straight, her gray suit accenting her dignified persona. For a high school girl, she now looked so much older, more sophisticated than a normal teenager. "The inherent problem with being able to solve poverty is a lack of jobs? A *structural* lack of jobs?"

"Yes!" Maria responded, throwing out her chest and raising her voice, desperately trying to sound confident but not able to do so. Her entire performance, especially at the end, emerged as forced, faked, and frazzled.

As hard as he tried, Randy could not recover. Long Beach watched this debate go downhill from Berens' cross-examination of Maria until the very end, when Randy finished in such a high pitch, his voice sounded as though he had attempted a Mickey Mouse impersonation.

When the postings came up again, Randy and Maria had survived. But so had Beverly Hills. Obviously, one or both of them had been previously undefeated and had just absorbed their first loss. Since both were still in the tourney, it was impossible to know officially which team won the debate, or even what their records had been before.

Mr. Palladin, stared at the posting and let out a primal scream. Both Long Beach teams were advancing; Redlands was not. Despite a hard-fought debate from which Ira complained of exhaustion and an inability to concentrate, Long Beach narrowly escaped with a 3-2 decision.

Since Long Beach could not debate another Long Beach team, Randy and Maria would have to mix it up with the Beverly Hills girls once again.

Knowing only three teams survived in the tournament, Ira and Margie now waited in the enviable position of having another debate, no matter what happened in Randy's round. And they enthusiastically discussed how that next round could be for all the marbles.

Randy and Maria did not have familiarity with Beverly Hills' affirmative case. In their only clash before State with a Long Beach team this year—one they had lost to Ira and Margie at Claremont in what many considered to be a fluke decision— Beverly Hills had been on the negative.

Mr. Palladin had judged the girls, but for that debate they also had been on the negative. Interscholastic debate, though grueling and competitive, fostered a code of ethics precluding the spying on teams or the exchanging of case or argument information between teams from different schools. So Randy and Maria would get no help there.

There was no buzz on the case they would face—no gossip, no leaks.

****

Almost five hundred people poured into a large auditorium at California State College at Fullerton, most of them to support Beverly Hills in their quest to repeat as State Champions. Both teams, refreshed from trips to the bathroom and decked out in their finest debate clothes, consisting of spiffy suits and elegant shirts and ties with matching coats, took their positions on the stage. With another Long Beach team waiting on the sidelines, at least one more debate most assuredly would follow. The debate at hand, though, had all the markings of the premier showcase for the California State Championships.

Karen Weller, a stately looking young lady who wore all gray with a white blouse, took her place behind the podium—and the microphone—to deliver the Beverly Hills first affirmative.

Nervously waiting, with their pens poised to write on their yellow legal pads, Randy and Maria both took deep breaths. It was now do or die.

In a loud, clear, crisp voice, Karen Weller, speaking from a Plexiglas manuscript, began: "The United States of America is the richest country in the history of the world. We Americans have passionately referred to our nation as 'the land of the free and the home of the brave…with liberty and justice for all.' And while it may be true that our country has been quite generous in our efforts to allow migration from all over the world. And while it may be true that even Americans who do not work, who are ill, who are elderly still have a very slight hope of getting a piece of the American pie, they will probably never realize those hopes. Not all Americans are afforded this opportunity, simply because institutional racial bias permeates our great land, with the ugly effect of throwing many Negroes and Hispanics out in the streets, sometimes with no food, and sometimes with no possible way of fending for themselves or their children."

Weller swallowed and took a breath, secure in knowing she was in the midst of delivering the most eloquent, powerful first affirmative speech of her life.

On the other side of the stage, also sitting at a table and open to the audience, Randy and Maria shifted in their seats. Mr. Palladin, positioned near the rear of the auditorium, watched intently. He observed a look of deep anxiety on Randy's face, as though he suddenly had been tossed into a hub of confusion. Certainly, Mr. Palladin thought to himself, Randy and Maria were ready for this racism case! What a break! Just yesterday they had demolished Redlands with the help of the *Newsweek* material.

So why did Randy appear to be in such distress?

Weller continued in an even stronger voice. "The affirmative, to support this resolution, will present three need arguments and

340

then a plan that will fully implement the resolution..."

Weller kept speaking, of course, but Randy had discontinued listening to her around the time she had finished her contention about the majority of Americans in poverty coming from one minority group or another.

He leaned over to Maria, who was nervously writing as fast as she could on her legal pad, and whispered in her ear, "Maria, I need for you to do me a favor..."

Maria continued writing as she listened to Karen Weller.

Randy gently grabbed her by the edge of the elbow. "I want you to let me do the first negative speech this time."

Maria caught what he whispered but didn't believe it. She cringed without looking at him. On second thought, maybe she hadn't heard him right.

"What?" she inquired with incredulity.

"Maria, life is more important than this debate. If you care about me, you'll trust me."

Between her teeth Maria said, "We should have discussed this first, Randy."

And, of course, Randy knew this to be the truth. He replied, "It just hit me, Maria...I have to do this. Please." He put his hand on her arm and stared into her eyes. "I love you Maria..."

By now Maria had lost track of Weller's words. She saw the judges writing frantically, as they captured Beverly Hills' case on their flow pads. Maria would have to get up and speak in less than four minutes, and Randy just had dragged the rug from under her. She asked in a very weak voice, "What do I say in *my* speech?"

"You'll know what to say. Don't worry about that now. Trust me," he repeated.

By this time, Maria had no choice. Part of her seethed because Randy had just thrown away their chances of winning the State Championship, a wholly unfair, confusing—perhaps—selfish act. The other part of her did trust Randy and had total confidence in his decisions and his willingness to protect her. But she didn't have the slightest idea what now possessed him.

Weller concluded her speech. Maria's head lingered in the

clouds. But Randy rose for his usual spot in cross-examination.

"Hi, Karen," he smiled politely, boyishly, almost bashfully.

"Hi, Randy!" Karen Weller enjoyed her powerful talent for fighting back with oodles of charm.

"Karen, is America a racist country?"

"Lots of racism here," she answered.

"Yeah," Randy grinned, "I know, I know, but I was just wondering, would you call us a *racist country*?"

Weller's face turned a little red. No one had asked her this question point-blank before. Not like this. "Well, I would say…" She knew what she would *have* to say to win inherency. "I would say yes, Randy. Laws and policies are engrained in American culture, discriminating against a significant portion of the society. This makes us a racist country."

"You're familiar with President Kennedy's views on racism and civil rights?"

Randy's body shook. This had never happened to him before in a debate.

"Of course…but, Randy, President Kennedy is dead. He's not our President anymore." Weller winked, thinking she had cracked a funny.

But no one in the audience laughed, not even slightly, including her debate partner.

"Well, Karen, if he *were* alive—and good for you that he's not—you would lose this debate right now." Randy had mocked her, making a statement instead of asking a question, which is a technique usually to be avoided, except to make a sarcastic quip. "So—yeah—allow me to ask you a *question*: Aren't you glad that President Kennedy is dead?"

Weller looked pained. The debaters on stage could hear some whispers and even a few groans in the audience. Mr. Palladin almost fell from his padded auditorium chair, wondering what a seemingly delirious Randy planned to do here—and why.

With this, Weller's actual age belied her alleged maturity and intelligence. "Nooo!" she squealed like a little girl.

"Isn't it true that if Kennedy were alive today, your case would have no inherency, and you'd lose this round hands down?"

"You can't expect me to answer a question like that, Randy."

"Well, Karen, his drive to enact civil rights legislation—protections for minorities—those barriers you have structured in your case, they would not be there if not for the assassination of President Kennedy—correct?"

Karen Weller could only remain stubborn. "Kennedy is dead, Randy."

Mr. Palladin thought, an unorthodox way of getting there, but Randy is setting up the *Newsweek* evidence about President Johnson's proposed civil rights legislation, cutting into their inherency.

Randy saw the timekeeper flash him a signal indicating he had only one of his three minutes of cross-x time remaining, so he fled to another topic. "Karen, is America the best country in the world?"

"What are your criteria for judging *best*?" Weller replied—a smart response to a nebulous question.

"Greater opportunities for its citizens, more freedoms, better standard of living, protectors of the free world…you began your speech by saying how wonderful America was—and I agree—I'm just asking you if we're the *best*?"

"Sure," she said flippantly. "But I suppose we could do a better job of feeding the poor."

Murmurs among the audience pervaded the auditorium. The unusual nature of these questions perplexed debaters and coaches alike. One of those confused was his own partner, though Maria tried to remain stoic. Where was Randy going with this?

"Do you think Lee Harvey Oswald killed President Kennedy?" Randy abruptly asked her.

"*What?*"

"Did Oswald kill Kennedy?"

"Who cares!"

Again, Weller thought she had been humorous. Although she was right about the apparent irrelevancy of this question to the debate topic, her little shriek did nothing to endear her to the judges or observers in the audience.

Randy refused to smile. "Say *I* care. Humor me."

"I don't know."

"Do you think anyone in this room cares about who really killed President Kennedy?"

"What?" she grimaced.

"Last question: If you had been in Dallas, Texas, on Friday, November 22, 1963, and you had seen a man about to assassinate the President of the United States—I mean just *before* he actually did it, and you were standing right there—what would you have done at that moment?"

Mercifully for all those in attendance, the timekeeper shouted, "Time!" which meant Weller had the option of answering the question or not answering the question. Since she saw no point in doing so—and neither did anyone else in the room—in silence she gathered her materials from the podium, turned, and walked back to her seat next to her partner.

Randy, dreading a return to his seat and the inevitable questions Maria surely would ask him—with desperate, panicky incredulity in her voice—sauntered directly to the podium instead, carrying with him only his clipboard and the yellow legal pad he had used during his cross-examination session with Weller.

Mr. Palladin noticed a couple of judges were squirming. One judge, an elderly speech coach from the North, crinkled her face in a pronounced scowl and put down her pen. Mr. Palladin wanted to leave the room, his mounting anger and embarrassment tearing him apart. He felt an obligation to rush the stage immediately and stop this so-called debate, but he restrained himself. Maybe Randy, as weird as this conjecture seemed, had a definite plan, an unorthodox scheme for winning this debate against Beverly Hills. And if Mr. Palladin halted the proceedings or left the room, he would lose his chance to witness high school debate history.

A hush, a deeper silence, a more penetrating deadening of the decibels than ever before in a room this size with this many people stuffed inside, hugged the auditorium. Randy's dramatic pause at the microphone heightened the suspense.

Then suddenly, Randy became someone *else*. Oh, he was still *Randy*, but no longer did he sound like Randy the *debater*. And it would take a long time, endless analysis, and countless heated discussions to discern the merits, the appropriateness, and the ethical relevance of Randy's approach in this important high school debate against Beverly Hills. For Randall Walter Whitman geared himself to explore territory no other high school debater had ever ventured before.

—CHAPTER 52—

Like a streak of lightening, Randy shot across Elm Street, reaching the grass on the other side. He passed two women—one who wore a bright red dress—and a man with a little boy. As he drove his body up the low grassy hill, Randy figured if a policeman hadn't stopped him, the cops weren't concerned enough to intervene. The motorcade had not reached the corner, so perhaps it was still permissible for someone to move from one side of the street to the other.

Randy turned around and saw several policemen on motorcycles heading north on Houston Street, toward the corner where the big records building and the red book building stood. Small American flags fluttered from the handlebars of those motorcycles. Randy Whitman knew that close behind them rode his hero, the President of the United States, John Fitzgerald Kennedy.

Panting from excitement and out of breath, Randy clutched his camera. Now in his clear view, the motorcade crawled slowly toward the busy corner of Elm and Houston, where it would make a sharp left turn, move past the Texas School Book Depository, and continue onto the Stemmons Freeway. At the Dallas Trade Mart, the President would address an assortment of rich investors and economists.

Having eyed the exact spot from which he wanted to take pictures, Randy turned again and this time headed to the top of the hill. At first grateful no one else seemed to be staked out in the vicinity, Randy now felt mildly spooked. Suddenly more conscious of an absence of surrounding spectators, he experienced a temporary sense of isolation, as though this current moment in his life was not real—perhaps a movie he had been watching on television.

He stood far enough from the street that he sensed some solitude. But then he remembered the significance of what was about to happen, of which he would become a part: he, with his trusty camera on this side of the street, and Ira Cushman, with his dependable camera on the other side of the street.

And then for just a few seconds, Randall Walter Whitman, suspended in time, entertained a surreal vision and a distortion of reality.

One hobo was kneeling, shouldering a rifle, readying to point it across a concrete barrier atop the hill. The other hobo sat on his knees, looking behind him in the direction of the railroad tracks, his gaze seemingly fixed on nothing, yet seeing everything.

Randall knew immediately the incongruence of what he witnessed: men dressed like lousy renditions of tramps, one pointing a gun at a street—toward a spot in the road that in less than thirty seconds from now would hold a car carrying the President of the United States.

Randy's thought processes choked, a flustered response to a scene he would never be able to clear from his memory.

He said nothing.

He did nothing.

Paralyzed with inaction brought about by shock and confusion, he let his camera slip from his hands and drop to the grass. He could have bent over and picked it up. It would have taken less than a second. But when the camera fell from his hands to a spot directly between his legs, he stiffened. One of the hobos —Randy would never be sure whether it was the rifleman or the railroad tracks watcher—snarled in a voice he eventually heard over and over in his nightmares, "*What the hell!*"

Reflexively, Randy dove toward the hobo clasping the rifle, pushed him with his body, and threw him off balance against the hardness of the concrete barrier. Out of the corner of his eye, he caught the other hobo beginning to rise from his kneeling position, determined to launch violently in Randy's direction.

With the dynamics of what he had learned from a full year of karate training that had led him to his Brown Belt, Randy hurled a right-footed round kick into the kneeling hobo's head. This mighty maneuver sent the hobo sprawling, paralyzing his ability to be a further threat to Randy or anyone else.

As the rifleman began to right his course after Randy had pushed him into the wall, Randy immediately threw his left foot, implanting it in the man's face, and the hobo fell to the ground near the spot he had been standing.

The commotion caused those below them to stir.

But Randy had to be sure, absolutely certain, this disruption would be enough—enough to stop the parade, enough to startle any other assassins from pulling off well-aimed shots. He put his body into full-throttle, racing down the small hill like a sprinter taking off on the hundred-yard dash. Screaming at the top of his lungs, he bolted into the street directly in front of the lead motorcycle policemen who guarded the front of the motorcade. "Stop!" Randy yelled. "Stop! They're going to kill the President! *Stop!*"

By this time, Kennedy's car was making a left turn onto Elm Street. The Lincoln halted. Secret Servicemen filled the President's car with their bodies, shielding the Kennedys from any bullets that might come in their direction. Much to his dismay, Oswald saw that a window post now blocked him from getting off a clear shot into the President's stalled car on the street corner, and he could not fire.

Guns drawn, several policemen hurried to the area behind the concrete barrier in front of the brown picket fence.

And Randall Walter Whitman, thinking he saw a glimpse of President Kennedy in the back seat of his limousine, made long-distance eye contact with his hero. Though certain to be in a panic, but with an incongruent smile, the President waved at Randy as though to say, "Thank you, son, for saving my life."

But just as Randy waved back, to salute his President, to let him know his *thank you* was quite unnecessary, he felt a sudden, sharp pain in his chest. The last thing he remembered was seeing a policeman's revolver aimed in his direction—and how difficult it suddenly had become for him to take another breath.

Although never aware of his legacy, the late Randall Whitman would be adored by Maria Barquin, John F. Kennedy, and the rest of the world for becoming one of America's greatest heroes. For generations to come, people everywhere would study the strength, the courage, and the character of this young martyr: a young man who had saved the life of the President of the United States—a sixteen year-old high school student, a protector of women, and a pretty darn-good young debater from Southern California.

Even his father and Tommy Wright—and Mr. Lott in heaven —would marvel at this boy's uncanny ability to make such an absurdly dangerous and difficult decision look so easy.

—CHAPTER 53—

Randy Whitman corkscrewed his head back to look at Maria, his debate partner and his potential steady girlfriend, as she madly scrawled notes on her yellow legal pad. When Randy then mentioned her name, a startled Maria lifted her eyes. "Maria, I'm sorry," he apologized.

He turned around and faced his gawking audience.

Randy's voice, now weary from three days of breakneck verbal speed and an overtaxed larynx, began to crack. This very untimely bout of strained vocal chords added an oddly effective emotional by-product to his delivery.

He then spent about four minutes with the mundane but devastating *Newsweek* material. And half-heartedly he dwindled Beverly Hills' case inherency.

But then he said, "Maybe the only point on which we agree with the affirmative: America, for a whole host of reasons, *is* the best country in the world. But one of the reasons we both said this so easily is because our system is basically fair. It is orderly and protected by the most beautiful document on the face of the earth: the Constitution. Transitions in government are clean; they're systematic. Political assassinations are not supposed to happen here—not in the United States of America. But they do—and one just did."

Randy stopped to fight back tears—not for dramatic impact. In shock, Mr. Palladin was strangely moved by Randy's amazingly powerful youthful eloquence. And he guessed Randy's destination long before Randy would arrive there.

Randy no longer delivered his first negative speech from notes or with cited sources and researched evidence. He spoke entirely from his heart. His innate ability to logically and clearly organize his ideas had become essential, and he took full advantage of this skill.

He continued, "Only a few people in the world know about this: But in Dallas Texas, on November 22, 1963, at approximately 12:30 in the afternoon, I stood on a grassy hill in Dealey Plaza. As President Kennedy's motorcade approached where I was standing, I saw two men behind a concrete barricade, and one of them was preparing to shoot Kennedy with a rifle. The men looked at me, and I panicked. I dropped my camera and ran. I can't remember the next few hours; they've become a blur. If I had been coherent, maybe my life today would be different. Maybe my state of mind would be saner. For sure, I wouldn't be telling you this here.

"But no one would listen to me. Except for Maria, no one believed me. Not really. My debate coach told me to analyze and report what I'd witnessed, but there was no place in this experience for analysis—only for emotion. And it was my emotions that ruined me that day. I ran; I fell. I forgot. And so when the FBI interviewed me, I came off as a scared kid who had freaked out and was totally traumatized—because I had loved and admired President Kennedy so much. And I *did* love and admire him. My greatest ambition at the time was to one day shake his hand. He was the inherency attack in our negative philosophy—until President Johnson's civil rights legislation!"

A ruffling of laughter went through the audience. But Randy had begun to speak haltingly, his face red. For the first time in three days, his suit coat was drenched with perspiration.

"They pinned this thing on a total loser named Lee Harvey Oswald—and I don't know if he fired a gun that day or not. Nobody knows for sure. But I'm certain he was not one of the men I saw on the hill. Our government is investigating this crime, but no one who saw anything different from a shooter in the book building is being taken seriously. They're going to get it wrong! They're going to blow this, and there's not a darn thing I can do about it! I realize that you think I should be locked up in an asylum —but I saw what I saw: two men on that hill killed President Kennedy. And I saw them!

"So you see, the real inherency in this affirmative case, the limitations and ineptitudes of government on any level—local, state, or federal—causes the affirmative a real double-standard. Because the true barriers they could site, not the stupid stuff about racism—excuse me—would also prevent Congress from passing *their* plan and, thereby, prevent them from adopting the resolution.

"Finally, because I see my time is running out, I wish to make a plea to all the judges—and to the debaters in this room who will live to debate again at another tournament, another time—because I may not."

He turned and bowed slightly to the girls at their desks. "This is also to the ladies from Beverly Hills High School: High School debate has gotten out of control. Help us to rake it in. Comments from unseen, unproven, so-called experts—it gets kind of tiring, doesn't it? I mean, just how many debates have these people judged in the last three days—always having to render their decisions based on such unimportant terminologies like *topicality*?

"So come with us down a road where you understand the realities of the world: where people of all cultures *do* have opportunity, if they work hard, play fair, and plan their futures; where those who are discriminated against can look forward to new laws protecting them from people whose bigotry may go back even several generations.

"But, unfortunately, this road also leads us to a place where fairness and equality and opportunity lie diluted in a government that is layered with selfish agendas and an expedient blind eye, all guided by an alarming amount of incompetence."

Randy's passion gripped the audience. Simultaneous with a thirty-second signal from an adult timer in the front row, he began to breathe heavily. Having found this intense breathing impossible to hide, he decided to speak very slowly and let the chips fall where they may. "My former debate coach Richard Lott, who would have been here today had he not recently lost the most important competition of his life to leukemia, always—always taught us to seek truth...to find a way to honor and respect our integrity and the integrity of this activity...and to work for a better world, a world where good triumphs over evil."

Randy stopped. He had little remaining ability to forge forward. His next few words would wrap up his position; he would not speak in this debate again. The judges either accepted his point of view, or they didn't. But no matter what, he had won a moral victory for truth and goodness.

Finishing with much less passion—and more businesslike—than in the previous several minutes, Randy regained his control, maintained his composure, and summarized, "The affirmative team has no inherency. The ladies have looked at the wrong structural barriers for solving the problem. With individual kindnesses, acts of compassion, and displays of decency, along with hard work and respect for the worth of the individual, we make a lot of headway fixing what is wrong with our country. Started by President Kennedy, carried out by President Johnson—a war on poverty, and new, sweeping civil rights laws will relegate overt acts of racism to the annals of history."

It was the kind of finish people in attendance might have been expected to give a standing ovation. But there was no thunderous roar from the crowd—or even a few scattered claps; instead, stony silence filled the large, crowded room.

Randy remained at the podium waiting to be cross-examined by either one of the young lady debaters. But the girls from Beverly Hills huddled.

They huddled for a long time.

The judges grew impatient. So did the audience. The structure of high school debate did not lend itself to a designated period for a partner powwow. Questioners were expected to immediately rise from their seats and begin their cross-x. But the unconventional conference between the Beverly Hills debaters alerted the masses that something further would be askew.

Finally, Karen Weller rose from her seat and said in a loud voice. "We have no questions."

Which also was shocking, because debaters *always* had questions—even novice debaters had questions—especially at the State Tournament. So when Lori Berens walked slowly to the podium without so much as a legal pad in her hands, everyone in the room sensed that Long Beach had drawn Beverly Hills into its trap. But what would the judges think about this fiasco?

****

Berens, a shorter girl than Weller, didn't smile. Normally serious, she hardly ever smiled during a debate round. But now she oozed tension, and her curly brown hair stood straight up. Gripping the microphone—another act debaters rarely performed—she said, "We think this debate is over. The negative has offered nothing substantial against our case. All their real-world, personal experience, I've-seen-it-all rhetoric may sound surprising, may appear refreshing, and may even *be* refreshing, but it doesn't answer our arguments—*any* of them. The fact is, a large segment of America's poor is with no hope of getting help, enough help to feed their children or put some sort of roof over their heads. The negative speaker, though eloquent and passionate, was pretty hollow. He didn't even attempt to attack our plan."

She paused and then shrugged. "Please look over your notes. What could you have possibly written down during Randy's speech? That Johnson is going to pass civil rights as a tribute to Kennedy? So what? Does this guarantee the poor will be able to eat? That the U.S. government covered up a conspiracy to kill Kennedy? So what? What does *that* have to do with poverty? Seriously. *What*? The government is corrupt? Really? I thought the negative was *relying* on the government for new anti-poverty programs and new civil rights laws. Sounds like a contradiction to me! That their late coach—and I do remember him as a good man, too—wants real world debating? Well, that's what we have offered to you: real arguments for a real world.

"You have heard some very strange, very weird ranting by the first speaker from Long Beach High School. I do hope the second speaker from Long Beach actually tries to *debate*, because that's why we all came here, didn't we?"

That second speaker from Long Beach High School, Maria Barquin, as though someone had flipped a switch on a machine, picked up on Randy's direction and was hell bent on getting with his program. Maria now debated not for the State Championship; she did it for Randy: for his trauma brought on by his experiences in Dallas; for his love and loss of Mr. Lott; for his devastating disappointment in his parents; for his passionate trust in *her*. Maria knew that winning this debate—securing three of the five judges' decisions—had become superfluous in its significance. A lot more rode on her presentation than a redundant indulgence in intellectual masturbation.

Though finishing only her sophomore year, Maria looked like a college student, as she rose for cross-examination. And she also looked stunning. Dressed in a conservative black suit, her dark hair reaching down to her shoulders, where it flipped up in small curls, Maria Barquin appeared to have her way with the world. But, in fact, she was on a mission.

Her questioning time short, she picked up on what Randy had established as the negative team's flavor: "So you do not like our approach tonight? Is that it?"

Maria came off as amiable, so incredibly genial. And real. When she appeared relaxed and didn't succumb to any pressure to measure up, to *win*, Maria's personality *radiated* likeability.

Berens sagged. "Is that what you got out of this? You didn't attack anything in our case, Maria. Nothing. Our case stands. Why are we even debating anymore?"

She smiled. Maria knew, as a contrast with Berens, the Miss Congeniality award went to her—a hundred times over. Berens looked ready to fold.

"We didn't attack your case?"

"No."

"What about inherency?"

"No."

"Laws will be passed to relieve discrimination? Didn't you hear Randy?"

"There are no guarantees the poor will get the money— because of racism, Maria."

"What if these people are no longer discriminated against?"

"You can't guarantee this."

"Can *you*?"

"Yes."

"How, Berens? Who's serving on your board of directors— John Kennedy?"

"Our plan does it," Berens explained. "We guarantee four thousand dollars a year to poor families."

"There is no discrimination on the federal level?"

"The money's *guaranteed*, Maria."

"How can you do this, Berens?"

"Do what?"

"Just *guarantee* everything? You talked about all these racist people, and they are from the same branch of government that will regulate your guaranteed annual income?"

"Free from racism and corruption, yes."

"No corruption on the federal level, right? No hiding of truth, right? No lack of ability to solve major problems, right?"

Berens exhaled irritation. "What happened in Dallas has nothing to do with this. Nothing." And then she let slip, "Jesus, that is such a stretch!"

Debaters never uttered *Jesus* in a round. The profane was forbidden.

"And your plan is not? Let's see here, Berens: you are *giving* four thousand dollars a year to poor people, all of whom you say are victims of racist government bureaucracy, even though most of them seem to flourish just fine. And *then* you are telling us that this contemptible human behavior would be *absent* from federal bureaucracy? Come again?"

Berens paused, eyes glazed, face looking forward. She replied deliberately, "Yes, that's what we're telling you."

"Again: no racism on the federal level, Berens?"

"You're missing the point, Maria."

"No corruption on the federal level, Berens? No hiding of truth, twisting of fact? No heads buried in the sand?"

Lori Berens lost it. "This has nothing to do with Kennedy, Maria! Jesus, Maria, have you and Randy lost your marbles? You're both crazy!"

Maria grinned, her face settled, calm, and confident. "You can't solve the problem, though, can you, Lori? In fact, you make it worse, don't you? Government officials, investigative agencies, commissions for reform—they can do whatever they want, can't they? Hide facts. Distort reality. Shirk responsibility. Is that not true, Lori? Is that not what *you* told all of us here today?"

Mercifully, the timekeeper cut them off.

Randy Whitman had made a conscious decision to wage arguments that really mattered. The importance of ambiguous, immaterial ideas about giving money to poor people paled next to the significance of the issues he had raised in this public forum. To Randy, the girls' comments about the poor and minorities being categorically incapable of protecting themselves against an evil white power structure seemed as racist, as demeaning, as condescending, as patronizing, as those ideas he had heard from people who were obvious bigots, including his own parents.

Randy didn't know which way the judges of this debate would vote, but he had taken some real initiative to do *actual* good in the world. He was ready to move forward in his life, to no longer question himself about his behavior in Dallas—or to seriously wonder if he had imagined all that he said he had seen.

—CHAPTER 54—

On the Monday after the tournament, the *New York Times* expanded on their previously obscure story about witnesses to the assassination who thought they heard shots fired from the grassy knoll. One witness, a man who claimed he dove to the ground with his small son, adamantly maintained, "I heard a firecracker go off behind me and immediately—because I'm a hunter—grabbed my little boy and threw him to the ground. Then I heard two or three more pops, and, I swear, I felt something whizz right through the top of my hair. I was scared to death."

The *Times*, supplementing their previous story from months before, again referenced "three shabbily dressed men" the police had detained for questioning. Curiously, these men wore primitive clothing—suits, however—and possessed a slight growth of facial hair. None of these men wore a tie under their gray coats, and each of their shirts was white, with very wrinkled collars. The writer encouraged the investigators to find out where these men had come from and to carefully examine an ambiguous connection to an old, ramshackle railroad car behind the knoll.

Surely, Randy thought, the Warren Commission would thoroughly investigate these hobos and others who were somehow linked to the grassy knoll, especially those who had referred to gunshots that came from behind them near the top of the hill.

Randy's sense of personal relief cascaded every time he heard another media account of gunshots from the grassy knoll. Yes, he knew the truth. But he finally concluded that officials hadn't taken him seriously. It boded unlikely that the FBI would offer him up before Earl Warren's Commission.

Randy Whitman, debater deluxe, brilliant in so many ways, goofy and clumsy in so many other ways, accounted for but one of multitudes of strange, oddball accounts of what happened in Dallas that Friday afternoon.

And making Randy even less credible: at the time he had been only sixteen years old.

****

The Tuesday afternoon after the State Tournament, Randy Whitman walked Maria Barquin home from school. He held her hand tightly in his, and with their books tucked safely away in the crook of his right arm.

This is precisely when he had his epiphany. He had one more task to perform, one more ugly event to experience. Only then could he commence with his recuperation, fully benefit from the adventure of his healing process.

Randy accompanied the dark-skinned beauty to the walkway leading up to the front door of the Barquin home. He took both of her hands and extended her arms so he could look directly into her eyes. "Maria, I have something to do. I'll call you tonight," he said with masculine resolution.

He leaned forward, brushing her lips with his. They stayed locked together a few seconds longer than Randy had intended.

"Okay," she said. "I am going to do homework."

He nodded, but his serious, stern face, his jaw locked, brought her concern.

"Where are you going, Randy?"

"I need to talk to Carmen's cousin."

"Her cousin?"

"The guy who tried to scare me. The creep is old enough to know better than to throw crap on our driveway."

"What are you planning to do?" she asked, remaining calm.

"Have a talk."

"Randy…"

"No, really. He needs to hear me out. I want it to be in broad daylight and when he's alone, so Carmen's parents don't get the Puerto Rican Mafia after me."

"They still might," she only half-kidded.

"I doubt it. And I don't think he wants to mess with me."

"He's *big* from what I hear."

"But he's stupid, from what I *know*."

"Randy, if your karate teacher finds out about this—"

"Nothing's going to happen."

"Randy…"

And with that, Randy kissed Maria again and then sought after Carmen Pedro's live-in, twenty year-old cousin, Juan.

When Carmen saw Randy swaggering up the driveway of her house, her heart leaped. But she knew that if Randy wanted to make up with her, possibly mend a few bridges, they were already beyond repair. His rejection of her, his secret lusting for another girl, his unwillingness to tame the racism of his evil parents— didn't Randy understand how much she had been hurt by him? He eventually discovered how *angry* and resentful she had been. But would he never grasp the pain she felt from the wounds he had inflicted?

And Carmen's brief, unpleasant interlude with Tommy Wright—of all people—had done nothing to bind Randy and her back together.

Yet, Randy's familiar face still charged her with comfort, a cavernous yearning for the way things used to be.

Awkwardly, she greeted him at the top of the driveway, a bland concrete pour. Its holes, bumps, and bruises detracted from the aesthetics of the house.

Without the kind of formality Randy normally used to greet those who had *never* attempted to sabotage his life, he cut right through the chase. "Carmen, I need to see your cousin."

Carmen had begun to greet him with "Hello," but her former boyfriend's coldness, his icy demeanor, frightened her. "He's not home," she informed him.

She could fling short, terse sentences with the best of them.

Juan stood in the doorway behind his cousin, his eyes fixed in a curious gaze.

Juan Pedro was an anomaly in the Pedro clan: he was not good-looking. Small, beady eyes under a thin forehead, topped with black, greasy hair and a face full of acne never made Juan feel as though he fit in with this physically glamorous Puerto Rican family. As he stood there in his straggly, torn, white T-shirt, he seemed much less imposing, less significant than he had before: in the days he had haunted Randy, defecated on his family's property, and threatened him from the safety of an anonymous automobile.

Toe-to-toe with Carmen, Randy glared, "Do you know what it is to be ashamed, Carmen? You should be very ashamed." He shook his head. "I thought you were a decent person. But while I was going steady with you, I learned a lot, and I've gone through a lot since. I've accumulated a lot of lessons. I've also discovered what a good person *is*, and you're not one of them. I'm so embarrassed that you had me fooled."

Proud of himself for his self-control and his containment of any physical expression of rage, he finished his point softly. "Your parents are decent people; otherwise, I would have come after *your* house with a heck of a lot worse than cow dung."

"Juan did this without my prior permission, Randy," she said awkwardly.

"But you gave your permission, Carmen. You knew about it."

"Only later did I—"

"*You* taped that note to my locker."

How she now wished that she hadn't let Juan talk her into such an idiotic plan to get back at Randy and his racist family! Her eyes lowered. Her face advertised guilt, but she never used the words to admit any remorse.

Not even, "I'm sorry," formed on her lips.

By this time Juan had made his way down the length of the driveway. Relieved that Juan's false bravado had kept him from carrying a weapon, Randy noticed the expression on Juan's face changing: from a broad machismo to a little trepidation, the closer he came to Randy.

Randy was not exceptionally tall. But at this moment, in *righteousness*, he towered over the bulkier Juan Pedro, who outweighed him by twenty-five pounds.

Slinking away, the diminishing braggart asked Randy, "What do you want?"

"I hope you enjoyed your turn in jail. Did you like the

mashed potatoes and gravy in there?"

"I'm gonna' kick your ass!"

Randy smiled at Juan's bluster; it amused him. "Rather than put a hole in your face, I'm going to consider the fact that you're not very smart; in fact, when I think about you, Juan, the word *stupid* clearly comes to mind."

Randy saw Juan's clenched fists at his sides. The older boy's face bulged with the kind of anger a man feels when someone has stripped him of his masculinity in front of a female—in this case, his teenage cousin.

Carmen moved quickly to Juan's side. She remembered Randy's devotion to karate and sensed that her defenseless cousin was about to discover firsthand the timeless code of all students of the martial arts: *You don't hit first, but if you get hit, you take the other guy out.*

"Juan, just let him talk. Just let him."

"Yeah, Juan," Randy goaded. "Just let me talk, and let your little cousin—a *girl*—do the talking for you."

Juan almost spit at him but did not. "You were cruel to my cousin!"

Randy flinched. "Cruel?"

"First you told her nice things. You needed her for your own emotions, and then you dumped her!"

Suddenly, Randy felt less smug. He *had* dumped Carmen. There was little doubt about that. But up until today's taunting and badgering on his part, he had always been willing to accept responsibility for the breakup. Even on a good day with Carmen, he could list at least ten reasons for ending their relationship. Besides, he simply had been with Carmen too long. He knew her too well.

Then Maria walked into his life.

Now, however, Carmen's creepy cousin, who had been encouraged by her to taunt and frighten Randy and to deface his home with excrement, stood before him. He practically *begged* Randy for a kick directly under his ribcage.

"Your cousin and I broke up," Randy fired back. "And that, *amigo*, was none of your business."

"She's my cousin, man!" And the whites of his knuckles appeared.

"And your sweet cousin ordered you—*ordered* you—to throw *crap* on my parent's lawn. What did my mother ever do to either of you?"

Carmen interjected, "She's a racist!"

"No, no," Randy denied. "She never did anything to you, Carmen. Never. So you blamed my parents for what happened betweens us? That's just wrong! Sure, she had some problems with your Puerto Rican heritage—but I already set her straight on that."

Juan exuded more false macho. He asked Carmen, "Want me to take care of this punk?"

Carmen knew that if she said *yes*, her cousin soon would be lying flat on his back in the middle of their driveway, and with a huge imprint of Randy's shoe in the middle of his forehead.

She calculated the risks in this scenario.

She wisely said, "Just leave him alone, Juan."

"No man!" Juan stepped forward. "I wanna' teach this queer a lesson!"

Juan's head hovered above Randy's, his chin at Randy's eye line, offering an inviting target for contact from one of his feet. Juan's right leg began to paw at the ground, much like that of a horse before it gallops off with its rider.

The seconds on the clock slowly ticked off. Carmen briefly imagined her cousin's head spun around by Randy's fist, with blood spatter winding up several feet away on the trunk of a large sycamore tree.

Randy, without landing a finger on the Puerto Rican's face, poured his eyes through the soul of Juan Pedro.

The karate student had been taught to use words first. He had been trained to resist temptation. He had been directed never to punch or kick another, unless in the act of self-defense or in order to protect another human being who was defenseless and in need of his help.

Provoking Carmen's cousin into losing his temper so Randy might knock him into unconsciousness would not have satisfied him today, no matter how much he would have loved to see Juan pay a painful price for his destructive blind family loyalty and his unsavory acts of aggression toward him and his family.

Juan didn't follow Randy down the sidewalk. But he called after him, swearing in Spanish and English, imploring him to come back and take his licks like a man. Randy heard Carmen scolding Juan in Spanish, probably advising him not to go after Randy—that he knew karate and was not afraid to use it.

"Ah, those karate punks!" Juan waved off his female cousin as he teemed with his grandest bravado. "They're all nothing but a bunch of mama's boys! If he comes back here, I'm gonna' cream him!"

Carmen wanted very badly to laugh at her cousin's audacity, the earnestness of his last comment. She chose not to laugh; instead, she walked silently inside her house and immediately began working on her challenging algebra homework.

Even for a girl with the bottom-dwelling ethical fiber of a Carmen Pedro, working algebra equations could be a daunting, but welcome, distraction from becoming further dragged into life's moral gutter.

****

On the last day of school, the Long Beach Pilots were thinking only about their pending summer vacation and not at all about the concluding, end-of-the year awards ceremony in the high school's gymnasium.

The bleacher seats offered uncomfortable reclining for nearly two thousand chatty, self-absorbed teenagers. The June sun had already heated the interior of a large basketball court area. Approximately a hundred students sat on folding chairs at the base of the court. They were to be honored in a one-hour festivity celebrating the academic accomplishments of Long Beach students during the 1963-64 school year. Their principal would announce scholarship awards for seniors.

Mr. O'Shannon, tall, freckled, and red-faced, one who could easily measure up to the physical stereotype of his Irish ancestry, spoke in a booming voice through a hand-held microphone hooked up to a couple of enormous speakers on both sides of the gymnasium. He called off the names of student award winners, mentioning GPA leaders, science project achievers, spelling bee survivors, and so on.

And then he came to the debate awards: "Ladies and gentlemen of Long Beach High School!" he announced, with what seemed like more enthusiasm for this distinction than he had already broadcast for other student achievements. "Our school's all star debate team rose way above the competition at the California State Championships last month!"

He paused, rechecked his notes, and continued, "Winning Third Place from a field of the best high school debaters in the state: our own team *of…*Maria Barquin and Randy Whitman!"

Their faces full of joy, Randy and Maria went to the podium to accept a school-awarded certificate for their Third Place achievement at State.

Ever since they found out they had lost a 3-2 decision in that very weird, controversial round against Beverly Hills, they were nothing but gracious—even grateful—for their opportunity to debate those girls in the first place. For Randy it had been the chance of a lifetime to communicate what truly mattered to him. Losing a debate to last year's State Champions was a very small price to pay for that opportunity. Maria respected Randy beyond reproach after their mutual experience, and *she* vowed to do something crazy at State next year.

After the applauding multitudes had settled back in their seats—with Maria receiving the requisite cat calls from the less mature of the adolescent boys seated in the backless gym bleachers —Mr. O'Shannon continued, "And now I would like you to greet the 1964 California *State Champions* in high school debate, on their way to the Nationals in Cincinatti, Ohio: Margie Pendergrass and Ira Cushman!"

A thunderous ovation rattled the building. No sports team, no other event in the history of Long Beach High School had so unmistakably shaken the gym from its rafters. The crowd must have cheered for three minutes, as the school band joined them with a chorus of, "Happy Days Are Here Again!"

Well-rested from their bye and with blood in their eyes, Ira and Margie had faced Beverly Hills in the final round. The girls, racked with exhaustion and engulfed by confusion, had barely eluded a second loss in the tournament and elimination at the hands of Randy and Maria. They then faltered into the final round. On the affirmative, Ira and Margie had debated dynamically, their arguments crystal clear and overwhelmingly persuasive. Beverly Hills had stammered, stuttered, and stumbled, and looked defeated from the onset, lacking passion and punch. The final judges' tally: Long Beach 5, Beverly Hills 0.

Ira and Margie had done it again to Beverly Hills, but this time in the debate they coveted the most: the victory that would crown a State Champion from Long Beach High School's debate team—achieving Mr. Lott's last goal.

Mr. Palladin walked to the microphone after the ovation simmered. Clad in denim trousers and a red, flannel shirt, Mr. Palladin looked more like a candidate for rodeo riding than he did for debate coaching. But the debate coach now, he was.

Mr. Palladin spoke with confidence and enthusiasm and pride. To an amazingly hushed audience, his voice resonated from wall to wall. "What a remarkable achievement! What an amazing experience this was!"

The Long Beach students and faculty again broke into tumultuous applause. And again Mr. Palladin waited patiently to regain their attention. He now lowered his voice, still quite audible throughout the gymnasium. "But for me—and I know for *all* the debaters on the team—this has been such a bitter-sweet experience. As you all know, the debate team's coach, their anchor and their rock, died a few months ago. He wasn't present—in body anyway —at the State Tournament; nor is his physical presence with us today. But I know I speak for Ira and Margie…" He paused and looked admiringly at the debaters standing next to him. "And for Maria and Randy, and all the rest of our Long Beach Pilot debaters…we know you're listening to this, Mr. Lott. And we know how pleased you are with your students. They competed at the State Tournament in ways that *you* taught them—that make us *all* proud. We love you, and we miss you, Mr. Lott. Your legacy is this high school, these students, and this debate squad…onward and upward, Pilots of Long Beach High!"

Mr. Palladin thrust his fist in the air, and everyone cheered. They cheered their school; they cheered his words. But only a few of them comprehended the true meaning of what Mr. Palladin had said about competing at the State Tournament in a way Mr. Lott would have been proud. Most students, teachers, administrators, community members, and even some of the debaters in attendance that day figured Mr. Palladin was talking about *winning*.

A few people were aware that Mr. Palladin's reference to Mr. Lott's pride had not been about winning at all.

Randy and Maria, with the help of Mr. Palladin and Ira and Margie, had brought real life to the debate world. And this is what the debate world—and, perhaps, *winning* itself—meant to Mr. Lott.

EPILOGUE

In November of 1964, the Warren Commission released a twenty-four-volume report of their research, interviews, and proceedings entitled, *The Warren Commission Hearings*. These several books were later summarized in a single book. The many volumes were made amazingly readable by adept editors and called, *The Warren Report*.

The *Warren Report* immediately became the official word of the investigation into the assassination of President Kennedy. The Warren Hearings had modeled the quintessential method of investigating political and social disasters and debacles.

According to the *Report*, using an Italian Mannlicher-Carcano bolt-action rifle, a lone gunman fired three shots from the Texas School Book Depository Building. One bullet missed everyone, possibly bouncing off the curb, its fragmented metal spraying into a bystander's leg. Another bullet hit the President in the back, exited through his throat, entered Governor Connally's back, transversed his right rib cage, traveled through his left wrist, and lodged in his left thigh. While the governor lay mortally wounded, the bullet rolled onto the stretcher technicians had been using to transport him throughout the hospital. The third and final bullet had torn into the rear of President Kennedy's head. Exploding the President's brain matter and skull bones throughout the limousine, that bullet alone would have been enough to bring an end to Camelot.

The *Report* fingered Lee Harvey Oswald, an order-filler for the Texas School Book Depository, as this lone assassin. Approximately forty minutes after murdering Kennedy, Oswald shot and killed Dallas patrolman, J.D. Tippit. He had been arrested after seeking refuge in a movie theater. And then he was murdered two days later by a Dallas nightclub owner named Jack Ruby.

Ruby, the *Report* officially contended, had killed Oswald to prevent Mrs. Kennedy and her children from having to go through the ordeal of Oswald's long criminal trial.

So that was it: *one assassin*—and from the book building.

No shots fired from the grassy hill—no assassins there.

One insignificant, little loser who wanted to get his good-for-nothing name into the history books had murdered Kennedy. The convenience of his place of employment, lax security, and the clearing Texas skies that allowed the Presidential party to remove the climate-protective bubble top from the Lincoln Continental had all added up to the unthinkable: John F. Kennedy, 35th President of the United States, was assassinated in Dallas, Texas, on Friday, November 22, 1963.

But Randall Walter Whitman knew better.

He folded away the newspaper containing the advanced summary account of the *Warren Report*, scheduled to hit newsstands soon. He turned his face to Maria Barquin, her head now nestled comfortably in the crook of his arm. Her fragrance and touch reminded him of how happy he was to be alive.

No one from the government—the FBI, the Secret Service, the Justice Department, or anywhere else—had contacted Randy since a few months after the assassination.

Several more official news publications asked him to tell his story, but he always refused. He had already given his account on several occasions: many times to friends and family and others he could trust, once to the government, and once to a large, intelligent, attentive—and appreciative—audience at the State Debate Tournament.

Randy knew he wasn't crazy, but he believed that the truth he grasped would go with him to his own grave. He needed to enjoy the *now*—to lap up the present. He now had what he wanted more than anything else in the world, what he cherished the most: his life, his integrity, and his girl.

He had stopped dwelling on the possibility of clandestine, sinister entities—forces bent on demolishing him and those he loved—still lurking in the fissures of America's anal cavities. Randy figured that once he had jetted past any opportunity to testify in front of the Warren Commission, no one was concerned about him anymore. No one any longer worried about what the boy with the camera had seen on the grassy hill.

He was safe: out of sight, out of mind.

Randall Walter Whitman, glowing in the false safety of the moment, gently kissed Maria Barquin on her soft, inviting lips. He then looked appreciatively to the sky, oblivious to the menacing evil still aching to destroy him.

ADDENDUM

Numerous reports of hobo sightings after the assassination did absolutely nothing to influence the Warren Commission's conclusions about Lee Harvey Oswald being the lone gunman in Dealey Plaza.

Of all the theories as to what happened in Dallas that morning almost fifty years ago, the speculations about the weird-looking hobos have intrigued me the most. When I look at the black-and-white still pictures of these hobos that have been published in books written by critics of the Warren Commission, I can't help but wonder about the hobos' presence on the grassy knoll right before, and right after, the murder of John F. Kennedy —and how they just seemed to disappear, never to be seen or spoken to again.

Who were they? Nobody really knows, but the fictional account in this novel offers one possible theory as to the significance of the three hobos on the grassy hill.

After a lengthy trial, Jack Ruby was convicted of the first-degree murder of Lee Harvey Oswald. His attorney, the renowned Melvin Bellae, fought for a new trial for Ruby, and won his appeal. However, in 1967, while awaiting that second trial, Ruby suddenly contracted cancer.

Jack Ruby's cancer killed him, but only after he had begged government officials to remove him from his jail cell in Dallas, so that he could be flown to Washington D.C.

He wished to talk, he said, but did not any longer feel safe in Texas.

Ruby's request was never honored. Whatever secrets—*if any* —he harbored about Oswald or the Mafia or the CIA or others will never be known.

Bruce J. Gevirtzman
December 31, 2009

© Black Rose Writing